CIRQUE de Vol MYSTIQUE

A Young Adult Circus Anthology

Constance Roberts

Christis Christie

CM Lander

Elle Beaumont

Jessica Julien

Helen Vivienne Fletcher

and KM Robinson

Crescent Sea
PUBLISHING

Come one, come all. For one book, and one book only, we present to you, Cirque de vol Mystique.

Let the circus capture you again...

Stories

Circus of Scales by Constance Roberts

Blood Is Silent by K.M. Robinson

Game of Bezique by Elle Beaumont

Circus des Spirits by C.M. Lander

The Ringmaster by Jessica Julien

We All Fall by Helen Vivienne Fletcher

The Dollhouse by Christis Christie

Circus of Scales

Constance Roberts

CHAPTER 1

Written in Flame

THE NIGHT'S CHILLY BREEZE TEETERS THE PLATFORM BENEATH ME. THE plank of wood is only wide enough to hold my two narrow feet. I am too high up to see anything below, but I can feel it all; the pulse of the crowd, the sting of the whip, the lick of the flames. All the energy from the audience surges through my blood as if it were my own.

That's why, when the dragon's flames rise up to meet me on the tiny iron platform, I do not quake in fear.

I dive.

The firestorm that swirls around me is a comfort of sorts. Always has been. I know that no matter what, Celestia will always catch me. Not just because that's what she's trained to do, but because she is the truest friend I've ever had in this world. And I am hers. Our bond is as unbreakable as the chains that tether her to the to the center of the ring.

My hands reach, ready to clutch the ivory spikes above her wings at the precise moment before it's too late and I crash to the ground. Even now—after I've emerged through the fireball, meeting the cold and the black of the night once again—I still do not fear. I could close my eyes and I would still know that those white wings will swoop in to catch me.

Celestia is as quick and quiet as a flash of moonlight. She's learned over the years what makes a good show and what our master, Gorio, expects of us. Let the crowd believe I have just jumped to my death.

9

Let them believe they are about to witness something gruesome and horrific. Then, at the last second, just as they are about to turn away and shield their eyes from the gory sight of my fall, a miracle saves me. A majestic, opalescent, fire-breathing miracle.

I land with ease on Celestia's back. She plumes another fireball for effect and we soar over the crowd. The audience erupts with applause. They are enchanted by the sight of Celestia's shimmering white scales and crystal-like talons. She flies low, but not so close that anyone is singed as she huffs flames over their heads. Once we make a few circles around the ring, Gorio directs us back to the center where he is waiting with a proud grin on his puffy, pink face. As we've done a thousand times, Celestia poses regally while I slide off her wing into the arms of the ringmaster. I smile brightly as Gorio takes my hand and holds it high. I swear to the Stars, it is the only time I ever let that slimy man touch me and lasts only as long as the crowd keeps cheering.Not a second more.

Our act in the Circus Of Scales has been called one of the most dangerous stunts ever performed. Even Gavriel Tarthe, the warlord of the west coast, was said to have held his breath when I plunged from the platform during a special performance in his camp. Our caravan moves from town to town, but people cross oceans to come see wild dragons dance and drink the enchanted potions made from their blood. There is no show more spectacular on the Emerald Continent than the Circus Of Scales.

As much as the applause fills me with pride, it is barely enough to keep my feelings of guilt at bay. After the show is over, I will return to my plush dressing room while Celestia will be locked away in her cramped livestock car. From the window in my own vardo, I will be able to see the folded tips of her wings poking through the iron bars, glistening like moonstone in the starlight. She will be fed her ration of one goat a day and sleep on a bed of soiled hay.

I constantly reassure myself that the Circus Of Scales is the best place for her. Well, the *safest* at least. Out in the wild, if she were not eaten by a bigger dragon, or stolen as an egg from her nest, she would have been hunted for the blazing orange crystal in her throat that gives her the ability to breath fire. Magic crystals and dragon blood are highly sought after and fetch a fortune. As it is, the dragon species is disappearing. As much as I hate to admit it, without the circus, Celestia would have been lucky to live to her second hatchday. At least here, she is protected by guards at all times. Gorio goes to great lengths to ensure no one else gets a hold of his precious meal ticket.

But it still doesn't change the fact that this isn't the life she was meant for. I see the longing in her ember-colored eyes when she looks to the sky, and I feel her pulse race with mine when we are soaring around the ring. She longs to take flight and never look back. She longs to do what she was made for. To do what she deserves.

During the show, the second Gorio drops my hand I discreetly wipe my palm on my bedazzled costume. The revealing garment is covered in white sequins to look like Celestia's scales and my hair is dyed a brilliant orange to match the dragon's blazing eyes. Together we look like the were-form of the other.

Part of the price of admission includes that spectators get to marvel at the dragons up close after the show. The crowd parts as Celestia and I are led by two guards to our pedestal outside the ring. We pass a parade of other trained dragons, as well as my fellow performers, Luna and Sable. The two girls are aerial artists that breathe streams of light and shadow from their throats. Where Celestia and I were fashioned to look alike, Luna and Sable are paired as complementary opposites; Luna glittering in white diamonds and Sable robed in black ribbons twisted around her dark skin.

As in the set list, Celestia and I are placed at the very end, right next to a gilded cage of singing hatchlings. The baby dragons are so tiny they could fit in my cupped hands. They flit around like birds, emitting little puffs of purple smoke and emerald glitter that blot the cage. I wonder if Celestia was as playful when she was little.

Now, my white dragon is perched stoically on her pedestal as children point and people gape at the majestic wonder before them. This is the part of the show where I must answer the most ridiculous questions - always with a smile on my face, of course.

"Has it ever let you fall?" A man tilts his head back to take in Celestia's full form. The dragon stands about a half a person taller than me.

"Not since the last time, when they had to scrape pieces of me out of the dirt," I jest.

"Does the beast bite?" a woman asks, clutching her child's hand tightly.

"Only if you get too close." I wink.

"Is he your pet?" the little boy asks. "Can I have one, Mummy?"

"She is not my pet. She is my partner." *And my friend*, I want to say, but I find people look at me strangely when I say that out loud. Gorio doesn't like it when I answer like that either.

"Could you make it shoot a fireball at my little brother?"

"I could, but the flames would singe you as well." Would serve the brat right.

"How come you can touch the fire and not be burned?" a little girl asks.

This question always stings a bit. I swallow my guilt and answer, "Before each show, I drink a vial of a potion made with Celestia's blood. It makes me immune to fire and even be able to summon the flames for a short time." The next part always lays heavy in my mouth like lead before I get it out. "The same potion is available for purchase just over there."

I motion to a caravan set up with merchandise and souvenirs. Little stuffed dragon toys and jewelry made from colorful scales hang on the racks, but the dragon's blood potions are displayed right in front. Gorio keeps every size stocked, from fullsize ale bottles to little vials you can wear around your neck. Several patrons are already strolling around summoning flames in their palms and puffs of purple love spells through their fingertips. I lose a few spectators to the exotic wares of the merchandise cart, but neither Celestia or I mind. We're both used to the gawking, but the interaction is exhausting. All I want to do is go back to my room and wash this itchy paint off my face. Perhaps if I'm lucky, Nix will have saved me a tangerine tart from the sweets cart.

I can't help but notice a peculiar patron that stays in the outskirts of the crowd. He's a tall, lean figure that hides his face in a hood. In my experience, anyone wearing a hood is never up to anything good. The circus attracts it's share of creeps, but there's definitely something off about this fellow. I can't exactly see his eyes, except for an occasional flash of green in the shadow of his hood, but it seems as though his gaze never leaves us. He watches the guards closely but doesn't approach for a closer look at the circus's main attraction.

"Are you ever afraid the dragon will try to eat you?"

I'm snapped out of my suspicions by another ridiculous question. After I answer, I turn back to the hooded creep, but he's moved on to the sweets cart. I feel a little silly for being so paranoid, but I can never be too careful when it comes to Celestia's wellbeing.

For a few extra crowns, patrons can purchase a printed sketch of Celestia and I and I will sign it for them. I never learned how to read or write, but Gorio had me practice a loopy script that spells out my name. For the signatures I use a special rusted gold ink that makes the letters "IVY" shimmer as if they were written in flame. I usually sign a few dozen before the crowd disperses, the patrons skipping off back to their ordinary lives with a trinket or two to remember the magical evening.

The minute the last patron is gone, the colored lanterns are snuffed out and we all return to our own ordinary lives, which are much less glamorous than the ringmaster would have his audience believe. With guards flanking me, I escort Celestia back to her cage, my hand caressing the smooth scales of her neck. Gorio is already waiting for us, still dressed in his velvet jacket and ridiculously tall hat. He is paired with the troupe "physician" whom I never like to see. Rupert always wears a snide expression, accentuated by his thin brows and long, dark mustache. His pointed face always reminds me of a rat with something to hide.

I feel Celestia tense beside me. She lets out a huff of smoke through her nostrils.

"What are you doing here?" I demand, not bothering to hide my contempt. And I know very well what they are doing here. "Celestia's harvest isn't scheduled for another two weeks."

Ignoring me, the guards take Celestia by the chain and lead her into her livestock car.

Gorio smiles innocently and spreads his hands apart like he has no choice. "Stock sold well tonight and is running low. We'll need more dragon blood for tomorrow night."

I cross my arms, hoping the gesture will quell my anger before I do something rash. "So just water down the stock you have. Stars know, you do it anyway."

Gorio's grin darkens and he leans in close. The breath coming from behind his pearly teeth smells like blood and chocolate. "Watch your tone!" He warns. "How I manage my wares is none of your business, girl. When I found you, you were nothing but a flea-ridden brat one cold night away from starvation. I gave you a home. I made you into a star! And in return, I get nothing but back-talk and sullen glares."

As well as all the money I earn you. This show wouldn't be half as profitable without me and Celestia.

A while ago I made sure money was the only thing Gorio took from me. Once he started stumbling into my dressing room drunk in the dead of night, I started bunking with Celestia in her livestock car. Let him go through a fire-breathing dragon before ever getting the chance to touch me.

Behind Gorio, I see Rupert climb into the cage with his extraction kit. Celestia is shaking. Rage boils in my blood.

I can't help myself. I hate seeing my friend in pain.

I lunge for Rupert and tug on his coat until he loses his footing and falls to the ground. The tubes and needles of his kit scatter in the dirt. I swear, Celestia's screech sounds like a laugh.

"Savage little wretch!" the physician cries. The guards scramble to help him up.

"Serves you right!" I spit on his shoes as he stands, brushing the dust off his fine clothes. "You won't take another drop from her until her harvest!"

Gorio's face burns crimson. He grabs a hold of my arm and squeezes so hard I almost give him the satisfaction of a whimper. His lips come close to my ear and he speaks gravelly and low.

"Now listen here, girl. You will do as you're told and not interfere with my work on my animals, or I will bleed you right along with her!" He drags me away from the livestock car as Rupert reassembles his kit and climbs back in. We stop in a patch of dry grass where my white costume will not be soiled in the dirt. My back hits the ground with a thud and the stars above me spin—until Gorio's fat hairy face brakes into my vision.

"Now if you have any interest in eating tonight, you'll go get yourself cleaned up and not say another word." He pauses, and I think he is going to turn away, but instead he runs his beady eyes over my scrawny form lying on the ground. "A girl like you was made for looking at...among other things...but *not* listening to. You'd do well to remember that."

I shiver under his gaze. When his back is finally to me, I sit up and gesture a curse I learned from Sable that is supposed to bring him bad luck. I doubt it will work, but it makes me feel better, anyhow.

I stand up and brush myself off. My costume was spared from the dirt, though I think about dousing it with dragon's blood just to spite the ringmaster. I know better though. I can't risk Gorio taking out his anger on Celestia. She's already been through enough.

I swear I can feel her wince as the needle pierces the soft spot between her leg and gut. I watch them drain her, too loyal to turn away. I remind myself once again that the Circus Of Scales is the best place for her, but it's getting harder and harder to believe my own lie.

CHAPTER 2

Life in Chains

It's late by the time I make it to the dining tent after cleaning up and putting on normal clothes. There is nothing special about my brown dress and tattered green belt. In fact, the ensemble looks out of place with my otherworldly orange hair. It's rare that I'm not with the rest of the troupe, but it's then that people look at me as though I've stepped out of a fable realm.

As if announcing my arrival, my belly rumbles when I pass through the flap in the tent. The air inside is stuffy but holds a savory aroma of beef gravy and cider. The scattered tables are nearly empty, except for Terie and a few other stagehands scraping their bowls clean. Luna and Sable are there too, drinking mugs of something hot and comforting. They are also in their street clothes, similar to mine. Luna's golden hair is piled in a knot on top of her head while Sable's dreads flow freely, still adorned with onyx beads.

"We saved this for you," Luna says as I take a seat beside her.

"We almost thought you weren't coming tonight and nearly sold your supper to Terie," Sable says.

I thank them as I take the bowl of stew. It's cold, but will fill me just the same. "Gorio bled Celestia tonight and I didn't want to leave her."

Luna's pale brows knit together as she frowns. "I thought her harvest wasn't for another few weeks."

"It isn't, but the ringmaster can do as he pleases," Sable says, her dark eyes staring into her mug. "It's no wonder, though. Fire blood potions do sell out the quickest."

She and Luna also need to drink dragon blood before their act so that they can emulate the sun and shadow dragons. The blood is harvested from two adolescents that are still being trained and not part of the show yet. The aerialists don't like it any more than I do, but like me, if they want to eat every night and sleep in their own bed, they put aside their scruples.

"At least it doesn't hurt them," Luna says. Her voice is like the chime of a bell. I know her words are meant to be a comfort, but she can be kind of a ditz sometimes. Harvesting may not be painful, besides the initial prick, but Celestia is completely worn out afterward. She's always lethargic and grumpy the next day. It's like the life has literally been drained out of her, which is why the procedure is usually scheduled for an off night.

I've suddenly lost my appetite for my cold stew. "Worst part is, he expects her to perform tomorrow night. I'd like to bleed that bastard dry then make him dance around like a buffoon. See how he likes it."

Sable looks to the entrance as though she is afraid the ringmaster will come through the flap at any moment. But I know better. No doubt Gorio is midway through his second cigar and soaking in a hot bath. I wouldn't care if he heard me anyway. I prefer that my master know exactly where he stands with me.

Luna's tone is still light when she says, "At least she'll have the whole way to Clovery to rest up. I'm sure she'll be good as new by tomorrow night."

"Probably. I just wish there was something I could do for her. I feel so helpless sometimes." I slink down in my chair and rest my heavy arms on the table.

"Don't be so hard on yourself," Sable says. She reaches out and rubs her calloused palm along my arm. "It's not your job to protect her."

I don't have the words or the energy to explain just how wrong she is.

Terie must have noticed the half-eaten bowl of stew I'd abandoned because the stagehand comes sauntering over like a stray cat. "Evening, ladies. Care for some company of the gentleman variety?"

"Of course," Sable says dryly. "If you see one, do let us know."

Terie smirks and his dimples come out in full bloom. He takes the chair next to me and sits down. I scoot my bowl in front of him.

"In the meantime, you can have this," I offer. "I know it's what you're really here for."

"That, and to gift you with the latest rumors to hit this side of Feathered River," Terie says, already his mouth full of chunks of stew. I swear the boy eats more than Celestia, but he can't keep it on him to save his life. I figure he burns a lot of energy running errands and hauling cargo from this end of the camp to the other, but Terie could probably eat an entire dragon in one sitting if allowed.

It's easy to see why the local girls always fawn over him. His slick, auburn hair always falls in a way that frames his bright blue eyes and draws attention to his statuesque bone structure. He may be a bit cocky, but there's no doubt his smile is contagious. Terie charms his way from town to town, leaving many brokenhearted damsels in his wake.

In fact, I'm surprised to see him unaccompanied on such a nice night. I don't mind though. Terie's cheek sometimes has a way of cheering me up. Besides, I'd like to get my mind off the unsavory events of the evening.

"Let's have it," I say perking an ear up to him. "What's the biggest news this side of the river?

He leans his sharp blue eyes over the table as if he's about to divulge a juicy secret. I admit, I'm intrigued. "Some are saying the Lost Prince was spotted here just the other night."

My interest deflates like one of Nix's butter rolls.

Sable rolls her eyes. "People say that constantly, but he's been dead for almost two years! Don't you think if he was alive he would have returned to the palace by now?"

Terie raises an auburn eyebrow. "Not if he doesn't want to be found."

I scoff. "If Prince Dashell doesn't want to be found, then he isn't going to show his face in public. Besides, why would a royal fake their own death? Why would you ever leave the safety and luxury of a palace? 'The Lost Prince' is just some dumb tavern tale."

The truth was, Prince Dashell was killed two years ago in a skirmish with a large savage tribe on the edge of the kingdom. His body was never found, but that's because savages take warrior bodies and eat them as some sort of trophy ritual. Dashell was the sixth—maybe seventh? I don't really keep track—prince in line for the throne so it didn't really upset the line of succession. The king decreed a month of mourning and everything. The one that started the rumor that the prince was still alive is said to be his heartbroken fiancée, but everyone knows that is only a manifestation of her grief. Everyone *should* know that anyway. Everyone who's not thirsty for the tiniest drop of gossip.

Terie pays no mind to my logic. "And it's not just Clovery. The Lost Prince was sighted at a cemetery in Dilshire before that. This time with a woman, dressed all in black."

"Dilshire?" Luna perks up. "We were just there two nights ago!"

"And did you see any handsome royals lurking about? Cuz I sure didn't," I say.

"Well of course not. You wouldn't have seen any because the circus wasn't set up anywhere near the cemetery."

"Nor would I ever go near there." I shiver at the thought. Graveyards are sacred homes for the dead, not the living. No wonder the Dead Prince was sighted there. It was probably just his ghost.

"All I'm sayin'"—Terie shrugs—"is that we should be on the lookout."

"Right. You do that," Sable says. "And when you see the prince you tell him there are plenty of lost princesses here to keep him company." She earns a snicker from me and Luna.

Terie sits back and crosses his arms over his chest. "You laugh, but there's plenty chance for it since we're getting a late start tomorrow."

"We're delayed?" I ask. "Why?"

"Word is there's a dragon's nest in the hills just outside of town. Gorio is sending out a hunting party at midnight to retrieve the eggs."

"Of course, he is," Sable says dryly. "A fine prize for his ever-growing collection."

"I hope the mother is a fire dragon and she scorches him to a crisp," I say, but I know the likelihood of that happening is slim. One reason being that wild dragons are nocturnal hunters, so the mother will be away from the nest. Another thing being that Gorio rarely goes himself on such excursions. Then again, we all need dreams to get us through the day, right?

"At least we'll all get to sleep in tomorrow," Luna says cheerfully.

As if tempted by the promise, I yawn. "I plan on getting started on that right away," I announce, rising from the table and bidding everyone goodnight.

The night air is alive with a sticky mist and the chorus of insects when I come from the dining tent. Near the edge of camp, I spot a small wagon loaded with weapons and supplies. A few stagehands and all of Gorio's men that serve as guards are gathered around as if discussing strategy for a battle. It must be near midnight.

With everything going on, there's little chance of an unwanted visitor tonight, but I won't be able to entertain any thoughts of sleep without checking on Celestia first. I find her unguarded, curled up with her tail wrapped safely around her. From a distance, she looks like a crescent moon someone captured in a cage. But she is my moon, and one day she would live free in the sky where she belongs, I swear to the Stars.

I must be tired. My thoughts tend to stretch far when it's late at night and the darkness feels big and expansive like it can hold any and every possibility.

Celestia is snoring peacefully when I approach. Because of my rigorous training and the ringmaster's meager meal rations, I'm thin enough to slip through the bars. The floor smells of fresh hay. At least Gorio had the decency to give her a fresh bed before bleeding her. Rupert always does a clean job. Besides the bandage wrapped around her leg, there is no sign the harvesting was ever done. Beforehand, the dragons are always given a sedative so they don't get any ideas of harming the physician while he works. Celestia must not have woken up yet because her dinner is still lying in the corner, bug-eyed and staring blankly at me.

"Poor girl." I run my hand methodically over the scales on her neck. The gesture is as much of a comfort to me as her. Feeling the pattern of her scales on my palm fills me with a calm I can get nowhere else.

I sit with the sleeping dragon in her cage and watch the small company of hunters ride off toward the hills. I think about how Celestia was taken as an egg from her nest in the same manner, probably in that same wagon. Part of me hopes the hunters come back empty handed– or not at all. And another part of me repeats the lie I tell myself every day. In the circus, the dragons may live a life in chains, but at least it will be a long life, where they will be safe and cared for–if Gorio doesn't decide to sell them instead.

I decide to end the night on a note of gratitude, thankful that I have Celestia beside me. I curl up in the nook between her neck and belly and let myself be lulled to sleep by the comforting sounds of her slumber and warm, rhythmic rise and fall of her chest.

Since I'm a light sleeper, I will wake at the first intrusion on my slumber. It doesn't feel like long after I'm floating in the depths of sleep before something seems…off. The natural rhythm of slumber is disturbed, the sounds aren't right. There's a rattling of chains, a churning of wheels and a motion of propelling forward. I pop my head up out of Celestia's embrace, my eyes taking a moment to adjust to the dark of night. There's a wind that's picked up and dark silhouettes of trees wiz by outside the bars.

We are moving.

CHAPTER 3

Fierce Little Thing

THE STARLIGHT DOESN'T OFFER MUCH INSIGHT AS TO WHERE WE ARE exactly, but we can't have gone far. I was barely asleep a minute, it seems. There's enough light to make out the rears of a wagon team in front of us, not the usual caravan that tows Gorio's prized dragon from town to town.

I may be on the verge of panicking but when I check on Celestia, her eyes are still tight slits. A tendril of quiet smoke curls out of her nostrils with each slow breath. She is unharmed. If the thieves were going to just slit her throat to get her crystal, they would have slaughtered her quickly and be done with it. Which means, whoever wants her, wants her alive.

A quick glance around tells me there's no one else in the cage with us—unless someone is stupid enough to hide at the hind end of a sleeping fire dragon—but on instinct, I reach for the knife tucked away in my boot. The hills pass us on my left side, which tells me we are headed south. But how far south? All the way to the shore? How long do these people think they can outrun horseback guards while towing a two-ton dragon cage?

From what I can make out, there is a man and a woman leading the team of horses down the rocky path. The man wears a tight cap, but the woman's dark locks are loose and shining in the breeze like a raven's wing. When I reach my arm through the bars, I can *almost* grab the wavy ends. My plan was to yank on her hair as hard as I could, and hope that would cause the thief to pull back on the reins, halting the wagon team. Looks like I'll need another tactic to get them to stop.

I take out the knife I keep hidden in my boot.

"Filthy savages! Forgot to check something before you ran off with the loot?" I call from behind. The man turns toward my voice, but I barely get a look at his young face before my vision suddenly goes black.

Before I can reach up to slice the hand in front of my face, the wrist holding my knife twists to the side. In a reflex to the pain I drop the blade, losing it in the piles of hay. A whimper escapes me, but I don't give my captor the satisfaction of a scream. I wriggle and kick, but the captor's grip only winds tighter. I feel the sharp curve of a blade at my throat and a dark voice comes to my ear.

"Don't make a sound or I'll split you open."

I obey, simply so the man believes I'll continue to cooperate. The second his guard is down, the bastard will find a chain wrapped around his neck.

Still blindfolded by his palm, my captor leads me to the far end of the cage. He's careful not to bump me into Celestia, which gives me an idea. If I can wake her somehow, not only will he be distracted enough for me to escape, but anyone else near the cage will be charred to dust. I wonder if the dragon's blood I drank will last long enough to spare me from Celestia's flames as well. I swallow a lump forming in my throat.

"You're not supposed to be here," the thief grumbles. "No one was supposed to be here."

"*You're* not supposed to be here," I throw back at him. He's removed his hand from my eyes and is now fastening something on my wrists behind me. A coarse rope to the iron bars.

He hardens his expression as he works, but he doesn't reply. His face is close to mine. It's not a bad face. Not at all. His features are smooth and unmarked by age. Strangely, I can tell by the dark roots of his hair that the color has been lightened. Straw colored strands frame his sleek brows and moss green eyes–the same green eyes that haunted me in the circus grounds only hours ago.

"I've seen you before," I accidentally blurt out in my astonishment. "You were at the show tonight."

The captor finishes a tight knot and quickly stands and faces away from me, as if he still doesn't want me to see him. His hands hover at his shoulders as if he is going to pull up his hood, but instead puts them back down at his sides. "You're a quick one. Perhaps there's something underneath that rotten orange hair after all."

I calm my tone, adding a sweetness to it. "Please, what's your name?"

Perhaps if we keep talking, I can get him to trust me. I don't care what happens to me, but there's no way I'm letting these creeps hurt Celestia.

Mr. Creep fails to answer me.

"What do you want with Celestia?" I try again.

His fists clench at his sides. As if this is a nervous habit of his, he loosens his hands and shakes the energy out of his fingers. "No one was supposed to be here." He turns his profile to me. "No one was supposed to get hurt."

"What are you going to do with me, then?" I try to keep my tone neutral.

The starlight flickers in his hard eyes as we pick up speed. We both know he doesn't know what he's going to do with me.

"Please, just tell me what it is you want. Maybe we can come to some sort of agreement. It's only Celestia I'm thinking of. And you," I add.

"Me?" He frowns, as if he suspects he's being tricked.

"I don't want anyone getting hurt either," I say. "Gorio and his men will hunt you like rabid dogs until he gets his prized dragon back. And when they catch you, you'd better pray to the Stars for a quick death."

Mr. Creep laughs. "Your threats are hollow. We'll be halfway to shore by the time Gorio's lap dogs get back from their little hunt in the hills."

Realization pierces me like a winter gale. "The lot of you set this all up! You're the ones that started the rumor of the dragon's nest. You knew the camp would be unguarded tonight."

"Figure that out all by yourself, huh?"

I shrug. "I admit it's a brilliant plan, except for one thing..."

"Oh? And what's that?" Mr. Creep looks down at me with an amused smile.

"I'm just not sure what you're planning to do once this wild fire-breathing beast wakes up and finds a stranger in her nest."

I'm a little concerned when Creep's smile doesn't instantly disappear. He keeps his gaze on me and slowly opens his cloak to reveal an array of sharp blades and insidious instruments. He pulls a syringe half filled with a clear liquid.

"There's no worry of that," he says. "There's enough juice here to make sure she doesn't open her eyes until she's locked away where she can't hurt a soul."

That's it. I'm done with this game. Blood burns in my limbs when I look into his smug face. "You come near her with so much as your fingernail and I will wring your throat and watch the life slowly drain out of you."

Creep's smile only widens. "Be careful with your threats or I just might have to carve your orange head up like a pumpkin."

I lunge for the bastard, forgetting that my wrists are bound to the bars. The coarse rope scrapes across my skin. Creep laughs when my motion is jerked to a stop.

"You're a fierce little thing, I'll give you that," he says. "Stupid, but fierce."

Before I can throw out a retort, I notice the cage slowly coming to a halt. We are both quieted by the shuffle of loose stones and impatient horses.

"Titus! What's all that ruckus back there?" a male voice calls in the darkness. I hear the thump of two sets of feet dismount from the wagon.

Creep's—or rather Titius's—sneer turns downward into a frown upon hearing his name used. He never intended on sharing his identity. Titus curses under his breath.

"Everything's fine, just get us back on the road."

"I heard shouting," says the other male voice as he comes around the cage. "What's going on?"

Titus's eyes dart in panic as he thinks up an excuse. Before he can speak again, I decide to make myself known.

"Oh nothing! It's just me," I call over my shoulder. Titus shoots me a look that could cut glass. "I was just explaining to your friend here how the lot of you will be cooked like skewered piglets once this dragon wakes up. That is, if my master doesn't find you first."

"Stars blaze!" I hear the other male voice behind me, and by Titus's sigh I know the other fellow has spotted me tied to the bars. "We've kidnapped Ivy the Fire Tamer! This is what you call fine?!"

Perhaps it's the performer in me, but for effect, I peer over my shoulder and shoot the man my best stage smile. Except, it's not a man. It's a boy. I'd bet my life he was younger than even me. The raven-haired woman stands beside him and her dark eyes take me in. Her petite nose crinkles as she crosses her arms. She seems more disgusted by my intrusion on their plan than surprised.

These people sure have some nerve. They're the dirty thieves, not me.

"You said everything was clear," the woman says to Titus. Her voice is like clashing steel.

"I'm handling it," Titus says through his teeth.

"Clearly." The woman rolls her eyes. "Just cut her loose. We've got to get moving."

"We can't just let her go," Titus argues. "Not now that she's seen our faces and knows my name, *thankyouverymuch!*" He stares hard at the boy.

The woman huffs. "I don't care if we toss her down a ravine. Let's just get rid of the circus whore and be on our merry way."

If I wasn't tied up and had access to my full range of motion, I might do something about her comment. But I'll worry about that later.

"That's the last thing you want to do, trust me," I speak up.

The raven-haired woman cocks her head to the side as she turns her cold gaze to me, as if she's shocked I have the audacity to speak. "Oh, and why's that?"

"Look—" I try to match her icy stare. "I don't know what you're planning to do with Celestia, but you won't get anywhere without me. I can keep her calm and keep her from roasting you all like the dirty pigs you are. But if I'm not here when she wakes up, I can't protect you."

"She's lying," the boy speaks up. "She's not really a dragon tamer. She's just a pretty face for the show."

"No. I think we need her."

My attention turns to Titus who sizes me up with his calculating glare.

"I think she's telling the truth," he says. "How else could she be sleeping in the cage alongside a wild, fire-breathing dragon? *Why* would she be in the cage with it in the middle of the night if they didn't share some sort of bond."

"Hmm...perhaps there is something underneath that fake blond hair after all." I smile.

My comment is ignored as the team of thieves mull over what to do with me.

"We can't take her all the way to The Sanc–the *island*," the woman corrects herself before she reveals too much. "There's just no way."

Titus throws up his hands in exasperation. I get the feeling these two argue a lot. "Well, I'm not about to just let her run off! And before you say it again, 'getting rid of her' is not an option. That's not what we do. That's not who we are."

Raven woman raises her voice so loud that if Gorio is already on his way she's about to lead them straight to us. "Since when do we care what happens to the orange ditz? What makes this girl different from the hunters and the masters? She may not hold the whip, but she uses and profits off the dragons just the same."

I scoff. "I'm sorry, but did I just hear a pot calling a kettle black? And if you think two coppers a night is a profit then you're obviously not very good at this thieving thing."

Raven woman draws a crude knife from her belt and points it at my face. "Keep your whore lips shut if you don't want me to cut them off."

"Greta, enough!" Titus snaps. "No matter what she is, she's more use to us alive. She can keep the dragon under control and if she's here, then there's no way she can run back to her master and help him hunt us down."

The thought brings bile to my throat. I wouldn't run back to that man even if he turned into a giant sweet-roll. But they don't need to know that.

I notice Greta lowers her knife, but she doesn't sheath it. "And what do you suppose we do? Drag her along with us?" she asks venomously. "We can't trust her. And even if we could, we don't have the resources to keep a useless tag-along."

These thieves really are terrible if they can't afford to feed a scrawny thing like me. How exactly do they expect to feed Celestia?

"Titus is right," the other boy speaks up. His eyes quiver as he peers up at the sleeping dragon. "Ivy's not useless. She'll keep the mare calm and safe until we get to–"

Greta slaps her palm over the boy's mouth before he can give up their destination.

"Clodhead!" she curses. "Is there a slug where your brain is supposed to be?"

The poor boy cowers under her glare.

Still standing in front of me inside the cage, Titus sighs heavily. "We need to get back on the road before we're spotted."

"Then I suggest you make a decision, fierce leader," Greta says, although her tone is anything but respectable.

Titus shoots her a warning look and then turns his sharp gaze to me. Somehow, I can see his mind right through his green eyes, quickly calculating a dozen different scenarios at once.

"Does anyone care about my opinion?" I ask with a singsong voice that I hope breaks the tension.

"Definitely not," Greta answers flatly.

"The tamer stays," Titus declares. "For now. Greta, Tatum, get back to the wagon. I'll stay here and keep her under watch."

"She stays bound," Greta says and obeys her leader, but not before a low growl escapes her throat. There is an instant lift in the air once Greta is out of my sight.

That is, until I turn forward and see my blade I'd dropped in the scuffle. Titus, crouched in front of me, points the crude tip at my heart.

CHAPTER 4

Horns and All

I TAKE IN A BREATH, READY TO SCREAM. WITH ANY SHRED OF LUCK, Celestia will hear it and wake from her sleep. I'm halted when a soft smile graces my captor's lips.

"I won't hurt you," he says with a steady voice. "I'm going to cut you loose."

I believe him, but stiffen just the same as he draws closer.

"No," I say. "Give it to me. I'll do it."

One of his eyebrows hooks upward. "How are you going to do that with your hands bound behind your back?"

"I'll manage, just give me the knife. Place it in my palm."

He hesitates. "It'll be much easier if I do it. You'll probably end up slicing a finger."

"I won't. I've done it before. Just please give me the knife."

His smile disappears, replaced with a sympathy I neither appreciate nor need. "I promise, I'm not going to hurt you."

"I believe you," I insist. "But please, just let me do it myself. I don't like men touching me." My words fly out of me urgently before I can take them back.

Titus recoils, as if he was about to wound me. The pity in his expression deepens. "Oh. Uh…of course," he stammers. He flips the blade into his palm so that the handle is facing me. "I'm just going to reach around and slip this into your palm."

He moves slowly and gently, as if he's trying not to spook a horse.

In order to bestow the knife to me, he gets uncomfortably close. But only for a moment. I accidentally breath in his scent of earth and pine. Perhaps he sleeps in the forest. Though his gaze is averted from mine, I can see the fractal pattern of his irises as my fingers maneuver to grab the handle. His eyes are like cut emeralds.

"Thank you," I mutter once I have a grip on the dagger.

He nods and slips away, settling on the other side of the cage. Celestia's form rises and falls peacefully between us.

I work without words, carefully sawing the rope that binds my wrists. I try not to think about when I had done this once before with a shard of broken glass. I try not to think about how much younger I was and how hard my heart had pounded against my protruding ribs. That part of my life was before I was found by Gorio and started training with Celestia. That part is over now, I remind myself before residual panic rises.

"Thank you, again. I know this goes against what Greta said." The rope snaps free and I bring my hands forward. I roll out my aching shoulders and caress my raw, red wrists.

Titus lets out a sad laugh. "Don't take anything Greta says to heart. She likes to act tough until she gets to know a person. Trust issues."

I scoff. "You don't say? Doesn't sound like she really wants to know me."

Before Titus replies, his face twists like he's holding in something rotten. "Look, don't take this the wrong way, but she doesn't take well to people…like you."

"People like me?" I ask slowly. I'm not sure whether to be confused or offended.

"People who profit off the exploitation of innocent animals. Dragons in particular."

I stare at him blankly. I can't tell whether he's joking with me. "Again, I'm not the one who profits from Celestia's tricks. I barely have a copper to my name! And need I remind you that you're the ones who snuck into a circus camp in the middle of the night and ran off with a fire-breathing dragon and her tamer?"

"Fair enough, but…" Titus begins his speech with a quick lick of his lips. I hadn't noticed before, but they were plump like tulip blossoms and were the color of wet sandalwood. The mannerism catches me off guard and sends a trickle of heat down my spine. "First of all, we didn't 'run off' with you. We had no idea someone would want to spend the night in a dragon's nest."

"An honest mistake," I deadpan.

"And second of all…" He continues, but his voice drops off and his eyes cast down into the hay. Whatever it is he wants to say he doesn't want to look at me when he says it. "It's a lot more complicated than you think."

"Sure it is." I wave dismissively. "Regardless of what you lot hoped to accomplish tonight, you need to get one thing straight." I pause intently to make sure what I'm about to say sinks in. He beckons me on with a curt nod. "I will see to it that Celestia and your crew make it to your destination safely, but know this: I love that dragon more than my own life. Wherever she goes, I go. And I'll be cursed before I let you lay a hand on her."

Titus's crooked smile enrages me. "Alright then," he says with a shrug of his shoulder.

"I mean it," I reiterate. "If you or your sullen underlings go anywhere near her, I'll beat the life out of you myself."

His tulip lips flash me an amused smile. He may think the threat is hollow, being that he is twice my size, but let him. I'll have the element of surprise when the time comes.

"I'm pleased to tell you that won't be necessary. We've absolutely no intention of harming Celestia."

In the passing light I try to read his expression. I've been around lying men all my life. There is always a tell, a tautness to the muscle in their jaw, a tiny quiver of their eye as they speak. I see none of it in Titus. I'm confused.

"Why steal her, then? What are you planning to do with her?"

"I told you, it's complicated. But given your terms, I think we'll get along just fine."

I roll my eyes. "You'll have to tell me eventually. I refuse to leave her side." To make my point clear, I settle in against her spine; the same spot I straddle while riding her.

Titus draws in a pensive breath. "If and when the time comes. For now, rest assured that you and your beloved dragon are safe with us."

I chuckle. "I cannot rest," I say, even though as the words are spoken a yawn churns in the back of my throat. It is the late end of a long day. I imagine by now Gorio and his men have figured out the ruse and are headed back down the hill. It won't be long before they're on our trail. If given the choice I wonder if I'd rather have them find us and return to the circus or escape to the unknown with this crew of assorted ruffians.

A long stretch of silence passes between us as I imagine the outcome of both fates. If I stay with Celestia and run off to wherever it is she's going, I'll never see Luna or Sable or any of my other friends again. They're more than friends to me, I realize. They're more like the only family I've ever known. As much as I despise the circus, I can't imagine my life without them.

I look out the back of the cage and picture Gorio on his chestnut stallion, leading the charge to my rescue. His men would easily flank the wagon and halt us on the road. Gorio would take the thieves out one by one and slit their throats.

I don't want that either.

"I promise you, Ivy. We all want the same thing," Titus says, breaking my dark thoughts.

"How could I possibly be sure of that?"

He smiles warmly. "Just trust us."

Something in his bright emerald eyes makes me want to do just that. But I know better. I've trusted before.

"I don't think I can stop Gorio and his men if they catch up to us," I tell him.

His warm grin slants and becomes cocky. "That fat fool? I've dealt with far worse."

"If you say so."

A yawn overtakes me and I stretch out, laying my chest and arms over Celestia's back. Her scales are hard, but are a comfort to be touching. I feel as if her warmth and energy flow into me, becoming my own. It feels like what people call home.

"Don't say I didn't warn you," I whisper just before my eyelids fall.

It is sometime later when I'm stirred awake. Feels like mere minutes have gone by, but the cool blue light of dawn breaking through the trees tells me morning is not far off.

Beneath me, Celestia chortles sleepily and stretches her hind legs.

"She's waking up," I mutter to Titus, who is still perched on the other side of the cage. He doesn't look nervous about the waking dragon, just fighting his own exhaustion. Now that more light filters in through the bars, I can see dark crescents hanging below his eyes and a translucence to his pallor. I wonder when the last time was he caught a wink of sleep.

"I'm excited to meet her," he says cheerfully despite his weary expression. "You promise she'll be…alright?"

I look at him pointedly. "She may be a little startled by the presence of a stranger, but I'll make sure she doesn't scorch you." I stand and hitch my leg over Celestia's back so I can climb to her other side. I move up to her front where her eyes are cracking open and the uneaten goat carcass is starting to smell.

I crouch down and lean in close. "Good morning sweet one," I coo softly. I hum her a tune as her eyes gradually open and she huffs herself awake. The smell of her smoke is intoxicating. Like warm embers in a snowy wood.

"Mind you, she'll probably still be drowsy from the sedative you gave her," I tell Titus with a sideways glance. He has inched his way closer. Mesmerized by my dauntlessness perhaps, judging from his wide, weary eyes.

I continue my tune and we both watch as the dragon's eyes slowly open to reveal bright amber orbs. I expect Titus to scoot back a bit, but he doesn't. When I look over at him, I spot something I don't expect to see in a dragon trafficker's gaze as he peers at Celestia. Wonder, admiration, concern. He's being cautious, but he's not afraid of her. I gather Titus has been this close to dragons before. It's almost as if he's *comfortable* around them.

"She'll be alright," I say after a quick examination. Celestia doesn't move much, but her breathing is normal and she acknowledges me with a nuzzle.

"Oh, so you're a physician now, are you?" Titus smirks. I can tell by his tone he is only teasing, but I answer in full seriousness.

"Much better than her *actual* physician," I say dryly.

"Why do you say that?"

I can't hide the disgust in my voice. "The only thing Rupert ever does for his patients is harvest their blood and make sure they're fit to breed on time."

"That's outrageous," Titus says. I'm surprised to see his scowl matches my own. "Has Celestia ever bred?"

"No. She's too much of an asset to the show. Gorio can't have her fat and laying eggs all the time. Though he does get extra coin off her by harvesting her blood. I imagine, that if for whatever reason she can't perform, he'd start breeding her then."

I watch as Celestia methodically takes in her surroundings. She's especially familiar with this cage, as well as traveling, but what the dragon's not used to is the strange man crouching by the bars. A low rumble forms in her throat as she turns her narrowed eyes on him.

I lay my arm around her neck and rub her on the soft spot under her chin. It's how I get her to relax during thunderstorms. "It's alright, girl. This is Titus and he's not going to hurt you." I put emphasis on those last words while staring down the trafficker. He doesn't look at me, but he nods and slowly extends his hand out to her, his fingers lingering just inches from her nostrils. A bold move, considering she could snap his arm off without a blink.

Celestia has no interest in the peace offering, though. Instead, she turns her attention to the rotting goat laid before her. In less than three bites, the meal disappears, horns and all. It's good to finally be rid of the stench.

"She takes a while to warm up to people," I tell Titus. "As I'm sure you can imagine."

If I didn't know any better - and I don't really - I would swear dragons can understand exactly what we're saying. The way Celestia looks at me, I would swear she could see right into my soul. It's not so hard to imagine, really. This majestic species has been around since the dawn of eternity. They possess the rarest and most powerful form of magic. Who's to say they're not capable of mastering the art of our language?

Titus clears his throat. His brow scrunches as if he's contemplating an impossible decision. "What would happen to you if Celestia couldn't perform anymore? I mean, you two are kind of a double act, right?"

The question trips me. Instinctively, I run my palm down the scales of her neck. I literally trust this dragon with my life on a daily basis. I'd never thought of what would happen to me and the act if she were no longer a part of it.

"I don't know," I admit. "I don't have another skill like the aerial artists or illusionists. I guess I could train with another dragon, but it could take years to form the same bond of trust I have with Celestia. Ultimately, I suppose it would be up to Gorio to decide." The thought turns my stomach.

"Well, what if, say, the circus was no longer an option for you? What would you do then?"

I stare at him blankly. "The circus is my only option."

"But what if it wasn't? If you could do anything –anything in the world–what would you do?"

I scoff. "That question is a fantasy." The idea is so preposterous, I'd never considered it before.

"Come on," Titus says. "Just think about it. We've got the time." He looks outside to the soft orange light breaking through the trees. The color reminds me of the fire I dive into every night.

"Oh, I don't know," I sigh. "I guess if the circus wasn't around anymore, I'd want to take Celestia up into the mountains and just hide from the rest of humanity. We'd live among her kind and she could fly free." As I speak, I peer into the depths of her glowing eyes. The dragon purrs and I feel as though she's pleased with this idea, too. "Even if she chose to fly away from me and never return, I'd be okay because I would know that is her choice. I'd stay in the mountains and try to protect the other dragons as best I could."

I almost forget I'm talking to a trafficker. I expect him to snicker at my answer, but when I glance at Titus, he wears a hopeful smile. I hate the fact that his lightheartedness is somewhat alluring. I don't come across many men like that. No one that's ever asked what I wanted. But it's all an illusion, I'm sure. He's only trying to get me to open up. Maybe he wants more inside information about Gorio and the circus.

Titus doesn't say anything for a moment. Then suddenly a light comes over his expression as if he's made a decision.

"In that case, Ivy..." He smiles excitedly. "There's something I need to tell you."

I don't get to hear what that 'something' is. The rumble of dozens of hooves snags both of our attention. Barreling down the road behind us is a horde of Gorio's men, whipping their horses, closing the distance between us.

I shoot to my feet at the same time Titus rises and draws his blade.

"They've found us." I shudder.

CHAPTER 5

Inferno

Titus hisses a quiet curse.

"Not part of your masterful plan?" I ask in an *I-told-you-so* tone.

"I just don't see how they could've caught up so fast." A bit of sweat glints off his brow.

"As much as it pains me to admit it," I say, "Gorio is smarter than you think."

Titus shakes his head. "We can still outrun them," he declares with a half-mustered confidence.

Beside me, Celestia turns her head to the commotion behind us. She immediately screeches at the approaching horde. The sound can be deafening to people who aren't used to it. I notice Titus doesn't cover his ears, only winces a bit against the abrasive sound. When the dragon's cry is over, Titus yells over his shoulder for Greta to speed up and not stop for anything. I hear the cracking of the whip over the rumbling of hooves as she signals for her wagon team to pick up the pace.

The command does little good as Gorio's guards close in on us.

One of them locks eyes with me.

"The girl's here too!" He shouts over his shoulder to the others. Celestia lets out another screech, as if she knows they're speaking of me. I can smell the fire burning in her throat. I feel the flames like they are billowing in my chest.

"We may not have to outrun them," I say. An idea sparks as I watch the fury stir in my dragon's eyes. "Tell Greta to slow down."

"What?!" That's insane!"

"Trust me. We *want* them to catch up to us." I give Titus a hard, sideways glare.

He hesitates only a moment before shrugging. "Not like I have any better ideas," he murmurs under his breath before moving to the front of the car. He and Greta argue a moment before I feel our momentum slowing.

The guards inch closer. The darkness below their weary eyes is visible in the blooming morning and sweat drips down their faces and necks. By my guess, they've been riding this hard all night.

The heat in my blood rises, and, I imagine, so does Celestia's fire. The smoke unfurling from her nostrils is denser now, thick with smog and fury. It won't be long now.

Footsteps approach behind me as Titus makes his way up the wagon again. I turn and push him back the way he came. "Take cover!" I command as I crouch as far from the end of the wagon as possible and pull him down with me.

A hair of a second later, Celestia releases her blaze in a burst of rage and heat. A firestorm shoots out of the back of the wagon. The inferno blinds me and the backlash of air burns my cheeks. When the pain becomes too intense, I cower in the solid crook of Titus's arm. I feel his arm hook tightly around me. My instinct is to push him away–despite the possibility of burning alive without him. But another feeling overtakes me; wraps me up like a thick, warm blanket. Something I've only ever felt in the presence of Celestia.

Safe. Protected. Home.

The roar of the blaze seems to go on forever. Celestia concludes the attack with a menacing growl. When the heat dies down, I cautiously peek out of Titus's embrace.

Celestia's tail weaves back and forth in front of us, like she does once she finishes a satisfying meal. Beyond the bars, an air of smoke and a pile of scorched, blackened bones recedes in the distance.

Titus is still holding me when the ashes of Celestia's wrath disappear under the crest of a hill on the road. I don't think either of us realize it until Greta's voice pulls us from the silence of shock.

"You guys alright back there?" she yells over her shoulder.

Titus clears his throat and scoots an appropriate distance away from me. "Yeah. All good here."

Tatum is completely turned around in his seat, still staring wide-eyed at the carnage beyond the iron bars. "I guess they won't be a problem for us anymore."

"Oh, they will," I say, stroking the soft spot under Celestia's chin. She returns my affection with a low purr and a nuzzle. "You've taken Gorio's best act and his most lucrative dragon. He won't rest until he has us back. Celestia's bought us some time, but more hunters will come."

Titus looks at me, taking in my words. "Was Gorio not among them just now?"

"I didn't see him." I shake my head. "It wouldn't be like him to come himself, either."

Titus whispers a curse, admitting I'm right. "I didn't see him either."

"We don't need to worry about him," Greta says confidently. "No one can find us where we are going."

I look at Titus skeptically. "And where exactly *are* we going?"

"That's none of your business," Greta snaps, still manning the reins and focused on the road ahead. I notice we've picked up our pace again.

"Lay off, Greta." Titus sighs exasperatedly.

"Actually," I say, "it is my business, seeing as how you've kidnapped me and I just saved your lives. Do you have any idea what Gorio's men would have done to you if they'd caught you?"

"Do you have any idea what I'll do to you if you don't stop this whining?"

"Enough Greta!" Titus explodes. "Ivy's right. We are alive only because Celestia was protecting her. The dragon could have done the same to us if Ivy wanted her to. I think she deserves to know the truth."

"Don't you say a word, Ty," The raven-haired girl's words are sharp as talons, but there's also a hint of pleading in her voice. As much as she argues with him, Titus's opinion holds weight.

"She's not how you think she is, Greta. We can trust her," he says. He turns to me. "We can trust you, right?"

It takes me a minute to believe he's actually asking me this. I cross my arms over my chest. "Can you really trust anyone?"

He nibbles his lip as he considers the answer.

Greta huffs from the driver's seat. "Really, Titus. You've known the girl all of four hours and you think she's one of us?"

"She seems nice," Tatum comes meekly to my defense. I'll remember it.

Greta groans. "Honestly, you men are all the same! 'Nice' isn't the same as *safe* and *loyal.* 'Nice' could mean a knife in your throat while you're sleeping."

I'm growing weary of all the bickering. "Listen, I don't want to hurt any of you. And honestly, I don't care where I go as long as I'm with Celestia. So, if you can promise me she won't be harvested, or sold, or killed for sport, then yes, you can trust me."

Silent looks of deliberation pass between the boys. Greta just shrugs her shoulders. "Fine. Whatever. But if she kills us in our sleep, I'll find whatever Star Realm your spirits end up in and torture you both for eternity."

When Titus looks back to me there's a spark in his eye, like when Terie is about to spill a secret he's held onto for far too long. "We're not going to sell Celestia. Or do any of those other horrible things," he says. "We're going to set her free."

CHAPTER 6

Free

FREE.

In Titus's bright voice, the word rings like the echo of a bell. Far away and unreachable. He waits for my reaction.

"I don't understand," I say. "You can't just set her free. It's not possible. Out in the wild she'll be exposed to too much danger. She could be eaten or hunted–there's a hundred things that put her in danger. Besides, she's been tame too long. I don't think she'd even know how to take care of herself. You wouldn't be doing her any favors."

"She wouldn't be out in the wild," Tatum explains. The boy is completely turned around in his seat and engaged in our conversation. "We have an island, a sanctuary of sorts, where dragons hunt their prey and fly free. She'll be safe there."

My eyes flick to Titus. He smiles warmly. "It's true."

I have to step back. Instinctively, I reach up and Celestia puts her snout in my hand, as she's trained to do. But the gesture feels like something more. A comfort. An encouragement. A message that everything will be alright.

Such a place can't possibly exist. The seas between here and the Ruby Continent are vast, but there's no hiding an entire island of dragons! I can't even imagine it.

"You're not serious," I say. "The three of *you* run a dragon sanctuary in the middle of the ocean?"

"Just what's that supposed to mean?" Greta asks from the driver's seat.

If Titus is offended, his face doesn't show it. "We currently have charge of twenty-three bulls, thirty-six mares, and two dozen nested eggs," he says proudly.

A hunter's and trafficker's gold mine.

"Any as big as Celestia?" I ask.

His eyes trail the dragon's neck as if doing a comparison from memory. "None yet. She'll currently be our biggest but there are some promising hatchlings that Dr. Grove suspects will be the size of a finback whale come next Spring."

"Dr. Grove? You have a physician?" I ask.

"The best," Titus beams. "She's patched wings, set broken limbs, even nursed abandoned hatchlings. If there's any sort of grounded dragon, she'll get them flying again. Dr. Grove's the one who developed the sedative that's safe for the dragons."

"That's not just some horse sedative?" I ask, pointing to the pocket inside his cloak.

"Not this, no. This is a special blend of seaflower and ripeweed that will keep a dragon dreaming all day without damaging their circulation."

I must admit, even I'm impressed. But don't let on. I cross my arms and ask, "This island must be massive to hold so many dragons peacefully. How big is it?"

He doesn't even have to think about it, "Nearly two hundred leagues of shoreline," he answers nonchalantly.

"Two hundred leagues? That's huge! How did you even get the land?"

"Titus owns the island," Tatum speaks up. Titus shoots him a warning look.

"My family owns the island," he corrects.

"Your family?" I narrow my eyes on him. Only ridiculously wealthy and powerful people could own an island that size. A marquess or perhaps a merchant tycoon. Come to think of it, I thought only the royal family held all the outer islands.

I find myself taking another good look at Titus. Underneath his scruff is a strong jawline that suggests prestigious breeding. But what's more telling, is the dark streak at the part in his straw-colored hair, as if it's been manipulated that color and the new roots are growing out. Could just be the shadows cast upon him, but it's curious, nonetheless. What reason would he have to disguise himself?

Terie pops into my head and his silly story of the lost prince. But that's all it is, a silly story for barmaids and bored housewives. Prince Dashell may be dead, but he's much more entertaining as a runaway rouge.

Titus must notice my scrutinizing because he turns away from my gaze and calls to Greta.

"How much farther till port?" he asks.

"Only a few more leagues," she answers. "We've made good time."

"Good," Tatum says. "Brock and Crow are waiting on us."

"Brock and Crow?" I mull over the names. "Friends of yours? Just how many of you dragon snatchers are there?"

"Not enough." Titus sighs. "But besides the three of us, we have the two shipmates at port, the physician and her two assistants, Millie–our cook–and half a dozen sentries to patrol the island. And then there's Alister's wife and their daughter."

I barely believe what I'm hearing. Part of me doesn't want to believe it–to save myself the disappointment if it's all a trick.

"And all of you just…" I search for the right word, "coexist in this sanctuary full of wild dragons?"

A humble grin tugs at Titus's lips, but he can't hide the pride in his voice. "The wild ones roam the island, yes, but most of the dragons we've rescued were born in captivity or even brought to us as eggs."

Rescued. The word hits me. Is that what's happening right now? Is this our chance for a new life?

"They're pretty tame," Titus continues. "Until they are able to support themselves, we keep them in the fortress with us. They're free to wander the courtyard and those that need care are housed in the infirmary."

As Titus rambles on, that word still tumbles around in my mind. A thought occurs to me. These people came to save Celestia. A show girl like me was never in their plan. What if they don't want me to stay once I get them safely to the island?

Hogwash. Just let them try to separate us. They'll regret it.

When I glance up at Celestia, her amber gaze is already cast down at me. A chortle rolls in her throat and she nods, reading my thoughts.

That's right, I imagine projecting into her mind. *If this doesn't turn out to be as good as it sounds, I'll hop on your back and we'll get the hell out of there.*

"We're here!" Tatum calls excitedly from the front seat. I hadn't even noticed that we'd entered a town, but here we are, rolling down a cobbled street with sandstone buildings sprouting up on either side of the main road. There's a breeze, I also notice, cool and damp, drifting up from the shoreline on the horizon, carrying a soft scent of salt and fish.

Trilliant Bay. I recognize the port town, named for the fact that it is a facet port that connects three of the gemstone continents. The circus performed here last winter, right on the beach, as we toured the coastline. There aren't many noteworthy places on the Emerald Continent that I haven't been.

I'm sure the people of Trilliant Bay are used to all sorts of cargo coming through to the port, but a dragon is not an everyday sight. Titus fidgets a bit nervously as onlookers stretch out their necks to get a better view as we roll by. A few children dash out into the street, almost touching the iron bars before their cautious parents snatch them back.

"You sure she's going to be alright?" Titus asks, eying Celestia warily. "She won't get too agitated?"

Celestia huffs as if in response to his implications.

"Celestia's used to gawkers," I tell him. "As long as she doesn't feel threatened, everything will be fine."

Titus's jaw flinches. "We've seen what happens when she feels threatened."

"Well, that's why you have me, remember?" I reach up and caress her neck. "I will keep her calm."

He nods, then turns his attention back to the road. The docks are in sight now and we're coming up on them quickly.

"I'm curious," I speak, Titus's back still to me, "I know you were planning on Celestia being sedated, but she's still a giant dragon. A pretty famous dragon, at that. Aren't you worried about all these people talking and word getting back to Gorio?"

When he turns, the rising sun glows on his face and I finally see the worry etched in his features.

"Oh, I've no doubt," he says. "She was supposed to be covered with a sheet and reported as meat cargo for the soldiers on Silver Coast, but now...I guess there's nothing we can do about that."

A pang of guilt hits me. Still, I just couldn't let her be drugged again. I couldn't let her be treated like cargo.

I'm not sure how to respond, but luckily, I don't have to.

"Look! That's our ship." Tatum points to a large cog vessel with some sort of boxed structure on top of the quarter deck. A single sail billows in the wind, so white I almost mistake it for a cloud. The cloth looks brand new, which is contrary to the worn condition of the rest of the vessel. Two male figures pace the deck. One looks about my age with dark skin and hair, which is more common on the Citrine Continent than here. The other man I have a hard time placing. His skin is dark also, but looks more tanned and weathered by long days in the sun. He seems a bit more seasoned, as well, poking about the ship, tying ropes, and checking nets.

I've never been on the seas, but I've heard nothing good about it. Sickness from the endless rocking. Merciless storms that will throw you off course if you're lucky enough to survive them.

"Don't worry," Titus says. He must see the hesitation all over my face. "We'll only be out there a few days. It'll fly by."

Somehow my gurgling stomach isn't convinced. I remember I haven't eaten for almost a day. I suppose I can inquire about food once we are on board but decide against it. There's no telling if my body has plans of spewing the meal back into the sea.

An official looking gentleman saunters up to the wagon as we stop next to the dock. "My, my! This ain't something you see every day. That is some fine cargo you got there, Mr. Stone."

There's something off about the way he says Titus's surname. "Stone" is probably the most common surname on the continent. It would be almost impossible to hunt and pin down a particular Mr. Stone. The man's tone suggests he's dealt with a few "Mr. Stones" and that he knows exactly what sort of "cargo" this is. In no way is it illegal to sell or ship dragons, but the glint in his thin smile tells me he's seen Celestia before. And me. He knows how valuable we are to the right people.

"Ain't she a beauty, Samuel?" Titus plasters on the fakest grin I've ever seen. "Now you can understand why I can't have word getting out about this shipment, right? Gotta make sure I deliver them both in one piece to my…impatient buyer."

Hearing Titus talk this way, acting like a completely different person than the one I was speaking to moments ago, sends a shiver through me. He's once again the man who held a knife to my throat.

"Right, right." The uniformed man scratches his hooked nose. "I'm sure we can come to an understanding." He holds his hand out for Titus to take it in an official agreement. Titus accepts, passing something silver and shiny into Samuel's palm. I almost would have missed it, had I not been familiar with the simple sleight-of-hand tricks the illusionist had taught me.

I don't believe for a second this man will keep his mouth shut. Not when Gorio's new work hounds start coming around with much more sharp and persuasive kinds of metal.

"Appreciate it, friend," Titus says.

"A pleasure." Samuel dips his head. He helps guide the cart and wagon team directly onto the ship. Once we are on board, the four horses are unhitched and led into what I thought was the captain's quarters, but what is instead a makeshift stable. Greta and the two seamen settle the horses in.

Celestia, Titus, and I are still inside the cage. I look around the deck, then stop at that strange box structure. "Where are you planning on putting us?" I ask warily.

"Most of us sleep below. There's a bunk for you, if you like. It's definitely close quarters, but it's clean and free of rats."

"Sounds cozy, but I'm staying with Celestia."

Titus half frowns in a *suit-yourself* sort of expression. "We've got special quarters for dragons." He points to the box. "The inside has been lined with flame resistant steel just for Celestia."

"Looks like you've thought of everything," I reply dryly.

"We can get the ramp and wheel her car straight in, so she doesn't even have to leave her cage. I thought it would be more comfortable for her if she stayed in familiar surroundings." He acts as though that's supposed to be a comfort to me.

"Locked up, you mean."

Exasperation droops his features and I can see just how tired he is. I wouldn't be surprised if he went straight to bed once we set sail. I just might, myself.

"Look," he sighs, "things didn't exactly go as planned. Celestia was supposed to be asleep for most of the journey. We're trying to help her, but we're going to have to make a few adjustments. All of us are." He looks pointedly at me.

I make a quick decision to use what energy I have to press my point. "You want to lock her up in another cage, for days. She's not used to being confined for so long. Even in the circus she's allowed to get out and roam around every few hours."

"Well that's just not an option in this case." Titus pinches the bridge of his nose. "Maybe that's why Gorio has never taken the circus overseas. But in any case, don't forget we are trying to *help* Celestia. Once we get to The Sanctum she'll be able to roam and fly around as much as she pleases, day and night."

The Sanctum. I can't help that my heart bursts with excitement at the thought. "Well I'm staying with her, even if she's in a cage for a whole month."

"Be my guest." Titus relents.

With the help of Brock and Crow, the two seamen, Tatum and Titus wheel Celestia and I up the ramp and into the new cage. The light caught inside is dimmer, and even though the space is a bit bigger than the car, the room feels much more cramped with the steel walls. At my request, they leave the door open to let in some light and so that we can see out into the wide, blue ocean. Celestia's ember eyes take in the cobalt terrain for the first time.

Celestia's pulse beats faster and I feel her tremor beside me. I wonder if she can feel my nerves or if the anxiety is all her own. I coax her to lay down, and nestle in beside her. I take a few deep breaths and try to steady my heart beat. To comfort myself, I imagine I'm at the top of that skinny platform, ready to plunge into the fire, except this time, it is the sea and a world of the intrepid and unknown.

CHAPTER 7

The Sanctum

IN THE TWO DAYS THAT FOLLOW, I ONLY WANDER FROM THE CAGE TO retch what little is in my stomach.

"Don't worry lass." The older seaman tries to comfort me as I hang my head over the rail. "Your sea-legs will sprout soon and the worst will be over."

I learn he is the one named Crow and he gives me some herbs that are supposed to calm my stomach. Eventually, I vomit those up too.

But I find Crow was right about one thing: by the fourth day the cage stops spinning and I begin to feel farther from the edge of death. Lying against Celestia's warm belly eases what's left of my nausea and by nightfall I'm able to venture out into the fresh air for some dry biscuits.

A shroud of glowing stars spreads out above the dark sea as I emerge. I hadn't been on deck during the night, and the sight takes my breath away. I feel as though I am suspended in a realm of dark, enchanted dreams.

The wind has died down to a soft breeze and the rest of the deck is quiet. I don't see anyone on watch so I assume everyone must be below. I wrap my arms around myself and drink in the moment of solitude. In the circus, I'm rarely alone. Out here, I feel like I'm the only person in the world.

But I'm clearly not.

"Mesmerizing, isn't it?" Titus leans on the rail beside me. His sudden words are like ice touching the curve of my neck. They are followed by an involuntary shiver.

I turn my head to Titus. It is the first time I've seen him in days. His features are brightened and contoured by the starlight, much like the night we first met. Perhaps that's why I feel comfortable speaking with him out here in the dead of night.

"I'd think you'd be used to such a sight," I say.

He shakes his head. "Nah. I only come out here at night when I'm on watch. I'm too superstitious and it kind of gives me the creeps."

"The creeps? Big bad dragon savior afraid of the dark?" I tease.

"No, it's just, you know what they say." He gestures up to the stars.

"That our ancestors' spirits dwell in the Star Realms, so they can look down and watch us while we live out our lives," I finish for him.

"Yeah that," he says, now looking down at the wooden rail. "Just kind of feels like a lot of pressure, you know? Generations and generations of other people's expectations."

I let out a quiet laugh. "I've never really given much thought to it. I don't even know my ancestors."

"Orphan?" he asks. His tone is light, as if he's asking which fruit I prefer. I wonder if it's because he's one himself and null to the constant sympathy from others.

"Yes. You?"

He takes in a breath before answering. "Sort of."

I'm not sure how one can 'sort of' become an orphan, but I change the subject anyhow. I don't like wasting thoughts on people I've never met, or my life before I came to the circus. Before I met Celestia.

"So how did you get into all this?" I ask. "How did you start rescuing dragons?"

"Ehh…" he keeps his gaze on the rail. "It's a long story."

I gesture around us. "I've got nothing but time. Two days' worth, I'm guessing."

"Less than that," Titus says. "The winds have been in our favor. We'll be in Sanctum by sunset tomorrow."

"Really?" I can't hide my excitement. My blood races at the thought of what the dragon hideout will be like, and the promise of getting off this ship in less than a day.

Titus notices my enthusiasm. A prideful grin sweeps over him once again.

"The Sanctum is my life," he says, gazing out over the quiet waves. "It's the only life I've ever wanted, you know?"

I shrug and stare out at the twinkling stars in the water. "I've always just wanted a home, I guess." *Have I found that home already with the circus?* I wonder.

"What was your life like before?" I ask. "What made you want to risk your life to save dragons?"

He takes a long time to answer. I can feel a secret there, burning deep within him like the crystal burning inside Celestia. And just like with my dragon and her crystal, I feel I'd almost have to kill Titus to get it out of him.

"I grew up with a privileged family," he finally says. Not surprising at all. I was wondering how he'd had the money for a team of horses, his own ship, and not to mention a private island. "Dragons were always around my home, one way or another. Some were trained for combat, some we stuffed for decoration. My sisters even kept a few as pets. I'd always been fascinated with them, but I hated seeing them caged and treated like slaves. Sold, slaughtered, harvested, and used. It felt wrong - like they deserved more than that.

"There were a lot of expectations for me as I got older. Most of my siblings moved away and moved on with their lives. I continued my studies and duties, but nothing sparked my interest more than those magnificent, complex creatures. I got to a point where I couldn't live a life that wasn't meant for me, so... I just left."

"You left? With a ship and your own private island," I point out.

"My family owns so much land they won't notice one tiny mound of dirt in the ocean," he answers confidently.

"What about your parents? Won't they come looking for you?" I can't imagine ever walking out on a family if I had a real one.

He gets quiet again. There is a darkness in his eyes that is deeper than the matrix of the night sky. And that's when something he'd said strikes me like a surge of icy water.

"Some were trained for combat, some we stuffed for decoration."

Three years ago, only a little bit after I'd begun my act, the Circus of Scales had been invited to perform for the royal court. Knights riding on armored dragons met us at the palace gates. The throne room had been draped in scaled curtains and stuffed dragon heads.

"My sisters even kept a few as pets."

The two princesses had light and shadow dragons, just like the ones Luna and Sable used before their act.

Understanding floods into my thoughts as I'm able to piece it all together. "They won't come after you because they think you're dead," I blurt out.

Titus snaps his gaze back to me. "What did you say?"

"You faked your own death. You're Prince Dashell."

He laughs. So hard that his eyes squint, but it doesn't hide the panic trembling in them. "You...you're more than just seasick. You're delirious with fever."

"I'm perfectly fine," I insist.

His laugh turns into a nervous chuckle. Desperate. "You haven't eaten in days. Your mind is playing tricks on you. Come on, we'll find you something to eat."

I don't reply at first, only watch as his demeanor changes from playful to panicking. "Don't play games with me, Dashell," I say evenly, almost as quietly as a wave whispering over the sea.

He stares at me, lips parted, moss green eyes pleading. "Please, don't use that name."

"I won't," I say. "If you promise to be honest with me."

He hangs his head; his straw-colored hair hides his eyes. "I wanted to tell you. I was going to once we reached The Sanctum. Greta was against it till she knew we could trust you."

"It's alright," I tell him, finding myself inched closer to him. In this vulnerable state, he radiates that comfort I felt with him in the cage behind Celestia's fire. "I understand. We all have our secrets. We all have our pasts."

"How did you figure it out, though?"

I shrug. "A lot of little things. Mostly because I've been to the palace. I knew exactly what you were talking about when you described your childhood. And the dye job," I add.

His fingers run through his lightened hair. Watching one strand fall into his eye sends a tremor through me. "You were at the palace with the circus?" he asks. "I definitely remember Celestia, but I don't remember seeing you there that night."

"I didn't have orange hair yet. Gorio added that detail later. I don't remember you either, but that's because Prince Da—the prince didn't have blond hair."

The corner of his lip jerks into a half smile. "Well, I guess it's like I said."

"What?" I ask as he moves in close. I'm enveloped in his scent of oakmoss and embers.

"Perhaps there is something beneath that putrid orange head of yours," he says, his eyes tracing the lines of my lips. I know what he wants to do.

And for reasons I don't quite understand, I let him.

His own lips are soft but driven with an unyielding force of longing and heat. I take in that force and reciprocate with my own. Our lips weave together like a choreographed dance, and I'm not sure how I already know the steps. His arms pull me closer while I reach up to rake the lightened hair I just can't resist. His tongue effortlessly finds its way in and glides over mine, sending tingles down my neck–until something turns those tingles into cold like ice prickles.

Somehow Gorio's face manifests, a lascivious sneer plastered on his pink cheeks. A freezing jolt strikes my core. I break away from Titus, breathless and shaking.

"Uh, I…I'm sorry. I shouldn't have done that." Titus flusters behind me. I can't bring myself to look at him.

"No, it's–don't worry about it," I spill out all at once. I grab onto the rail for support as a tremor ravishes me.

"Ivy, I'm really sorry. You said you don't like to be touched. I don't know what came over me. I won't do it again."

"Really, Titus," I insist, my tone harsher than I mean it to be. "It's fine. It's just…"

"Ivy, you're shaking."

Instinctively, I jump away before he can touch me. The look on his face is pitiful.

"It's just late," I say. "I should…I should be alone."

He doesn't try to stop me as I scurry back to the cage and Celestia's warm belly. The cage where I am guarded and safe and where I plan to remain.

I don't show my face again until late the next day when I hear a rowdy commotion on deck. For the last dozen hours, I've locked myself away with Celestia and the pile of boar bones she has accumulated in the corner of our cage. I'm still groggy from being sick, famished from skipping meals, and embarrassed about the events of last night.

Never in my life have I been kissed like that. Never have I let anyone. And just when things were getting good, I panicked and ran away like some foolish damsel. I don't know how to face Titus now that he's made his feelings known. I don't even know how to face my own feelings.

Let's forget for a second that Titus is a prince in disguise. It doesn't matter if he were the bastard son of a baker. All I've ever wanted in life was a home of my own and Celestia by my side. I've never pictured myself in the arms of anyone, let alone a secret royal. Whatever last night was, I'm just not cut out for it and it can never happen again.

Let's also forget that I've dreamt of nothing except his lips on mine since.

Outside on the deck, Crow hollers that we've spotted land. Sounds of scurrying boots creak the old wooden planks. For the umpteenth time, Celestia huffs and shifts her weight. She's never been locked up this long and she's starting to get agitated. The poor dragon needs to stretch her legs and spread her wings. I'm thankful this part of the journey is nearly over.

It is Tatum that sticks his head in the cage to retrieve me. "Come on. You're going to want to see this," he beckons to me with an extended hand. I accept his invitation after I assure Celestia I'll be right back.

The day is overcast, but the light is bright enough to sting my eyes as I emerge out of the dark hole I've called my home for the last four days. Tatum presses something into my palm. After my eyes adjust, I see it is a hard biscuit topped with a spot of carmine colored jam.

"Figured you were hungry after missing breakfast," he says sheepishly.

"Starving," I say before taking a generous bite. "Thank you, Tatum."

The boy's rosy cheeks bloom as he smiles. He reminds me more and more of a sweet boy that I remember from my first orphanage. He was sickly, but always shared his porridge with anyone who asked and even gave me his blanket after mine was thrown in the mud for a laugh. I can't recall what happened to him, but I can't imagine he made it far in a cruel world like this. Now, I don't think I even want to know.

Someone clears their throat beside me. With a mouth full of biscuit and jam, I turn to see Titus with a pained expression. Perhaps he's as unsettled about last night as I am. Though I don't see why. I'm sure as a dashing prince he's kissed many a fair maiden.

"I see you're finally up and about," the fallen prince says in a very tight, official tone. "Glad to see you're feeling better."

Since I haven't yet swallowed the giant gob of biscuit in my mouth, I simply nod in answer.

"Good," he says. "You'll be happy to know we'll be docking soon."

I look out over the bow of the ship, expecting to see a lush, green island in the distance. Instead we are headed straight into a dense, murky fog.

"I can't see a thing," I say squinting into the mist.

Now, a wry smirk spreads across Titus's face. "That's the idea. No one can."

"The western shore is lined with crystals that make fog on cloudy days. It's a rare kind of magic," Tatum explains.

"Superstitious sailors avoid the fog," says Titus.

I nod in complete understanding. "If you've met one sailor, you've met them all."

It isn't long before the ship plunges into the mist and we are shrouded in a cool cloud. I hold up my hands and they disappear in front of my face. Something about the fog actually *feels* enchanted. There's a buzzing of energy and the mist sparkles as if it is infused with tiny bits of glass.

We glide like this for a minute or two until the vessel jerks to a crunchy stop. We've hit land.

Crow drops the anchor and Tatum leads Celestia and I down a ramp. To my surprise, the boy was easily able to pick the lock to her heavy chain, and I wonder where the fallen prince found such a versatile lad.

Celestia grunts as she tries to get steady on her feet. Through the soft scales under her chin I feel her heartbeat quicken. Not being able to see things clearly is making her nervous, and I do my best to soothe her with a quiet hum.

Soon, sand shifts under my feet, and I follow Tatum out of the mist to a beach at the edge of a lush, grassy meadow. My eyes twitch, as if not believing the sight laid out before me. Deep green hills stretch out for leagues, leading into dense forests and rocky cliffs. A waterfall pours over the edge of a crag and forms a crystal pool at the base. The air is alive with the sounds of birdsong and the scent of magic and wild roses. As if announcing our arrival, a crimson dragon circles overhead and screeches a welcome.

This is what it feels like to find what you're searching for. This is what it feels like to come home.

"Welcome to The Sanctum," Greta says dryly as she passes me. I realize I've been standing in place, gawking at the landscape.

It is a long walk to the fortress, but I enjoy every moment of it. I suspect Celestia does too. It feels good to stretch our legs and experience the stillness and certainty of dry land again. We walk through the meadow and cut into an overgrown forest, thick with brambles and fresh moss. I can't help but think of Titus's sharp green eyes. He's positioned behind me as we follow the worn trail through the woods, so I can't look over to him to read his expression. The walk feels even longer with the silence between us.

Although it is not all silence. Tatum and the other seaman, Brock, are talking about some hatchlings they want to check on in the nursery. Greta is looking forward to cinnamon bread and a hot bath. I completely relate. Perhaps she's not a soulless harpy after all.

The fortress itself is nearly as hidden as the western shore. The base is covered in overgrown brush while thick ivy scales the weathered walls. An agile, lizard-like dragon jumps off a nearby branch and skitters across the battlements as he chases a stray leaf carried by the breeze. The structure is barely taller than the trees which is why I must not have seen it on our way inland.

"We've got some renovations planned for next spring," Titus says as he comes up behind me. It's as if he can read what I was thinking. "It might not look like much now, but we're going to reinforce the keep and add a southern tower."

"It's amazing," I say, just as the little lizard dragon has abandoned his quest for the leaf and chosen to watch me studying him instead. He cocks his head to one side and introduces himself with a screech. Celestia chortles back, and the two exchange a dance of some sort.

"Hey, Rex," Titus calls to the dragon on the rampart. "Looks like Celestia's already making friends."

I steal a glance at him –then immediately wish I hadn't. His emerald eyes are glowing in his warm expression. I see the love he has for this place and what he does all over his face. It makes it so hard to forget about the moment we shared under the stars.

A flash of raven hair darts past us. "Are we going to stand out here all day? I'm hungry." Greta pushes open the heavy oak doors and disappears across the threshold.

Titus and I share a nervous laugh. "After you." He insists with a sweep of his hand.

I guide Celestia along with me as we enter the fortress. Celestia has to crouch in order to fit inside the front room. There are dusty bookshelves and a few benches scattered about, but nothing that suggests an organized operation in the rooms beyond.

"We're planning on sprucing up this entrance, but it's not very high on the priority list. Come, the main hall is much more interesting," he says, ushering us along.

He is right. I've never imagined anything like this place. A dozen dragons varying in size roam about freely as if they own the place, grazing on potted plants that line the walls, batting at leather balls that are littered about the floor, bathing in the shallow pool in the center of the room. One dragon sends strands of a sapphire smoke curling through the air.

The ceiling in the main hall is much taller, so Celestia can stand at her full height. Light and warmth pour from the hearth at the back of the hall. Several large nests are placed by the fire, one of them occupied by a pair of thorn dragons curled up together like tree roots.

Upon noticing our arrival, a little black dragon the size of a hound darts towards Titus and stands on its hind legs until Titus bends down to shower the creature with affection.

"Misty had a fractured claw and a tear in her wing when we found her. Dr. Grove stitched her up, but she still doesn't fly very well," Titus explains between black tongued kisses. "We keep her in here with the rest of the dragons that are no longer suited to the elements."

I don't say anything, afraid I might succumb to tears instead. Watching these creatures play and swim and dream safely in the comforts they deserve, it's more than I ever thought possible.

Titus shifts uneasily during my silence. "Let me show you the infirmary," he says. "I can introduce you to Dr. Grove. Come on, it's through the courtyard."

Outside, more dragons roam about, rolling in the dirt and lazing in the late afternoon sun. Structures are built all around to resemble mountains and caves. Nearly all of them have a dragon or two poking around.

"You've put so much work into this," I say, impressed.

Titus beams like a praised child. "It's not much, but I wanted it to feel like a home for them."

With so many dragons around, it feels like a home for me.

"If I were a dragon, I'd want to live here," I say.

His smile grows wider. "Maybe you can," he replies quietly.

Before I can answer, Celestia leaves my side to go investigate a golden horned bull slurping from a fountain. Upon her approach, the male spreads his royal blue wings out to her in a display of his prowess. She snorts a puff of thick smoke in his face.

Titus and I laugh.

"They really all get along? Living together like this?" I ask.

Titus watches as the golden horned dragon dances around Celestia. "For the most part. The ones that prefer to live in solitude are scattered about on the island. They're just like people, you know, with their different personalities and preferences." He leans down to scratch the scales on the cuff of Misty's neck. "But I think most are happy here. We try to provide them everything, so there's not much to compete for, so there's not much to fight over."

"What do they eat, exactly?"

"We try to get as many as we can on a diet of vegetation, but for those that prefer meat, there is an abundance of wild boar on the island. A lot hunt on their own and return here to the courtyard to sleep."

"I doubt Celestia can hunt," I say.

"She won't have to. We're able to sustain enough meat for those that can't, but that's why we try to switch over their diet to roots and fish."

I have to laugh. "Good luck with that. I don't think Celestia's ever had anything to eat but goat."

A glint shines in Titus's eye. "So, you're considering letting her stay?"

I scoff. "I was told I didn't have much choice."

He smiles devilishly. "Something tells me you don't always do as you're told.

I leave Celestia with her new admirer as we continue to the infirmary. This part of the fortress seems to be the busiest and is occupied by the most humans. A tall woman, with gray streaks running through her ponytail hunches over a desk strewn about with papers. A young girl is rotating palm sized eggs under a lantern. Tatum is kneeling by a kennel of a dozen squeaking hatchlings, handing them bits of meat. Shelves line the walls filled with notebooks, scrolls, and potions, but what my eye lands on is a case of crystals all arranged and labeled.

Titus must notice my gaze turn dark, because he quickly explains. "We've acquired these crystals from all over the continent. Some I even stole from the private collection in the palace. They help Dr. Grove with her research and…occasionally, we'll use them to assist us on a rescue operation."

I shrug. "Makes sense, as long as you didn't harvest them yourself. Better they be used for good, I suppose."

"Let me introduce you to our physician," Titus says, eager to change the subject. "Dr. Grove!" he calls to the tall woman.

Dr. Grove pops her head up, looking bewildered, as if we'd just interrupted some deep deliberation. Perhaps she hadn't noticed anyone entering her domain, but at the sight of us, an open grin spreads through her cheeks.

"Titus, dear, when did you get back? Who's our new friend?"

I already like this Dr. Grove. It's good to know not all the women in this group are callous and hostile. The physician wears a tattered blouse and trousers with a stained apron to match. I can't see her hands covered under her rough leather gloves, but if I could I would bet they would show a lifetime of hard work. There is a warmth in her light brown eyes and an air about her that tells me she loves what she does.

Titus clears his throat. "This is Ivy." He gestures to me. "She is… our guest." He gives me a sheepish look, probably wondering if he'd used the right word.

"I see." Dr. Grove's eyebrow raises slightly, but she doesn't pry. "Well in that case, welcome. Please, make yourself at home. If you need anything, don't hesitate to ask. Just, make sure you watch your step—Little Spryer got out of his kennel yesterday, and I don't know where he's scurried off to."

"You'll want to check the kitchens. He's probably hiding in the sugar sacks," Titus says.

"We have." Dr. Grove sighs. She looks to me. "That's what got him admitted to the infirmary in the first place. Millie thought he was a field mouse and whacked him with a ladle."

"Poor thing," I say.

"We'll keep an eye out," Titus offers. "I'm sure he'll turn up."

The physician clasps her hands together. "Right, well. Lots of work to do. A pleasure to meet you, dear. Titus, be sure to give her a tour, we don't get guests often." She turns to go back to her desk. "Jessa? Did you find that tonic I asked for?"

Titus shoots me a half smile. "I don't think that woman ever sleeps."

"Well, when you do what you love…"

"Guess that's why I don't sleep much either," he says dryly.

I'm gravitated toward the kennels. Almost every one we pass is full. A gray shadow dragon sleeps carefully with a cast on his hind leg. A luck dragon wheezes in the kennel next to it. Her almond eyes are clouded as if her magic is diminished.

"These guys are all on the mend. Most of them just need a bit of isolation and rest before they can leave." Titus assures me. Perhaps he can sense my worry as my fingers graze the iron bars of the cages.

"What's wrong with her?" I ask, I reach through the bars to caress the golden scales of the luck dragon.

Titus's tone turns solemn. "Felicity had been viciously attacked before we found her. Someone had tried to slit her throat to get her crystal before she fought them off. The cut left irreversible damage to her trachea, which is why she has trouble breathing. The magic of her luck crystal kept her alive until Dr. Grove was able to stitch her up, but her magic was drained in the process. It's going to take a while before her crystal is charged again and she can recover."

"Poor thing," I whine. It's no wonder she was attacked. Luck crystals are among the most rare and valuable magic. I try not to imagine the same thing happening to Celestia if she were out in the wild.

"Would you like to meet our newest arrivals?" Titus asks, his voice light again.

"Of course," I say, and he leads me to the kennel with the playful hatchings.

Ice dragons. Five little hatchlings, no bigger than kittens, climb on top of each other, nipping and licking each other's scales. The babies are all shades of winter, from light gray to a frosty blue. Their wide eyes glimmer like sparkling snow. The little squeaks and screeches that come from their tiny mouths are like music to my ears. I am in love.

"Do you want to hold one?" Titus grins. He places a limp hatchling in my hands and my heart melts, despite the cold that radiates into my palms. The little dragon looks up at me with their crystal fractal eyes and huffs a frosty mist as it coos. I snuggle it to my chest and its nubby little horns burrow into my bosom.

"I think he likes you."

I hug the tiny hatchling tighter. "I don't care if I get frostbite, I never want to let him go." The baby chortles as if to agree.

"You can hold him as long as you like," Titus says. "You can stay as long as you like," he adds more quietly.

I don't meet his eyes—it's hard looking away from my cute new friend—but I smile. This place is a dream. Now that I'm here, I don't ever want to leave. Celestia could be safe here. She could make a home among her kind and among people who will fight to protect her. The Sanctum is the Stars' answer to the only wish I've ever sent up into the sky. It is the home I've been longing for.

Which is exactly why I have to leave. The sooner, the better.

CHAPTER 8

Anchor in The Sky

CELESTIA SOARS IN CIRCLES AROUND THE FORTRESS, THE BEAUTY OF HER pearlescent scales rivals the moon in the night sky. She's made a habit of this the last two nights before she nestles into a cave in the courtyard until dawn. I sit and watch her from the balcony, sipping a calming tea and preparing for my early departure at first light.

The only thing that makes it easier to leave, is knowing Celestia is safe and happy here. In the short time we've been at The Sanctum, I believe she's already started making this place her home; claiming a nest, roaming the grounds, taking to the skies whenever she pleases. She's even warmed up to Greta, which only gives further evidence that I may have misjudged the woman. I've found that Greta has as much fire in her heart as Celestia and I'm grateful she is on the right side. Titus may have forsaken his title of Prince and thought he left his duties behind, but he has turned out to be the greatest leader I know.

The people here are *good* people. They live to take care of the dragons not because someone ordered them to, or because someone is paying them, but because it is their calling. I believe it could even be *my* calling, if not for the fact that my very presence here puts everyone in danger.

As if the Stars could manifest my thoughts, Titus strolls onto the balcony and leans his arms over the railing, much like that night on the ship I still can't seem to put aside. He perches a safe distance away, shifting nervously.

His voice shakes my core as it pierces the still air. "I came to try to change your mind one last time."

I smile sadly. "I wish that were possible. I really do."

Titus is quiet for a moment as we both watch Celestia in flight. There is no other spectacle like it, watching a dragon command the skies. Tonight she's like a creature I've never seen before. Freedom has given her a new grace that I could watch all night.

"She's going to miss you," Titus finally says. "I'm going to miss you."

I dare to look at his face and I wish I hadn't. So much heartache and hope glints in his starlit eyes that I feel for a fraction of a moment that I might actually change my mind.

But I can't.

"I know," I say. "I want more than anything to stay, but, it's just not possible."

Titus turns to me and fidgets with his hands. He speaks quickly in an awkward stammer. "If this… if this has anything to do with the other night…I shouldn't have done it and I promise–"

"It doesn't," I cut him off. Better to keep those feelings under lock and key. Though they bang on the cage like a wild animal, they will do me no good now. "Like I told you all yesterday, Gorio is a proud, persistent man. He will search the ends of the earth for his prized dragon. If I go, I can convince him that Celestia is gone and to stop looking. If I stay, I put you, all of the dragons, and everyone's hard work at risk.

Titus cautiously puts his hand over mine. When I don't flinch, he takes them both into his own and holds them gently. His voice goes low and dark, so quiet I move in closer to hear it. "I swear, Ivy, I will protect you. I'll never let that bastard or any of his hounds near you again. You belong here. I can't bear the thought of you going back to that man. To be used like his property…"

"I have to," I insist. My voice squeaks as tears rise to my eyes. I blink them away and grip tighter on Titus's hands. "I can't bear the thought of this place no longer existing. Of these dragons being slaughtered or their freedom being snatched away. I can't bear the thought of you dying because of me."

I have more to say, but I'm hushed by his firm, warm lips. If only for this moment, if it is to be our last together, I let myself drink in his worry, his desperation, his hunger. I have all those things too, and between us they flourish into a bond that burns as bright as the stars. It's as if wherever his hands touch me, they ignite a fire that has been forever dormant. A fire that couldn't be doused even by an ocean between us.

I'm nearly breathless as we pull apart. When I look up into his eyes, they are alive with the same fire that runs in my veins. "A kiss, even one like that, won't convince me to stay," I tell him.

"I didn't think so." He smiles sadly. "But it might be enough to convince you to come back."

I abandon words and let my lips answer for me. How long can we stretch this moment? How long can I beg the Stars to keep away the dawn?

Reluctantly, I pull away. I want to look him in the eye with my next words. "Titus, I will not stop fighting until I can return. Until I know you and Celestia, and everyone else are safe from that scoundrel forever."

A shiver forms under my skin as he strokes my cheek. "Neither will I," he says before our lips meet again.

The Stars do not grant me my wish - not entirely. When our moment inevitably ends, I spend the rest of the time I'm given on the back of Celestia, gripping her spikes like my anchor in the sky. We soar over The Sanctum and the night wind whistles past my ears. I know the Stars are listening as I make the same promises to my dragon.

ABOUT CONSTANCE ROBERTS

Constance Roberts is a retired flight attendant who turned in her wings to stay at home with her adventurous children and to write. She and her husband live in St. Louis, Missouri where they spend the weekends playing board games with friends. She is an avid bookstagramer and you can find her book photography on Instagram @imagery.in.pages. She is currently working on another gender bent fairy tale, and has big plans for another fantasy series.

CONNECT ON SOCIAL MEDIA

www.facebook.com/onyxmoontrilogy
instagram.com/imagery.in.pages

ALSO BY CONSTANCE ROBERTS

Sigil in Shadow

Lost

Onyx Moon

Blood Is Silent

KM Robinson

A Little Red Riding Hood Retelling

CHAPTER 1

"You need to worry more about the world," he warns as his eyes flick over to me. "You're not invincible, Sienna."

"Neither are you, Ephraim."

He eyes me with a grin. "Actually, that's exactly what I am, madam." Ephraim motions down to his abs as he tightens them.

"Just because they advertise you as the Invincible Man, doesn't mean you are, Eph. I've seen you in training, don't forget."

Spinning, I twirl my silks around me like a cape, clutching it under my chin. I consider sticking my tongue out at him but decide to pretend to be mature instead.

"I don't think that's how that's supposed to be used." He smirks.

"How would *you* know? You're on the ground all the time."

I wrap my foot around the fabric and begin to climb using my other foot to hold the fabric in place, pushing myself higher as Ephraim watches me. My hands and feet take turns pushing and pulling my body into position.

"You've had me in the air enough times that I can *pretend* to do your job, Sienna."

"Yes, and flawless as you may be, I still look prettier up here," I counter playfully. I separate the silks and lift myself up into a double foot lock. Josephine starts the organ music across the tent as we all warm up for the evening's show. It's muggy in the tent and the crickets have started chirping early this evening.

"Indeed." Ephraim turns and makes his way over to a bench where he starts curling his arms as he lifts his weights, showing off as several of the girls walk by. They ignore me in favor of ogling Ephraim.

Can't he just practice throwing knives instead? He has more than one job here.

"Where is she?" An icy voice cuts through the organ's deep tones.

Turning, I find Samuel standing in front of me. I lift both hands above my head, leaning forward as I cross the silks behind my back. Moving my hands to grasp the fabric, I lean back to invert, legs out to the side as I dangle upside down from the silks.

"Who?" I reply, facing away from him.

"Ida, of course," he snaps. "She's been gone for three days. Where is she?"

"You know as well as I do that she's out in the woods working on a new routine." *Or something.* We don't ask questions about Grandmother's magical ways. She always returns with something new that changes the face of the show though, so we let her get away with being mysterious.

"Your grandmother can't just go running off whenever she feels like it." I don't have to see him to know his fists are clenched at his side. Samuel's reactions are as dependable as rain on the first night of the show in a new town.

Of course, my grandmother can do whatever she wants. She's responsible for three-fourths of the acts that perform in this tent. Samuel may own the place, but Grandmother is the one who keeps it running. If she wants to wander off to one of her many cabins along the route, no one is going to stop her—she comes back with magic every time she leaves and makes Samuel a ton of money.

"If she's not back by tomorrow, you're going after her." He's most definitely clenching.

"Mhmm," I murmur, pulling my legs back up from the sides to lift myself to face him again. He glares at me for a moment before looking around at the other's warming up under the enclosed tent.

"We don't have time for that!" Samuel shouts to them. "The people are here. We're starting early tonight! Places!"

I can hear one of my grandmother's many little sayings float through my mind. She's always coming up with strange things to say that make the most perfect sense…and then she uses them over and over as reminders to the crew.

Smoke for fire, she always says about Samuel. For as much as he tries to breathe flames, he's all talk.

Josephine's playing only slows for a moment as she registers his words, transitioning into the song she reserves for signaling the performers to hide from the incoming audience. We still have time before the people make their way to the tent, but many of us aren't allowed to be seen by the public until our appearance in the show, and have to get out of the main part of the tent.

Several of the men and women walk out of the tent to engage with the audience who has come to see the show before they take their seats inside the tent colored by yellow-tinted lights. I duck behind a curtain that separates the main ring from the area we've designated for the performers and walk toward my dressing room.

My trunk sits in the corner of my fabric-encased square room. There's enough space to change wardrobe and do my makeup. The walls of the tent don't block the sound, so Josephine's swelling music crashes through the backstage area loudly enough that it sounds like I'm in the center of the ring.

"Ready, Sienna?" Fannie's voice frightens me. I whip around to face the closed curtain that acts as a door.

"Almost," I answer, dipping my shoulder down as I slip the sleeve over my arm. The flesh-colored fabric settles snugly against my body, ribbon-like strips of red fabric wrapping around me dramatically to mesh with the silks as I perform. I loop the elastic over my finger to hold the sleeve in place, a sharp point dividing my hand in half.

The curtain moves as I push it open and step out in front of Fannie and Blanch. The two sparkle in deep purple tones adorned with silver accents. Both girls wear curled hair pinned back to the sides, the only difference in their ensembles is their hair color— Fannie a chestnut brown and Blanch the darkest raven-black I've ever seen. Grandma Ida did the girls a favor when she chose purple as their signature color.

"Trying to impress someone tonight?" Blanch muses, kicking her hip out to the side as she raises an eyebrow.

"No more than you are," I counter, releasing the curtain behind me.

A rush of wind passes by as Harriet rushes through with her batons. Had they been ablaze, she would have burned the tent down with the way she is moving.

"Slow down, Harriet, opening act isn't for another two minutes!" Fannie calls after her playfully. The girl ignores her.

"One of these days she's going to turn around and breathe fire at you," I warn with a laugh.

"You mean I'd finally get a solo act?" Blanch grins. "I'm in."

She winks conspiratorially at me before turning to playfully yell, "Hey, Harriet!"

Fannie shoulders her friend like she does when one of the horses is being stubborn. Blanch holds her ground, barely swaying. Rolling my eyes, I push between the two toward the main part of the tent, ribbons in hand.

"Time to go, ladies."

Someone shifts the curtain concealing the backstage area from the main tent, allowing me to glance through it for just a moment. People file in, taking their seats as they wait for the show to begin. Josephine pounds out the notes on the organ, swelling enough to get the crowd ready for our grand entrance.

"I heard Ida still isn't back," Harriet murmurs, shifting anxiously next to me. She always arrives at the entrance before the rest of us, even though she's near the back of the lineup. "She's supposed to be changing my act when she gets back."

For a girl who works with fire for a living, she certainly is nervous before a performance. Working with fire may be the *only* time she's confident.

"If she's not back this evening, I'm being sent out to find her in the morning," I promise. She nods.

Suddenly, the music stops—our cue.

The lights on the other side of the curtain dim and the crowd falls silent. The lights go out completely, leaving us in the dark. Fabric rustles as Orville or one of the other boys whips open the curtain. As one, we rush into the ring and take our places, bathed in darkness.

Whispers fill the room from the audience as they wonder why it's taking so long without the lights on. Josephine presses one finger lightly on the organ key, followed slowly by another.

Deep breath.

Lights.

Roaring music crashes over the audience as the lights go on at full strength, drenching the ring in yellow. Throwing my hand up into the air, I release the ribbons. My face follows my initial move and I catch sight of rows of sparkling lights running from the center of the tent to the edges, mixed among chiffon fabric that matches my silks in an array of colors.

Looking back down, I see the crowd as the other performers start swirling around us. I dance with my ribbons, twirling them into the air to catch the attention of the onlookers. Most of us can't give our acts away yet, but the opening number still has to shock and awe the audience.

Fannie and Blanch find their horses across the tent and mount, standing on their saddles as they race around the outside of the ring. Ephraim juggles knives, concealing his true abilities for later.

Fire spins in the air as Harriet beams brightly, getting just close enough to the children to make their eyes grow wide. Orville leads in one of the elephants who circles the tent. Everyone glitters in the wardrobe picked by Grandma Ida for each individual person—no act has the same color or outfit design—we're all unique.

Red.

I'm only allowed to wear red when I perform. Grandma saved the color specifically for me. It was my mother's color before me and I inherited a different shade of it when I started my own act.

Blood. Fire. Intensity. Passion.

Grandmother always told me red was the color of war and strength, power and determination, desire, love, and passion. I love and loathe it all at the same time.

Grandma is a bit of a kingmaker. If the other circuses are to be listened to, she has the magic touch. Some even say she has real magic, but what she actually has is highly trained talent. Her skill at finding new acts is unparalleled. But even if Samuel brings in a new act, they have to pass Grandmother's tests to stay. Her word is final on a talent's success or removal from the show—she's always right. Samuel learned the hard way when he kept someone she turned down or dismissed someone grandma insisted we keep. With the way she always knows, it wouldn't surprise me if she was some magical creature sent to watch over us. If anyone in this world has *real* magic, it's Grandma Ida. I hope I've inherited some of that magic too.

My ribbons swirl around me as I move, contorting my body as I dance. Samuel stands in the center of the ring, eating up the attention in his black-and-white striped suit with accents of red and top hat, cane in hand, every bit a ringmaster.

The music grows as we finish our opening number. The crowd's gaze is fixed on the colorful spectacle. I run to the center of the ring, positioning myself—only a few notes left until all eyes will be on me.

The final notes.

I pass my ribbons off to Ephraim to carry out for me.

The lights go out.

Everyone else runs to clear the area. I remain, twirling the fabric one of the men lowers for me around my arms in my beginning pose, showing off the silks, one toe pointed gracefully in front of me.

A single light falls on me.

The group is transfixed by me as I start to move, leaving the fabric to fall behind me as I step forward, distracting them as the remaining performers leave the ring. Each step matches Josephine's music.

My costume matches the silks and once I'm in the air, it will look like it's part of the fabric, making me one with my apparatus.

I greet each section of the crowd, taking small bows or holding my arms out as I move around the center of the tent quickly before taking my place by the silks once more.

Lifting myself onto the silks is easy and I quickly climb high into the air—high enough to be seen by everyone without them having to struggle to look around the people in front of them. Just as I've been taught to do, I move into a double foot lock, wrapping the silks around my feet. Grandmother knew I needed to put on a show if I was to be the opening act for the circus and her routine never disappoints.

My wardrobe is overly hot in the sticky summer evening air, but it makes for a flashy show, which is exactly what Samuel demands of us. Twisting the silks behind my back, I drop into a cross back straddle, dangling my arms to the side high in the air, matching my outstretched legs. The children in the crowd gasp, shouting questions to their parents about why I'm hanging upside down.

I smile to myself as I move, twisting the silks counter-clockwise until I start spinning clockwise in the air. I've always loved the feeling of the lights dancing behind my eyelids as I close them just long enough to see the vibrant colors piercing through my makeup-covered eyelids. Opening my eyes, I reach up to right myself and climb higher as Josephine's music guides the viewers through my act's story.

The routine is only a few minutes long, but I've heard the audience say they were amazed by how it seemed I was up in the air for an eternity. I suppose to people who don't see it every day, it does seem like a rather long time. Samuel would never allow for a routine to last more than a few minutes though—he keeps us on a tight schedule, and we pack far too many acts into the show to dawdle. My body would be screaming if it were any longer, so I don't mind staying on task.

Nearing the end of my silks performance, I climb higher and make a show of wrapping the silks around my body. Inverting, I wrap one knee around the silks and grab the dangling end with my free hand. Looping it behind me, I wrap it around my lower leg. I twist my body around, positioning myself properly. The fabric wraps around my leg again, crossing in front of my body and around my back until it dangles freely again. With both hands, I clasp the fabric flowing beneath my head, knee still wrapped over the top part of the silks above me.

I take a breath to focus before straightening my leg and releasing my right hand straight out. My left hand guides the fabric as I finally allow myself to tip over, spinning into a triple star drop. I cascade down toward the ground, toppling over myself as part of the audience screams. The rest gasp.

My body stops, bouncing up slightly as the silks cushion me a few feet above the ground. My legs come together, pointing my toes as my hair sweeps the dirt. I only hold myself there for a moment before pulling myself upright. Using my legs, I spin myself, freeing my body of the final part of my wrap, then slide down the fabric to the ground.

The entire tent is silent. One breath. Two breaths. *Applause.*

I smile as Grandmother taught me to do, bowing to the corners of the tent. A little girl in the crowd catches my eye. She claps furiously, grinning at me.

Just then, the tent door rips back, revealing Blanch and Fannie. They ride in on their horses, a team of them in their wake. The two take turns leading their entrance, and the second rider always comes for me.

Still in my final pose, arms in the air, I wait until Blanch angles her horse at me at the last second. I run at full speed toward her, catching her wrist. I'm not sure how the girls manage to pull me onto their horse at a full gallop every night, but I hold on to them as we race around the ring.

Both girls slow their horses as we reach my exit, allowing me to easily dismount before they rush to the center of the ring to perform.

"Nice work out there," Blanch calls before preparing to deposit me into the waiting arms of Orville.

"Thanks!" I yell before I fling myself off the horse's back, twirling in the air with a hand from Blanch. I land heavily against Orville's chest. He swings me, completing my motion and I fly through the partially open curtains into the backstage area.

I crash into Samuel and he makes sure I'm standing of my own accord before turning away, giving me a moment to stabilize myself. "Nice work out there, but you're still responsible for finding Ida in the morning. You were good, but not good enough to earn a morning off."

"Thanks, boss," I mutter under my breath as I push away from his chest and make my way back to my changing area to switch for my work on the lyra.

"Hey, Sienna," a deep voice says behind me. I don't have to turn.

"Hi, Elijah." My heart speeds up. I blame the triple star drop that was only supposed to be a double star drop.

Sometimes a girl likes to show off.

"That was impressive," he croons.

"It was supposed to be." *Confidence…I can pull this off.*

"It's nice to see a woman who knows what she's doing." He peels off, fading into the crowd of people backstage.

"*Wow,*" Ephraim says, sidling up next to me.

"Leave it alone, Eph." I roll my eyes.

"Fine, if that's what you want." He shrugs. "Do you want help tracking down Ida tomorrow, or should I leave that alone too?"

I've gone out numerous times to track down my grandmother on my own, but the majority of my friends protest. They don't like when I travel into unknown woods by myself. This town is particularly less high-end than where we normally travel, but Grandma Ida and my mother always taught me to be braver than I felt. Showing weakness never helped a female's case.

"I'll be fine. You get your beauty sleep," I quip. Glancing at him up and down from the corner of my eye, I add, "You need it."

"Fine," he jokes. "Be that way. But when you get kidnapped, don't expect me to come save you."

"Last time you thought I was going to fall down a pit and die, suddenly it's abduction?" I turned to face him as I walk. Spinning, I move backward. Ephraim reaches out to take my wrists, steadying me as I walk quickly backward. My hands rest on top of his, fingers tracing his forearm as I balance myself on my tiptoes to walk faster. We've always worked well together, even though we don't share an act.

"I'm just saying that I won't be the one to come and save you." He cocks an eyebrow.

"Elijah can come rescue me instead," I tease.

"Good luck with that," Ephraim mumbles. "He's more interested in the mirror than rescuing pretty girls."

"That's true." Harriet brushes past us, equipment in hand. We both pause to look at her before laughing.

"This is me," I say as we reach my dressing room curtain. I kick my leg out behind me for show, leaning onto his arms a touch. Ephraim bows his head slightly to say goodbye before leaving to get ready for his own act. It scares me when he has people attack him in the ring for show, but he always emerges unscathed.

"Wear something sparkly!" he shouts as he walks away.

"Always!"

While silks will always be my favorite apparatus, I love that working on the lyra gives me more freedom with my wardrobe. While everything has to be streamlined for silks so that nothing catches on the fabric, I can wear anything while working with my hoop.

"Sienna!" Ephraim pauses, glancing back. "Don't forget to wear something red when you sneak out early to look for Ida."

I wave him off and duck into my changing room.

Grandmother, though incredibly good at her job, is starting to lose her sight. She recognizes most people by their voice and their blurry signature color now. Wearing red helps her to identify me from a distance—I'll have to find something to wear since I can't take my wardrobe out of the circus without drawing too much attention and my jacket is ripped thanks to Hoyt and his tigers.

I'll figure it out later though—first I need to decide on my next show piece.

I rummage through my small trunk until I find the dress I want. Setting it over the top of the trunk, I turn to my small mirror and examine myself in my silks outfit before changing.

Strips of red fabric move over one shoulder and down my chest, wrapping around my waist. A second piece covers the other side of my chest, wrapping behind me. A large piece of red moves around my waist to swirl between my legs and around each thigh. It twists down around my knees, making me look like I'm wearing ballet slippers with incredibly wide ribbons tied around my calves.

While I have many different outfits, I wear this one when I'm feeling particularly bold. Mother never cared for it, but Grandmother said it made me look brave—perhaps I should wear *this* out to find Grandmother in the morning. In truth, this town makes me nervous and I don't like the idea of roaming around where I could run into anyone—best not to draw attention to myself.

What if I go out when I'm sure no one will be around?

The thought sparks in my head, making me duck as if I've been struck.

I *could* go out when no one was around. It would probably be safer. If I skip the end of the show and leave right after my next act, that will give me at least an hour to wander in the dark before the people start straying from inside the circus limits—likely two hours before the majority of them start to file away. It could be my best opportunity to avoid the townspeople.

I tug down the sleeve of my outfit, sliding it to the floor. Noise fills the area outside of my dressing room and I quickly hurry into my next outfit. The translucent skirt drops to the floor in front of me, slits all the way up to my waist. The bodice wraps similarly to my last outfit, coming to a point in the middle in various shades of sparkling red. Behind me, I clasp the high collar, adjusting the feathers off of my right shoulder. I consider leaving the detached sleeves off for the evening, but they really *do* complete the outfit—we all have to suffer for our beauty in this heat.

Tying my curls back into a high ponytail, I give myself at least a little grace when it comes to dealing with the sweltering heat. The tent makes everything so much hotter with all the people in it. Perhaps I'll leave my hair up when I slip out later.

Stepping out of my changing area, I look for Samuel to tell him I'll be leaving tonight. He doesn't do well when Grandmother isn't around to oversee his circus, so I'm sure he won't mind if I skip the closing number to retrieve her from the woods. I'll have to find out if she took anyone with her or not—Grandmother likes to disappear without telling anyone she's going, occasionally taking a performer or two with her for training.

Before I can take more than three steps, Fannie has me cornered. After she gives me the full rundown of their part of the show, I mention I'll be slipping out early so they can cover for me in the finale. Blanch nods but looks worried, as does Fannie. They know better than to argue.

I find Samuel, explain what I'll be doing, and get his approval before making my way to the ring to wait for my next call time. My lyra performance goes quickly enough and I block out Samuel's instructions to return immediately to the tent with Grandmother this evening. He almost sounded worried for my safety...*almost*.

I change into all black, wearing pants and a fitted top with a belt to the side to hold my knife, water, and a few extra things I carry with me when I go out. Without a jacket to wrap myself in, my only option is my red cloak. Once my boots are tied, I pull the cloak around my shoulders and step out into the night air, leaving the hood off. Not wanting to deal with the warmth of the fabric, I push it off of my arms, behind my shoulder, leaving it to hang from my neck. It's uncomfortable but not as bad as the sweltering heat.

Stars glisten in the sky as the crickets shriek their high-pitched songs. Darkness surrounds me, leaving only the faint glow of the lights outside the tent to cast my long shadow over the dark grass. The noise from the tent silences in my wake as I walk away, and I pray everyone remains at the circus and not prowling around in the dark.

Ephraim was wrong—I don't need to be more worried about the world. I'm already terrified of it.

The noise I hear next gives me good reason to be.

CHAPTER 2

A MAN GROWLS BEHIND ME. I SPIN, READY TO DEFEND MYSELF.

"Did clearing my throat scare you?" Elijah grins arrogantly at me.

"Don't you have a show to do?"

"Do I?" he questions. Elijah takes a step toward me.

"You're supposed to," I challenge, crossing my arms. The wind kicks up at just the right moment, making my cloak shift behind me. If only Grandmother could see me now—she'd be so proud of my wardrobe-moment.

"I'm going with you," he replies. "The woods are no place for a woman this time of night."

"Everyone is here at the show. I'll be fine," I counter.

"You want me to stay and deprive you of my company?" he asks. "I hardly think so. I promise, I won't make your boyfriend jealous."

"Boyfriend?"

"The *invincible* one..."

I reach up to tuck my hair behind my ear. "Just friends."

"I know." Elijah grins. "That's been made *very* clear; I just like testing the waters."

The new act is a troublemaker.

"Perceptive."

"I'm aware of many things, Sienna." Elijah runs his hand through his hair as he steps toward me. "Shall we?"

"If you want to test Samuel's wrath, be my guest." I motion for him to walk with me. Turning, I lead the way, pretending I know where I'm going.

We walk in silence until the glow of the circus lights is completely in the distance. The moon's glow illuminates our path, brightly reflecting the hidden sun.

"The last circus I worked in wasn't as brightly colored." Elijah makes small talk. "They focused on a black and white scheme."

"Sounds macabre," I muse.

Elijah's hands are clasped behind his back as we walk and I fight not to mimic him. Grandmother taught me not to copy others—it suggests that they are the leader and we are the followers. I hold my hands at my side, tucked just behind my cape as it billows out behind me.

"Why are you wearing that?" He nods to my cloak.

"So that Grandmother Ida can see me. She can't always make out faces from a distance, but colors help."

"I've heard she has magic—real magic. That's what all the other circuses are saying. I'm surprised she can't just heal herself so she can see again."

People have been claiming Grandmother was magic for the majority of my life. She took a small circus and transformed it into one of the best-known shows in the country in a matter of months. She teaches our people to do things no other circus can pull off. In truth, I think she enjoys being mysterious about it—she plays into what people say about her. I've believed it a time or two myself—how else can I explain some of the things she's capable of?

"Why red?" Elijah asks before I can respond.

Stepping out of the field and into the woods, the fallen leaves start to crunch under our feet despite it being the middle of summer. The trees are far less dense than many of the woods I've been in, allowing the moonlight to easily pass through to us.

"It's a family color."

"Ida doesn't wear red," he points out.

"That's a story for another time," I interject. I don't feel like talking about my mother right now or why Ida doesn't dress like me anymore. "How are you finding the circus?"

"I'm settling in," he drawls, hands in his pockets.

"I've seen your act a few times," I mention. "You're pretty good."

"I was trained by the best." His words come quickly and easily.

"Yet, you left…"

The breeze picks up slightly, rustling the leaves in the trees. My hair brushes across my face from behind, tickling my cheekbones and chin.

"I went out on my own. You can't be an apprentice forever, Sienna."

"But you're willing to throw it away to walk into the woods in the dark of night," I point out.

"Protecting one of Samuel's star acts hardly seems like an offense." He glances at me from the corner of his eye, barely turning to acknowledge me. "He'll get over it. Besides, it's only been two months —I'm hardly of value yet—and the closing number is just showing off. There's no real magic in it."

"I'd still be afraid of getting in trouble."

"You're afraid of a lot, aren't you, Red Girl?" He uses the nickname some of the other performers call me. We all have one, but I've been here longer than most and my color stuck.

"No," I lie. If only Ephraim could hear this conversation. "I'm out in the woods alone at night—do I seem like a coward to you?"

"You seem stupid." He pauses, realizing he insulted me. "Going out in the dark in a strange town isn't safe. You shouldn't just go out on impulse."

"Didn't you just tell me I was timid?"

"You can be timid and still make poor decisions, Sienna. You need to be careful whom and what you trust. Putting your faith in a fabric tent to keep people in while you wander out alone is hardly a wise choice."

"I didn't see you stop me."

The trees open back up into a small clearing of tall grass. I don't like walking where I can't see, and there's very likely ticks and other creatures in there, but Elijah doesn't hesitate, so neither do I. The grass tickles my elbows as I hold my hands up out of the way—at least my pants will protect my legs, but my arms are bare.

The earrings I put on before I left dangle around my chin. Every few steps, one swings into my line of sight, catching the light from the moon. I walk more intentionally in order to swing them more, the light soothing me and giving me something to focus on as we walk through the tall grass. Something scurries away from us in the dark and I fight to control my breathing.

"Where are we looking?" Elijah asks, changing the subject.

"I don't know. Ida goes where she pleases. I'm not sure if she took anyone with her this time to train." I speed up to keep step with Elijah. "Honestly, I thought she might have taken *you* out here. You were gone when she slipped off, but I saw you the next day. I heard she might have found some new talent, but I'm not sure. It's always a guessing game with Grandma Ida."

He chuckles. "Keeping tabs on me?"

I laugh, trying to play it off. "I notice everything."

"Did you notice me noticing you?" His pace slows, as does everything in my world.

"No," I reply cautiously. "I didn't notice that."

"Maybe you haven't been watching carefully enough." He laughs quietly again. "Magicians like being watched closely, Sienna. You're hurting my feelings."

He's definitely trouble.

"Is there some way for you to know where Ida went or are we going to be wandering around all night?"

I shake my head, clearing my thoughts.

"Usually she leaves me some markers." My eyes start sweeping from tree to tree as we step back out of the small clearing. "I'm the only one that can spot them though."

"Ah, a secret. I can back that."

"You like secrets?" I ask, absentmindedly as I start to look for Grandmother's signals to me.

"Secrets are the fuel the world runs on, Sienna. The more secrets you have, the more power you hold."

In the bush, I see the mark my grandmother has left for me—three broken branches in a row, all bending down toward the ground, even though they've been snapped at a sideways angle.

"This way," I mutter, pulling us off to the left.

Elijah raises an eyebrow at me but doesn't ask how I know.

He's not supposed to know how we communicate, so I try to distract him.

"How long have you been performing magic?"

"A few years." He takes his left hand out of his pocket and loops it through his belt loop, allowing it to dangle next to me. My companion steps to the side just enough to shift closer to me. A few more shifts and he will be touching my arm. "A few different shows tried to poach me over the years, but I was loyal. Once he felt I was ready, my teacher sent me out to find my own work."

"Which is why you joined us."

"No, I was with another circus first, but they didn't have what I was looking for, so I moved on after a time."

"Are you finding that here, or will you be leaving us too?"

Elijah pauses for a moment, not answering. When he finally

speaks, he says, "I think I might have found what I've been looking for." He waits again. "I'm very interested to meet your grandmother. We've talked a little, but I haven't been able to see any of that magical wisdom she's become known for."

"I'm sure you'll get a chance when we find her."

"Samuel seems very anxious to find her."

"He is." I step around an exposed root, nearly catching my toe on a rock instead. "Perhaps you could teach me to do a few simple magic tricks sometime. We haven't had a magician in the show for years, but I was always mesmerized by sleight-of-hand when I was younger."

"Are you trying to get me up on your silks, madam? Because that won't happen. Unlike your friend, I have no use for spending time in the air."

"I wasn't proposing a trade unless you wanted one."

"But you will offer *something* in exchange for my time and knowledge…"

"The pleasure of my company, good sir," I quip. I spot Grandmother's signal again and keep us to the left once more.

"A fair trade, then, I see." He nods. A small smile tugs on his lips.

"Babur!" a yell pierces the otherwise quiet night. I whip around.

"What is it?" Elijah asks, turning with me.

"Babur?" a second, less-certain voice takes up the cry.

"Orville?" I yell.

Silence hangs between us for a moment.

"Sienna?"

"Here," I call back, walking toward the sound of his voice.

"Careful, Babur is loose." He crashes through the trees until I can see him. Hoyt follows behind him, chain in hand.

"Babur is…?" Elijah asks uneasily.

"Tiger," I respond. Orville approaches, taking my outstretched hands in his. He ducks, looking into my eyes in the moonlight.

"Babur escaped, we don't know how, but we have to find him before the show gets out." He glances at Elijah. "Let's split up. Elijah, go with Hoyt."

He tugs on my hand as Elijah protests.

"He's right," I interject. "Hoyt trained Babur—you're safe with him. Orville works with the elephants and has more experience with animals than either of us. We'll have to find Ida tomorrow—this is more important. We need to get Babur home before the townspeople notice him wandering and try to hurt him."

A strange expression flashes on Elijah's face—I can't tell if he's relieved or upset. After a moment, he nods, accepting the arrangement. Without another word, we split.

"How could this have happened?" I mutter to Orville.

"There was no damage to the cage. It looks like someone let him out." His words hit me with the same force the ground does when I occasionally slip off the lyra in practice when I'm not paying attention. "Babur!"

I listen through the darkness and trees, hoping to detect the sound of a tiger's paws. Nothing.

"What do we do if we can't find him?"

"Tell the town. Likely get run out."

"We have to find Ida before we get run out. I just hope we find Babur before the townspeople do."

"We will. He can't have gone far—he never strays from Hoyt for too long. The guy practically raised him since he was a cub."

"Are you saying Hoyt is his mother?" I snicker at the image of Hoyt as the compassionate, caring type.

"Something like that." Orville grins. He runs a hand through his long, blond hair. If their faces weren't different enough, I'd say he and Ephraim could be brothers, but cousins is close enough. "Nice cape, by the way."

"Hoyt ruined my jacket last week; it's all I had."

"No luck finding Ida then, I take it?" We duck under a tree branch.

"Clearly didn't get that far."

"Babur!" Orville suddenly shouts, interrupting my final word. Turning back to me, he adds, "Did you really think it was wise to come out at night?"

"I thought everyone would be in the tent for another hour and I'd have time."

Just as we step out of the trees and into the clearing, something rushes at us. It tramples through the grass, nearly colliding with Orville.

"We found him!" Elijah gasps. "Come help."

CHAPTER 3

"YOU CORRALLED A TIGER?" BLANCH ASKS IN DISBELIEF.

"That's not the important question here!" Fannie practically shouts, turning on Blanch. "She was surrounded by three of the most gorgeous men in this circus and you're worried about a *cat?*" Fannie protests.

"We *really* need to realign your priorities, Fannie." Blanch glares at her shaking her head in mock disbelief.

"A tiger, huh?" Ephraim interrupts. Fannie and Blanch beam at him. "I knew you wanted to expand your act, Sienna, but a tiger? Are you going to start getting a big head too like the other trainers?"

He sits down next to us on the edges of the benches that we moved to the side of the food tent.

"Hoyt's been looking for a new partner, I hear." Fannie bats her eyelashes at Ephraim.

He leans forward, placing his elbows on his knees. "Well," he drops his voice conspiratorially, "if *you* switch to work with Hoyt, Fannie, I'll be available to work with Blanch."

He swings around to face the raven-haired girl. Blanch laughs, leaving Fannie shocked for a moment before she laughs too. Ephraim has endured Fannie's flirtatious side for years and enjoys teasing her back.

"I accept," Blanch finally struggles to say. "Lose the shirt and we're good to go. Training begins tomorrow."

Ephraim's grin grows as his eyebrows shoot up. Reaching for his collar, he begins to unbutton his shirt, pretending to leer at our friend. I laugh and swat at his arm. He sways sideways a little with my strike, fixing the top button.

"Are you going to let me accompany you today, Sienna? Since you have such a tendency to find vicious creatures out there." His grin turns into a sincere smile as he looks over to me.

"You'd better not be calling my tigers *vicious*, Ephraim." Hoyt sits down next to us, balancing a plate of food on his knee.

"I was actually referring to the wolf who followed her out into the dark." Ephraim shoots an icy glance at Elijah across the tent.

"There's something off about him," Hoyt agrees.

"You mean the fact that he's gorgeous?" Fannie counters.

"Who's gorgeous?" Josephine sits down with us.

"Elijah."

Josephine's eyes grow wide. She's usually fantastic at schooling her long, oval-shaped face into compliance, keeping us from reading her expression, but not this morning. Her gentle features spark to life as she glances down.

"My point exactly." Fannie crosses her arms triumphantly.

"Yes," Blanch replies, also crossing her arms at her friend. "But his attention isn't on *you*, is it?"

"I'm willing to share the attention with Sienna for now," Fannie says benevolently.

"Back to the point," Ephraim redirects us. He points to the group. "Can we walk you, Sienna?"

"You know Ida doesn't like big productions," I reply. Everyone looks at me.

"You realize where we are, right?" Orville points out from his place by his cousin. "This thing is called a tent. It's similar to the big one we perform under *every night* for *thousands of people*."

I roll my eyes at him.

"I don't need a keeper, thank you."

"At least take *one* of us with you," Ephraim pleads. "A few of the townspeople saw you bringing Babur back last night—I'm sure word has gotten around by now."

"Which means they'll be looking for a tiger, not a girl."

"Which means they'll be in the woods *looking*." Orville jumps in before Ephraim can argue.

"Take someone, Sienna," Hoyt encourages. He grins viciously at me. "*I* volunteer."

"Yeah, go with Hoyt; I'll keep Elijah company while you're gone."

Fannie smiles brilliantly at me, bobbing her head from side to side as if she won.

"I'll go." Harriet sits down with us, her long, dark hair free from the bun she wears it in while performing. One dark finger points back to herself. "After all, I'm the one who works with fire every night. The only one who does more dangerous work is Clarence."

Ephraim looks affronted. "You think the man getting shot out of a cannon into a net has a more dangerous job than the man who gets punched in the gut by a strongman every night?"

"*Nobody* could get past *those* abs, darling." We all turn to Blanch, shocked that wasn't Fannie's answer. "Oh. I need to stop spending so much time with my partner. I'm so sorry." Blanch looks horrified that she spoke.

All of the men look quite pleased with her outburst. Ephraim's eyes sparkle. "Thank you, Blanch."

"I'm still going to be more helpful to Sienna than *you* lot." Harriet declares. "Samuel isn't going to fare well if we don't get Ida back soon."

She sits back as her nervous side comes out. Whenever she's anxious, her bravado fades.

"I'll be fine," I protest. "It's light out; nothing is going to happen."

I refuse to look at Ephraim, but I can feel his eyes on me.

"Let her go," Josephine's quiet voice stops everyone. "She's done this before. She does it all the time when Ida wanders away to work. We're better off here doing damage control from Babur's unplanned walk last night. We need to show them that it's business as usual and no one here is worried that another tiger might escape."

She doesn't say it, but she also means they need to figure out who let the tiger out in the first place.

"I can take Caleo for a walk," Orville suggests. "She hasn't had a good walk since we arrived the other day, aside from running around the ring."

"Good, take the elephant for a walk," Josephine directs.

"Someone want to help with Brisheet?"

I stand as they debate what they should do to maintain appearances around the tents. I make it to the exit before Ephraim catches up to me.

"Be safe," he says quietly into my ear as he leans in behind me. Ephraim presses a knife into my hand. I tuck it into my belt that sits over my long, gray skirt.

He brushes away from me, not waiting for an answer.

The circus is a different place in the daylight. Outside of the colorful tent, everything is bathed in white light from the sun. The circus lights won't be on for hours and I miss the colorful glow of red, blue, green, and yellow from the bulbs strung across the tents.

It's not nearly as warm as it was last night, but it's still early morning; there's time for it to warm up more. The noise from the animals mixes with performers calling to one another. Many of the men are working on projects, building new set pieces, repairing damage from the night before, or moving feed for the animals. I slip past them quietly.

Thinking twice, I move the knife Ephraim handed me to my boot, just in case. I check the knife that was already sitting on my hip to ensure I can remove it easily should I need to use it, and then I set out away from the circus perimeter.

Having already discovered part of the path last night, it's easier to get on the right track today. I quickly locate the broken branches and make my way along the path. The birds escort me as I walk.

Unfortunately, the tall grass is just as concerning as it was last night now that I can see the spiders everywhere. I go out of my way to walk around the area.

I make it several more markers before I notice the noise behind me. At first, I think it's the wind in the trees and bushes, but as the noise persists, I convince myself that I'm not alone.

My hand automatically reaches for the knife at my hip.

"Planning to cut my heart out?" A familiar voice asks. I relax as Elijah steps into sight.

"Sneaking up on women in the woods isn't encouraged, Elijah," I remind him.

"You knew I was here."

My eyes involuntarily sweep the length of him taking in his dark clothing. In return, he slowly looks me over.

"Shall we?" Elijah holds out a hand, pointing away from where I'm walking. Without waiting, he takes several long strides toward me, grabs my elbow, turning me, and propels me forward in the direction of his choosing—the wrong way.

"We shall." I pull my elbow away. "But we're going *this* way."

I wonder if he's going to argue for a moment. He pulls out a few cut ropes instead. Holding them up, he shows me the three different lengths.

"Let's make a wager. If you can turn these ropes into three

matching ropes of the same length, we'll go your way. If you can't, we go my way."

A smile tugs at my lips as I indulge his game. This might prove interesting.

With a big flourish, he shows off each rope he's holding in his left hand. Elijah draws out the process, talking about each one in great detail as he loops the ends up into his waiting fingers. Once he's displayed each of the three ropes, he grabs onto three ends and pulls. Each of the three ropes has transformed into the same length—a trick that would shock anyone.

The magician grins flirtatiously at me, then crumples the ropes into the palm of his hand. Pulling them out one at a time, he reveals three vastly different lengths of rope. Raising an eyebrow, he hands them to me to inspect.

I tug on each, ensuring that they are solid pieces of rope. Nothing has been cut, there's nothing sneaky about them. The trick is pure magic.

What Elijah doesn't know is that I also know how to perform this trick. I might not know much about magic, but I know enough to get by if I ever need to entertain a group of people. Our last magician taught me this one.

Placing the ropes in my hand, I pretend to mimic him. I let my voice waver just enough as I'm repeating his words to make him think I'm uneasy. Each rope is held out in my hand, displaying the length before tucking them up to create the loops just as Elijah had. At just the right moment, I dart my eyes away to something behind him. Just as I knew he would, he tracks my movements.

As he glances back, I take a deep, steadying breath. Repeating everything he said, I pull the ropes down, revealing the same length ropes dangling from my hand. His jaw drops.

After a moment, he meets my eyes and grins. "Well played."

I swirl my hand over the ropes, moving differently than he did to reveal the ropes returned to their natural, uneven state. Elijah reaches out for his ropes. I place them in his hand, and he tucks them away. I spin before he has a chance to protest.

"Nice of you to join me again," I comment, cloak billowing out behind me with my quick steps.

"You still shouldn't be out here alone."

"Don't pretend you're here for me. We both know you're here to see Ida."

His footsteps suddenly stop behind me. I walk a few more feet before turning around.

"What if I'm here for *you*?"

A single rose made out of lace fabric rests high on his left lapel, just below his shoulder. From it, three silver chains so dark they're almost black dangle across to his right side, halfway between his hip and shoulder. They sparkle in the sunlight dancing through the swaying trees.

Elijah's jacket is long, resting over a brocade fabric vest in a steely gray color that's nearly black as well. Black boots stick out under tight, black pants, completing his look. He's left his gloves at the circus, apparently, or tucked into one of his many hidden pockets. He looks every bit a renowned magician, even if he's only been in the public eye for a few months with Samuel's crew.

"Perhaps I'm here for both." He takes my silence as an accusation.

His strides are long once more as he moves toward me. Just as I think he's about to bury his hand in my hair, he moves, tipping my chin up to him. His other hand grabs my waist roughly, pulling me toward him.

"Is that really such a bad thing?" he murmurs inches from my lips.

Elijah pulls away, moving around me. Stunned, I don't move for a moment. I nearly contort myself around without taking the time to turn my feet to see his reaction.

"I imagine it is." I finally turn, stalking toward him. "I'll forgive you *this* time, but—"

His lips silence me. This time, he tugs on my hair, opening my face to his. One hand slips low on my back, making me shudder. I did exactly what he wanted.

Elijah slams me against a tree a few feet away, kissing me the entire time. My fingers run over the chains on his chest until I reach his shoulder. I've never been kissed like this before, but I quickly learn that I don't mind it.

I brush over his ear, pinning it to the side of his head as I work my fingertips into his dark hair. Elijah's high cheekbones are sharp against my skin as he moves to the spot just below my ear, making me gasp.

It's only a moment before we pull away, but it feels like something has changed. I look down at the forest floor and focus on the crumbling leaves that are attempting to cling to their last bit of life now that they've fallen.

"I want to know everything about you," he murmurs. I giggle; I can't help it.

"I'd like to know about you too, Elijah."

"You first." He sounds breathless as he pulls away, leaving me resting against the tree. I force myself to push away from it, testing my legs gently to make sure I won't fall on my newly-weakened knees.

When I'm sure I can walk, I join him, letting him guide our path for a few minutes as I search for the next marker. Thankfully, he continues in the direction I had set us on before his interruption.

"How long have you been with Samuel's circus?"

"My entire life," I answer. The birds seem extra happy today as they sing to us. "I grew up there. Ida has been with Samuel since the beginning and my family has always stayed."

"When can I meet the rest of your family?"

"It's just me and Ida now." I try to keep the emotion out of my voice.

He makes a small noise and nods.

"You and Ida seem to be doing well for yourselves. Have you ever considered working anywhere else? You might be paid better elsewhere, especially with both of your talents."

"Oh, we'd never leave. As rough as he is, Samuel is family, and so are the others. Besides, Samuel would be lost without Grandmother."

"I can believe that—it certainly seems like Ida does a lot there."

"She does. She's been training me to take over for her, and it turns out that she does *so much more* than I thought. I don't think anyone is really aware of just how much Grandmother does to organize and run that show."

"It's nice that she's letting you take over," he says casually. "How much are you doing now?"

"Can you keep a secret?"

He perks up as I transition into being conspiratorial. "I'm a magician; what do you think?"

"Good point—you're probably the best of us all at keeping secrets." I pause for effect. "Grandmother has been training me for a while now. She's stepped back quite a bit. I don't know it *all* yet—and *Samuel* has no idea—but she's been letting me make most of the decisions and then she communicates them to the team. She wants it to be a seamless transition one day, even though she's not ready to retire and just come along for the ride yet."

"Samuel's going to let her retire?"

"No." I laugh. "That's why we're doing it this way. He will never know I've taken over until it's just me completely handling everything and Ida shows him proof that I can handle it."

"Will you be taken off your act at that point?" Concern hitches his voice slightly.

"I'm not going anywhere." I bump his hand with the back of mine. "I might transition some of my duties. If I really need to, we can find a second aerialist act to work with me and alleviate some of my duties, but only if we need to. I'll begin training people at some point over the next year or two, as well."

"So, you'll be disappearing on these little trips too?"

Elijah is good at putting the pieces together. I suppose I'll have to start making some disappearing trips of my own so people don't put it together when Ida and I both disappear all the time.

"Any chance you'll need company? Magicians are pretty good at disappearing acts—I could help."

He grins without looking at me. I tear my eyes away as we split to walk around a tree in our path, each taking a side. When we converge, he takes my hand, holding it tightly.

"I have a confession." Elijah's words are rushed.

Is he nervous?

"We need to go this way." He points. Before I can protest, he continues, gripping my hand tighter as if I might run away. "I've been working with Ida. I wasn't supposed to tell anyone. We've been trying something."

What?

Grandmother never tells me who she's bringing out into the woods to test new acts with, but I never would have guessed that she'd bring Elijah out so early—especially since he was still with us for most of her time away. She usually waits several months for new performers to establish themselves before she helps refine their act... and to make sure they stick around that long.

"She's not over there anymore—she left last night. We had to move for what we were working on."

"What are you working on?" I start to pull away. He holds me in place.

"Magic. *Real* magic."

"Real magic doesn't exist, Elijah. It's all sleight-of-hand and trickery. We make them believe, but there's logic behind it all."

Right? Something ticks inside my brain. If *anyone* had access to *real* magic, it would be Grandmother. But surely, she doesn't...

"Not in this case. We've discovered something. You'll see. Come on."

He pulls me along behind him. It takes a moment while I'm processing his words, but I catch up to him.

"You're sure this is the way?" I ask after a few minutes of him explaining why he didn't tell me he had been working with Ida again, reiterating the same thing in four different ways without giving me any additional information.

That's when I hear her voice. It's a quick shout in the distance. Before I can run to Grandmother, Elijah drops my hand, flinging his arm in front of me to stop me from rushing forward.

"It's part of it!"

"What's happening?" I struggle to get around him.

Spinning, he faces me, using both arms to pin mine against my body. Elijah puts a foot behind him to brace himself as he pushes against me to counter my momentum. Neither of us are able to break the force of the other, pinning us to our place in the middle of the forest.

"Sienna, you can't go over there, it's part of the process." He glances back over his shoulder, struggling against me.

"What is happening?" I demand as her next shout is cut off. I scream around Elijah since I can't move past him. "*Grandmother?*"

Everything goes silent but Elijah.

"You...can't—" His words are separated as he tries to counter my movements. An angry male voice cuts him off.

"What is this?"

My blood runs cold as I make eye contact.

CHAPTER 4

"IDA, I HAD TO TELL HER." ELIJAH CUTS ME OFF. HE REFUSES TO RELEASE his grip on my upper arms.

Throwing my left elbow up between us, I bring it down on his forearm and break his hold. Twisting, I wrench my right side away from him. He holds his hands out at me as if he had just encountered one of Hoyt's tigers and was trying to tame it with his words.

"I'm sorry, Ida," he addresses the man again. "I had to tell your granddaughter about the new act we were working on." He turns back to me. "Sienna, I'm sorry I couldn't tell you before. I knew it would be hard to believe and you'd have to see the transformation for yourself."

He glances at the man again. His dirty blond hair is stringy, falling past his shoulders. His brows are dark and far thicker than the bit of facial hair that surrounds his lips and chin. The man glares at me as Elijah continues.

"Ida"—he turns and nods at the man—"and I have been working on transformation magic. It's your grandmother."

He looks desperately at me before turning back to the man. Elijah walks quickly to his side, the man's gaze fixed on him. The man's eyebrows furrow, but he quickly raises them, nodding.

"Hello, my dear," the man addresses me.

Elijah turns, reaching out to me, waving me over. "Come."

I blink. There's no way the man in front of me is my grandmother. She's a woman and two generations older than the man in front of me.

They can tell I don't believe them. The man steps away from Elijah. Reaching down, he pauses until he's sure I'm watching. He snaps one, two, three branches right next to each other—Ida's signal that I'm moving in the right direction.

"Grandmother?" I ask in disbelief. He nods.

"We've been working on this for a while now, Sienna," Elijah supplies. "It's why Ida brought me into the show—I have a gift and so does she—even more than me. We weren't sure we had it right, but she insisted on trying it before she would let any of us test it. We're planning on using it as part of my act originally, but then we're going to expand it to several of the other acts as well.

"I know you're *taking over for your grandmother*," he glances at the person next to him, "but we wanted to make sure we had this right before we told you in case it failed—we didn't want this bit of it coming back on you if it didn't work. Your grandmother wants you to succeed in taking over for her and she knew you'd push this once you knew about it, even if it failed. She didn't want you constantly working to make a failure succeed. But it's worked, Sienna! It's worked!"

The man beside Elijah watches him carefully, nodding slowly, then faster before turning to look at me.

"What is this?" I ask skeptically, locking eyes with my...*grandmother*.

"Magic, dear. I knew Elijah would be the one to help us figure it out." The voice is dark and low. Even if Grandmother had transformed herself somehow, I can't imagine this is what she would sound like posing as a man.

"How are you doing this? Even if you *could* change your appearance, how are you getting your voice to do that?"

When did I start believing this man is my grandmother?

"Come, I'll explain everything." Grandmother motions to me, her fingers now long and gnarled much differently than her aged skin. "But I need to *show* you. It's not just magical words, my dear. It's so much more."

"And it requires a great deal of additional space, which is why we moved," Elijah interjects, earning a glare from Grandmother—something I'm well accustomed to.

I take a cautious step toward them. Elijah takes his place by Grandmother and elbows her slightly—I don't think I was supposed to notice.

"It may be hard to see you, dear, but even *I* can tell you're hesitating. Come along now."

I feel like I've been struck. It *has* to be her, right? If she still can't see, that means even though her appearance has changed, she's still in there.

"Come, come." *Impatience*. Perhaps it *is* her.

Lifting my skirt, I follow. What choice do I have? If Grandmother has discovered something, I need to learn what it is.

"Why were you shouting?" I ask, standing alongside them as they begin to walk.

"The transformation process," Elijah jumps in. "It's a bit painful at first, but it seems to be getting easier."

"How many times have you done this?" I ask in horror, looking at my grandmother posing as someone else. She looks far too dark for the Grandmother I know.

"A few." I wonder if she means to sound like she's grumbling or if it's a byproduct of the transformation process.

"Can you change back now?"

They both turn to look at me.

"No. It's not possible because—"

"No, the effects last for several hours at a time." Elijah quickly supplies. "Ida *just* changed, so she'll be like this for a bit. Don't worry, it will make traveling easier, won't it, Ida?"

Grandmother nods.

"You're still unsure," Elijah sounds disappointed. He looks to the man next to him.

The man reaches into his pocket and pulls out a red ribbon crossed over itself in a loop with a point where the ribbons meet. Grandmother has worn it on her left wrist under her sleeve since the first day I started training on silks.

It's her. There's no doubt in my mind that this is her.

The man—*Grandmother*—smiles at me. Tucking it back into the pocket it came out of, my grandmother nods at me.

"This way, children." Grandmother has always called everyone *child*. It's a term of endearment, but also a reminder of who is in charge. Even Samuel has to endure it.

Grandmother leads the way, clad in her signature dark clothing. I wonder if her outfit changed in the transformation process or if she had donned those clothes before it began. I've heard rumors about another circus having the power to change a person's being, but until this moment, I thought they were only rumors sent out by the ringmaster himself to try to drum up more business and downplay Ida's renown—very few circuses get the attention Samuel's show gets.

Elijah takes a place next to me, allowing me to walk just slightly ahead of him. Grandmother's new strides are long—even longer than Elijah's—and I have to hurry to keep pace. We move so fast that I can barely keep track of where we're going.

I try to ask questions along the way, but they both keep telling me they just have to show me. After twenty minutes, we reach the edge of a clearing that could have also been a fantastic place for Samuel to set the tent up.

Past that, there's nothing but more trees and small clearings. I give up asking questions and let them lead me further away. Birds chatter in the distance. Once in a while, a pair of squirrels will chase each other across our path.

"We're close," Elijah informs me, taking my hand surreptitiously. He drops his voice to a whisper. "No matter what you see, just stay by me and hold my hand."

Fear pricks the back of my neck. The light streams through the trees ahead, suggesting we're about to walk out of the forest and into the open. Despite the summer heat, everything feels cold.

I balk.

Elijah turns to look at me, tugging on my hand. There's fear in his eyes, pulling slightly at the corners just enough to make him look concerned. "You have to come."

I don't. I stay rooted to the ground as he pulls harder on me.

"Come along," Grandmother says matter-of-factly. "We don't have time for this."

"It will be fine. Can you trust me?" Elijah asks, changing his demeanor. He's no longer trying to be forceful, but his words from before have a lasting impact.

Grandmother moves forward, not waiting.

I take a tiny step forward.

"See?" Elijah asks. "I'll be right here with you."

Slowly, I let him guide me to the clearing. Across a cut-down meadow, there's a caravan of wagons and small tents—another circus traveling through.

"What is this?" I demand. Whatever this is, it isn't right.

"Come along," Grandmother insists again. "We haven't time for this."

Her outfit is similar to Elijah's but far less showy. It's dark-colored with a long jacket that sways around the knees. Tall boots sit over long trousers. A billowy shirt peeks out from under the jacket—it's not a show piece.

"It's a circus," Elijah whispers. "Just come inside and see."

A large tent is set up similar to our food tent. It's large enough to hold the crew of a circus, but not big enough to perform in. The fabric is dark, just like both of my companion's outfits.

There are enough animals around to hear and smell from the tent, even though I can't see them. Glancing around, I note a number of cages laying about, though none of them appear to be homes to animals—they're far too pristine. Chains sit on the ground, forcing us to maneuver around them.

The tent is relatively empty save for a few performers dressed in black and white wardrobe. Their lines are sharp and piercing, high-lighted by the commanding contrast of their colors. They look over to us pointedly and wait.

"This is that aerialist I was telling you about," Grandmother addresses the group. "She'll be joining us today."

A man and a woman painted nearly white with pink makeup around their eyes look at me in shock. A third who looks to be some sort of court jester from books looks at me with a reaction I could almost classify as pity, though it's hard to tell with the strange makeup on. The rest simply nod and look away.

"Sit," Grandmother commands.

"Are you hungry?" Elijah asks. He's still holding my hand tightly. I shake my head no.

Elijah sits beside me. Grandmother walks away toward the small crowd of performers.

"Where are we?" I whisper.

"Ida just needs to talk to some people first and then we'll explain." He pats my hand with his free one.

After a moment, Ida walks back, and I hope she transforms back to herself soon. It's disconcerting to be staring at her in the form of a younger man like this.

Grandmother steps forward, looming over me. I didn't realize how tall she was in this form. I nearly stand up, but something in Grandmother's expression tells me not to move.

"I'm going to show you something." Grandmother holds her hand out to me. "It will wear off soon and I need to show you before it does."

Elijah quietly nods next to me. I take Grandmother's hand and rise. We leave the tent and the strange performers behind.

The sun is high overhead, making the heat unbearable again. I wonder if I can take the cloak off since Grandmother knows I'm here now, but I dare not ask as we walk.

Stepping into another tent, Grandmother adds, "We perform closer magic here. This circus provides a more *personalized* experience to our clientele at times. We have a big tent like Samuel does, but here, we allow our audience to step into the ring and investigate the acts for themselves at the start of the show. What you're seeing here is our close-up endeavors."

Grandmother lifts the curtain back that blocks the tent from the outside world and places a hand on my back to shove me forward. I stumble and Elijah loses his grip on my hand.

When I find my footing and look up, I discover a dimly lit tent full of apparatuses and dark, sparkling things hanging from the ceiling. A lyra is suspended in the middle of the tent.

"We want you to perform here, Sienna," Grandmother addresses me. "We don't need Samuel anymore. I want you to design the shows *here*."

"You...want to *leave*?" I couldn't have heard right.

"I've already left. I'm bringing you with me."

"Run—" a voice screams from the side of the tent. It's followed by a loud metal clang. I look over just in time to see a handler slamming a metal rod against the bars of the cage again. A girl cowers on the far side, only inches from where the metal struck.

"What is that—"

"Part of her act," Grandmother cuts me off. "We have unique acts here aside from our main show."

Grandmother waves a hand in the air. Knowing I'm meant to follow, I watch the movement.

"Will you lead?" Grandmother addresses me without looking.

"They want you to be the star act, Sienna," Elijah announces. "They want to feature you. Well, you *and* me."

Nothing makes sense. Why would Grandmother leave Samuel's show? She was training me to take over for her. The people there are like family. Why would we ever leave for someplace so...*dark?*

Trying not to be too obvious, I carefully move my gaze around the room as I examine it. The slow, deliberate movement gives me a minute to think.

"Grandmother, why?"

"Are you questioning me?" Grandmother whips around to face me.

My grandmother doesn't snap at me. She doesn't even raise her voice to me. She's a master at leveraging disappointment to make people feel a thousand times worse than if she yelled at them.

The magic spell breaks around me. They lied.

Magic isn't real, my inner voice reminds me.

I was foolish to think it might be true. It was ridiculous of me to believe the whispers of the people calling my grandmother magical. I was naïve to believe that a pretty boy who brought me stories of magic might actually be telling me the truth...might actually want to be with me instead of manipulating me.

What if he doesn't know?

"Elijah," I whisper, stepping back.

The man posing as my grandmother drops his façade. He steps toward me dangerously.

"Elijah!" I whisper harshly again, trying to step back to run.

The man I thought was my friend grabs my wrist, clenching down on my bones, refusing to let me leave.

I'm going to pay the price for my wishful thinking.

"Hold her," the tall man growls at Elijah.

Elijah instinctively wraps his other hand around my wrist and I'm certain it will bruise. If these men want me to work for them, they should be more careful of damaging my hands—I need them to climb.

Elijah transforms, no longer pretending to care, leaving me no doubt that the man I thought I was getting to know can't actually be trusted. I drive my heel into Elijah's foot, and he yelps. Thankfully, my dominant hand is free of his grasp, leaving me the ability to strike. I connect with his nose violently. His head reels back—both with the force of my punch and with the shock of the assault— and blood trickles down his upper lip as he glares at me.

"*Stupid* girl."

Pain radiates through my jaw as his knuckles connect.

CHAPTER 5

There's one spot of bright light behind my eyelids. I can tell it's not natural light—it's sharper. It resides only on my left side. It's painful.

I don't open my eyes—I know better. I might not know enough to not trust co-workers who are actually strangers, but at least I know *that* much.

Listening, I pick up the sounds of a circus. *Am I home?*

The more I hear, the more I'm certain I'm not.

Elijah hit me.

No. Elijah *retaliated* when *I* hit *him.*

I'm at their circus—him and that man that was with us.

Grandmother. Where is she?

I had heard her before Elijah and that man talked me into leaving. They must have her too.

I was such a fool.

"Release her at once!" Ida's voice fills the room. She's here. They have her. I can hear her struggling against them, but they're much stronger than she is or ever has been.

My eyes fly open—I can't help it.

Through my bars, I see Grandmother standing between Elijah and the man, two other men standing near them to provide support. The man who tricked me holds onto Grandmother's upper arm, just above her elbow as she snarls at him.

"What have you done?" She turns, glaring at Elijah. "I gave you a home."

"And he's giving *you* a new one, so even trade," the tall man snarls back. His hair looks greasier than before, but his face is still drawn down into a permanent scowl—I should have seen this coming.

I let a pretty face and cunning words seduce me into letting my guard down. The names I call myself aren't nearly harsh enough.

"She's in a *cage!*"

"Are you volunteering to join her?" The man raises an eyebrow.

Pushing myself upright, I grab hold of the bars. I'm in a giant birdcage, covered in ornate swirls. There's a short, but wide chandelier inside with a hook for what I'm assuming must be a lyra. The bottom is open, leaving the dirt exposed—if they leave me in too long, I'll dig myself out.

Elijah notices me and grins, though it's more like a sneer. He saunters over to me, never taking his eyes off of me. Removing one hand from his pocket, he grasps the bar above my hand.

My nostrils flare as my ears pull back like an animal's might. Every sense is heightened as I watch him.

"Come now, you didn't really think it would be so easy to win a man over, did you? Who do you think I am, your little friends?"

"I'm impressed you can still talk after the way I hit you, Elijah. I figured you'd have at least a few broken teeth with the way you reeled back." There's nothing I can do inside the cage except use my words to lash out at him. He glares.

"You were so willing to believe I'd ever consider caring about you..."

"You were so quick to run your hands down my backside while you kissed me. You didn't seem to mind that." I'm loud enough that the tall man and Grandmother hear me, each making a face. I wish I had Harriet's talent for spitting fire right now so I could singe the fool in front of me.

The tall man's expression changes for a moment—perhaps I've made him wonder who Elijah is loyal too. It's certainly not me, but if I can use it to drive a wedge between them, I'll do it, even at the expense of humiliating myself further.

Looking down, I run a single finger over the bottom of Elijah's hand still resting on the bar above mine. He pulls back in disgust. I smile.

"Luther, you will release my granddaughter," Ida demands.

Luther?

My mind explodes in seven different directions. We've all been warned to stay away from Luther and his unsavory circus. Reports said he was nowhere near us, though. He shouldn't be here.

"He's been following us," I whisper to myself.

"Figured that out, did you?" Elijah whispers back, keeping our conversation private as if it's some sort of game. He pauses as if considering me. "You know, we *could* have some fun while you're here…"

"Dismemberment?" I ask, knowing he doesn't mean kissing.

Elijah scowls at me. "You don't need all of your fingers for your act, do you, Sienna?"

"You take one, I'll take one." I grin back at him, threatening him. He can't risk losing part of his hands—he needs them for his magic act.

"Elijah!" Luther snaps. The boy whips around. "Handle her."

Luther shoves Grandmother toward Elijah. She stumbles for a moment but catches herself. When Elijah reaches her, he pulls her across the tent.

"Sienna!" she screams. I reach through the bars, but since she was never close to me to begin with, it's just an emotional reaction. I call back to her as Elijah drags her away.

I will not cry. I will not cry.

Grandmother is pushed into a cage across the tent similar to my own. I know she can't see me from so far away, but I see her. I'll make it my mission to watch over her from my prison.

Once the men stalk out of the tent, I look around. The girl who tried to warn me is eyeing me from her cage. She's far enough away that we'll have to raise our voices to be heard—we'll have to be careful if we try to talk to keep from being overheard. It's too dangerous to risk now and she raises a finger to her lips with a slight shake of her head.

With nothing else to do, I examine my surroundings. The cage is made of dark metal and made to look worn even though it's kept in relatively good condition. While it looks like part of it is flaking, the entire thing is smooth.

Glancing up, I eye the hook inside the cage. It's high—higher than I can reach. It won't do me any good, unless—

I slip my cloak off. Draping it over one arm, I move to the side of the cage and try to scale the bars. It's not as easy as climbing my silks, but it doesn't take too long until I reach the curved top. Inverting, I hang upside down off the bars, hair dangling behind me.

My wrists and feet wrap around the bars, and I extend one arm, holding the cloak. Upside down, I attempt to hang it on the hook for the lyra. Folded in half, it's long enough for me to reach the ends from the ground, but not long enough to use to wrap. If nothing else, I can use it to swing and propel myself at the men when they open the cage door.

In the air, I realize the knife has been taken from my belt. Shifting my ankle against the bars, I discover that knife missing as well—Elijah must have seen me hide it there. I wonder what other information he's given to Luther over the last two months. Clearly, enough about Grandmother to capture her.

Once I'm sure the cloak is secure, I hold the bars with my hands and dangle my feet. When I'm positioned correctly, I drop to the ground. The girl squints at me from her own cage. For a moment, I almost use hand gestures to point out my plan, but I can't be certain she hasn't been planted here by Luther and Elijah to spy on me. Perhaps it's best not to make friends here.

An hour passes before anything happens, leaving me to study my surroundings outside of the cage. Two men walk in, appearing to be guards. One sets a tray in front of the girl in the other prison. She waits until he's backed up before reaching through the bars to get the food he brought.

A light switches on, plunging the edges of the room into darkness as the light focuses on the lyra hanging from the top of the tent. Black beads glitter all over the ceiling in the form of strings and chandeliers.

The light catches the dust in the air. It sparkles as it floats around the black lyra. It would almost be beautiful if it weren't so terrifying.

A click sounds and the lyra begins to lower.

The men step toward me, pulling their hands out from behind their backs where they had been in resting position. I take a step back, feeling every muscle in my body tighten. Now isn't the time to fight, but I want nothing more.

The one who hadn't approached the other girl unlocks my cage, opening the doors. He motions me forward, lips in a tight line. I breathe out before stepping forward.

They turn, aligning themselves with me as I step out. I walk toward the lyra, assuming they want me to go where they have lowered it to hover above the ground.

"Cooperating. Good." Luther steps out of the shadows. "I'm sure you're aware that your grandmother is just over there."

He points through the shadows to where Grandmother's cage is hidden somewhere in the darkness. I can barely make out things a few feet away with the blinding lights on me, much less determine where they're holding my grandmother.

"You will perform this evening. You will perform *every* evening," Luther informs me. "If you don't, she pays the price."

Grandmother gasps somewhere in the darkness. Elijah chuckles from the same direction. I grit my teeth. If I have the opportunity to destroy Elijah for this, I will.

"How did you get her here?"

"Elijah proved to be a very good source of information for us. He's been spying on you for months. He tried to follow Ida, but lost her. Thankfully you pointed him in the right direction, and while you were distracted with that tiger escape, he was able to get information to us. We reached her before you did."

So, Elijah was the one who released Babur. He let the tiger go then wandered into the woods with me—that was brave of him. Or perhaps he's as clueless as he believes *I* am.

"Clearly not by much."

"We moved her locations, didn't we?"

"And then Elijah brought me right to you," I remind him.

"As he should have. You're going to be more useful to us than your *magical* grandmother will ever be, assuming you prove to be as good as he says you are."

I glower at him.

"All this based off a ridiculous bracelet." He pulls it from his pocket and drops it on the ground, grinding it into the dirt with his heel. "Good thing I pulled it off her while she was trying to escape."

"Good thing Elijah told you how she speaks and acts so you could pretend to be her," I spit back.

"Yes, that was rather helpful." He runs his hand over the edge of his long jacket. "Elijah can clean this up when you're done."

He taps the bracelet with the toe of his shoe before looking back up at me, mouth drawing down into a scowl once more.

"Move," Luther instructs, nodding toward the lyra. "Show me what you're capable of. You'd better live up to expectations, girl."

I close my eyes once I reach the apparatus and take hold of the metal. It feels familiar under my touch. If Luther wants to be impressed, I'll impress him.

I twist, starting to spin the lyra. While still on the ground, a lyra can spin exceptionally fast. Once in the air, it's not nearly as quick, so I keep my feet down and let it carry my body in tight circles. Once I feel I'm moving enough to be impressive, I lift my legs to the lyra. Threading them through, I pull myself up with my arms to sit inside the lyra.

I pull my legs back so my knees hook over the edge of the apparatus, arms stretched above my head to support myself. Stepping my feet onto the edge of the lyra one at a time, I push myself upright so I'm standing hunched over. Pushing my knees away from myself, I shift my weight directly over my toes to balance myself and push my chest and head outward into a cameo, hands sliding down slightly while I drop my knees just a bit.

Luther comments to Elijah who has joined him, but I can't hear their words from my place on the lyra. Raising my hands higher, I shift to place my head behind the hoop and hook my toes.

Now that I'm closer to the top of the tent after having been raised in the air, I can easily see the chandelier beads—they look cheaply made, but who am I to judge? Instead of dwelling on it, I extend my arms out, leaning back. My legs straighten, pushing the base of the hoop away from my body. I dramatically release one leg and extend it backward in an oversplit before bending it back even further, angling my leg and knee.

"You can do better than that," Elijah calls.

Glaring at him, I lift my leg back to the lyra and walk my legs back onto it until my knees are hooked. Pulling myself up, I continue to walk myself forward until I'm sitting on the hoop in the seated position.

The lights flash, changing color and direction as I move one hand low on the lyra and shift my position to sit sideways so the hoop is resting directly down my spine and seat for balance. Somewhere, music starts to play a creepy melody. I've always enjoyed dramatic mood music, but something about this feels off—perhaps the out-of-tune C sharp messing up the A major chord.

My long leg lifts up to rest inside of the lyra, pushing against it at a right angle at the same time I lay back into the hoop. I rest the muscle alongside of my spine against the lyra and concave my back into it as I position my other leg below the first. My higher leg extends to the top of the lyra and I point my toes up while pressing in with my ankle for balance. I release my hands, using the rest of my body to hold myself in place.

I fall into rhythm with the music, moving along with the tempo as they lower the hoop again. Pulling myself upright, I sit sideways, twisting back into the seated position. Dismounting, I reach back up with an underhand grip far enough apart that both of my ankles can fit between them.

The lyra spins as I lift my feet, hooking them over the edge of the lyra. I flex my toes back down toward myself and release my hands, gracefully straightening my spine until I'm hanging by my ankles as I spin.

If they want a show, I'll give them a show.

I pull myself into an amazon, resting my weight on my neck and shoulder as the rest of my body dangles in the air. Reaching back, I lift one of my legs back with my free arm, nearly touching my head.

Twisting a leg over the lyra, I pull my body up and over until I flip around entirely, circling the hoop several times as it spins. Turning again, I sit on the hoop, leaning back into it to release my hands. I dip my head back to help spin faster, then lift both legs up to the top of the hoop, wrapping one around the tie at the top.

With each turn of the lyra, I maneuver my legs, spinning my body as the men working the rigging raise it up again, following my movements. I flip around a few times until I drop into a Russian split. With one leg high in the air, I arch around until I'm dangling from the lyra upside down, leg still pointed out as the music continues plunking away.

With a quick movement, I drop my legs so one rests in front of the hoop and one rests behind. I sit on the apparatus, straddling it. As soon as I touch it, I release my hands, dropping my upper body below me. Luther gasps beneath me and I try to hide my satisfied grin.

Extending one leg, I rest on the back of one knee from the hoop. I use my hands to pull myself through my leg, contorting myself around it as I spin. The lyra turns as I reach up and pull myself through the hoop, flipping over it until I drop down, dangling by one elbow as the lyra lowers once again.

Once my feet touch the floor, I spin the lyra, releasing it as I bend over backward to look at my captors. They look hungry—like they just found their meal ticket.

The music continues, but I do not. Righting myself, I turn on my heel to face them. Luther no longer looks impressed.

"You've done well, Elijah. Take her backstage and get her ready. She will go on tonight."

Elijah grabs my elbow roughly. I bump into him, hoping to pick his pocket while he's busy paying attention to his master. Maybe he still has my knives on him and I can stab him before threatening Luther until he releases Grandmother.

Jerking my arm away from Elijah to cover my movements, I find only a pack of cards too big to hide on my person. If he had been wearing one of his costumes, I would have known exactly where to look in the secret pockets—I saw Grandmother and Josephine making his wardrobe.

He pushes me across the tent, past my cage where my red cloak is still hanging. He notices it and grumbles a question about why it's there.

"It was too warm to wear it and I didn't want it getting dirty on the ground," I respond.

Outside, the sun glares so brightly that I have to lift a hand to shield my eyes. It leaves a green hue everywhere I look.

"Move," Elijah commands. He doesn't bother to pull the cloth back before shoving me into another tent.

This one is covered in bolts of fabric and trunks. A young girl looks up from where she's bent over a dark steamer trunk. Her hair is knotted and snarled, making a tangled mess of her white-blonde hair.

"Dress her." Elijah's words are harsh. He clearly went into the right business—he's very good at deceiving people and making them see exactly what he wants them to see. I once thought he had been charming.

The girl scurries over to me, sizing me up.

"What do you do?" she asks quietly.

"Aerialist."

She hovers around me for a moment, grabbing my arm and moving me around. When she's satisfied, she motions me across the room to a trunk. Elijah watches closely from the entrance.

The girl picks through outfits in the truck, handing me things to hold. I fold them over my arm and wait.

When she's done, she directs me to a screen that's clearly thin enough to see my outline through with the light in the background. Elijah doesn't appear to be moving. The girl flips on a light in front of the screen to help compensate.

Behind the thin fabric, I'm ordered to strip off my clothing. I drop it in a pile on a small stool with ripped fabric. The girl has the decency to look away and hands me my new wardrobe. Horrifyingly, Elijah and I would look stunning together in an act if we didn't hate each other. My dark outfit sets off my eyes and hair in the tiny scratched mirror behind the divider.

Elijah doesn't look impressed when I step around from behind the screen, though his eyes spark, telling a different story. He controls his face well.

"Happy?" I ask.

The skin-tight black costume hugs my curves—at least I won't get caught if they have me work with the silks. I miss my vibrant reds—they set my hair off more, and any reminder of Elijah's deceit only serves to infuriate me. Then again, upon further reflection, I suppose I fit more along the lines of Samuel's black and white stripes with red accents than Elijah's all-black outfit. If only they'd let me have a few pops of color like our real ringleader wears.

I wonder if anyone noticed we are missing yet.

"Over here," a new, female voice interrupts. I hadn't noticed the older girl standing off to the side. She must have entered the tent while I was changing.

I take a seat where she motions, Elijah close behind me. He hovers over the girl intimidatingly and she ducks slightly, cowering in his presence. I didn't realize Elijah had such power.

"Just keep them closed," the girl whispers loud enough for Elijah to confirm she isn't conspiring with me. She lifts a brush to my eyes and I lower my lids in compliance.

My fingers wrap around the bottom of the stool's seat, grounding me while I have my eyes closed. Brushes flick over my face, adding powders and creams while the girl paints on my makeup. The girl who gave me my wardrobe, moves behind me, tugging at my long, dark hair. Thankfully, she's careful of my jewelry and doesn't pull at my earlobes.

If it were Fannie and Blanch working on my styling, I would be relaxed and enjoying myself as I was pampered. Instead, my muscles start to burn from being so tight and on edge. Pain creeps into my neck and shoulders where the tension is taking hold. I have to fight against cringing each time the brush comes in contact with my skin and my only thought is whether or not the tools are sanitary.

"It's *fine*," Elijah grumbles as the girls continue to work on my appearance. I don't think I've ever sat in hair and makeup for so long in my life—and it *never* takes this long when I do it myself, which is almost always.

I open my eyes just in time to see the girl with the brushes swipe the soft bristles at my face again, missing as Elijah jerks me away. I stumble across the tent to the door, this time he flings the fabric open as we move exiting at the same time.

The sun is starting to sink into the sky. It's still light out, and will be for a few more hours—well into the show this evening—but it must be late afternoon already. Men stand around talking to each other. They look like they've been doing hard labor all day, clothes and skin covered in dirt. I wonder if any of these men were the ones who brought my hostage grandmother back to this madness after Luther and Elijah tricked me into joining them.

"You're performing tonight. Don't give us any trouble," Elijah instructs, hissing in my ear. "We don't have time for you to come up with a new routine, so you'll just have to figure it out as you go for a few days until we have time to work on this. You *can* base it off of the music, *can't* you?"

He looks at me as if he's actually concerned. I blink, refusing to nod. He knows I can develop a routine as I go—he's watched me do it before. I wonder if his own standing is on the line since he's the one who brought me into this mess. If Grandmother wasn't locked in a cage here, I'd mess up my routine just to hurt Elijah.

"Starting tomorrow, you'll be assisting me in my show as well."

The last thing I want is to be his assistant.

"What does Luther do? Isn't he your magician here?" I realize, wondering why his mentor allows him to take the spotlight off of him.

Elijah turns, glaring at me. "Of course not. He's in charge—he's our ringmaster."

"I thought you apprenticed for him."

The tents flash by us as my captor directs our path. Instead of going back to the main tent, he wheels us around it. I have to jump over piles of rope as we go. He walks much faster when he's on a mission.

"Luther took me in. I apprenticed once, but it was a lifetime ago. I've been with him for years."

"What is your stake here?" I ask, pulling my elbow away from him so I can walk on my own. "You had a home with us—why give it up for *this*? It seems so oppressive here."

Elijah's steps hesitate for a moment and I move my hands, ready to block him when he tries to throw me against something. He doesn't.

"I have more power here than anywhere else. I'm in charge here."

"I thought Luther was in charge."

"I'm second in command. He trusted me enough to come get you, didn't he?"

"You were really sent on a mission to kidnap *me*?" I ask incredulously.

"I was sent on a mission for Ida. It was easy to gain her trust. When I showed up in the woods with some story about accidentally running into her, it was easy for me to talk my way into staying. I made sure she was in the exact right spot for Luther's men to capture her.

"In case you don't realize, I spent an awful long time trying to keep you away from her out in those woods. It wasn't until I realized you were just as valuable that I allowed you near her."

He turns to grin cruelly at me. The low, dangerous music slithers through the fabric of the tent to us, accentuating his vile reaction.

"You were foolish to believe your grandmother could have actually found magic—there's no such thing, Sienna. There's only reality and deceit. We sell a lie to the people who come to watch us—we make them believe there are good things in this world when it's really just shrewd people that are cunning enough to outwit the commoners ruling over the gullible ones."

"Are you saying you're some kind of king?"

"I'm saying that people are shocked by *your* show—but they truly *believe* mine by the time they leave this tent, Sienna. Give it a few weeks after a show and they'll forget your flashes of red in the sky, but they'll never forget the man who broke their idea of reality. I give them a fantasy that they want to believe in, and then prove to them it's true—and only the best can exist in a world where magic is *real.*"

"It's *not* real," I protest.

"It's as real as the chains you're going to be wearing if you don't cooperate, *Red Girl.*" He stops at an entrance on the far side of the main tent. "Remember—you will do everything I say, or Ida will pay the price."

Directly inside the entrance to my right, is the cage Grandmother is sitting in. They've given her a small chair, but it can't be good for her hip.

"Grandmother." I announce my presence, knowing she won't recognize me without my signature color on. I grab the bars as she stands.

"Sienna," she whispers. "Are you all right?"

"I'm fine, Grandmother. Are you okay?"

"I'll be fine, dear. Just do what they tell you to do—we don't need you getting hurt." Her fingers, gnarled with age, brush over my hand. "They're keeping you across the tent?"

"Not for long," Elijah interrupts. "We'll be clearing the tent for this show. You'll all be moved. We need the apparatuses."

"Boss said to leave them," a man announces, walking over to us from across the tent. "They perform or they lose a finger."

"The old lady can't perform anymore," Elijah protests. "Besides, who would want to see that?"

"Boss said she works, or she pays." The man shrugs.

"You expect her to flip around on silks all night?"

"Give me a lyra," Grandmother interjects. "I can sit and do some limited moves. At the very least, I can spin and move inside the hoop."

"You can't be serious!" I exclaim. "You haven't done aerial in the last decade."

Grandmother turns to the men proudly. "She's been the star since she was eight."

They both narrow their eyes at her.

"You can't make her work." I look pleadingly at Elijah.

"Looks like you'll be staying here, Ida." He ends the debate. "Sienna is going back to her place as well. Move, Sienna."

"You don't look like yourself, dear." Grandmother turns back to me. "You're hard to recognize with all of that on your face."

She's warning me.

"No one will recognize you," she adds.

Maybe she's waiting for Samuel to find a way to save us. I wasn't smart enough to leave a trail—I thought I was among friends. I'm not sure how long it will take them to find us, but I heard the men say that we're moving on after tomorrow's show now that they have Grandmother in their custody. If they don't locate us in time, it's *my* fault.

"Blood is silent, dear," Grandmother calls. *Another code.*

She used to say that to me when I was practicing on the silks. She'd say it looked like I was entwined in a waterfall of blood as I was twisting high above the ground during training. I would constantly talk my way through it, and she needed to remind me not to ruin the effect by distracting people with my murmured words. *Blood is silent* was her reminder to keep my head down and turn out a good performance.

Play the part. Put on a show. Do what you must to keep their attention where you want it. Blood is silent.

I don't fight with Elijah as he guides me back to my cage. If Grandmother believes our friends will find us, I'll believe it too. I'll play along until they arrive to help us escape. If I'm unrecognizable, that might be a problem, though. I'll need my own signal to give them —perhaps my cloak hanging in my cage will help.

"When you're not in the air, you'll be performing here." Elijah opens the door and motions me in.

My cloak is sitting in a pile on the ground, replaced by black silks. *So much for my idea.* I consider picking it up, but it's a miracle they left it there at all, mixed among the shiny fabric pillows tossed inside.

"Consider yourself a bird." Elijah grins. *A caged bird, maybe.* "Inside your nest, you show off, but don't over exert yourself, and *don't* take the focus off of the person in the center of the ring.

"We have other aerial acts. You just happen to be the best of them. You'll go at the end of that segment of the show right before I go on. You'll wow the crowd with your show, then lead the way for me to come on. While I'm performing, you will sit and watch me closely, swinging—you will not detract from my performance, do I make myself clear?"

"Support the other aerialists. Don't show you up. Got it." I tilt my head, giving him my best unimpressed look.

"See that you don't. He wasn't kidding when he said we'd take fingers. It's not like you're a *magician*, Sienna. People come to this show for magic. You're a clown at best."

"A clown that has climbed higher than you have, Elijah. In every sense."

He frowns, placing a hand on one of the bars of the cage door.

"Test me, and I'll work you until you can't go on any longer, Sienna. I'm willing to allow you to be featured in this show in your own right, but people come to see magic and illusion—you're not needed for that. I can push you until you wither, and it wouldn't even matter. And even if we *did* need aerialists, there are more of you here.

"Remember, Luther doesn't need you in the air to survive, Sienna. He needs you in a chair, doing what your grandmother does. You don't need to perform for that, and you don't need all of your body parts for that either. I can take whatever I want from you."

"With Luther's permission," I remind him. I shouldn't push him— I'm supposed to be laying low—but I can't help it. "I'll do as you say, Elijah. I'll cooperate to protect my grandmother, but if you touch her, I'll burn this circus to the ground and you'll never even see it coming. I'll play the part perfectly and when you think you have me in compliance, I'll destroy you all. If you keep Ida safe, it won't come to that."

"Get ready for the show," Elijah growls, ignoring my words as he steps away.

I turn, kicking pillows out of my way. The men have obviously just dumped them into the cage instead of arranging them around the outside to give me a place to stand.

I bend to fix them when my world suddenly goes black.

Looking up, I see dark fabric draped over my cage, concealing me from the world until it's showtime.

CHAPTER 6

I PACE AROUND MY CAGE IN THE SEMI-DARK. ONCE MY EYES ADJUST, I can see my surroundings very dimly, giving me the ability to walk without tripping, but I'm forbidden from touching the fabric until my new handlers remove it.

Elijah hasn't spoken to me since my world went dark, despite me begging him for more information on how this show was going to work. I don't know if there is an opening act or if I'm banished behind the curtain until the aerialists go on. I don't even know *when* they go on in the lineup, leaving me to hover near the silks so I'm ready when I'm exposed to the world.

The music seems to go on forever and I eventually decide that I'm not a part of the opening act. I can't even tell what the opening act is. No one speaks from the center ring. If there's a ringmaster, he's nothing like charismatic Samuel.

I prop the pillows up, trying to display enough of my red cloak to remind me to stay grounded and keep my head down. I don't know what to expect and I don't want to lose my head at the wrong time. The crowd won't know it, but it's a symbol to them too—I'm not of this dark, gothic place. I'm Red.

Once the music shifts, I wonder if it's all been an interlude up until this point and the show is actually *just* beginning. Beyond the curtain, I can hear the crowd so close it's almost like they're right outside of the cage.

When the fabric moves, I jump. I hurriedly pull myself into the silks, ready to perform. The curtain drops around me outside of the cage, revealing men. They gawk at me through the bars, some with their wives. A few couples have children with them, clinging to their legs. These are nothing like the people who come to *our* circus for the shows.

The children look horrified at me while their mothers pale, unable to look away from my face. My makeup must be very strange.

"She looks like she's been hit and died," one boy says.

"It's just pink makeup around her eyes," his father replies, picking him up. "And she's very pale, but never you mind."

They must have used a white powder on me and pink eyeshadow like they did for some of the performers I saw earlier. What a strange choice.

The wife looks down at my outfit with obvious disdain.

More men crowd around to watch me as I swing in the silks, having forgotten to put on a show. Through the bars, I spy another cage—the girl from before—wearing white powder and pink diamonds over her eyes. Her hair is frizzy and voluminous.

I still don't know what they did to my hair, but from what I can tell, it's similarly styled, enough product in it to form an actual bird's nest.

On the other side, another cage is occupied by a man wearing a large cape made of black feathers that reaches partway down his chest and back. He wears a dark, sharply pointed crown on his head with black powder makeup stretching from his hairline down below his eyes to his mid-nose. Black chains cover his arms, and he wears black, short half-trousers as he swings. His lips are outlined in dusty pink that matches the girl's makeup next to me.

The majority of the group standing in front of me moves on to the next cage as more men and women rotate in front of me. In the center of the ring, workers are rolling several cages around the ring through the spectators. They watch closely as a girl in a white corset and skirt twists around a lyra that she obviously doesn't know how to use. Her faux rabbit ears accent her pink lips and she adjusts the ruffled collar she wears, oblivious to the fact that I'm watching her from across the room.

It appears the opening act is designed to let people peer into the cages up close. I hadn't understood what Luther meant this morning, but now I do. The cages shift and wind their way through the crowd, looking at each man and woman behind bars, twisting to the music. Some men linger by the acts that fascinate them, following them if they're in moving cages.

Outside of a cage, several thirty-year-old men dressed all in black with pale makeup and dark eyes circle around the spectators, frightening children, harassing women, and drawing the attention of the men to the girls in the cages. They wear black hats with white accents on them and black folded collars so big that if they sat on a chair, leaned their necks forward, and pulled up their legs, the collars would consume them entirely, hiding everything but their faces. One wanders next to me and reaches in the bars toward me. I know better than to kick him, but I have to fight every instinct to avoid doing it.

The girl in the cage next to me catches my attention, giving me a look to snap me out of my haze. I agreed to perform and I'm not.

Stretching up, I lock myself into the silks and start to move enough to be interesting. I avoid my signature moves or anything complicated that would better serve the show I must give later this evening.

Every time a leering man reaches into the bars to try to brush against me as I move, I shift, avoiding his touch. Unable to see the entire way around myself at all times, many of them manage to touch my legs, lingering against my skin, making me feel sick.

A new cage rolls past me. The girl's hair is braided tightly in buns on either side of her head above her ears. She wears pale powder and has a beauty mark painted high on her cheekbone. Her lips are partially untouched, only a smear of purple is painted down the center of her mouth like tiny lips. Purple, orange and pink crowd her eyelids with no blending, making her face look stark and harsh.

Another hand touches me and I flip over on instinct, avoiding him. When I right myself, another cage spins past me. Elijah is inside —the spinning cages must be for those who cooperate—moving cards from one hand to another as he performs small illusions in an overly pronounced way. His lips are dark, with strange, uneven lines painted out from each side. Hair wild, it stands out as much as the short black tulle collar around his neck.

If this is Elijah's idea of a good costume, why on earth did he pick that gorgeous wardrobe that he wore when he was with us? I wonder if his personal style doesn't fit the aesthetic of his master's show. Or maybe he has more than one style. The gigantic buttons on his white shirt under his sharp suit jacket suggest he might be compensating for something here at this show.

A blonde girl suddenly appears from a lyra high above the crowd at the center of the tent. Her hair is short and curly, topped with a plumb colored feathered hair piece. She holds a cane in her hand. She poses with her high-heeled feet up against the inside of the lyra, lace tights on full display as she opens the show. After a moment, once the crowd looks up to see her, she uses the cane to direct people back to their seats before she continues.

A hand grabs my outer thigh from behind and doesn't let go, cupping his hand around my skin and I panic.

"I'm here, Red," the voice murmurs. He leaves his hand on me, waiting for me to recognize him, then pats my leg twice before slipping away, dragging his hand across my skin.

Ephraim is covered in black as he walks away from me. His fair hair is pulled back into a tight ponytail behind him, barely long enough to hold. He reminds me of Samuel with his hair back like that. When Ephraim turns and sits, his eye is covered in a deep bruise.

He nods before tearing his eyes off of me.

Ephraim is here. He knows where we are and he's here to help us.

I'm surprised Ephraim recognized me the way they have me painted, but maybe my cloak in the bottom of my cage served as more than just a reminder to myself. I glance down at it and see it's been pulled slightly away from the pillows I tucked it between—he's definitely seen it.

My friend glares off to the left from his seat. I follow his gaze for a moment as he watches Elijah's cage spinning in the distance out of the way.

He clearly knows Elijah is in on this and he's trying to keep Elijah from identifying him in the crowd—that's why he's dressed so strangely and has his beautiful locks pulled back into that hideous look. Ephraim scoots over, blocking himself as much as possible with the people sitting in front of him as the cages in the middle of the ring move around, bringing our former coworker closer to him. I can't take my eyes off of him.

A sharp bang on the bars of my cage does the trick as one of Luther's men glare at me. Pulling myself higher in the silks, I move into a cross back straddle, hanging upside down with my legs out to the sides.

The workers clear out the cages from the center of the ring and I realize other acts were also in the moving stages. Elijah gives me a wild look as he's wheeled past me. I pull myself up in response.

Once he's out of eyeline, I turn back to Ephraim. He catches my eye and I immediately lift both legs up into the air, pointing harshly at Grandmother's cage across the tent. He nods sharply once, indicating that he understands.

The bruise on his face takes the most getting used to. I'm terrified of what he had to endure to get to us. Did Luther's men find him? Did he run into Elijah and that's how he discovered us here? Regardless, he's been hit. Ephraim has endured a great deal of injuries over his time with Samuel's circus, but usually his face is protected. I don't even remember the last time someone was able to get the upper hand on my friend.

The girl on the lyra begins her act, only stumbling over a few of the transitions as the people below gasp and call out in response. Under our training, she could go really far with her performance. Here, I imagine, they will work her until she falls to her death and then immediately replace her without a second thought.

I take my time progressing through different moves on the silks. Why waste my energy before my actual performance? The beads glitter from the ceiling, the chandeliers are lower now to give the audience a better view, and I slowly move my legs out while locked in the silks to show I'm making an effort.

After a while, I fall into the rhythm of the music, finding beauty in it where there's meant to be none. Once the lyra is lowered, the girl runs off as the handlers bring a new performer in. They attach silks to the hoop, limiting some of her movements. She doesn't seem as experienced as the first girl so I don't think it matters as much. The girl goes through her act and they lower her back to the ground.

Two more cycle through, both on silks. The second girl—the one who tried to warn me—nearly falls, prompting the audience to gasp as she tangles in the black and white striped fabric.

Luther opens my cage door, motioning me out. He's dressed in dark show clothes. He wears a feathered collar but leaves his stringy hair hanging down in front of him. Sequins sparkle on his jacket, demanding the world watch him.

He holds his hand out to me without smiling—no one smiles here. I take it with my left hand, allowing him to guide me out into the open. I rush to keep up with him as he spins me around in front of the audience. I dip when I feel pressure over my wrist, thrusting my free hand out to the side in a slight bow.

Luther guides me to the silks, bowing to me before running backward. In this show, he is the guide and the whole audience watches in rapt attention for where he leads them. If he tells them I'm the one to watch now, they will.

I catch Ephraim's gaze in the audience, still clearly watching for Elijah so he doesn't give himself away. He nods again, telling me to perform.

The music starts and I climb the silks, blocking out everything but the off-key music. I invert, wrapping the silks around my body in preparation.

The audience gasps each time I drop, cascading toward the ground only to catch myself at the last second. Luther stands to the side, watching and waiting in case he needs to run in to control me if I step out of line.

Before the music slows, I release my hold on the silks and rush across the tent to where a lyra still hangs low to the ground out of the way. Luther starts to run after me and I smile, knowing I caused him to work when he didn't have to.

I twist onto the lyra, spinning it quickly on the ground before pulling myself up. I catch a flash of Luther halting his run when he realizes I was improvising in the show. He dips into a low bow, directing the audience to applaud me.

I move into an amazon, dangling by my neck and shoulder to much applause. If Luther and Elijah want me to make a name for them, I'll give them a show to remember once I've escaped.

Looping around the lyra, I slip to the ground. Once again, I spin it, this time lifting myself up enough to get my head above the bottom of the hoop. Tipping my neck back, I hang, releasing my arms so I'm spinning on the lyra by only my neck.

I reach back, grabbing my legs to pull them up toward the back of my head as I spin in the air slowly. The audience erupts as I reach up to steady myself before I pull my body up onto the lyra, swinging my legs until I can walk myself onto the hoop into the seated position.

The men handling the rigging move me up into the air and I sit inside the hoop, moving my legs until I'm perched inside it without using my hands.

When they finally bring the hoop back down, I dismount and rush toward Luther to take my final bow. He grabs my hand, squeezing it tightly enough to know that he's angry I tricked him. I act innocent.

"Get back in your apparatus." His words are threatening. He spins me to bow to the other side.

In my peripheral vision, I see Elijah rushing into the ring.

"I've been told to make this good," I mumble to my captor. He noticed Elijah and nods deftly to me. With a final twirl, he releases me.

I duck under his arm and rush toward Elijah. His eyes grow wider when he notices me, but I don't change my path. My hands collide with his shoulders as I use the force to spin him around. I kiss him on the cheek, surprising him, but the men in the audience shout loudly, making any decent mother in the crowd regret bringing her children to such a show where catcalls are encouraged, and men leer at young girls on stage.

I drag my hand across Elijah's shoulders slowly, leaving my left arm up in the air as if we were lovers being dragged apart and all I could do was reach for him. After a beat, he raises his arm and pretends to reach for me, even though I'm halfway back to my cage by that time.

Throwing myself in the cage entrance, I leap at my silks, catching myself as I swing. Spinning around the cage, I pretend to keep my gaze on the magician, knowing the audience is still watching me in that moment. Once the silks stop spinning, I quickly step into foot locks and extend into an inverted oversplit, staring at Elijah. When the audience refuses to look away, I release a hand and point, palm up, at Elijah, to ensure they focus on him.

After a moment, I pull myself upright and wrap the silks around my body, finding a comfortable position to hang in, legs extended, body tipped for the audience's benefit, as I swing and stare in Elijah's general direction as he performs. When I'm tired of one position, I move into another, knowing the audience is now mindful of what I'm doing as I keep my attention on the main act. I pretend to watch him dreamily.

If Elijah wants me to keep the focus on him, and has no interest in being with me, I'll make him suffer while I do exactly as he asked me to do.

I risk a look at Ephraim covered by a sweeping gaze across the audience. He gives me a look before turning back to watch Elijah. Reaching up, he tugs on a strand of his hair. I assume it's some sort of signal, but I don't understand it.

Now that I have nothing to do other than stare, I focus on the intricate design of the edges of the tent. Luther's people have taken the time to black out everything but where they want the audience to focus—the performers.

Unlike Samuel's circus, the environment isn't part of the experience. There are no lights aside from the spotlights used to illuminate the many acts in their cages and the main performer. No ribbons litter the space. The only accents are the beads at the top of the tent and the black cages spread around the room.

Elijah finds his footing after my shocking twist to his performance and works through his illusions, making people disappear before the audiences' eyes, working through a small mentalism act, and creating something out of nothing over and over as the crowd gasps.

Taking a woman's hand from the audience, he guides her down into the ring. He appears just as interested in her as he was in me and I roll my eyes. She giggles as he makes her a part of his act.

I turn, inverting into a cross back straddle again. It's far more entertaining than Elijah and his magical lies. From upside down, I try to find Ephraim in the audience, but he's not there.

Unable to search for him without giving myself away, I have to force myself to stare at the show. Across the tent, grandmother is in her cage, sitting in the lyra. Thankfully, they gave her a piece of fabric to wrap around her waist, lengthening her skirt. It hangs down in her hand and she twirls it to spin herself in the lyra in the seated position. The chair she had earlier has been removed.

I pull myself up and watch her as she performs. She can't pull her legs up dramatically like I do, but every once in a while, she crosses her legs, or switches to the opposite side of the lyra to add some motion to her time in the hoop. I know she's capable of a bit more, but she's clearly not going to let on that she's capable of more than they think—that will be valuable later.

Grandmother wraps the skirt around her arm, making her look like she has butterfly wings each time she moves to the top of the hoop. I wrap the silks around my arm and mimic her movements gracefully as I rest, tangled in the silks. She can't see me, but it's my silent way of speaking solidarity to her from across the ring.

A movement catches my eye in the audience—Ephraim.

He shuffles to a different seat, moving nearer to the front of the group, inching closer to me. Wisely, he chooses not to look at me, but a few minutes later, he moves again, making his way through the crowd.

Elijah leaves the ring, ushering in a new act. Each one is ostentatious and slightly grotesque. I've never seen a circus so dark, both in color and in feel. Elijah seems to be in his element, as does Luther. Fannie would have a fit if she could see this.

Ephraim looks at me, staring until I turn to look at him instead of watching him from the corner of my eye.

"Trust me?" he mouths.

I nod once, making it look like I dipped my head. I quickly turn in the silks, wrapping them around me to make sure I've covered myself if anyone was watching. I can't let Ephraim get caught—there's enough men here that they could force him into a cage like they did to me, and surely Elijah would make him suffer here; far more so than he will make me pay while under his control.

When I look back to him, he mouths something else. "Tomorrow."

He stands up. I blink. Ephraim makes his way down the remaining steps and walks toward the exit with a scowl on his face as if he's had enough of the show. Without stopping or hesitating, he walks swiftly toward the exit, collar high on his neck to cover part of the short ponytail he's wearing.

I want to call out to him, to beg him to stay, but instead, I twist, dropping in the silks enough to get attention. I don't bother looking; I know he's already gone and walking away from the dark circus tent into the twilight evening.

Tomorrow. He promised me he would be back tomorrow. I just have to survive the night.

CHAPTER 7

Sleeping on the ground is the last thing I want to do, but they don't give me a choice. Once they cover my cage over to prevent me from talking to the others, I tie the ends of the silks together, one higher than the other, to form a hammock they didn't expect me to build for myself. Settling back into it, I cover myself with my cloak even though it's warm out—it's a form of armor for me, protecting me from the world.

Poor grandmother was given a cot, thankfully, but it's anything but luxurious. Even Hoyt's cot near his tigers looks more comfortable and I've sat on it before—it's like sitting on a plank.

Sleep eludes me, but eventually, I sink into a bit of rest. I'll need it for whatever Ephraim is preparing. I worry about how Ephraim got that black eye for an hour before my mind shifts to the escape, and eventually, I find myself lost in sleep.

When I wake up, the fabric surrounding my cage is still there, but bright enough to let me know it's morning. I don't want the men taking away my silks, so I force myself up and untie them before kicking some of the pillows around on the ground—at least they had the consideration to leave those for me. Or maybe they are just lazy.

Blood is silent, Grandmother's words ring in my mind. I will be silent and these men holding us captive won't realize we're escaping until it's too late to stop us.

Before I can sit, the curtain around my cage is ripped away. Luther stands before me. He turns and nods to the man standing beside him. The man opens the door and steps back.

"You did well last night. You might find it easier here than you thought, assuming you don't try to mess with me again." Luther raises one eyebrow at me. "Go get cleaned up and then we'll talk about your future here."

He's awfully willing to work with me knowing I'm likely to escape the first chance I get. I wonder if this is how he controls the others too—holding a family member to leverage against them, forcing them into submission. I wouldn't be nearly so compliant if Grandmother wasn't at risk.

The man with Luther grabs my arm, but I elbow him. "I'm perfectly capable of walking, thank you."

He escorts me to a small tent to wash up and use the bathroom. A scared girl scurries away as we approach. Inside, I dip my hands under the water and brush it through my hair.

I take a breath and dip my head under the water. It's warm enough that my hair will dry, and I hate going with an unwashed mane. Pulling the water up my arms, I brush it over my shoulders. Not caring if I'm taking too long, I wipe water over my legs, attempting to clean off the dirt. The man yells to hurry up, but I dismiss him, claiming I can't be covered in dirt for the show later.

Wringing my hair out, I let it drip before tossing it over my shoulders. When it air dries, it will become curly and soft, though I'll have to work to brush it out after the tangles they added to it last night. Picking up a towel, I scrub the makeup off my face. I hope it won't be painted back on until after Ephraim finds me.

He must have been alone last night if the others were nowhere in sight. They would have made sure I had seen them if they had been there. They likely would have broken us out during the evening's performance if they had had the numbers.

The man eyes me when I exit the tent dripping wet. My hair is plastered against my back, dripping down in cold streams of water despite being wrung out—long hair holds in water much longer than shorter hair and has a tendency to release it like tiny waterfalls at the worst times.

A few drops hit my ankles as I walk alongside the man. He returns me to my cage, but before he can lock me in, Elijah appears. I sigh and follow him.

Like our own circus, this one has a tent for food. Elijah hovers over me as I sit. He takes the seat across from me and a short man with a wrinkled face waddles over quickly on unsteady feet with two plates. Elijah's is covered in food. Mine has decidedly less.

Picking up a fork, I poke at what some might describe as a food. Elijah doesn't seem to notice and eats his meal.

"That was quick thinking last night," he acknowledges me. "I don't like being surprised, though, so we're going to have to work on it."

He doesn't like being surprised, but he *does* like when I make him look good. Star-crossed lovers being pulled apart by separate acts is certainly good for conversation in the audience and he knows it.

Luther enters the tent and saunters over. He reminds me a bit of Hoyt with the way he walks, but their personalities aren't the same at all—Luther is far too sullen—though they both have huge egos.

"I want you to plan our acts," he addresses me.

"I noticed they fell pretty flat," I murmur, picking up a piece of what I think is egg with my fork. I take a bite. Definitely egg, but not very good. "Have you fed Ida yet?"

Luther ignores me. "We obviously have different acts than you're used to, and quite a few aerialists. You'll need to take that into consideration when you and your grandmother are planning the new show."

At least he plans on letting me see her.

"The makeup needs to go," I say flatly.

"The makeup and wardrobe stay," Luther corrects me as the short man sets food in front of him. Luther eats without looking at me as the older man waddles away. I'm terrified he might fall and break something, like the ankle that clearly never set right the *last* time he broke it.

"Why do you keep people in cages?"

"The apparatuses are for the show," Luther replies, shoving another bite of food into his mouth. I wrinkle my nose—men are disgusting at times. Maybe Ephraim and Orville are extra considerate around us and I've become spoiled.

"I slept in one last night," I point out, setting my fork down. I'm slightly surprised they gave me something I could stab them with.

"That's only for people we can't trust." Luther looks up. "Elijah doesn't sleep in the bird cages."

"Everyone else does."

"Look around, Sienna," Elijah cuts in. "How many people do you see roaming around?"

"You mean the men who threatened the people in cages?" I lock eyes with him. I definitely want to put the fork through the back of his hand.

"I mean the handlers and performers. Work with us, Sienna, and you might even be able to share our quarters with us." He glances at Luther who nods.

"We're willing to give you some freedoms if you work with us," he concedes. "Just don't cross us and you can earn our trust. Like I said, you could learn to like it here. I saw the way you fell into your performance—you could do well with our type of circus."

"How long have you been here?" I cut him off.

"Two performance engagement. We were only here to find you, Sienna. We don't need to stay, nor do we need to impress these lowlifes. They don't have money to pay for extras and there's no point in wasting our time.

"In fact, we don't even need to stay this afternoon. We could move on to our next stop and it wouldn't hurt our purse one bit."

"We're just doing it to rub it in Samuel's face. When he finds out you're *with* us and performed in the next town over, he'll be livid."

Luther's lips quirk up on one side. "There's nothing he'll be able to do about it. He won't be able to track us, and by the time he finally finds us, you won't want to go back."

This guy is delusional.

He turns his wolfish grin on me. "I'm willing to give you the world, Sienna, if you'll join us. You can run this place. You can be the star act. Your grandmother can help you as long as she's alive. Turn this circus into the most successful one in the country, and I'll give you everything. You'll only have to answer to me."

He'll swallow me whole and spit me out, he means.

"Why are you so willing to give me *everything*?" I ask skeptically.

"He needs to keep this circus open. We've put far too much into this to fail," Elijah answers for his boss.

"So, you're failing?" I respond, picking up my fork again. "Kidnapping all those people isn't getting you anywhere?"

"If you don't want me coercing people to work for me, give me enough star acts that make other performers come to *us* for jobs. I won't need to force people into working if the talent is coming to me."

He makes a good point.

A horse whinnies outside the tent somewhere. A man yells at him as the horse apparently balks. I tune it out and focus on Luther.

"How are you getting all of these people to cooperate, Luther?"

"Same reason you're complying, little girl." He and Elijah share a conspiratorial grin, confirming my suspicion.

"Fine. If I'm going to do this, I still get to use red."

"Excuse me?" Luther drops his smile.

"You heard me. Red silks this evening or I don't go on. If I'm the star, then I'm the star. He gets his weird sparkly suit"—I wave my hand at Elijah—"and I get my silks. There's no room for discussion on this."

"I—"

"Give me my silks and I'll train that little bird in the cage next to me. She almost killed herself last night. I'll even wear that stupid outfit you picked out for me."

Luther starts to object but quickly realizes the merits in my argument and nods. "Fine. You'll have your silks. You'll work with Candace once you're done eating. If I don't see dramatic improvement by this evening, *well...*"

He brushes his hair back as he trails off. Standing, he walks away.

"The show is this afternoon, by the way. You've got five hours. We're moving tonight." He yells over his shoulder like I don't already know that information.

Elijah catches my eye. "I always knew you were reasonable."

"Get my silks, Elijah."

He looks like I slapped him.

"Oh, Elijah." I laugh at him. "Really. Did you honestly think that you'd be above me? I'm saving Luther's circus. I'm training his people. You're doing what—an act? Your moment of glory was bringing me to Luther to work for him. You had your moment, Elijah. This circus is now what *I* say it will be.

"I'm going to train those people in those cages. I'm going to make them greater than you. I'll train them all to do exactly what I do. I'll turn this into a circus of the best aerialists in the country. No one will rival us. By the time I'm done, we won't even need a magician. I'll make the aerialists magical enough for the audience.

"You just took away your own job, my friend. With one *kiss*, you sealed your own fate. You've destroyed yourself with your ambition. You work for me now."

He reels back as I remind him of our searing kiss in the woods yesterday.

"Now." I bat my eyelashes. "If you want my mercy, go get my silks, *boy.*"

Elijah snorts, furious.

I stand up and sway away from the table, leaving the plate and the steaming man behind. He shouts at me, but the men don't dare touch me as I march to the main tent, leaving them scrambling to keep up with me.

Throwing the curtain open, I step in.

"Open the doors," I command loudly, confusing the workers. "Do it."

The man behind me nods as I turn sharply toward him. He heard Luther give me power and knows better than to test me.

I stomp over to the cage next to mine. "Unlock her."

The girl looks at me, terrified.

"I told Luther I'd train you so that you don't kill yourself tonight. I get red silks in return."

She looks terrified at me that I would give in so quickly. She has no idea that it's all an act until Ephraim launches his rescue mission.

"To the lyra, Candace. We have work to do."

She quickly scurries across the tent to the hoop. I motion for the men to lower it and set to work teaching her basic safety for the moves she had attempted and failed to do last evening.

Five hours pass quickly as I instruct her, avoiding all personal conversation and hoping she catches on.

Ephraim is radiant in red. Whoever decided he should exclusively live in those gorgeous blue costumes was a fool, though, to be fair, he's more striking in his signature color than mine. He still looks incredible sitting in the audience, watching me.

The black eye is gone, leaving me to realize that it was makeup he wore yesterday—Josephine taught him well. He's wearing fake facial hair to hide his strong jawline, but I could identify him anywhere. His eyes spark from across the room as he locks eyes with me.

The entire group is here, spread around the room in disguises. Orville's easy features and soft eyes are trained on me from several rows away from his cousin, also dressed in a variation of red. Hoyt looks as angry as Babur when he isn't fed on time, hunched forward in the front row on the far side of the room.

Blanch sits near Clarence in the back—I nearly didn't recognize her in that wig—and Fannie and Harriet hover near the door, hair wrapped up in scarves to avoid detection. Out of the hundred people who work for Samuel, half of them are in the audience, and I imagine the other half is waiting outside to help us escape without detection. Samuel is nowhere in sight, though I didn't expect him to show up in a situation where Luther could easily spot him. The two have known each other for many years.

The only one we have to worry about is Elijah—no one else here knows our faces. My friends perceptively watch the show, keeping an eye on me, Grandmother, and the men holding us captive.

Candace does much better this afternoon. I watch from my perch in my cage, wrapped in my silks.

My outfit this evening is different than before. Lace covers my legs under my solid black outfit. Elijah walked into the wardrobe tent and demanded I wear the most uncomfortable outfit possible and I let him have the victory. If he thinks he gained a bit of the upper hand, he's less likely to watch me this afternoon.

When it's my turn, Luther escorts me from my cage and I dance my way over to the center of the ring. My silks drop from the top of the tent, cascading down in red.

Blood. My people are out for it this afternoon.

Hoyt and Ephraim lean forward onto their knees as they watch me. Orville leans back, glancing sideways. I don't know their plan, but I have to be ready for it. I need to get Grandmother and help as many of the caged people as possible before I flee.

"Boo!" someone yells from the audience. It's low and hard to pick out at first, but a second quickly follows.

"We're tired of this!" a female calls—I think it's Fannie using a strange voice.

"It's the same thing over and over!" Orville yells. The crowd picks up their chant and demands something new.

Luther's face crumbles as he realizes his plan is falling apart.

"Do something," he hisses at me as if I would have an answer to saving his precious circus.

"What do you want me to do?" I hiss back as he tightens his grip around my hand, making me feel like he's going to shatter bone if he presses any harder.

"Give them a show!"

"I'm an aerialist—my act is exactly what they *don't* want to see!"

Behind Luther, I can see Blanch and Clarence in the background. She waves at me, trying to get my attention. I ignore Luther, waiting for some kind of signal from my friend. They started this riot—they must have a way to end it.

"Pick Ephraim," Blanch mouths, pointing in his direction. I squint as she repeats her actions.

"I have an idea," I say, pulling away from Luther.

I prance a few feet away, closer to the audience. Raising one hand, I ask them to silence. It takes a moment, but they eventually calm down.

"So, you want something new?" I begin. "If you think this is so easy, why don't you come up here and try it?"

"We didn't come here to do the show ourselves, lady," a man objects.

"What if I could teach one of you to go up there with me? What if I let one of you up close and personal while I'm in the air?"

Several people object, but Ephraim in disguise stands to his feet.

"I'll do it." He leers overtly at me. His eyes drag from my feet up to my face, lingering. He grins at me suggestively—not a side of Ephraim I'm familiar with.

I look him over as if disgusted by his obvious attention toward me. Holding a hand out, I wait for him to begin walking out of the stands toward me. Once it's obvious that he's joining me in the ring, I run toward the silks, bypassing Luther.

"Leave," I murmur.

The silks sway as I launch myself onto them, intentionally spinning. I hold myself between them, moving my feet as if dancing to the music that isn't playing.

When Ephraim gets close, he quickens his steps, and I fling one side of the silks toward him, lowering myself just enough to run on the ground. With one side of the silks in my hands and the other in Ephraim's, we run opposite each other. He moves slower than me as if trying to catch on. Balancing on one arm, I lift the other, signaling the men working the rigging to raise us into the air, holding my hand flat when we're a few feet off the ground to make the audience assume I'm teaching him.

"You okay?" I call to him.

"Keep going, Red," he calls back, smiling. "Teach me your ways."

Pointing down, I signal the men to lower us back to the ground and we both run once our feet touch the ground. Letting go, I spin, twirling the fabric around me until I run to Ephraim.

We hover together as I pretend to give directions for the benefit of the audience. Ephraim leans closer to me, hovering over me while holding some of his weight on his half of the silks.

"Are you going to tell me what's happening here?"

"We're performing, of course," Ephraim says. "I've always wanted to do a duo show with you."

"*You* wanted to do an aerial show with me?"

"You can't teach a man to work on silks and not expect him to want to show it off with a pretty girl every once in a while." He winks suggestively at me—again, for the benefit of the audience…*right?* "I've got seven different knives hidden on me, by the way. I have a feeling we'll need those later.

I point at his feet and he slips out of his boots. "They're not in there," he informs me. "At the end of the act, be sure to hide at least one on you."

"And where do you propose I do that?" I point as if I'm explaining where I want him to stand. Bending, I demonstrate a foot lock.

"Good point. Let me handle that," he comments. "Just play along."

"Fine." I back up as he does what I just pretended to teach him how to do.

"Come on, already!" an annoying man calls from the crowd. My head snaps in his direction, then I wrap the silks around my wrist and walk quickly in an arc until I lift my feet and spin in a small circle with one hand out, upright to the audience to indicate that I would comply. I point to Ephraim.

"Ready?"

"We'll talk up in the air."

He drops his fabric, letting it float to me. The music starts and I gather the silks in my hands, climbing up into the air. Once I'm high enough, I wrap my feet into a double foot lock and invert into a cross back straddle, gathering the flowing fabric into my hands. Looping each side so it dangles loosely between the ends of my feet and my hands. Grasping it tightly and locking in my wrists, I nod for Ephraim to climb up the silks I'm holding for him.

Ephraim signals the men working the rigging to lower the silks, but I'm only confused for a moment. I nod, giving them permission. They drop the rigging lower and Ephraim saunters over to me, grabbing the silks just under my hand. He points up, nodding to the men working the rigging, and then pulls back, stretching the silks as far as they will go to prepare to swing us.

He pauses before pushing forward. As soon as we move, he lifts his feet off the ground and the men pull us up, sending us toward the top of the tent. We move back and forth once before Ephraim drops, clutching the ends of the silks. He inverts in the air as I hold him. His feet make a running motion as the rigging men bring us back down— at least they're capable of following along with what we're doing in our act.

Ephraim releases his hold, freeing me to right myself. I quickly unlock my feet and wrap myself, twisting in the air for a double star drop. It takes me a moment, but Ephraim keeps the attention on me, reaching out for one side of the silks as it brushes past him.

I drop, leaving the audience in shock.

Twisting in the air, I cascade down toward Ephraim. He stands there smiling at me. I can barely see him as I twirl in the air, but somehow I feel like I've seen everything. Just as it looks like I'm going to crash into his arms, I jerk to a stop, still wrapped in the silks and he pulls away to let the audience see I saved myself.

"Not bad," he jokes.

I release myself and dance over to him, letting him spin me on the ground. His touch is warm and familiar.

Why haven't we done this before?

"My turn?" he asks. Before I can respond, he rushes to the silks and climbs up. Inverting like I had, he waits for me to join him in the air. I oblige, climbing.

He holds a hand out to me, and I take it, preparing to use him like an apparatus. We go through a series of moves where I contort in the air, held by only a foot and wrist, a single foot, or both feet.

Miraculously, Ephraim talks me through each transition, telling me when he's going to let go or move me. I follow his cues, bending my body as he directs. I didn't know he was capable of holding me like this, but he knows my act well enough to know what I'm capable of doing and he knows his own strength, making him the perfect person to direct our performance.

"Hands," he murmurs, and I turn to let him hold me by my wrists. Pulling my legs between our arms, I twist up around his waist. I lock my legs around him and we both let go, holding our arms to the side. I barely notice the audience cheering.

Looking up, I meet Ephraim's eyes. "We're going to get you out of here, Sienna. I promise."

The lights flash in my eyes, making a glowing ring appear around him, washing out his features. The fake scar stretching across his temple is barely visible.

I take his wrists, pulling my legs from around him. With my knees near my face, holding on only by my wrists, I wait.

"Trust me," Ephraim whispers, letting go of me. I drop.

He catches my ankles, stopping my decent. I twist in the air, facing the opposite direction and kick my feet up until I'm wrapped around Ephraim again. My back rests against his chest as we hang upside down. He pushes me up so that I'm upright. Reaching up, I take hold of the silks and pull myself up, standing on his outstretched arms.

Luther's eyes are wide below us as I glance down. There's no way he believes I *just* taught Ephraim how to do this. "He's onto us," I murmur as I lift myself up to stand on the inside of Ephraim's legs—it's a good thing the man is indestructible.

We quickly do a few moves before I drop back onto his hands, sliding down his arms. I contort in the air.

"When we hit the ground, get ready to go—this was a distraction to break Ida out." The silks start to lower us slowly, knowing they can't risk Ephraim dropping me if they move too quickly.

"The others?"

"We couldn't trust them, but we won't leave without them. Turns out, Josephine is pretty sneaky—I saw her near Ida for a second while we were working."

"Who is helping her?" I reach up and take his wrist as he flips me in the air. I kick my leg back, posing for the audience.

"Hoyt and Harriet. Fannie is covering them. The rest are here for us. Samuel is waiting outside."

I *knew* our people would be outside too.

"I'm going to beat Elijah to a pulp before we leave," Ephraim comments. "Just warning you now."

"As long as you let me get a kick in, I'm fine with that." I twist the silks in the air to spin us as he holds me in place by my feet.

"Confession: I followed you yesterday. Please don't be mad."

"Ordinarily I would be mad at you for not trusting me, but if you hadn't, I'd be on my way to...*wherever* Luther was planning on dragging us."

I drop the silks and Ephraim switches his hold, taking one ankle and one wrist in his hands. Turning, I look up at him.

"It's not that I didn't trust you." He tries to convince me. "I didn't trust *Elijah*. I saw him follow you and I followed him."

That means he saw us kiss. Embarrassment washes over me.

"He never should have done that to you," he says softly. "You deserve so much better than that."

Ephraim pauses for a moment, glancing down as we draw nearer to the ground. "Time's up, Sienna. Let's do this."

He holds me in the air until I wrap myself around his waist one more time. I flip forward, taking him with me so he's parallel to the ground, facing the top of the tent. I dangle off of his back as he slides us down the silks.

Once on the ground, the music continues to play, but Luther and his men converge on us.

Suddenly, Ephraim pulls me toward him, slamming me into his chest. He buries his hands in my knotted hair, twisted from how they designed my hair for the evening.

Ephraim's lips are searing against mine, kissing me over and over as he roams his fingers through my hair. I don't intentionally place my hands on his sides and run them up his back, making him shiver. He *definitely* means to make my knees go weak.

When he pulls back, I realize why he risked kissing me as the men converge on us—he's hidden one of his knives in my intricately designed hair. I can fight back.

The audience bursts into applause, cheering for us, thinking it's all part of the act. Ephraim quickly pulls on his shoes.

"What is this?" Luther demands. "You'll pay for this."

"Ephraim?" Elijah sounds shocked, dark features pulling back tightly. Ephraim rips off the fake facial hair he had been wearing—I'm excited to try kissing him without it.

Ephraim and I separate, pulling away from each other as we run in opposite directions. The silks guide us, pulling us back into the path of the men trying to take custody of us, knives and ropes in hand.

We have one chance at escape, and if we fail, it's going to be a bloodbath.

CHAPTER 8

Ephraim holds onto the red silk as he runs at my captors. Lifting his feet, he slams into Luther, knocking him to the ground. While I move, I wrap the silk around my waist, allowing my hands to be free to fight. The downside is that I'm tangled in a silk, which will make it hard to escape if I need to.

Lowering my center of gravity, I run at Elijah. I know Ephraim will have his say with our former friend and this might be my only chance. I grab hold of the silk with one hand and mimic Ephraim's move, kicking with both feet in the air.

Elijah sees me coming and tries to move out of the way. I collide with him, but he's prepared and grabs one of my arms, spinning me in a tight circle close to his body. He growls angrily at me, trying to slash at me with his fingernails.

I let go of the silk, letting it hold my weight in my lock. With both hands free, I attack, clawing at his face. The spinning motion continues, forcing Elijah to stumble over his own feet. I cry out as I attempt to take his eye—Grandmother always taught me to go for the eyes if I were ever being attacked, and surely this counts.

Elijah pulls back, giving me the briefest of moments to unwrap myself from my lock. Now is the time to run, not the time to fight tangled in silks.

Ephraim battles against Luther and his men as Orville and the majority of our men join us in the ring. The crowd's shocked gasps chorus around us.

Elijah punches me, snapping my head to the side long enough to see mothers scooping up their children, trying to escape the fight. I don't blame them for fleeing.

Turning back, I take my rage out on Elijah.

"Sienna!" Ephraim warns me. I look over in time to see Luther crawling toward me, ready to pounce.

I realize the music has stopped. It's a strange thing to discover as a man is running at me, but my brain focuses in on how silent it is aside from the people yelling around us and the sound of bodies colliding in battle.

"You belong to *me!*" Luther's words pierce through the chaos around us.

People scream from their cages, begging to be let out. They recognize that this is their chance. Someone else will have to save them.

Elijah reels back, but I don't have time to see what he's doing. Luther barrels toward me. I drop to the ground at the last second, forcing him to trip over my body on the dirt. Spinning, I kick out, connecting with his chin as he whips around to face me.

He curses at me, grabbing my ankle to jerk me toward him, dragging me through the dirt. Something catches in my sight and I duck instinctively as Elijah sails over my head, missing his target—the fool is trying my move on the silks.

Reaching into my hair, I pull out the knife. Drawing my arm back, I drive the hilt of the knife into Luther's cheekbone. I kick, forcing him to release his grip on me. Scrambling back, Ephraim grabs my wrist, pulling me to my feet.

"I will destroy him." Ephraim's growl is punctuated, looking for Elijah as he swings in the air.

"And I'll let you," I reply.

"Heads up, you two," Orville yells as he rushes past us. "No time for kissing!"

My face drains of color; I can feel it running out of my skin. Ephraim's hand on my hip doesn't help.

He spins us. Our people wrestle with Luther's men. Thankfully, most of them have resorted to hand-to-hand combat instead of using weapons against each other. Samuel's men have the advantage though —he's made sure even our handlers are trained. Luther appears to have only used his men for muscle around his circus and they falter when our men contort easily around their punches.

"You!" Luther bellows. Turning, I follow his gaze. Standing in the light pouring in from the open tent door, Samuel rides toward us on Caleo's back. She picks her trunk up when she spots Orville fighting.

A man snaps Orville's head back, dropping him to the ground. He quickly raises his hand and forces Caleo to stay in place. She obeys, waiting for Samuel to give her directions.

"You thought you could steal my acts?" Samuel yells from atop the elephant. He moves, echoing the commands we're familiar with Orville giving his charges. Caleo responds, stepping forward.

"Where did he go?" Ephraim whispers, pulling my attention away from the leaders of the two circuses.

"Who?" I ask, realizing my arm is wrapped around Ephraim's back, hand sitting on his hip. He turns, moving me with him.

"Elijah. Where is he?"

"I didn't see."

"We need to find him."

One of the chandeliers falls from the top of the tent, crashing next to us. The men working the riggings are trying to assist their boss by dropping things on Samuel's team. It shatters, sending black, metallic beads flying everywhere.

"Careful," I caution Ephraim.

He pulls a knife out from his boot—he must have slipped one in after he returned his shoes to his feet after our act. I, unfortunately, am still without shoes, leaving me to move around the ring barefoot.

"Give up, Luther. You're not going to take my people from me," Samuel calls down.

"Your girl isn't coming back to you, *Samuel*. She knows she can do more with me." Luther leaps to his feet, striding toward the elephant and our ringleader.

I wonder how easy it was to convince Elijah to betray people for fame. It's the only reason I can think of for Luther to assume I would be so easily swayed for power.

"I'm not staying with *you*," I call, still searching for Elijah. I can't find him anywhere.

"Sienna!" Samuel calls, stretching out his hand for me to join him, declaring my allegiance. Four men stand between us, making it nearly impossible. I'd rather fight for my freedom anyway.

"You won't take her or the old lady from me!"

"Ida is already halfway back to our camp, Luther. You lost her during Sienna's performance."

Luther whips around, looking for Grandmother's cage. It's empty, door open. He whips around, ready to attack.

Ephraim raises his left hand, balancing himself as he retracts his right hand, knife pointed up to the top of the tent as he prepares to throw it at Luther.

"Stop!" Ephraim warns him. He doesn't and Ephraim releases the knife, burying it in Luther's shoulder.

The tall man turns, wild-eyed.

"Knife!" Ephraim directs. I quickly drop my weapon into the knife thrower's hand, and he sinks it into the front of Luther's opposite shoulder. He staggers back, screaming in pain with two knives protruding from his upper arms. He throws curses at Ephraim and Samuel as if they matter.

Then he turns his sights on me.

Ephraim's muscles tighten next to me, brushing against my arm, but he doesn't sweep me behind his back as I expect him to do. Instead, he bends, retrieving another knife from a hidden pocket in his pant leg, and places it in my hand. He nods without looking at me.

I'm not going to kill Luther!

"Leg," he murmurs, as if reading my thoughts.

In the same way that Ephraim has tried the silks with me under our own tent, he's also taught me knife throwing. I'm nowhere near as skilled as he is, but the alternative was learning to be punched in the gut by a strong man, and I wasn't about to go through that training.

Arm in the air, I ready myself as Luther takes slow, heavy steps toward me, wrapped in pain.

"Stop, Luther," I threaten. I give him a few more chances to come to his senses. "I said stop."

When he doesn't, I embed the knife in his leg, forcing him to the ground. He pulls the knife out of his leg and tries to throw it at us, but by that time, Samuel is off of Caleo's back and walking up behind Luther. He pries the knife out of his hand.

"There!" Ephraim shouts. I jump next to him.

Ephraim takes off running, leaving me behind. I rush to keep up with him.

"Guess he's not so loyal now, is he?" I shout to Luther, swinging my arms at my side as I try to keep up with my friend. Luther's face crumbles, enraged as I shoot past him.

"Orville!" Ephraim calls, arms pumping in the air as he runs, the muscles in his back tight.

His cousin had somehow managed to work his way just outside of the tent as he grapples with one of Luther's men—the one that had been my guide this morning.

Ahead, I see what Ephraim saw: a red cape—*my* red cape.

The person turns around, looking over their shoulder as they run, hood high around their face to block people from seeing who it is. Several of our people dart out of the way, assuming the red flash is me. They let the person pass, running straight toward Brisheet.

Orville turns just in time to see Elijah leap onto Brisheet's saddle. He orders his elephant to stay still as Elijah attempts to force her to run. My cape settles around his legs as he kicks the poor elephant.

In the background, some of Luther's now-former captives are releasing the animals. I wished we could have talked to them before the escape to make sure they didn't just let the animals wander off to be hurt or killed by the townspeople. We'll have to collect them when this is all over and get them to new homes. Thankfully, Luther's circus consists mainly of people and not animals.

Ephraim runs to head off Brisheet while Orville shouts to her, trying to calm the poor creature. I run straight for Brisheet and her rider. Launching myself in the air while Elijah is distracted by Ephraim's approach, I pull myself up next to him.

I'm only sitting behind him for a moment before the magician reaches around his back—and mine—and pulls me forward roughly. I land in his lap, sideways. Looking up, I meet his glare.

"Fine, you want to play this way, we will." He pulls out a knife and holds it to my throat. "Back off, Ephraim. I'll do it, and you know I won't hesitate."

Ephraim's hand shoots out to the side, holding off Orville.

"Let her go, Elijah, and we'll let you leave."

It's sweet how Ephraim thinks Elijah will ever consider that as an option.

"No." Elijah laughs. "You won't touch me while I have the flying princess here. She stays with me.

"Besides," he adds, "I'm pretty sure I took her from you once anyway."

Not one of my finer choices. I let Fannie get in my head sometimes when it comes to boys. From now on, I'll ignore them completely.

Unless Ephraim wants to kiss again.

Hoyt runs up, nearly crashing into Ephraim. His eyes dart between Ephraim and me, trying to find some meaning in the scene as his jaw tips open slightly. For a man comfortable working with cranky tigers, he looks a bit bewildered now.

"Elijah, let her go!" Hoyt demands, glaring at the man who has me pinned on top of an elephant.

I try to right myself so I can see them from more than the corner of my eye, but Elijah holds me down, using his forearm to block my upper arm from moving. Unable to twist around, I wait, biding my time.

While Elijah's eyes are on the boys, I stretch a hand down Brisheet's side. Candace's eyes peer out from behind a barrel a few yards away. She holds her breath as she watches the scene. The girl looks like a scared rabbit about to bolt. I shake my head no and she sinks back.

"Trying to be a tiger, I see..." Elijah comments flippantly, still trying to get Brisheet to follow orders. She balks, stepping backward. He's clearly never worked with animals before.

The boys' protests chorus each other to distract my captor as Orville tries to sneak up to Brisheet without Elijah noticing. Unfortunately, he *does* notice, which is when I jerk forward, grabbing the end of the cape he's wearing.

Pulling hard, I force him back, causing him to lose his balance. Elijah grabs onto my waist, trying to steady himself. Instead, I inch my foot up along Brisheet's shoulder and push us over, toppling Elijah backward, while I plummet face first to the ground.

He slams into the ground, and it audibly knocks the breath out of him. I roll, using my hands to propel myself over and I tuck my head as I move, using my feet to catch myself.

I make it upright before Elijah grabs my ankles and forces me back to the ground in a heap. Brisheet rushes away from us heavily and Orville takes off after her.

Ephraim and Hoyt run up to us, but Elijah has found his knife again and is yelling threats. To the right, smoke drifts up into the late afternoon air, dark and twisted. A pile of hay meant for the animals is on fire. Harriet hovers a few feet away, watching the scene unfold, her tools in her hand, ready to assist with her fiery ways. She surprisingly doesn't look nervous. Blanch appears next to her, cradling a bleeding arm with her hand.

Elijah stands, towering over me, leaving me on my back on the ground. He points his knife at me. Ephraim and Hoyt slow their approach, trying to keep him from doing anything rash.

Threatening the wolf will do me no good—that doesn't throw him. If I want to distract him and give my people the upper hand, I have to do something to fluster him.

Raising my right foot, I drag it along his ankle, under his pant leg. My nose wrinkles as I come into contact with the hair on his legs.

How did I ever think he was attractive? His sharp nose and angular cheekbones should have been enough to make me reconsider my stance, but I listened to the other girls obsessing over him and when he turned his attention on me...

Elijah starts. *It's far too easy to make him do that.*

I use the opportunity to kick his hip.

He stumbles, dropping the knife, and then runs.

With his knife in my hand, I follow Ephraim's training. The knife sails through the air, digging itself into Elijah's upper leg as he turns to look back at me. He curses, running with painful, hobbled steps. Blood drips down his leg as he moves toward the woods.

Looking back, I see Ephraim holding out his arm across Hoyt's chest to stop him. "Let her go." My friend nods to me.

I turn, prepared to hunt down Elijah. I don't need to run—he's not going to get that far ahead—but I keep a quick pace as I track drops of blood on the ground the same way I look for signals from Grandmother.

The others follow several paces behind me, ready to back me up when I approach my prey. Orville calls out from atop Brisheet, telling us he plans to circle around in case we need him on the other end, though I doubt he'll be able to make it through the trees on the wide animal. The last thing I hear before I leave the area is that he's taking Blanch with him. Considering her injury, I think that's a wise choice.

Stepping into the woods is familiar. It's safe, even though it's in a town that I don't trust. With my friends trailing behind me and the town actively moving away from the fight that erupted at the show, I'm free to move without worrying about who else might be tracking me. Instead, I track down Elijah.

Leaves brush against my legs, my lace tights barely protecting me. I watch closely for anything that might cut into my flesh. The wind guides me, pushing at my back. I'm grateful for the breeze—it had been incredibly hot inside the tent and it whips the sweat off my back under my costume.

It doesn't take long to find my cape in a heap in the middle of the pathway. I pick it up, wrapping it around my shoulders. I can't afford to carry it, and neither can the others. It flows out behind me in the breeze I'm creating as I jog through the woods barefoot.

Unlike the circus tent, the woods are filled with quieter sounds. Everything seems more natural out here. The breeze. The birds. The crunch of leaves beneath our feet. I barely notice the twigs piercing my feet as I move across the layers of decaying leaves on the forest floor.

The sound of heavy breathing catches my attention and I turn. Elijah tries to muffle his puffing but is unsuccessful—he made it quite a bit farther than I expected. One shoe sticks out from behind a tree where he's resting, attempting to cover himself with branches from the nearby bush.

"And here I thought you could pull off a disappearing act." I let my words sound like a song as the others surround the tree in a wide circle, leaving me to talk to Elijah alone. "I guess you're not as great of a magician as you thought. You talked a big game for such a sad little sideshow."

He glares at me, grimacing. One hand rests over his leg where he's trying to stop the bleeding. Red peeks out from around his fingers, dripping down the back of his knuckles until it falls to the dead leaves below.

Grandmother was right—*blood is silent.*

"I knew you weren't worth the trouble."

"Then why *did* you go to all this trouble, Elijah?" I ask, hand on my hip. "You could have worked with us and made a *real* name for yourself. Instead, you worked with Luther. How did you honestly think that would pay off?"

"Luther doesn't have staying power, Sienna. A few years from now, this would have all been mine."

"A creepy circus with reluctant captives as performers? How do you think that would have ended up?" I shift my shoulders, letting the cloak fall around my arms—he doesn't realize how many times the cloak hindered his plans, but I do.

"They all had reasons for cooperating," he insists. "And they like me better than Luther. *I* wasn't threatening their families. They were grateful to me and would have been grateful when I gave them jobs after I took over for Luther."

Delusional. That's the only explanation.

Elijah howls and cringes forward.

"You know, Ida could fix that for you. In addition to everything else she does, she's quite good with healing people's injuries—she's learned so much in her years with Samuel and his crew." I can feel my eyes spark as if I touched the end of an electric lamp before it was all the way removed from its power source. "You can come back with us, Elijah. At least you won't bleed out in the woods alone."

"You wouldn't be kind enough to let me die in peace," he growls. His eyes narrow.

"You're right; I wouldn't let you die alone. I'd sit here talking to you the entire time, drawing it out as long as possible. The good news is that you aren't going to die from that wound…unless I want you to. Now stop being ridiculous and get up—we have places to be."

"I'm not going back with you." He pushes himself up until he's balanced on one leg, holding himself up on the tree.

"I don't think you're getting back on your own." I raise an eyebrow at him. "You can let us help you back, or we can force you back, but either way, by this evening, you're the only one who is going to be in a cage."

"*You* looked better there," he snarls.

"I look better in *color*, you pathetic—"

"All right!" Ephraim interrupts, stomping over. "I've had enough. She hunted you down and you're going back into a cage where you will stay for a very long time, Elijah."

"I—"

"No. You keep your mouth shut, or we're handing you over to the local authorities." Ephraim twirls his knife in his hand for show. "I sincerely doubt you want to be locked up *here* in the town where you caused so much chaos. They're not going to be happy about the fight, or the animals running wild, or the fire that I'm sure they saw smoke from. When we tell them it's all your fault and it's because you've been abducting people to use in your show, I can only imagine how they'll react. Based on what I saw of the way they treated your performers when you let them walk around those cages, I have a feeling they'll have some creative forms of justice."

"Move," Hoyt demands.

Moving in behind Elijah, he wrenches the boy's arms back, tying them. Harriett stalks behind him, flashing a match to remind Elijah that she doesn't mind burning things down for the fun of it. The others walk behind them.

Josephine glances back at me, her features soft and delicate, clearly concerned about me. I'm surprised she stayed behind after she got Grandmother out of her cage.

"You okay?" Ephraim asks quietly.

"I'm fine," I whisper, feeling the day crash over me.

"Can I help you?" he whispers again. Turning both hands over, he offers to carry me back through the woods to spare my feet. I nod heavily, tiredness dragging over me.

Ephraim scoops me up in his arms, my hip pushing against his abdomen and chest, melting into the sculpted curves of his muscles. I rest my head against his shoulder, arm curved around his neck as I try to support part of my weight.

"Are your feet okay?" he asks.

"I'll be fine," I murmur into his collarbone. His breath hitches, jerking my forehead slightly where it rests against his neck. I lift my head up, suddenly amused as I remember our show on the silks. "You were pretty magnificent back there."

His lips quirk up as he catches my eye. "Yeah, well, tracking down the bad guys is kind of my specialty, Sienna."

"Oh, no, I meant up in the air." I really *am* impressed with what he pulled off. "How did you figure out how to do that?"

"You and I practiced enough. And I've tossed people around for the show before." He shrugs, jostling me. "Sorry."

"We hardly practiced enough for you to pull that off. Have you been working on that without me?"

"Let's just say I've been watching you closely enough to have a pretty good idea of what we could do together."

"Oh?" I raise an eyebrow. "What exactly can we do together?"

He grins.

"Was one of those things you thought we'd be good at the ending of our little show?" I tease, referring to the kiss.

"Oh, I *definitely* knew we'd be good at that." He blows a kiss at me and I have to fight a giggle.

We both dip as he ducks under a tree branch. I turn as something catches Ephraim's eye ahead—Harriet. She gives us a look before turning around, and this time, *I* laugh.

"How bad do you think this is going to get?" I ask, nodding to our friends.

"Pretty bad, I'm going to guess. Orville has been rooting for us, but we'll never hear the end of it from Fannie and Hoyt."

"Good point."

"I'm pretty sure Ida will have some thoughts on this too."

"Ha!" I snort. "I'm sure she will."

"Is there anything I can do to sway her to my side on this?" Ephraim inquires. "I definitely didn't ask her permission before kissing her granddaughter, and that woman basically controls my future. I have a feeling I need to make it up to her before she spends the next five months making my life miserable to prove a point."

"You already rescued me, what more could she ask for?"

Ephraim laughs.

"What?" I ask, grinning.

"You rescued yourself, Red. *You*, Sienna, are one *star* act."

"I couldn't have done it without you, *Invincible Man*. Speaking of colors though, maybe we should dress you in red more often, what do you think?"

"If I have to perform in red, then *you*, have to spend a little time in blue during the show, my friend."

"*Friend*?" I challenge. His lips pull up in a wide smile. "What exactly does my appearance in blue require?"

"I can throw knives at you."

"No," I quickly cut him off.

"No?" he asks curiously.

"No. You have Fannie and Blanch for that."

"Fine, you can throw them at me and I'll catch them. It's the perfect crossover for my *Invincibility* act and knife throwing."

I consider it for a moment.

"That would probably require a lot of practice," I muse as we exit the forest. Orville has both elephants back under his watch. Our friends are turned, waiting for us to join them. Samuel calls out that we need to get back and check on Grandmother. Ephraim sets me down as Josephine runs for a pair of shoes for me.

"I wouldn't mind putting in a few extra hours every day until we get the routines down." He smiles at his cousin as Orville bumps into his arm. Orville looks around his cousin, giving me a look, trying to hold back a grin.

"Kiss her, or I will, Eph," Hoyt mumbles as he brushes by us, prepared to look for the animals the captives set free earlier so nothing happens with the townspeople.

Samuel splits us up, directing us on where to go to clean up Luther's mess. Everyone scurries off to help.

"Take her home, Ephraim. Make sure Ida is all right and then stand guard in case any of Luther's men decide to take matters into their own hands."

"What about the others?" I ask.

"They can join us if they like, or they're welcome to travel with us as far as they want until they reach home. I've let them all know they're welcome to stay with us this evening—we'll feed them and give them a place to rest until they can decide what they want to do." Samuel really does have a heart deep down somewhere. "They've all agreed to join us for this evening at least. Even a few of Luther's henchmen have requested jobs with us. They'll need to be tested first, of course."

"And the town?" Ephraim questions.

"If we get out of here quickly, they'll have no idea we were involved, and they won't find much of Luther's circus left. I've got Clarence and a few of the men dropping him off with the local authorities now though, with a full description of his transgressions.

"They're an odd bunch. I'm sure Luther will appreciate their unconventional methods. Elijah will be going with them."

Josephine reappears with shoes for me as Ephraim explains how I hunted Elijah down in the woods. I slip them on, grateful I no longer have to travel barefoot—I need my feet in one piece for tomorrow's final show before we move on from this place.

Elijah glares at us, hands bound in front of him, a cloth tied around his leg. His nostrils flare when I make eye contact with him.

Ephraim quietly takes my hand while he and Samuel talk, clearly ignoring Elijah so he doesn't beat him to a pulp.

"Good luck with Fannie," Josephine mutters as she backs away from me, keeping her voice low so only I hear her.

"Helpful, thank you."

"It's not *my* fault you felt compelled to kiss the most gorgeous man in this circus…" She rolls her eyes. "Aside from—"

She cuts her own words off as my eyebrows shoot up. I clutch the red cloak around my shoulders as I laugh, assuring her I'll find out whose name she almost said later this week.

"Come on," Ephraim tugs on my hand. "You can come with us, Josephine."

"Anyone want a ride?" Orville offers. Blanch holds his waist with her good arm as they sit on top of Brisheet. Caleo bends down to allow us on.

"I'm fine," Josephine runs off, leaving us standing there.

"She's on a mission," Ephraim muses.

"Let her go," Blanch calls, smiling. *She knows something.*

Ephraim helps me onto Caleo, and he and his cousin direct the elephants back toward our colorful circus tent. The lights will be sparkling by now as the sky starts to dim. My silks will be waiting for me, as will Grandmother, but I won't be performing this evening. The circus will be closed down to cater to the needs of the people we rescued today.

"Nice work today, Red." Ephraim leans back into my arms as I hold his waist. "You really drew some blood out there."

He references my grandmother's remarks about my silks. She'll be delighted when I tell her about what happened today. Perhaps blood *isn't* so silent all of the time.

"Nice work today, Invincible," I murmur into his ear. He purrs, turning his face to me slightly, no longer shy about his affections. "Want to practice on the silks tonight, *friend?*"

Maybe I can find out what that hair tug meant last night at the show. We clearly need to get better at working on our signals.

"I really don't think we have a choice if we want to get this right," he replies innocently as if I didn't have ulterior motives. "We need to start immediately…*without* an audience this time."

I fully agree.

ABOUT K.M. ROBINSON

K.M. Robinson is a storyteller who creates new worlds both in her writing and in her fine arts conceptual photography. She is a marketing, branding and social media strategy educator who is recognized at first sight by her very long hair. She is a creative who focuses on photography, videography, couture dress making, and writing to express the stories she needs to tell. She almost always has a camera within reach. Visit her at her website for free books and exclusive samples: www.kmrobinsonbooks.com

CONNECT ON SOCIAL MEDIA

facebook.com/kmrobinsonbooks

instagram.com/kmrobinsonbooks

twitter.com/kmrobinsonbooks

youtube.kmrobinsonbooks.com

Get free books and excerpts of other K.M. Robinson books at
excerpt.kmrobinsonbooks.com

ALSO BY K.M. ROBINSON

The Golden Trilogy

Book One: Golden

Forged: A Golden Novella

Book Two: Locked

Book Three: Edge

The Complete Series Boxset/Omnibus with Tempered: an exclusive bonus novella

The Jaded Duology

Book One: Jaded

Book Two: Risen

The Complete Series Boxset/Omnibus with exclusive epilogue

The Siren Wars Saga

Book One: The Siren Wars

Book Two: Darker Depths

Book Three: Beyond The Shores

Origins of the Siren Wars: Prequel Novella

Book Four: Forbidden Waters (coming soon)

The Legends Chronicles

Along Came A Spider: A Prequel Novelette

And They'll Come Home: A Prequel Novelette

The Archives of Jack Frost Series

The Revolution of Jack Frost

The Redemption of Jack Frost (coming soon)

Stealing Steam Series

Book One: Lions and Lamps

Book Two: Pistons and Prisoners

Book Three: Railcars and Rulers

Top Hats and Telegraphs: A Prequel Novella

The Complete Series Boxset/Omnibus with Vambraces and Victories: an exclusive bonus novella

Virtually Sleeping Beauty: A Novella Retelling

The Goose Girl and The Artificial: A Novella Retelling

The Sinking: A Little Mermaid Novella Retelling

Cindrill: A Cinderella Assassin Novella Retelling

Sugarcoated: A Hansel and Gretel's Witch Novella Retelling

Game of Bezique

Elle Beaumont

CHAPTER 1

"Try your hand at a game of chance," crooned Etienne Mercier. His card table happened to be set up in the market with the hope of snaring the attention of the patrons. Bezique was his game of choice, and it was not a game of chance so much as it was a game of thievery and trickery.

"You—fine *monsieur*! Care to dabble in a game? You could very well line your pockets with a fortune." Etienne's light-green eyes sparked with a challenge as he honed in on a passing gentleman, waving his hand.

"Why don't you get a real job." The man sneered. He wasn't the first to curl his lip in disdain.

Instead of lobbing a quick-witted retort at the man, Etienne let it go. It would do nothing but draw negative attention to him if he snapped back. His lips pressed into a firm line as he lowered his gaze to the card table.

His tanned, worn fingers combed his dark hair back. In spite of living in destitution, he'd managed to scrape together his earnings to purchase more exceptional-quality clothing. Just because he lived on the streets for a time did not mean he needed to look it—or represent it.

He dressed smartly—a white cotton dress shirt, coupled with a dark blue vest. The sleeves of the shirt were rolled up to showcase that he was not, in fact, stealing from the patrons. The joke was on them, he didn't need sleeves to take from them.

It wasn't his fault that he couldn't maintain a job. As soon as an employer discovered that he was fae, they banished him from their establishment. Fae were seen as a blight on the world thanks to the wicked council that ruined everything. It was all fun and games until one diabolical plan hatched, and evil rained down on innocents. Count de Clavière ruined the future for fae-kind, and painted them to be all the same: bloodthirsty, greedy, and willing to enslave humans.

Etienne's parents were victims of a proverbial witch hunt, cornered and killed by a fearful mob. As mercy would have it, Etienne had been at their next door neighbor's playing with their son while they had been at the theater. He had been given the news amidst eating an eclair, only eight years of age, and his world had been shattered.

Fortune had hardly smiled on him. He was allowed to live with the Collier's for a year until they had no choice but to turn him out on the streets. Forced to learn how to pick pockets, swipe food from tables, and use his magic to survive, he had become a savvy street urchin. Etienne had always been bright, and he ferreted enough money away so that he could rent out a dingy hole, buy food instead of stealing or rummaging through the waste bins, and most importantly, clothe himself to set him apart from the typical street rat.

"Come and try your hand at a fun game," he recited one of his several lines. His nimble fingers spread the cards along the table, and then with one movement, the cards shifted into the other direction. As he quickly shuffled them, he noticed he had caught the attention of a well-to-do woman.

Middle-aged, and yet still beautiful, he had the feeling she broke a lot of hearts in her youth.

"*Bonjour, monsieur,*" she offered and peered down at the table. "What is this?" she inquired.

"This is—" His words were cut off.

"*Non,* not that. What is this?" Her hand motioned to him, and she clucked her tongue. She leaned forward and scooped up the deck that he had spread out and shuffled them. "You have to have flair, *mon ami.*" She turned her back to him, her purple skirt brushing against the card table. The white wig on her head boasted of wealth. The curls that dangled from it only seemed to bring attention to that fact.

Whoever the woman was, she had played cards before. Her fingers traversed over the deck with skill, and though her fingers were gloved, they didn't stumble or slip once. Squeezing the deck of cards, they skyrocketed into the air and fell into a neat pile in her awaiting hand. "Attention, *monsieurs and mademoiselles*! Have you ever wanted to feel your heart hammer in your breast? Have you wondered what it was like to live on the edge? Try your hand at a game of chance, just one game…what have you to lose?"

Etienne's mouth gaped open, and he surveyed the attention that had been drawn to them. "Thank you," he murmured as he bowed his head, heat flooding into his cheeks.

She smiled at him. "Take care, *mon ami*, and *bonne* chance."

He blinked as he took the cards back from her. "Wait," he called out as she began to walk away. "Your name. What is your name?"

She fluttered white lashes at him, a curious smirk on her lips. "You may call me Marie, but don't let anyone know that." She lifted a finger to her ruby lips. "I shall see you again, no?"

"Will I?" His dark lashes fanned across his skin, feeling less confident under her intense blue gaze.

She twisted her lips and nodded her head. "I think we will. Paris is not so big, you know?"

Marie, he thought. No surname, no title, and yet she could maneuver a deck of cards as if she had been born in a gambling hall. He wrinkled his pert nose and furrowed his brow. Who could say who she was? The streets of Paris were full of tricksters just like him.

She may not have used magic, but her energy had attracted onlookers, and so he played, or instead, he played them.

Marie had taught him one thing: no matter what, it was always to put on a show. In that brief moment they shared, he knew it was less about seeming like a scam, and everything to do with enticing the onlookers.

Could he take their mind off their woes? Could he make them gasp, smile, or giggle? The more he could, he discovered, the deeper their pockets became. Bezique was a clever game, but so was reading a person and redirecting their attention.

Etienne pulled a card from his pocket and ran a finger along the smooth edge. Notre Dame's bells came to life and told him it was 4:00 pm. Soon, the 4:05 steam engine would be roaring to life. Tucking the card into his pocket, he folded the table up and strapped it to his back before he began to make the journey to the apartment he called his hole.

Colombe Street was a decent walk, but it was one he was used to by now. Etienne kept his hands shoved in his pockets to guard the coins he had earned. He was grateful the steps to his apartment were in front of him.

"You filthy fae scum!" a man a few rows down cried out. Lifting the cane at his side, he was readying to strike down a boy that must have been only ten.

Etienne curled his lip and removed his hands from his pockets as he briskly walked toward the greasy man. The sparse hair atop of his head was slick with oil, and his face gleamed in the fading sun. He smelled like aged body odor and alcohol. Etienne could have sworn he had bugs rolling in and out of the gaps where his teeth once had been.

"Fine *monsieur*, what seems to be the problem?" Gracefully moving so that he could help the boy up and pull him to the side, Etienne flashed the man a brilliant smile.

The boy was definitely fae. The tell-tale pointed ears and too-pretty features painted him as such. It was why Etienne grew his thick hair out—it hid the pointed tips.

"Disgusting Fae; they should have been wiped out when we retaliated. He stole from me."

Etienne clucked his tongue. "Ah, surely they serve some purpose, no? Shining shoes, entertaining the masses?" With his hands behind his back, he motioned for the boy to run along. "What did he steal?"

The stout man snorted and waved him off. "Maybe not even that," he muttered and hobbled down the street. "My watch."

"The very watch in your hand?" he asked carefully.

"I got it back from the runt."

"What a fine watch it is. Where did you get it from? I've never seen such workmanship."

"My father. It was his." The man's features softened as the moments ticked by. He must have been lost in his memories surrounding it, because when he lifted his beady eyes once more, he waved his hand in dismissal and walked away.

When Etienne turned around, he found the boy hiding behind a bin, his large, mismatched eyes peering at him. "Come here, *mon ami.*" He sing-sang his words to the boy, and crouched down to sit on a step. "The world is not a friendly place for our kind, but one day they will accept us. Until then, we must do what we can to survive, which either means not being caught, or being clever enough to weasel your way out of trouble." He reached into his pocket and took out some coins to drop into the boy's hands.

"No, *monsieur*, I cannot take this!" His eyes widened as he realized that Etienne was also fae.

Purposely, Etienne brushed his hair behind an ear. "But you could take that man's watch?" Etienne's eyes shone with laughter, his dark brows lifting in mock surprise.

"He was a jackass," the boy spat out. "You're… you're like me."

"In more ways than one. Keep it. Now, run along and don't get caught next time." He watched as the boy scurried down the street and shook his head. Hopefully his words were true and one day Fae would once more be accepted amongst the masses, but for now, they all had to be careful, especially the young ones.

Etienne cast one more look down the alley before he ventured inside the poor excuse for an apartment.

The walls of the apartment were paper thin, so the moment Etienne's neighbors began to crow at sunrise he was awake. Every day was the same, even on the weekends. He slapped a hand against his face and rubbed his eyes. Like it or not, it was time to get up.

Once dressed, he collected his card table, and left for the day. Reflexively, he looked down the alley to see if his little friend lingered around, but he wasn't there. *Good,* he thought, *he was safer for it.*

In the distance, smoke billowed high into the air. Paris always seemed to have a thick cloud of it, mostly due to the steam-powered engines that always seemed to declare their presence with a roar. In the past decade, Etienne had seen the steam-powered contraptions burst to life, and more than that, the automatons that seemed to replace the need for a living being. It wasn't uncommon to see an automaton dusting shelves or retrieving paper, but it was only recently that they made their way into storefronts. That fact stung because store owners preferred to employ an automaton over fae.

Eventually, he made it to his usual place in the market, set up his table, and donned his toothy smile. Etienne took care today to remember the brief teachings Marie was so thoughtful to bestow on him.

His green eyes locked onto a well-dressed man and he flagged him down. "Ah! Excuse me, *monsieur*! Do you wish to feel your pulse thrum in excitement? Do you want to feel as though you were living life on the edge? Step right here; come and play a game of bezique with me!" To his surprise, the gentleman lifted his salt and pepper brows and moved forward.

"Bezique, is it?" the man inquired.

Etienne nodded his head. "Are you willing to take a chance?" His eyes glittered with a silent challenge.

The older gentleman stroked his trimmed beard and strode forward. "I think I *am* willing."

Nodding his head, Etienne set up the table. "What are you willing to bet?" His pulse leaped. If this man were the adventurous sort, he'd put down a healthy amount, but if he were stingy, he'd likely put down a measly morsel, something that would barely feed Etienne.

The man was the former.

The amount placed on the table would feed him for a month, if not more. Gulping, Etienne ran his fingers over the cards and recited the rules and objective of the game. The man nodded his head that he understood, and the game began.

His dark eyes observed the cards even as he lit up a cigarillo and took a puff.

Flick, flip, flick, flip, slide became the pattern. To some, it would appear dull, but not when the players were focused and intent on beating the other.

When it became apparent the man was engrossed in the game, Etienne relied on his magic, blurring the image a mundane would see as he slid away a card that belonged to the gentleman.

As the game wound down, it was growing clear who the victor was, and it wasn't the gent in front.

A sigh slipped from Etienne as he was declared the winner. "I'm sorry. Care to play again?"

The man smiled and took a long draw from his cigarillo. "No, but I'd like to keep my money, *thief*." He didn't move as he eyed Etienne.

"You're mistaken, *monsieur*, I am no thief." He kept his voice low, not wanting to alert the nearby crowd. It was arduous enough to gain the trust of them, let alone being accused of stealing.

The man snorted, stuck the cigarillo between the corner of his lips, and folded his arms across his chest. As he spoke, he did so out of the other side of his mouth. "I'm calling you on that. I'm going to give you to the count of three, and if you return the card to the table with my money, I won't have those guys drag your can to the authorities." He jerked his head toward the two burly men hanging back.

There was a reason Etienne was still alive, and it wasn't because he rolled over when pressed by a challenge. His green eyes flicked between the man and the two approaching men. In a blink, he scooped up the man's money and bolted away.

Bellows rang out in the air as he charged through a crowd of people. He felt someone trying to snag his jacket to stop him, but he pulled away. His heart pounded wildly in his chest as he zig-zagged through the populace and darted to the nearest alley. Quickly, he surveyed the area and spotted a rain barrel. He leaped up onto it and jumped for the overhanging roof.

A grunt escaped Etienne as his fingers dug into the roof and his arms worked to pull his frame upward. Once he was on the roof, it was easy enough to leap to the other. He eyed the clothesline below and quickly weighed out his chances.

Just a moment—that was all it took. He leaped into the air, his hands readying to snag the clothesline, and when they did, it sprung loose from the building. His heart fell to the depths of his stomach, but Etienne was ahead of the game, and as the line readied to snap above, he let himself free-fall onto a balcony. It was a rough landing— one that jarred his entire body—but with his neck on the line, it was worth the risk.

With a slight limp, he began to walk inside, praying that no one was home, and for once, luck was on his side. Casually, he milled around the lavish house, his fingers itched to take something —*anything*—but the weight of the money in his pocket was more than enough right now.

A small flight of stairs led down to the front door. He peered outside, and when the coast was clear, he exited. He'd have to leave the card table for a few hours and hope that it would be there upon returning to it.

Smirking, he tapped at his pocket and sighed. "*Merci*, Lady Luck." His gaze shifted too late, and he found himself staring at a pair of bottomless black eyes.

"Nice moves. I commend you for your bravery, but not your stupidity." Somewhere amidst the chaos, his cigarillo disappeared. "Those men over there have flagged down the authorities, but I have to say I am impressed with your dexterity, and therefore I have a proposition for you."

CHAPTER 2

Etienne was still puffing from his efforts, but the well-dressed man scarcely had a hair out of place. Dread crept into the fae's bones —if it was a choice between facing the authorities or listening to the proposition, he supposed he'd don his listening ears.

"I'm listening," he said softly.

The man nodded his head and extended his hand. "The name is Baron Weaver." He paused and waited for Etienne's reaction.

Of course, he was a Baron, he thought miserably. Why couldn't he have been a clerk? Or some wealthy shop owner? Sniffing, Etienne reached for the man's hand cautiously and shook it. Everything in him screamed run, and yet he felt compelled to stay to see what it was this Baron had to offer.

"You may have heard of me, but if not, I run a company, and I'd be interested in having you work for me. You know, as payment for stealing what belonged to me." His head tilted to the side as he gave Etienne a once-over, as if trying to guess where the money was hidden.

No, he most certainly had not heard of him. Although, it wasn't as if he were up-to-snuff on the peerage. He gawked at the Baron and felt his skin prickle. Etienne could give the money back, but he was in dire need of it. "What sort of company?"

"Entertainment."

"What kind of entertainment?"

Baron Weaver chuckled. "Why don't you come and see for yourself?"

Why should he trust him? Etienne had just stolen from him, and yet he was offering him a job? People weren't that kind—not anymore. They would push a starving boy down the gutter without a thought. Perhaps, just maybe, Lady Luck was on his side.

There was a chance that the Baron had never seen real magic before, and, if need be, Etienne would use it to save his hide. He would risk revealing what he truly was to protect himself if he had to. Although, he wondered which fate would be worse: finding himself amidst a hunt or in the crosshairs of Baron Weaver.

Life was but a game of chance, and Etienne found himself rolling the dice.

As it turned out, the Baron wasn't a murderer, and he wasn't going to turn him in—at least not yet. He had, however, taken him across the city to Bois de Vincennes—the largest park in Paris— which hadn't been expected. The park alone was impressive, but it wasn't the size of it that caused Etienne's mouth to hang open; it was the dirigible anchored to the ground. Etienne had never seen one up close before, and he was confident that none looked like this.

The back of the ship looked more like a tower, including several windows and a rooftop, which was actually a canopy. From the side of the tower, a giant sail hung limply, the gold and wine color of the sails matching the awnings perfectly. The front of the ship was also covered by a canopy, and the windows were decorated by wine drapes so that one couldn't easily peer inside of the deck.

"You should see her when she's landing. We call her Étoile de la Tempete. Étoile for short." Baron Weaver chuckled.

She must have been impressive to watch, and it must have been even more impressive to watch the workers string up the canopy. Étoile wasn't part of where the shows took place, but she didn't disrupt the aesthetic by being there. A massive tent sat beside the dirigible—the same gold, and wine hue—and ropes tethered it in place. There was one thing that was missing though—the sound of animals.

"No animals?"

"Oh, no, I don't do animals. They smell, eat far too much, and providing food for a menagerie just isn't economical."

Etienne waited for a moment to see if it was a joke—it wasn't. "You're a people-circus?" He pressed his lips together and nodded his head. The furrow on Etienne's brow must have said he didn't understand how a circus full of people could be profitable, let alone entertaining.

A deep chuckle escaped Baron Weaver, and his arm slid around Etienne's shoulders. "Ah, son, you could say that, but we're more than that, too. Come! Come and see. It's early, which means you'll catch them practicing for tonight." There was no room to back out because the grip on Etienne tightened as the Baron pulled him forward.

Idly, Etienne wondered what the park looked like at night and how crowded it became.

"Have you ever been to the *Cirque*?" Weaver asked.

"No."

"How old are you?" Weaver's brow furrowed as he looked at Etienne.

"Eighteen next week."

"Yet, you've never been to this show—or *any* for that matter?"

Etienne's cheeks flushed. "There are more important things to spend coin on, Baron." As weighted as the words were, he spoke them in a cherry tone belying the fact his life had been a constant struggle.

Baron's eyes didn't miss a thing. He nodded his head and motioned toward the open flaps. "Go ahead. Explore *Cirque de la Tempete*."

From where Etienne stood, it looked as if he were about to enter complete darkness, yet as he moved inside of the tent, he discovered how wrong he was. It wasn't as illuminated as the sky, but the inside shone like the heavens on a clear night. Gas lamps twinkled, and torches blazed around the center ring. It was the most fantastic thing he had ever seen.

Above him, two individuals dangled precariously from thick swaths of cloth. He squinted his eyes to watch. *"No!"* he shouted, and leaped into the ring, just as the smaller figure began to tumble down the silks. He reached her at the same moment she hung suspended.

The girl had a constellation of freckles across the bridge of her nose and the largest brown eyes he had ever seen. He couldn't help but notice given that her face was inches from him. Her hair, which was a vibrant red, was held back in a neat braid, she was beautiful— and she was also scowling at him.

"Are you stupid? What are you shouting for?" Like a spider climbing its silk, she pulled herself upright and shot an accusatory glare at him. "Disruptions aren't welcome during practice."

He blinked and grinned lopsidedly. "No. I am Etienne, and you are?" Extending his hand, he opted to disregard the venom in her words.

"Too busy to deal with you. Get out of here. Take your smooth-talking and go."

"I thought you were falling to your death," he remarked, losing the cocky expression as a genuine smile formed on his face.

The scowl didn't leave her face as she spoke again. "No, I was practically born in these." She plucked at the ribbon and shook her head.

Beside her, an older guy slid down the ribbon. His torso was bare and covered in numerous tattoos—it was hard not to stare. "Is he bothering you, Lil?" His golden eyes flicked toward Etienne.

"No—" Etienne began to reply.

"Yes, he is, but he's harmless." She dropped from the ribbon and padded up to him on the balls of her feet. "Go, now. Get out of here." There was an edge to her voice and a hard look in her eye.

"I can't, I'm here with the Baron."

Etienne watched the two troupe members exchange glances and saw her features tighten.

"Leave before he comes back."

"He'll only find me again—he hunted my hide down before, I'm sure he'll do it again."

She let out a frustrated sigh and slammed her shoulder into his when she walked away, leaving Etienne with the muscled guy.

"Don't bother, you'll end up with a broken nose if you follow her," the guy teased. "I'm Taurus; you can call me Rus." He extended his hand to shake Etienne's.

Rus' hand dwarfed Etienne's, in fact, everything about Rus seemed to dwarf him. In truth, he looked like an ancient god come to life—bronze skin, gold eyes, sandy blond hair, and tall.

"Be careful where you walk around here—people leap out of nowhere and tumble from the sky." Rus winked and waved as he turned to leave.

Maybe that girl was right. Perhaps he could just go. He could leave the stolen money behind, and the Baron would let him be.

Deciding that was the best idea, Etienne took the bundle of money from his pocket and picked up a rock from the ground. Using a stone as a paperweight, he left the paper money on one of the bleachers.

One more glance around and then he fled.

Baron Weaver was nowhere in sight—praise the spheres! Etienne walked with purpose but did not run since he didn't want to alert anyone.

Ahead, the imposing Étoile's sails began to flap, as if waving adieu to him. Holding his breath, he began to maneuver his way through the park. His foot landed on the road, and just as the next one followed suit, a voice snagged him.

"Leaving so soon? And before we even sit to chat about business?" The Baron clucked his tongue.

"I left your money on one of the seats. I'm sorry, I—"

"Nonsense, I saw how you scaled those buildings, and I also saw you on that line. Imagine what you could do with some training. You'd be one of the stars like Taurus and Liliane. I've always wanted their act to be a trio." He jerked his head toward Étoile. "Let's go talk numbers."

Who was Etienne to say no? He needed the money desperately, and Baron Weaver was giving him an opportunity to not only learn a new trade but to earn an honest wage. Besides, he had a feeling that if he declined, perhaps the authorities would be involved.

Instead of returning inside the tent, Baron Weaver led the way into the dirigible. If the outside was impressive, then the inside was downright extraordinary. Etienne had never been inside a mansion—aside from the lavish townhouse earlier—but he imagined that it would have looked something like this. Teal and silver damask print adorned the walls, but they seemed to shimmer in the light that trickled in through the windows. Curious, he lifted a hand to touch it. "Holy... it's—"

"—Silk, yes, so I'd prefer it if you didn't touch the walls," Baron Weaver said dryly.

Pulling his hand back, Etienne glanced down at a chair that was covered in a vibrant purple velvet. After the Baron's remark, he was afraid to touch or sit on anything, and as they maneuvered through the hall toward an equally as opulent office, he remained standing.

"Sit, boy. Just sit." Baron Weaver motioned with his hand, his brows furrowing.

Etienne's mouth parted as if to decline, but the look on Weaver's face said it wasn't in his best interest, so he sat.

"Whether or not you're interested in becoming part of the show, I thought I'd toss some numbers around. You'd be starting off as a trainee, learning the ropes and strengthening, but even so, you'd be earning at least *this* a week." Weaver pushed the paper forward once he was done jotting down some figures.

Etienne laughed as he picked it up and stared. It had to be a joke, but no—Weaver wasn't smiling. He wasn't laughing either. He just stared, and waited for an answer.

"You're free to go, of course, but that is my offer, and you'll earn more once you're a regular—double or triple that price depending on how much the crowd loves you."

There should have been more hesitation, should have been more thinking on Etienne's part, but he picked up a pen and eyed the man across from him. "Where do I sign?"

CHAPTER 3

IN HINDSIGHT, ETIENNE WOULD LOOK BACK ON THE MOMENT THE TIP of the pen touched the piece of paper and scrawled his name—*Etienne Jaritae Mercier*—and perhaps, later on, regret it.

As his fingers began to loosen on the pen, something pricked him. His gaze darted up toward Baron Weaver, but he was no longer seated in front of him. Weaver had moved from his seat and faced a wall of books, his hands clasped behind his back. Etienne placed the pen down, and winced as a drop of blood fell to the paper, inwardly cursing his luck. *Maybe if he...*

Pulling on his sleeve, Etienne went to rub away the blood, and it only smeared the liquid. In the corner of his eye, he could see Weaver turning around, so he hurriedly pushed the paper across all the way.

Baron Weaver sat down, his forehead creasing as he took note of the smudge on the paper. "All right, my boy," he paused and took the paper as he opened the drawer to his desk. He put it inside and steepled his fingers. "For now, you'll be watching Liliane and Taurus. They'll figure out your training, and you'll be expected to clean up for now. If you have belongings waiting for you back at your place, you can grab them, but starting now, you live with the rest of us."

Of course, when Baron Weaver said *"us,"* he truly meant *"them,"* for he slept in his cozy dirigible while everyone else slept in tents adjacent to the big top. Etienne was accustomed to roughing it, and so sleeping in a tent would suit him just fine.

"That all sounds easy enough." Etienne shrugged his shoulder and saw a slow grin form on Weaver's face. It would have made him laugh if there hadn't been a dark glint in the man's eye.

"It will be something, that is for certain. Come on, let's go see where you'll be sleeping, and then you can scurry off to gather what you need." Weaver emphasized *need* as he spoke.

There wasn't much Etienne possessed that he couldn't carry on his person, but to leave those few things behind wouldn't have been acceptable. He followed Weaver through the ship's corridor, and upon exiting it, Etienne felt his skin prickle again. Somewhere, someone was watching him.

As he lifted his gaze, he caught Liliane glaring at him from across the way, her arms were folded across her chest, and her wild red hair was in a braid against her head. Pausing but for a moment, Etienne sent a quizzical look her way. She shook her head, scoffing before stomping off.

Such hatred sparked in her eyes and all he had done was show up.

"I'm sure you saw the tents before. That is where the troupe readies themselves, and it contains their living quarters, too." Weaver motioned and continued down the grassy path toward the adjacent tents. They looked massive close-up, whereas before, they had hardly seemed big enough to hold a few people. Up close, they were the size of a small cottage.

"The quarters are separated by positions here, and so you'd be..." His words drawled on as they approached the tent. "Here. How fortunate for you only two reside in here, Taurus and Liliane. Some of the others house up to six."

They were tents, consisting of fabric, and therefore, whatever was muttered—lest it was spoken in a hushed whisper—was announced to everyone. Those who had been in their tents peeped their heads out and shot him a curious look. Most of them were friendly, except Etienne had to leap backward as Liliane flung the flaps open. She didn't seem as bristled as before, but the aura she threw off told him he was not welcomed.

"Beautiful Liliane, I was just showing the new blood around." Weaver nodded his head as he stepped inside the tent. At the moment, there were two sets of bunk beds. Two beds were made, while the empty bunk had yet to be dressed. A carpet was strewn out in the middle of the abode and against the sides of the tent were dressers, and mirrors, too, for when it was time to don their makeup and costumes.

"Have a look around. There isn't much, what you see is what you get." Lili shrugged her shoulders and padded away from the area, but not without muttering under her breath.

A hum came from Baron Weaver, and he turned to face Etienne. "Breakfast is made in another tent. You dine with the troupe. Everything runs on a certain schedule. You'll get used to it, and I'm certain you'll find your company more than willing to aid you."

Was he joking? Didn't he see how chilly Liliane was to him? Or perhaps that was how she treated everyone and it was her standard. Lifting his eyebrows, Etienne scrubbed at the back of his neck. "I'm sure. I'm a quick learner."

"Good, now that you've seen where you'll be staying, I'll send you along with Monsieur Pepin and LaRoche to fetch your valuables." His tone brooked no room for an argument. "They can grab a cab for you." He nodded and tapped his hand on a dresser. "This will be yours, too." Weaver turned to inspect the dresser, a large mirror jutted from the back. "Time is of the essence, son, they'll meet you at the lamp post at the entrance."

Having spent most of his life on the run, Etienne felt the pull to do it again, but, he remained cemented against the lamp post as instructed. This was the first time in his life he would be making an honest wage. Perhaps it was about time.

The sound of hooves clopping on the cobblestone brought his attention to the cab approaching. A man hung out of the door and leaped from it as it came to a halt. "In," was all he said.

Alarmingly, Etienne took note that it was one of the men who had chased him with Weaver. Clenching his teeth, he hopped into the cab and sat opposite of one of the other men who had pursued him. "Don't tell me. *You're* LaRoche, and *you're* Pepin?" The two brutes remained quiet. "Did I get it wrong?"

"No," came Pepin's reply next to Etienne.

It was a fifty-fifty chance, the odds were in his favor.

"Just keep your mouth shut and when we get to your rat's nest, hurry it up." Pepin kept his honey eyes trained out the window, his body radiating animosity.

What a touchy, miserable lot, Etienne mused, but didn't let it color his mood any. Opting to remain quiet for the duration of the ride, he closed his eyes and focused on the sound of the hooves, the jangling of the bronze buckles, and swishing of the cab. When Etienne concentrated he felt the pull of the spheres in the earth—the magic that pulsed in his veins—he could easily touch it, but it had been ground into him to never do so in public. To never let anyone know what he was.

He couldn't say how long he had rested in limbo, toying with the idea of using his magic, but when the sound of the hooves began to slow, he knew it had been for the duration of the journey.

"Make it quick. We've got things to do, too." LaRoche finally spoke, and it was he who pushed the door open.

Hopping from the cab, Etienne quickly walked down the alley that would bring him to his hovel. A grimace appeared on his face as he pushed the door open. Rats nest wasn't entirely wrong, and as tidy as he was, it didn't take away from the fact that the plaster on the walls began to peel away, the wallpaper was long gone, and the draft was likely lesser in the tent than it was here.

"I don't have much," he said over his shoulder, looking at Pepin and LaRoche.

"Good enough." Pepin shrugged.

Etienne made his way to the corner of the studio apartment, grabbed a bag and put in the clothes he had and a deck of cards. His fingers came to rest on a necklace that laid on his dresser. Lifting it, the chain spilled over his palm, and a charm of a faerie hung suspended, a turquoise bead hanging above it. It had belonged to his mother, a gift Etienne had bought her with his own money for her birthday. It was what he was unwilling to leave behind—everything else could burn for all he cared.

Pepin went to snatch it from Etienne. That was a mistake.

Throwing up his hand, a shield formed before him, and Pepin's hand crumpled against it, pain contorting his face. "Never touch this," Etienne hissed. His eyes seemed to glow as the magic pulsed in his veins.

Etienne should have been terrified, and while his stomach lurched at the idea of Weaver knowing, something flashed in Pepin's gaze, the honey-color brightening. *Was he also something Other?* Which made Etienne wonder—did Weaver go around collecting Other-kind as his menagerie? "I'm done here."

LaRoche eyed Pepin's hand and shook his head. "That's it? Ah, well, at least you're a light traveler—can't complain about that."

"Take your last look around here, kid, and kiss it goodbye. The Cirque is your home now."

Home. Etienne hadn't possessed a home in some time, this hovel was a roof over his head, a place to rest and hide in. But was this home? No, he hadn't had one since his parents had been killed. He didn't need to look around and didn't need to say his goodbyes to the place.

Upon returning to the Cirque, the lights had already blinked to life, the sun setting which allowed the nightlife of the city to come alive. Etienne stood on the outskirts as the two brutes moved away from him, no need to carry his light luggage. It was there that Etienne felt entirely displaced, and not for the first time. He did not belong in society, and he found yet again he did not belong here either. He was a part of something and still not part of it.

Maybe this time it would be different. Lifting the necklace from under his shirt, Etienne kissed the flying faerie. "I will try," he murmured to it, as if the inanimate object could respond.

Making his way onto the grounds, there seemed to be more people than Etienne had seen before. They were dressed in costumes; some wore painted smiles, feathers, and gaudy outfits. Idly, he wondered, if he shouldn't be racing to his quarters to dress, too, and it occurred to him that he didn't own any pieces that would match the tone of the show.

The sound of gears cranking made him look to the side. Outside of the big top, there was a mechanical arm, and the gears turned. That must have been how the silks were levered and shifted during the performances. It was dizzying to see the show come to life and there were far more structures than he had anticipated. There were tent and living quarters, and games, too, booths and demonstrations. The Cirque spilled onto the lawn of the park and seemed to devour it, one quirky individual at a time.

"Hey, you!" Rus jerked his head. Unlike before, he was coated in what appeared to be gold dust, his skin glimmered like a gemstone, and instead of wearing an ounce of fabric that resembled clothing, he donned a pair of form-fitting shorts that scarcely came to the top of his thigh.

Etienne's eyebrows lifted as his mouth opened as if to say something. Only a breath escaped his lips.

"You didn't think I'd actually be wearing something like *that*, did you?" Rus thumbed a nearby clown. Atop of the ambiguous character's head was a pink curly wig and a wicked smile painted in red over a white face. Instead of wearing poofy clothing, it donned a pair of boots, leather pants and a blouse that further made it difficult to discern which gender it was.

Imagining Rus in that outfit made Etienne chuckle. "I hope I'm not expected to wear that."

"Gods no, you're one of us. You'll be wearing—or not wearing—exactly what I am."

Etienne had never been humble per se, nor had he ever claimed to be shy, but at the idea of being practically naked in front of a crowd had him balking.

"Not quite yet, anyway, I've got to find Lili, see you after."

Color rushed into Etienne's cheeks as Rus walked away. He shook his head and continued toward the tent. Pushing open the flap, he ducked inside, heaving a sigh.

A scream assaulted his ears, and he turned toward the origin of it, spotting Lili desperately trying to cover her bare skin. "Gods! You can't just walk in unannounced! Are you a creep?"

"Oh, oh! I'm so sorry," he stammered as he lifted his bag to his eyes and at the same time he felt something hard connect with his head. "I'm sorry! I thought you were outside! I thought...I don't know!"

"That's right, you weren't thinking, at all!" she spat out.

There was some rustling, the sound of objects being slammed around and curses filled the tent. Etienne didn't run from it, it didn't seem necessary at the moment. Since they'd be bunking together in the same tent, it was apparent some rules needed to be brought to his attention.

"You can move the bag now," Lili bit out.

Not daring to look at her yet, Etienne moved the bag to his dresser and took a chance looking into the mirror. Not unlike Taurus, Lili's body was covered in gold dust. She wore bottoms similar to her partner's, and a band of fabric that covered her chest. Dust coated her hair, too, but it made it look akin to a fire blazing instead of hiding it entirely. That suited her, he thought.

Padding up to him, Lili narrowed her eyes. "Watch us tonight, see if that's what you want to do. Not everyone can stomach heights—"

"Heights don't bother me."

She looked put off he had interrupted her. "It's more than just heights, just watch the show. No matter what the Baron says, you may find you're inclined to work elsewhere."

Was it his imagination or was she challenging him? Etienne watched as she padded from the tent. He sincerely hoped that she didn't try to snuff the life from him in the middle of the night. The fae thought back to earlier in the day when he had first laid eyes on her—a spider, he called her—venom and all.

CHAPTER 4

THERE WASN'T MUCH TIME TO FEEL USELESS, BECAUSE SOON ONE OF THE various hands came to fetch him, showing him what needed to be done. As per Baron Weaver's warning, he was to clean up after the crowd and ensure that all their garbage was discarded. He, however, had to don a pair of dress slacks, a crisp linen shirt, and a wine-colored damask vest.

As the crowd began to filter in, their murmurs filled the tent, and the various shades of their faces seemed to glow from the gas lamps. None of the troupe had made it to the center of the ring yet, but the excitement in the air was tangible. Etienne might not have been at the entrance, but he could hear the crowd begin to whisper "sold out" as he paced around, picking up the discarded programs.

Five minutes into admission, the crowd began to huff and puff as they grew impatient. Suddenly, the gas lamps extinguished, leaving the crowd in utter darkness. When the lights flashed back on, Baron Weaver stood in the center of the ring. He wore dark leather pants, a wine colored vest, cream cravat, and black tailcoat. A top hat rested on his crown, and he smiled adoringly at the crowd surrounding him.

"Greetings, Ladies and Gentlemen, welcome to a night you will surely never forget. Close your eyes, make a wish, and let *Cirque de la Tempete* take you on an exhilarating journey." He tossed his hat into the air, and it seemed to disappear, but above him unseen to the crowd, a gold hand caught it before allowing it to fall back into place on his head.

There was no mention of magic; there would never be. Even if it were an innocent mention of a magical evening, there were likely members of the authorities in the crowd, and Baron Weaver was no fool from what Etienne had seen thus far. What would the crowd do if they did see magic and hadn't a clue that it was actually that?

Shuffling through the bleachers, Etienne continued to pick up after the crowd. His eyes kept flicking toward the ring with every new act. It was mesmerizing to watch, and he understood why people would come here.

In the middle of the ring, a ballerina danced into view, colorful butterfly wings of fabric danced behind her. Music tinkled with her movements, and although no one spoke during the acts, their thoughts were displayed on the faces, during her the motions. The dancer twirled, crumpling to the ground, and then a cloud of steam erupted. A snort came, and another cloud of steam billowed so that the ring began to grow smoky. Beyond the smoke, a great, mechanical bull erupted, stomping, and looked as though he would trample the crumpled butterfly.

The crowd gasped, and Etienne did as well, but the bull approached the butterfly, bent his head and aided the lovely dancer to her feet. It was a beautiful scene, but above all of the performers, the show stopper was definitely Liliane and Taurus.

When it came time for them to perform, the gas lamps blazed, casting a heavenly glow on them as they seemed to plummet to their demise. Etienne had seen that earlier and still found himself flinching. Heights didn't bother him, but the prospect of dying did.

Of course, the sound of the blaring horns, banging drums and the gasps of the crowd seemed to add new tension to the air, too, as Liliane and Taurus soared above the crowd like they could indeed fly. The mechanical device outside lifted the silks into the air. Rus propelled himself off one of the posts, and put himself in a spin as he descended. Silk unraveled from above and hung by his side. Rus teased Liliane with it, and then they were soaring above the crowd, tangling in one another as they told the story of gods from long ago, and how one had fallen for a mere mortal woman. The show seemed to pass in a blur. Etienne found himself caught up in the thrill of it, and his adrenaline pumped along with the crowds. He had never seen anything so beautiful in his life. This was what he had missed by not escaping to the Cirque? A lopsided grin formed on Etienne's face as he weaved through the throng of exiting patrons. He stood off to the side, and once the last patron left, he was able to move to begin the big clean up.

Etienne blinked as he watched Lili hop from one bleacher to the next as if she were a nymph in a past life. "Hey," he called out. "You were amazing." He sounded breathless as he said it, recalling the way the silks slid over her skin.

Lili turned to look at him, a small smile on her lips. "I know." Surprisingly, there was no venom in her words or gaze for that matter.

"I still want to do it."

She spun on the ball of her foot and walked up to him, still wearing nothing more than two slivers of clothing. "Do you?"

"I'm partial to adrenaline rushes, I guess you could say."

Lili assessed him, some of the hardness returned to her gaze, but her shoulders slumped as if she resigned herself to the idea. "It's too late anyhow," she murmured and shook her head. "I think this belongs to you." She reached out and plastered a card against his chest.

Glancing down at her hand, Etienne lifted the card from his chest and chuckled. "A fool?" He shook his head and rubbed his thumb against the colorful card. He handed it back to her. "You'll see, *mon cherie*, soon enough you will see."

She placed her hands on her hips, assessing him once more. "Prove me wrong, Etienne."

And he would, he would prove her wrong and work his arse off to ensure he had a place here. Not sweeping peanut shells and popcorn, but to be a part of the show—to be worth something to someone. "When do we start?"

"Tomorrow; it's a free day, no shows and it's our downtime. So, please, have an ounce of talent—I'm spending my free time working on you." She eyed him pointedly and turned to walk away.

Dawn came far too quickly. Lili shoved Etienne's shoulder and then promptly yanked the covers from his form. "It's time to wake up."

Unlike Lili and Taurus, Etienne had spent the better part of the night cleaning the tent and making it look as if nothing had occurred hours prior. He groaned and sat up, knocking his head on the top bunk before he collapsed back into bed. "I'll take that as an omen."

"No, take *this* as an omen," she said and pointed to her face, a wicked look overcame it.

Muttering a curse to himself, Etienne thought *this was it—this was how he was going to die—a redheaded vixen smothering him with a pillow.* Etienne stood up. "Already? What time is it?"

Lili cocked her head and tapped a barefoot. "Judging by the bells, it's four o'clock."

Another curse came from him, he had only fallen asleep two hours ago. "Breakfast?" he inquired.

"It's being made—with coffee, if that suits you—which is why I was kind enough to wake you. I figured you'd be hungry." She turned her back to him and rummaged through a drawer until she pulled an article of clothing out. A black cloth—or so it looked like. "You can wear this, it belonged to...*someone*." Clenching her jaw, she thrust the shorts at Etienne. "Hurry up."

It took a wounded person to know one, and although Etienne knew better than to make assumptions, he took the shorts and nodded. "I will." He waited until she was gone to change into them. He felt entirely naked. His long legs not hidden by slacks, his slender, but muscled torso also bare. Not a speck of chest hair curled on his chest, courtesy of the fae blood.

Thank the gods that it was still warm out; otherwise, he would have been frozen. It wasn't quite light out yet, so when he moved around the structures to find the dining tent, he was more than pleased to discover a fire burning in a pit inside.

"New blood!" someone cried out as Etienne entered the tent.

Lili cast him a sideward glance and furrowed her brows before returning to her portion of breakfast.

"*Bonjour*," Etienne cheerily said, his eyes glimmering. Moving toward the food, he greedily loaded his plate, ashamed that his stomach was nearly audible even over the chatter.

"You sure you want to load it in that heavily?" one of the troupe inquired, pointing to his plate. "Lili's tough; she's not going to go easy on you."

Shrugging, Etienne rammed a sausage link into his mouth. After swallowing, he said, "I didn't ask her to go easy on me." He moved his gaze from the woman and locked eyes with Lili. "She can do her worst all she likes." He grinned and shoveled more food into his mouth.

Lili huffed and turned her back to him once again, her head shaking every now and then as Rus roared in laughter. She wasn't laughing though, and Etienne had to wonder what was being said.

Sitting down next to the same lady that poked at him, he turned to her and squinted. "Why does she hate me?"

"Who—Lil?" The woman wheezed a laugh and shook her head before patting his bare leg. "Child, she doesn't. Lil doesn't take kindly to newcomers. Once you settle in I think you'll find her warming up to you."

Warming up to him, Etienne thought. He smiled lopsidedly. "I hope so, I haven't exactly lived my life to the fullest. I'd hate to wake up dead."

The woman's mismatched eyes fixed him with a knowing look. "Let me see your hand."

Hesitating but for a moment, he offered his hand to her. "Do you read? My mother used to say it wasn't wise to know your destiny."

She ran her thumb along the back of his hand and then smoothed a forefinger over the several creases on his palm. "I do, and she's right. We're not meant to know, and when we do, 'tis a heavy burden. I won't tell you if you don't want to know." She hummed, and schooled her features, not letting an ounce of her knowledge spill into her gaze. "I will say, you are right. You have not lived your life to its fullest. Take care, New Blood. I'll see you around."

The woman said no more, and pulled away, leaving Etienne wondering if maybe he should have pressed for the reading. His eyes flicked to Liliane again, and when she wasn't scowling in his direction, he took note of her delicate beauty. Could he be faulted for finding Liliane beautiful? She looked as if she had walked from the pages of a storybook—especially when covered in gold dust...a winged faerie, leaving dust in her wake. He also wasn't going to overstep his boundaries, knowing that venom—and likely thorns—awaited him on the other side.

"Ready?" Lili stepped up to him and jerked her head in the direction of the big top.

"Ready or not, does it matter?" He stood up from the seat and chuckled nervously.

Without hesitation, she replied, "no."

"At least you're honest." Etienne rubbed at the back of his neck and followed Liliane to what he hoped wasn't his death.

The tent flaps were pulled aside to let the light filter in and illuminate the inside. From the ceiling hung simple ropes instead of the silks that had been there last night. Squinting, Etienne looked around. Rus was sitting on a bleacher a short distance away, and Lili was currently staring straight at Etienne.

"I want to see you climb the rope," she said, pointing up toward the top of the tent.

"All the way up?" He rubbed the back of his neck, peering up at the top.

"Is that a problem?"

"Not at all, I was just clarifying, *mademoiselle*." He feigned doffing a hat. Without another word, he leaped from the ground at the rope. This wasn't something new to him—he had fashioned ropes countless times with drapes and curtains to escape his foster home when he found himself punished. With his eyes focused on the top, Etienne inched his way up the rope, using his upper body strength to haul himself upward. His legs gripped onto the line.

Once he was at the top, he released one hand, dangling precariously. "Like so?" He tilted his head and looked down at Lili who gaped at him.

Rus roared with laughter and shoved Lili's shoulder. "That's my boy! You showed her, Etienne. Now you owe me a day's wages, Lili." He winked and nodded his head up at Etienne again. "Come down, now. Lili's stewing, but you did great."

Careful not to let his grip loosen too much lest he gave himself rope burns, Etienne made his way down and stood before Lili. She looked less sullen, like she was allowing something other than fury to bubble to the surface.

"Good job," she murmured. "You can climb a rope, and you're not afraid of heights." She shrugged a shoulder.

"I told you."

"That means little to nothing." She didn't snap; it was just matter of fact.

Some of the elation Etienne felt escaped him, but she was right. She didn't know him, and he could have been lying. "You guys don't use nets?"

Lili scoffed. "Of course we don't. When we're practicing some-thing new, and not on the silks, we'll put the net up. Other than that, it takes away from the show."

"Has anyone ever..." Etienne's words trailed off as he caught the sudden anguish gleaming in Lili's gaze. He didn't need a verbal answer; that one sufficed. "Okay, what else?"

Motioning to Rus, Lili moved up to Etienne. She was two heads shorter than him and looked the part of a fiery sprite. "Every day, you'll need to limber up. Working out, stretching, practicing. We'll start with some basics." She motioned for him to follow.

Off to the side, there was a contraption that held a silk. It wasn't as tall as the rope Etienne climbed, but it would serve its purpose. "Today we'll practice two things: climbing and flipping into the silk." Lili walked up to it, and instead of quickly running through the motions, she took her time to show him exactly where his foot should go, and how to wrap it, grab, and push up. Rus fiddled with the silk, so it moved upward. Lili demonstrated again, this time her hands slipping into the silk, and then she pulled herself up and over tit so that her belly ended up landing on it. She twisted to the side, crossing her legs, and perched on it. "Think you can manage?"

Etienne had been mesmerized, and while the last one looked the easiest to accomplish, he was bent on proving himself. "Of course," he said, confidently.

Inwardly, Etienne grimaced—there was no way he could pull this off. Grabbing the silk, he felt it and was surprised that it was quite flexible—it had to be, of course—but it still surprised him. Holding onto the silk wasn't an issue, it was wrapping his foot in the fabric, maintaining his core strength and pushing off to climb upward.

Etienne fumbled for some time, but Lili surprisingly gave him patient directions, and encouragement. They continued with these two moves until they became reasonably fluid, and his muscles could take no more.

"Good job, I'm impressed." Lili approached him after and gave his arm a pat. "I mean it, I'm impressed. Not many take to it as easily as you seem to. I mean, anyone can get up in the silks, but not everyone was born for it, you know?" She leaned on one foot and crossed her arms.

He nodded and laughed, regretting it because his stomach burned. "I do, but I think that's why I'm here." He didn't miss the frown that passed over her face, and as she went to turn away, Etienne snagged her wrist. "Lili," he said softly.

"You could be anything you wanted. There is more to life than painted faces and empty performances." She shook her head.

"No, no I can't." But if not this, what would he have been. If the world hadn't turned against fae-kind, what would he have been then? It didn't matter. Wishing and hoping for another life would get him nowhere. This was the hand that life had dealt him and the only thing he could do was make it work in his favor any way that he could.

"A simple life in Paris sounds great to me." She eyed him and said nothing more before she stormed off.

CHAPTER 5

The next few weeks passed by in an aching blur. Every day was mainly the same, and every day Liliane seemed to place one more brick up on the wall she was creating around herself. No matter how much he tried to make her laugh or encourage her to let down her guard, it did nothing but repel her.

Anyone else would have given up being civil, but Etienne plastered a smile on his face and teased her like he would any other. All of the other members of the Cirque seemed to accept him, except for Liliane.

It was a day like any other. After breakfast, Etienne made his way to the tent to practice. A blur of purple caught his attention as he looked up. Lili was twirling inside of a bronze aerial hoop. Clad in tight fabric, one leg seemed to be wrapped in bands, and the other was entirely covered. She twirled around, and her body shifted so that she looked as if she were tumbling down. Her strong legs caught her as she reached her hands toward the ground. Lili's eyes fixated on Etienne and a smile formed on her lips.

Again, Lili's body shifted, her hands gripping onto the ring. She allowed herself to fall to the floor the rest of the way. "Have you come for some more suffering?"

His stomach twisted at her words. "Is that what the hoop is—my doom?" He pointed upward.

"Truthfully? It could be, but you want to give it a go? It might be fun." A dark look gleamed in her eye, and the way she said *fun* made it sound anything but.

There was no hesitation in his words. "Absolutely."

Hitting a lever off to the side, the hoop began to descend so it wasn't as high up, that way, if one fell, it wouldn't be to their death. "You first." She pointed up at the ring and nodded.

Etienne lifted himself on his tiptoes and grabbed the ring. He pulled himself up and through before he allowed his legs to twine around the silk at the top of the ring. Lili pulled herself up, and together, they began to maneuver the hoop. She was the graceful one, and while Etienne's movements weren't as clumsy as they could have been, they weren't fluid either.

Lili instructed him to flip over the hoop as she lifted herself up. He bumped into her and offset his balance. He wound up tumbling from the ring and landed on his feet gracefully. Chuckling to himself, he looked up at her and opened his arms. "I'll catch you."

She slid from the hoop, and as promised, his arms wrapped around her, easing her to the ground. "I can't do this anymore," she whispered softly.

Whatever Etienne had been anticipating slipping from her mouth had not been those words. "Do what?"

Lili spun to look at him and motioned with her hand, but the sound of a slow clap cut them off. For a moment, her walls had been crumbling, and now she carefully constructed them yet again.

"What a beautiful show," came the man's voice.

Etienne had to clamp his mouth shut, so he didn't declare it wasn't for show. His eyes fell on the approaching form of Baron Weaver.

"Just the two I was looking for. I have been thinking, and seeing *that*—whatever you want to call it—it cemented the idea in my head: a new act for the show. We've recycled the mythology story. It's time for another love story, and I think it's time for Etienne to enter the show."

Lili's eyes shifted, and she sighed. "Uncle, I don't think he's ready yet."

Etienne snapped his attention to Lili. His stomach lurched. She was his niece? His breath escaped his lungs, and he felt dizzy. After a little over a month with the Cirque, he hadn't been privy to such facts. Although, if he were to be honest, there were a lot of secrets he held close, too.

"Nonsense, he's come a long way. Put together a simple routine, the hoop or silks, it's up to you, but I want to see that in our next show." Weaver left no room for an argument. His dark brown eyes flicked to Etienne.

"A month, Uncle, please. In a month he will be ready. We don't need any accidents during the show."

While Etienne felt pinned by Weaver's dark gaze, he managed a fairly confident smile. "If Liliane deems me ready, then I will gladly do the show, Baron, but forgive me for saying if she doesn't, would it be wise to push?"

Weaver's nostrils flared, but then a laugh escaped him. "Perhaps you're right, do what you can in the meantime. Find a compromise, if it can't be done... I trust you and your abilities, my dear." He moved forward and wrapped his arms around Lili, placing a kiss to the side of her head. "I like this kid. If you let him fall, let him down easy," he teased and pulled back. "Get back to practice." He waved his hand and left the arena.

"We don't have—" Etienne's words were cut short.

"We do. If you're expected to perform, then yes, we do." Instead of sounding short and snippy, Liliane seemed out of sorts.

Without hesitation, Etienne leaned down to whisper, "Fly high." He pointed to the big top.

If Etienne thought his muscles were sore before, then this was nothing. Every part of him ached, and they were not yet through with their practice. The hoop proved to be challenging to maneuver with the both of them manipulating it, and while it was only one day of practice, time was ticking away.

"Even *I* can't tolerate anymore. Come on Etienne, let's call it a day."

Standing, every muscle felt stiff. "Only if you tell me something about yourself that no one knows."

Liliane's eyes widened, and she peered around. "Tell no one," she began, and then lowered her voice to barely a whisper. "I don't want to stay in the circus. I want to get out. I want a normal life; to raise a family and be in one place—to have roots."

Hunkering down on the bleachers, Etienne leaned back and listened to her. "Does he know?" he asked carefully.

"No, only Rus, and he would never..." Lili sat on a bleacher next to his head, gazing off into the distance.

Spinning around so he was on his knees in front of her, he replied, "So we will get you out. Get me ready, and I'll help you out. I'll make sure that Baron has nothing to complain about with my performance."

With each word, a brick seemed to tumble from Lili's wall, and Etienne could swear he could see hope begin to ignite in her gaze.

"We have a deal." She nodded and held out her hand to shake his.

"A Mercier never goes back on a deal, *mon cherie.*"

That evening, Weaver declared the next stop would be London, and Etienne's stomach fluttered. He had never left France, and the idea thrilled him.

"Only a few shows left here in Paris," Weaver stated as he stood in the center of the ring, looking over his troupe. "Make the most of it. This also means the new shows you've all been working on will debut in London." Weaver leaned onto his cane, his worn fingers drumming on the decorated wolf's head.

"Ah! The English do so love their shows," a familiar woman's voice rang out, and Weaver's lips pulled back in a wolfish smile.

Etienne gawked as the woman flounced her way to the center of the ring and kissed Weaver. It was none other than Marie. She wasn't as dolled up, her wig was gone, and her face wasn't powdered, but there was no mistaking her crystal blue eyes.

Weaver's eyes met Etienne's, and the devil had the gall to wink at him as if he knew, and he must have. Marie must have scouted for Weaver. "So glad you decided to join us, *mon trésor,*" she called to Etienne.

Gazing at Baron Weaver, she added, "You cannot run from me, Weaver." Maria cooed and turned to face the troupe.

The rest of the meeting was blocked out as Etienne bowed his head to whisper to Lili. "I know her."

"My aunt?" She blinked, but then her eyes averted his quickly.

"Marie, *yes.* She came to me at a card table." He would have continued to whisper, except Weaver turned his black eyes on him and motioned for him to follow.

"Etienne, might I have a word with you?"

As everything seemed to click together, Etienne felt dizzy, and although he wanted to be anywhere but an office with Weaver at the moment, he had to go.

Mistrust began to build in Etienne as he walked to Weaver's office. He opted to stand against the wall, taking care to not let his bare skin touch the silk wall.

"How are you getting along here? I haven't had a chance to speak to you."

A friendly enough question, Etienne supposed. "Well enough." He wasn't sure how he was supposed to respond. "I haven't woken up dead yet, so there is that."

A chuckle escaped Weaver. "A bit of news came to my attention, and I've been mulling over it."

"Pepin said you're a fae." Weaver sat back in his chair and eyed Etienne, assessing him quietly.

Unfolding his arms, Etienne's body became filled with tension at once, torn between fleeing and fighting. "It's not something I share with everyone, sir." Glancing at the man, Etienne didn't note surprise or contempt in his gaze.

Weaver patted the air and leaned forward. "As you shouldn't. Settle down, this is friendly territory." Toying with a ring on his thumb, Weaver stood from the chair and moved toward the wall. "We've all got our secrets, son." He reached out, tilted a silver mirror on the wall and stared at Etienne's reflection. In the mirror, Weaver's eyes began to glow an unearthly gold, fangs elongated, and his nails started to grow.

A curse fled from Etienne's lips, and he reached for the doorknob to the office, ready to escape, but Weaver's laugh halted him for a split second.

"Relax, I'm only saying we're all something of society's misfits here, otherwise cast away into the gutter, or worse. What you are is not a surprise to me—I can smell you're an Other."

"You're a werewolf?" Etienne dared to ask and wondered if Lili were as well—or Marie—or anyone else in the troupe.

Weaver seemed to have read his thoughts. "I am, although my niece isn't. She's fully human. I was bitten in my teens, and it was a secret my family kept. Still, I was an outcast, and I wanted to do something other than what every other Lord and Lady seemed to be doing." He waved his hand around and strode toward Etienne. "You're safe here," Weaver said.

Everything in Etienne's person screamed for him to run. He didn't trust easily, especially when someone was trying to convince him he was safe—it usually meant the opposite.

"From time to time, we use our gifts to enhance the show—never in a way that would peg us as supernatural, lest one of those blasted hunts begin." He shook his head and sighed. "For now, I expect you and my niece to train for the new act." He nodded his head toward the door as if excusing him. "Oh, and Etienne, be careful with my Lili. That is all."

Be careful with my Lili, Weaver's words played over in his mind.

The man was a werewolf, which made Etienne wonder who else among the troupe was Other? Scratching the back of his neck, he made his way into the Aerialists tent.

"Are you all right, Etienne?" Lili asked from her bunk.

"I don't know," he answered truthfully.

She nodded her head. "You will be. Get some rest, we have a lot to accomplish before London."

"Yeah, in addition to that lovey-dovey act, we've got the war of the muses we have to perfect, too," Rus mumbled from his bunk.

When Etienne fell asleep, he wasn't sure, but he woke to Lili shaking his arm. Slowly, he came to and peered up into her brown eyes.

"*Sonnez les matines! Sonnez les matines!*" her playful voice rang out as she danced from the tent.

Shaking his head, he sat up and began the morning ritual of dressing, groaning, and meeting the rest of the troupe inside the dining tent.

Madame Lucille, the fortune teller, eyed him from across the way. She smiled warmly, her peculiar mismatched eyes gleaming with wisdom as she assessed him. In those moments, he wished he broke his mother's rule about knowing one's destiny.

Breakfast went quickly, which meant he was expected in the tent. Rus was missing, but there was Lili in the center of the ring, the silks wrapped around her limbs as she soared through the air. Without her, the show wouldn't be the same—life wouldn't be the same—and it made Etienne's chest ache.

When she took notice of him, she slid down the silks, descending with grace until she was in front of him. "Ready to work on the routine?"

His brows lifted, and when she didn't say anything, he raised his arm up to grab onto the fabric. Twining it around his foot, he began to climb it, pulling himself up, and together, they rose like two spiders in the same web—and there had never been a more appropriate comparison.

The sound of the mechanical arm whirring to life vaguely reached Etienne's ears, which likely meant Rus had made his way back to the tent, however, at that moment his focus was entirely on Lili. His arm stretched out so his hand reached her ankle as they spun around above the arena. Gradually they came closer to the ground so that Lili could stand and she moved beneath Etienne, twirling in such a way that it just looked as if she were dancing, but with each move, she wrapped the silk around his legs.

Inverting himself, he reached downward, and Lili lifted her arms so he could grasp onto her. He lifted and the entanglement began. Each move brought them closer, their bodies sliding against one another, trusting in their partner.

When the act was through, they slid from the silks still in character, their heads rested against one another, but Etienne tipped her head up and kissed her softly. Every brick in the wall Lili had put up that had been in place before came crashing down around them. Lili's arms wrapped around his neck and the taste of her drove him to madness.

His hands pulled her flush against him, and she eagerly leaped up, her legs were wrapped around his waist. A chuckle slid from him and into her mouth as he broke off the kiss and peered up at her.

"That wasn't supposed to happen," she said breathlessly.

"Maybe not, but I've been waiting for a while to do that..." He chuckled and kissed her chin softly.

A whoop and then a clap came from the corner of the arena, Rus shook his head. "Listen, doves aside, if you two can pull that off in London the crowd is going to love it. Etienne, you've come a long way in a short amount of time."

Lili hopped down from Etienne's waist, her cheeks flushed with desire. "Let's hope so."

"I'm up for more practice." Even if this complicated things, Etienne knew he'd have to let Lili go to live her life outside of the Cirque.

CHAPTER 6

The teardown descended upon them, and it was up to the troupe to disassemble everything. Weaver was inside of the dirigible mapping out the rest of their course, but when the last of the tents were folded up and stored on the ship, everyone flooded on board.

This was yet another new experience for Etienne, his hands gripped the side of the ship as it began to lift off. Not afraid of heights, but not overly keen on a flying vessel, he was forced to balance himself as the machine kicked to life and the sails flapped in the wind.

"Never flown before?" Lili asked.

"Never. I'm not sure I like it." His olive complexion seemed to blanch.

"I'm sure I can find some way to distract you."

Of that, Etienne had no doubt. Lili's barriers had tumbled down into nothingness, and as Madame Lucille had guessed, she warmed up to him. Trust was a part of their act—they had to trust one another—but aside from the act? Etienne trusted her, and that was the first time in a long time he could say that about anyone.

Weaver was another matter entirely.

"Come on, let's head inside." She tugged on his hand and pulled him to the stairs that led down inside of the living quarters. Leading them to a room, it held bunk beds similar to that of the tent, and, once inside, she spun around on the ball of her foot.

It was strange seeing her in regular apparel—not that she wasn't beautiful regardless—but with brown pantaloons, boots, and a simple blouse with a brown bustier on, it was more clothing than he had seen on her in…*ever*. He chuckled.

"What?"

"No, I just thought this is the most clothing I've ever seen on you."

She twirled a red lock of hair around her finger and laughed.

He moved to the window and looked outside as they flew over Paris, once his home, and it was now gone. Good riddance, he thought. It had brought nearly nothing but misery to his life.

"Etienne?" she asked softly. "Are you all right?"

Looking over his shoulder, he sighed and nodded his head. "Yeah, I am, just the first time ever leaving." He sighed and turned to face her. "Lili, I—"

Walkling up to him, she silenced him with a kiss that held more fervor than all the others. "We can talk after." Her cheeks had reddened with desire again and her arms looped around his neck to pull him into the kiss.

Each kiss, each caress of her fingers made the tension ease away, and whatever thoughts had plagued him moments before were gone. He didn't want Lili to leave—at least not without him. Etienne's mouth covered hers, and he walked her toward her bunk bed and laid her down softly. His fingers explored each delicate curve, and soon Lili proved to him that there was more than one way to communicate.

Afterward, Lili brushed the hair from his face, and her eyes focused on the pointed ear. "You're a fae. Why didn't you tell me?" She didn't sound angry or disgusted.

"I think the reasons are obvious," he said softly, burrowing his face into the crook of her neck. "I was about to when you said we could talk after…" He chuckled and pulled his head back.

"Etienne, when I leave—" her words cracked as she spoke them.

"Shh, *mon cherie*, we'll get you out of here." Even if it killed him to do so.

She sat up on her elbow and ran her fingers through his dark hair. "I will be waiting for you."

"I love you, Liliane." He pressed his lips to hers and savored the taste of her.

"I still think you're a fool, but I love you, so I suppose that makes me one, too."

He pulled against him again and reveled in the blissful moment.

A loud bang awakened Etienne just as the airship tilted, and Etienne had to stop himself from tumbling out of bed by using his foot. Lili's body collided into his, and she muttered a curse as she groggily sat up.

"We've landed already?" she asked and wiped the sleep from her eyes.

"Is that what that was? I thought we were dropping from the sky."

Rus knocked on the door and entered. "Wake up, lovebirds, we just landed, and you know what that means."

Etienne surmised it meant no eating, and that they were expected to put the entirety of the grounds together before they could relax again. There would be no show for the next several days; it would be preparing the grounds, testing things, and practicing.

Once Rus left, they both tumbled out of bed and rushed outside before they were beckoned again. With wide eyes, Etienne looked around. This was London? He took a deep breath and smiled broadly.

"Quit smiling and get to work!" Pepin shouted at him.

Squinting at Pepin, Etienne launched himself into work, hauling the tents, setting them up, gathering up the bickering automatons that would be sitting inside the ticket booths. It was exhilarating to be amongst the workers, but this was more exhausting than the training days.

By the time they were done, food was being passed around. There were still some pieces of the Cirque that had to be put together, but that was enough for a day's work. Everyone was elated to be in a new location and begin their new show—the overarching theme was new love and an untested heart, per Weaver's request. Each act reflected the theme in some way, and together it created a fluid storyline of new love from start to finish.

"Here's to a successful run in London," Weaver said as he lifted a tumbler of amber liquid. "May we all remain safe, and the gods keep us in their embrace."

They all whooped to the toast and drank down their portion of celebratory champagne.

Etienne had lost track of how long he had been with them all, and somehow it seemed as if he had always been with them. The painful memories of his past seemed to blur as new good memories took their place.

When he was finished eating, Etienne began to work on the ticket booth, the automatons were currently lobbing insults at one another which amused him to no end. They each had a way of performing their tasks and didn't agree with each other. Their quarrels always ended up with the lawn peppered in tickets—why or how Weaver didn't tear their gears apart for that was beyond him.

As excited to be in London as he was, Etienne knew this was where he'd kiss Lili goodbye, at least for a while. His fingers tugged one of the drapes into place over the booth, and he tapped on the window, the whirring of the automaton's head made him chuckle. "Be kind to your friend, he's trying at least." He shrugged.

Lost in his thoughts, he didn't hear the footsteps behind him or notice the reflection in the metal of the booth.

"Allo," Marie's voice rang out.

Startled, Etienne stood up straight and spun around to look at Marie. She looked strange to him without powder or a white wig. She had buttery blonde hair and a creamy complexion. "I didn't hear you."

"I know. So, let me explain myself," Marie began and lifted a finger to silence Etienne as he was ready to speak. "Richard—ah, Baron Weaver—knew you were in the market. The last thing he wanted to see was you suffer, so he sent me to scout. I told him a little more about you, and he wanted to see you in action for himself. I don't believe he took you for an aerialist, but he knew you had a quick wit about you." She shrugged her delicate shoulders and smiled. "He knew what you were and did not want to see you become dust like the others."

Dust was one way of putting it. Etienne grimaced, but in truth, he was thankful for Marie and for Weaver at this point. If it hadn't been for them, Lili would never have tumbled into his life.

"To think he wanted you paired with the illusionists." Marie tsked and lifted a hand to run her knuckles along Etienne's smooth face. "I am glad you are here amongst us. Forgive me for the deception."

Marie had been absent for the past few months, and although it was none of Etienne's business, he wondered where she had gone. She pulled away without another word and faded into the milling workers, leaving Etienne gaping after her.

That evening, as the workers began to set the mechanical arms in place for the tent, Etienne was able to see how it worked up close. Once a lever was pulled, the arm lowered the crane's neck, and when it was shifted to either side, it moved in the direction the lever was moved.

Lili stepped over to him and cocked a curious brow. "Thinking of changing your role in the Cirque?"

He laughed and shook his head. "Of course not." Leaning down, he captured her lips between his and sighed. Who knew love could bring such bliss to a broken life?

"Come. Come with me," Lili cooed and tugged on his rough hands.

He peered at the nearby worker, and when he received a nod in response, he followed suit. "What could be so important that you'd drag me away from work?" He tossed his hands up in a mock show of outrage, which earned him a glare. That look tempted him to throw her over his shoulder and run away, but he followed her—and Etienne knew he'd follow Lili *anywhere*.

"Look, same sky, same stars but different." She pointed up at the inky sky which was blanketed in twinkling stars.

Bending his neck, Etienne brushed a kiss against the side of her head. "And from anywhere, it is still beautiful."

"Come with me," Lili said again, but this time the way she said it implied something else.

"You know I can't," Etienne said sadly. There was nothing more he wanted than to follow Liliane until the end of the earth but now was not the time.

"Then promise me you won't wait too long to find me?" she whispered softly.

"That I can promise, *mon cherie*." Spinning her around to face him he kissed her softly, it was bittersweet, and it lingered. "After this show, is that it?"

She nodded, a lone tear streaking down her freckled cheek.

Wiping away the tear, Etienne smiled and kissed where it had ended. "Your tears are touching, but don't you know? There is nowhere you can go that I won't follow—that I won't go."

CHAPTER 7

ETIENNE SPENT THE REMAINDER OF THE WEEK HELPING TO SET UP THE grounds for the Cirque, and somewhere in between was able to continue to practice the new routine with Liliane. Each day he found himself tumbling further into the depths of love and unlike when practicing, there was no net to catch him.

Soon, the opening night for London was upon them. The smell of smoke stacks hung heavily in the air, and an eerie fog rolled in so that as the lights blinked to life around the grounds, it cast a strange glow and shadows on the terrain.

London, so it seemed, was more reserved than Paris, for when it was time for the troupe to make their way into the ring gasps filled the air and parents abruptly covered their children's eyes. Most of the performers showed more skin than was deemed socially acceptable, even if it was a woman donning a sleeveless blouse or lacking a corset. Some lacked clothing altogether, but no bodies were entirely bare to the eye—some wore paint in place.

Contortionists scrambled across the center of the ring, manipulating their bodies in ways that weren't natural, and their painted faces seem to fascinate as well as horrify the audience. Weaver's show was not for the faint of heart, nor exactly was it designed for a child's consumption.

It was awe-inspiring, though. Members of the troupe and mechanical device combined created a breath-taking show, and before Etienne knew it, their act was up.

A click-whirr-click sounded off to the side, and the silks dropped from the canopy. Music tinkled off to the side, and Weaver's voice emitted to narrate their performance.

"Let's fly," Etienne softly murmured to Lili.

She smiled in return, sliding her hand along his shoulders and twirled away from him, taking his vest with her in one fluid motion. Lili tossed it aside and strode back to Etienne, her hand lifting to twine the silk around her wrist and he mirrored her movements.

Etienne pulled himself up the silk, using one foot to wrap it around the other and once they were secure, the mechanical arm lifted them above the floor. As it did, he reached out to grab Liliane's ankle, and together, it appeared as though they were flying.

One small tug and it pulled her closer, she moved her body at the right moment, and Etienne shifted his leg so that he could wrap his around her smaller one, and together they entwined, becoming one as the story went on.

Weaver spoke of falling, taking the leap of faith. As he did Etienne and Liliane shifted once more, carefully, Liliane allowed herself to drop, and Etienne caught her, holding her suspended as he hung upside down by his legs.

They swung around above the gasping crowd, and Lili flipped herself upright, gathered silk in her hand and wrapped it around her waist. She tumbled down her silk like the first time Etienne had seen her. She gazed up at him and waited for him to do the same.

He did, and when his feet landed on the ground, he took her face in his hands and kissed her soundly. It wasn't an act—it wasn't part of the act at all—but it felt right, and the crowd loved it.

That night was a success, and London roared with reviews the next day.

There was a new energy that filled the troupe, one that made everyone's skin buzz with anxiety. What it was no one knew—until it happened. Perhaps it was an omen—maybe it was just fate—but during a routine practice, one of the contortionists met his fate.

The troupe rushed into the big top to see what the shrieks were about. In the middle of the ring, the spindly man lay in a pool of blood. It was the first accident that had occurred since Etienne had joined. It was horrific.

Blood pooled around the middle-aged man, his skull fractured by one of the iron pulleys that held the silks and hoop in place. His once-happy face now caved in, and it was a sight that Etienne wished he could erase from his mind.

"Gods rest his soul," Weaver said after everyone calmed down. "We know the risks, all of you do, but it's why we practice, and it is why we check things not once, or twice, but thrice and four times over if we must. Tonight's show is canceled, we will honor Angelico." He removed his tall hat and held it against his chest, murmuring a prayer.

Etienne squeezed Lili's hand, thanking whatever gods that listened that they hadn't been in the air—or that *Lili* hadn't been. He lifted her hand and brushed a kiss against her knuckles.

"There hasn't been an accident like this in years," she murmured, sniffling quietly.

They were all akin to a family to one another, and some *were* kin.

Pressing his lips together, Etienne pulled her in for an embrace. "Why don't we get out of here for a little bit, see the city—at least one of the markets." He tucked a strand of her red hair behind her ear and pulled free some coins. "I found some coin for you to spend." He smiled and extended his hand to her.

"Oh, Etienne." Sighing, she pulled herself to her feet and curled into his side. "Take me away."

That, he could do, for a little while and then for a lifetime.

London proved to be less flashy and more practical when it came to attire. While there was still a fair share of wigs, over-powdering, and flouncy dresses, it wasn't uncommon to see the less-pronounced fabrics. There were more shades of brown, and the city in general, seemed to be far more industrialized.

Seeing Lili dressed in attire that wasn't sleek, or, as the Parisian society would see it—*indecent*—Etienne found himself staring. She was dressed in a short-sleeved blouse, brown bustier that teased his senses, and she wore dark brown pantaloons. The light brown boots had a significant heel on them so the top of her head could nestle perfectly beneath his chin while he stood. She was currently glued to his side.

"It's soon, isn't it?" Etienne asked quietly, reading into how she had clung to him on the walk to the market.

"It has to be, or I won't go. I'll want to stay with you. For thirteen years, this has been my life, and while I'm grateful, I just can't do this —this isn't living."

Etienne's chest constricted as a torrent of emotions assaulted him. "I understand," he managed to say.

"Say something else?" Lili sputtered.

"There will be a day for us, Lil, more than these fractions we share, and together we will live. Find a life for us. I'll find you." Etienne pulled her along through the market and toyed with a few items.

A soft noise left Lili, and she picked up a pair of leather fingerless gloves. Brass buckles adorned the back of it, and she handed over money for them. "I will try."

"That's all you can do, *mon cherie*."

"London seems like the place to set some roots."

A half smile formed on Etienne's face. "It does, and so…"

"…and so, on the eve of the next departure, we should come to the market again." Lili didn't need to say anything more than that, she would be staying in London and Etienne would be forced to leave his heart behind.

"I suppose that means we shouldn't buy overly much today." He lifted a pair of goggles that magnified the size of his eyes. When he blinked Lili erupted in a fit of laughter, his green eyes lined with long lashes batted away, and he quirked a brow. "What?"

"Your eyes!" she sputtered and held her stomach. "Here, let me show you…" She held them up and batted her lashes which made him laugh. "I guess we shouldn't. I'll only bring what I can carry on myself."

With nothing else to say, the pair milled through the market, picking up trinkets here and there. Etienne came across a crate of metal, he bent down and picked up one of the objects—a skeleton key. He held it up and twisted it around in his grasp.

"Take it, it's junk." The man at the stall waved his hand toward the crate. "It's just scrap, so take it." He shrugged and turned his back to them.

Leaning over Etienne's shoulder, Lili peered down. "What is it?"

"A key." Grinning, Etienne spun it around his fingers.

"I gathered that but to what?"

"Paradise, perhaps." Gathering up the key, he lifted it and nodded to the vendor. "You said you can't take much, but you can carry this." He lifted the key, all he needed was a piece of leather.

A hum escaped her, and she nodded. "I like the sound of that —paradise."

CHAPTER 8

ONE DAY—THAT WAS ALL THE TROUPE TOOK OFF AFTER WITNESSING Angelico's demise. The memory of his body had been burned into everyone's mind, but if one good thing had to come from it, it was checking things over and not becoming too comfortable with how things were set up. Each day, each show, they meticulously went over their setups, as they should have done.

The next several weeks soared by grievously fast, and when Weaver announced their next departure, Etienne's heart plummeted to his stomach.

"The Americas are next up on the list. They have some neanderthal running about saying he's the best—he's not seen our show yet," Weaver shouted as he slammed his cane to the dirt ground.

"He has animals in his show—imagine traveling with animals," one of the troupe hooted with a laugh.

Weaver lifted a brow and shook his head. "This week, we will be tearing everything down. Baroness Marie and I have a few things to attend to. We'll be back by the time Étoile takes to the sky."

It would be the perfect time to whisk Liliane away, maybe they could even manage to find a flat for her to reside in. This would be a challenge, but the broader opportunity was ultimately freedom for Liliane, and to build a life beyond just a dream—beyond *Cirque de la Tempete*.

Amidst deconstructing the ticket booth, Lili approached Etienne, her face taut with tension. He hadn't noticed because as always the automatons were bickering, and this time it wasn't with one another, it was with him, and how he wasn't properly taking the pieces down.

"He's doing just fine," Lili chimed in.

In retaliation, Otto—the one with blue eyes—shot tickets directly at Lili's face. They harmlessly slapped against her face and fluttered to the ground like feathers.

"Really," she muttered and scowled. "I should rip open your gearbox and fry your circuits."

Etienne chuckled and swept up the tickets out of habit. "He's exceptionally grumpy today."

"Never you mind him," Oyo replied as he moved from the ticket booth. His eyes, unlike his counterpart, were a glowing amber. His movements weren't as clunky as Otto, and if one hadn't seen his insides, they would have sworn he was a person dressed in costume.

Lili shrugged her shoulders and nodded to Etienne, speaking with her eyes.

"I'll be back for you two," he murmured at the automatons and tossed the discarded tickets into a trash bin. "Wanting to run away already?" Etienne whispered.

She spun on her heel and brought a finger to her lips. "Quiet."

It was clear she didn't trust that there weren't listening ears, and Etienne didn't blame her. Instead, he followed her to the edge of the Cirque. It took him a moment to notice the leather strap hanging from her shoulder—she had a bag with her.

"I thought we could inspect…things." Her words were vague, but they didn't have to be any clearer than that.

"As the lady wishes," Etienne chirped and swept a bow in front of her. She swatted the back of his head, tickling him there. He grunted and moved forward, quickly lifting her onto his back, and he began to run away with her draped over his shoulder.

Lili swatted his backside and squealed as she flopped against his sturdy frame. She ceased when he set her down, her brown eyes wide and cheeks flushed.

"I think we're far enough away now that you can talk." His voice sounded far more somber than it had before.

There was this niggling feeling in his marrow that a storm was brewing, and he couldn't say he had ever felt that before.

"I think you should wait," he blurted out.

"I thought we'd look for a place today," Lili said at the same time as Etienne. She paused and arched a brow. "What?"

His gut twisted at the look on her face and he scrubbed the back of his neck like he always did when he felt unsure. "I have this feeling..."

"I have feelings, too, and I know if I stay, I won't want to leave. This isn't easy for me either, Etienne."

He reached out and cupped her face, bending his head so he could kiss her lips softly. "It's more than that, *mon cherie*, I can't explain it. I'm sorry, I..."

A mixture of emotions flitted through Liliane's gaze. "Don't stop me. Please, don't stop me from going, because I know myself...and it's hard enough."

Nodding, Etienne vowed not to bring it up again, but whether it was remnants of sorrow from Angelico's fall or something else, he pushed it aside, and together, he and Liliane began their search for a temporary home.

They combed what they could of London, and Lady Luck was indeed on their side. A women's movement in the heart of the city was currently renting out flats. It was as easy as that, which made Etienne's stomach churn.

Throughout the week, they deconstructed the Cirque, and Liliane made trips to her flat, dropping off small items that she could fit in her bag. Meanwhile, Etienne remained behind to help out the others.

"Where's Lil?" Rus asked while helping to fold the big top's tent.

She had been disappearing throughout the week, but it also wasn't uncommon for her to run off to the shops—even in Paris.

"I'm sure she's dropping coins on the latest trendsetter in town." That wasn't out of the ordinary, and while Etienne felt terrible for lying to Rus, he couldn't risk telling him the truth.

"Of course, she'd skip out on the work, the little demon." Rus shook his head and grabbed the folded tent. "She better not skip out on all of this." He motioned to the rest of the grounds that needed to be dismantled and packed away.

Etienne chuckled as he carried poles to Étoile and stored them away. He felt eyes on him as he turned around and found Madame Lucille looking up at him. Curiosity nibbled away at him, and he jogged up to the older, weathered woman.

"Madame, can I have a moment?" he asked softly, glancing around.

"Only just." She pulled a colorful shawl over her head as a cool breeze picked up, her eerie, mismatched eyes looking him over.

How could he ask without outright asking? "There is this feeling I have..."

Lucille hummed and nodded her head, allowing for him to continue.

"Like a thick blanket over the mood here, not just about Angelico —something else."

A laugh escaped from Lucille, and she took one of Etienne's hands in her firm grip. "Do you take me for a Seer?"

While she was the fortune teller of the Cirque, no one had elaborated whether she was a Seer or not. Since Weaver seemed to collect oddities, it wouldn't have surprised Etienne.

"You are," he said boldly without flinching, and in turn, Lucille's smile broadened.

"There is a black cloud about to descend on us. I cannot say anything else. Be careful, tread lightly, and take care of your heart."

That was far vaguer than he had anticipated, and in reply, he scrunched his nose. "There is already a black cloud on us, *what else*— what else have you Seen?" Etienne wasn't going to let Lucille inch away from him.

"I cannot say."

"Can't or *won't*, Madame?" he ground her prefix out.

"I cannot, Etienne. In time you will see." She took a quick step forward and a manicured nail pressed into his chest. "Take care of your heart, because it is your greatest tool." Madame pulled away and produced a card for him. It wasn't a tarot card that decorated her table during the Cirque nights; it was a playing card—the King of Hearts.

Etienne grasped the card. He had a fool tossed in his face twice over and now a King of Hearts. When he lifted his eyes to look at Lucille again, she had already left and was nowhere to be seen. He had the urge to crumple the card in his moment of anger but decided to pocket it instead and stormed off to the tent to wait for Lili.

Etienne had fallen asleep before Lili arrived, and when she did, she crawled onto his bunk bed and kissed the tip of his ear. It jolted him awake, but when his eyes focused on the freckled face, he smiled and kissed her chin.

"It looks so lovely," she said quietly. "It's starting to look like a home…a *real* home."

He knew what she meant—it wasn't a ship. It didn't continuously move, and it wasn't this infernal tent—it was a real place that she could dwell and develop healthy friendships.

"Tomorrow, my uncle and aunt return, which means I'll be leaving." His hand swept over his face, and he struggled with being happy for Lili when it felt like his heart was in a vice grip on the verge of shattering.

"Only for a little while. I know what his trajectory is. Americas, then back here again. Apparently, the English loved the show so much that even the Queen herself wishes to attend." She leaned down and pressed soft kisses to his lips, peppering his face in feather light touches.

He moved his hands and quirked a brow. "The Queen?" Etienne twisted his legs around hers and bucked his hips so he could then spin her and pin her down onto the mattress. He held her wrists in his grasp and kissed her palms.

"Mhmm…she heard about us—how could she not—and wishes to see us back again." She winced as she referred to herself as '*us*' when she would not be part of the performance again. New energy surrounded her; instead of being controlled, she seemed far more energetic than she had been.

Etienne watched the excitement flitter across her eyes, and he wondered if it was more for the attention the show seemed to be garnering or for the fact she was finally getting her wish. He decided it didn't matter and instead occupied her mouth with his own.

"I love you, Liliane." His words spilled out against her lips, and it sounded less like a declaration of love and more like a heart-wrenching goodbye.

She must have heard it because she began to speak about the plan. "Tomorrow, when they return, things will be hurried and scattered. Amidst the chaos, I'll slip away. No one will know. Why would my uncle think for a moment that I'd slip away? Besides, he doesn't do head checks."

That was true, for as controlled as Weaver was, he never seemed to scan the troupe for any missing members. Didn't he ever worry about runaways?

"No more talking." She twined her arms around his neck and pulled him down for another kiss, letting her body do the talking, letting each touch and kiss erase his worries and doubts.

Her touches seemed to ease him for a moment, a welcomed respite amongst his mounting anxiety when it came to leaving her. He poured every ounce of his love into this moment—their last moment—for a few months at least.

CHAPTER 9

In the morning, the sound of Weaver's baritone rang out through the park. Etienne had been up long before the sun had peeked over the horizon. He wanted to absorb as much of Lili as he could in their last dregs of time with one another.

"Good morning, Etienne," Weaver called out as he strolled by. "Ready to hit the wild west? They say real card sharks swim in those circles." He cackled.

"I doubt they could manage to keep up with the likes of me, Baron." An easy grin formed on his face. The notion of flying again didn't settle well with him, but he was excited about the experience. His eyes flicked to the automatons that were hauling neatly folded tents toward the dirigible.

Nodding his head, Weaver winked. "I'd pay to see that. Don't go running too far off, we'll be loading up the troupe, and you don't want to be left behind." He hummed a tune as he walked away.

Etienne rushed to find Liliane, knowing that they were leaving soon. He wanted to taste her lips one last time. When he found her, she was hugging Rus, whispering something into his ear.

"We'll be leaving soon," he said, jerking his head and hinting toward Rus to leave.

Rus kissed Lili's cheek. "I'll see you soon." He left without another word.

If Father-Time himself stopped the hands of time so that Etienne could express how much Liliane meant to him, there surely would never be enough time to do so. Every piece of his heart belonged to her, and he believed that this was proof—letting her go so that she could be happy before thinking of his own happiness.

"Gods, Liliane...I'll miss you." His voice broke, and he leaned forward to kiss her lips, tasting the salt of their tears. His arms wrapped around her as he held her tightly. "Until next time, *mon cherie*." He kissed her soundly and pulled away.

"I'll see you soon, Etienne," she whispered and turned away.

Every step he took away from her shattered him anew, but it was for the best, wasn't it?

With the grounds cleared and Étoile officially packed, everyone filed into the dirigible—everyone except for Liliane. The sound of the ship came to life, but a distressed snarl brought everyone's heart to a screeching halt.

"Where is she?" Weaver growled. It was an inhuman sound that tore from his throat. His dark eyes gleamed gold as he scanned the several faces in the hall. "I said where is she? Liliane!"

The ship hadn't yet taken off, and to Etienne's knowledge Weaver hadn't performed a head count. Perhaps he could smell the loss. Opting not to find out how he knew, Etienne leaned against the wall next to Rus. He hadn't noticed before but in Weaver's clutches was a black feather.

"If I have to ask again where my niece is," he paused to control himself, but every muscle in his face was tense, and he looked on the verge of shifting. "She's not safe, and I know she isn't here. So, come forth and tell me, tell me why she would leave. She can't leave." Weaver shook, a frantic look in his eyes as he stormed toward the door of the ship.

A flock of ravens flew by, sounding off with their caws which seemed to send Weaver over the edge. He ran outside and began to scream his niece's name.

Etienne moved forward, he had to tell the man something— anything—not where she was, or what their plan had been, but she was his family. "Baron," he called out, but the Baron had taken off into a run toward the tree line. "Wait, Baron!"

"She can't leave, she can't leave!" Baron Weaver kept reciting the words, and the more he sad it, the more he sounded like a mad man.

Etienne felt a knife to his heart each time the man said the words, because he felt them, too. He felt them more than he wanted to. Wiping fresh tears from his eyes, Etienne grabbed hold of Weaver's jacket, but the older man turned around to snarl at him, baring elongated fangs.

"Did you do this, son? *Did you*? She's here—I can smell her," his last words came quietly.

The sounds of a shriek rang out, followed by that of another flock of ravens crying out, but they seemed to laugh.

"Too late, too late," they seemed to cackle.

"No!" Weaver roared and blindly ran through the trees. He swore and collapsed to his knees, fumbling after the fallen girl. Leaves clung to Liliane's hair, her dark eyes stared blindly up at the sky. On her torso were several gashes that bled profusely, and her neck had been cut, too. Beyond them a large raven sat, watching.

"Oh, my gods, my Lili," Etienne found himself crying out and crawling on the ground to Lili's prone body. Tears fell anew as he picked up her lifeless body and cradled her against himself. "Why? Why?" he shouted amidst tears, half glaring at Baron Weaver.

"This is my doing, my beautiful, Lili!" Weaver clawed at the ground, howling in dismay, but then his gaze snapped to the raven and snarled. The corvid simply looked at him and ruffled its feathers. One inky feather made its way to the ground. "You! Why, you wretched..."

Sobbing, Etienne kissed Liliane's face, he felt for any life that may be lingering in her body, but none was there. She was gone, his love— his heart—gone.

Weaver lunged at the bird, it flew upward out of reach, leaving a cluster of feathers behind.

The troupe had pooled out of the dirigible by the time Etienne and Weaver returned. An array of gasps went out, and a few cried the moment they saw Lili's limp form. Rus was the first to run up and hug her body, sobbing as hard as what Etienne was.

Anger built up inside of Etienne, Weaver had done this—had known something like this would have happened.

"Liliane is dead," Weaver said in a lifeless tone as if he hadn't just screamed until his throat was raw. "We will bury her properly, and then leave for the Americas as planned." With an effort, he controlled his voice as if this were nothing more than another act.

Etienne gnashed his teeth together, bent his head and kissed

Liliane's cold cheek. When he looked up he saw Lucille's mismatched gaze on him, and fury erupted—she knew, she had Seen and had not warned him or Lili.

Carefully, he passed his beloved off to Weaver and decided to press Lucille once more. Etienne ensured most of the troupe had walked away with Weaver and Liliane, and when Lucille was left behind, he rounded on her like a wild cat, his eyes darkening. "You knew, and you let it transpire. You knew." His hands were balled into fists at his side—Etienne wasn't a violent individual but losing Liliane had broken him. "You are a wretched thing, Lucille."

Lucille had the good graces to look away and wept silently. "There are things I cannot say, Etienne, and to say anything would reveal your fate."

"My fate was to live and die with Liliane!" he shouted and moved his hands as if he were about to shake Lucille, but instead he grabbed his hair and sank to his knees. "And she's dead. She's dead."

"It was not your fate, and it was not the way. Guard your heart, Etienne, mark my words, guard it…" Lucille moved her hand as if to touch him, but thinking better of it she walked away.

How could he guard something that he no longer possessed?

Weaver had ensured that his niece received a proper burial, that she was laid to rest properly, and that she was more than deserving of a decent service. Etienne couldn't agree more, but the entire thing was drawn out, which served to shred any surviving piece of his heart.

After the service, Weaver walked up to him and handed him a necklace. "I thought you might want this," he said quietly and laid the skeleton key into his hand.

"The key to paradise." Etienne turned the key over in his grasp, reminiscing on that excursion. If he had realized these would be the last memories he had of Liliane, he would have made them something more.

"I am certain she found it." He lifted his hand and patted him on the back.

Nothing would ever be the same, and when Etienne met the dark eyes of Weaver, he wondered just how deep his guilt ran. It was a demon that did it—so Weaver had later told him. A beast that walked amongst mankind and lurked in London, waiting for its victims. But

Etienne didn't buy that, not when he heard Baron Weaver crying that she couldn't leave, or cursing the birds as they cackled in the sky.

Not for the last time, Étoile took to the skies and headed toward the Americas.

Nothing would ever be the same.

C'est la vie.

EPILOGUE

Two years later...

Etienne's biceps were wrapped in silks, and as he flipped head-over-heels in rapid succession. The silks unwound from him, traversing down from the top of the tent down to the floor.

Just another day of practice, but when he heard a gasp the moment his feet touched the ground, he looked up and saw a green-eyed girl staring at him.

"I thought you were going to fall! That was amazing!" Her voice came out rushed, and although she spoke French, it was rough—as though she hadn't spoken it much or it had been a while.

"Isn't falling one of the best teachers?" he asked playfully and peered behind her shoulder. "Are you lost?" Had she come with someone else—or worse, had Weaver pulled another straggler in?

"No. I mean, yes. I mean..."

"Turn around. Go home. We're not hiring." He didn't growl at her, but he wouldn't be welcoming either. The Cirque was a trap—a death trap waiting to snap shut on its next victim.

"My name is Celeste. Nice to meet you, too."

"Names would imply that you are staying, *mon chaton*, which you are decidedly not." He spun on his heel and saluted to her. "*Au revoir.*" He winked and walked away.

ABOUT ELLE BEAUMONT

Elle was born and raised in Southeastern, Massachusetts in a little farm town by the harbor. She grew up fascinated with all things whimsical and a strong love for animals.

As she grew so did her passion for reading and writing. Although she prefers devouring all genres she largely enjoys dark fantasy.

She is married to her best friend and has two lively sprites who inspire madness, love and a sense of humor in her. They also have a menagerie of animals, two dogs, three cats and a horse. In her downtime, Elle enjoys creating candles, crocheting, horseback riding and running.

CONNECT ON SOCIAL MEDIA

ellebeaumontbooks.com

facebook.com/ellebeaumontbooks

instagram.com/ellebeaumontbooks

ALSO BY ELLE BEAUMONT

The Hunter Series
Hunter's Truce
Royal's Vow

Galathea Saga
Brotherhood of the Sea
Binding of the Sea

Veiled Allurement: A Cinderella Retelling Novella

Cirque des Spirits

CM Lander

CHAPTER 1

THE PICTURE WAS BURNED INTO MY MEMORY—AS CLEAR AS THE FIRST time he talked to me, the first time his hand brushed against mine as he borrowed my pen in second period math class.

My stomach lurched as I looked away, but I couldn't tear my eyes from the computer screen for long before the memory dragged itself from the back of my mind and forced me to look again and again. There he was. Robbie. My Robbie. Kissing Ellee, captain of the girl's volleyball team, in front of his house. His tan arm was draped loosely around her bare shoulders as he pecked her on the cheek. She smiled brightly at the camera, her face scrunched into a beaming smile that told the world of her perfect contentment, as the photographer captured their relationship bliss in one still image.

They seemed comfortable and that felt more like betrayal than anything. How many hours had I spent, nerves wound tight in knots, trying to find the words to tell him that I so entirely loved his every quirk and imperfection? That he was my soul mate and we were meant for one another? I never did though. It never seemed like the right moment and math class after math class passed by without a word from either of us to suggest what I had held in my heart for so long: that we were perfect for one another.

He obviously didn't see it that way. I stared at the computer for minutes on end, my heart heavy with grief, but unable to cry. I wanted to sob and shout and cry every ounce of tears in my body. The prospect of having to speak to my stepmom, Carissa, about my feelings if she overheard made me muster whatever strength I had to stifle my emotions until a night where she and my father were out on one of their date nights, and I could finally be left alone.

It must be nice to go out on a proper date: hair and makeup done, little black dress that compliments every curve zipped up and comfortable. I had picked out just the one in the off-chance Robbie came to his senses, but that seemed like a silly fantasy now.

I closed my eyes, forbidding myself to look at the screen once more. I shut my laptop and stood up just as my stepmother shouted from downstairs, "Amelia! Are you ready? We have to get going, honey."

I sighed. Spending my Friday night at the circus with my six-year-old half-sister and my overly bubbly stepmother was not my idea of a fun time. But then, staying in my bedroom with all its hidden memories of Robbie—the olive green bomber jacket I hung on the back of my door because green is his favorite color, the poster of The Sinner's Lament, his favorite band, tacked to the inside of my closet door, my velvety pink throw pillow that I kissed a thousand times imagining it was him—didn't exactly seem like the ideal place to spend my night either.

Instinctively, I went to grab my green jacket from my door and stopped my hand in mid-air. I didn't need to wear my memories tonight. I blindly reached into my closet to pull out the denim jacket my stepmother bought me for my sixteenth birthday. Something about no woman's wardrobe being complete without one. At least I was thankful for it now. I threw the jacket on and caught a glimpse of my reflection in the mirror above my dresser. The light blue of the denim set off the darkness of my almost-black hair and eyes. Everything about me seemed the same color. Plain. Ellee had such pretty blonde hair.

I closed my eyes and tried to shake the picture from my thoughts. I would be miserable enough at the circus all night. No need to punish myself further with Robbie reminders every five seconds. As I ran down the stairs, I smoothed my hair into a ponytail and hopped off the last step into the foyer. I do have to give Carissa credit. She did have pretty good taste when it came to interior decorating. This foyer was a banged up mess before she set foot in it eight years ago with dingy, marked up walls from where I rolled my toy cars all over them to a ratty old doormat that was older than my dad and fell apart a little more every time someone stepped on it. The wood floors were dull and broken in places. Now it was freshly painted in a cool, pale gray with white crown molding at the intersection of the walls and ceiling. Thick white baseboard trim set off a stark contrast of the gray walls and the newly repaired floors that she had stained a deep brown. The floorboards gleamed during the day when sunlight poured through the transom and sidelight windows surrounding our crisp new front door, complete with elegant etchings in its glass that created little flowers of light on the floor and the soft, new rug with gray circles on an ivory background. A small crystal chandelier hung down in the center of the room as if it had always belonged there.

Carissa stood by the door, smiling at me as I tousled my sister Sophie's wispy blonde locks. She wrinkled her nose in protest and checked her reflection in the hall mirror. It was then that I noticed her red lips and purple eyeshadow.

"Someone's all dressed up," I said.

"I have to look my best in case they ask me to perform," Sophie replied, directing a curl back over her ear and hopping away from the narrow table she had rested on to get the best view of herself. Carissa laughed to herself and shook her head as she opened the door. Sophie took the lead and I followed her out, Carissa locking the door behind us as we headed to her black minivan in the driveway.

Carissa, Sophie too, always seemed so put together. Style just came easily to the two of them. They could fall into their closets and come out looking cute. I looked down at my ratty shoes, splotched with mud from running outside in gym class after it rained. My dark jeans that were a completely different color than the denim jacket I was wearing. The heavily stained navy blue t-shirt. My entire outfit was various shades of blue that somehow clashed with each other. I didn't even know the same color could clash. I looked like I actually fell into my hamper and got dressed in the dark. Carissa had her blonde hair pulled back in a ponytail like mine, but her black top, blue jeans, and black booties were all free of ketchup and mud, unlike my outfit. And Sophie, in her white fluffy dress, really did look like she was ready to perform.

Maybe that's what having a mother around does for you. She teaches you how to put together outfits and do your hair the right way. I didn't really give Carissa the chance. I was eight when she came into our lives and I wasn't too thrilled about her in the beginning. It seemed too new, too sudden. I didn't understand why my dad had to start dating, but now, ever since I first noticed Robbie really, I understood.

Seeing someone, loving someone. It's not really something you can stop.

I buckled myself into the passenger seat as Carissa secured Sophie into her booster and took a moment while Carissa's back was turned to focus myself. If I could get through tonight without letting on that my entire world had just come to a crushing watershed, that the life I imagined for myself over the past two years no longer existed, then I would be okay. Just a few hours at the circus.

What could go wrong?

Carissa finished helping Sophie with her buckles and came around to the driver's side. She flashed her smile at the two of us and started the car. "Ready?" she asked.

"Ready!" Sophie called out.

Music started playing immediately as the car shifted into gear and we pulled out of the driveway—a jaunty pop song that Robbie would have rolled his eyes at if he'd heard it.

Just a few hours, I reminded myself, and then I can cry endlessly into my kissing pillow.

CHAPTER 2

WE ARRIVED AT THE MASSIVE PARKING LOT WITH THIRTY MINUTES TO spare. Soon enough we would be in our respective seats, in a dark auditorium, and I'd be left alone in a crowd full of people to lament over my heartbreak in the veiled privacy of darkness. Night had descended over our small town and the moon hung full and low in the autumn sky. Out of habit, I searched the cloudy horizon for my father's plane, but he wasn't even flying today. He was due back from his trip in two days. His business trips were a welcome reprieve if I'm honest. My birth mother left us when I was little and even my grandparents said he changed after that day. I wouldn't know though. He's always just been a sort of roommate to me. We'd pass each other in the hallway, eat together occasionally, but, for the most part, we left each other alone. Carissa changed things a bit. There's certainly more family photos and dinners than before, but not much more of an emotional attachment between my father and myself.

Carissa is really the only parent I've ever had—and I hate to admit that. She and I are such utter opposites, I don't think she could ever understand me. But she does try. And I give her points for that. It's more than most people have done for me.

My phone vibrated in my pocket and I checked the message. It was from Jessica, my current best friend. "Did you see that pic?" she messaged. I knew exactly which one she was talking about. I ignored it, but my phone buzzed with a follow-up message from her. "What a jerk. I can't believe I let him copy my homework last week." I clicked the screen dark once more and shoved the phone in my pocket. This was not something I wanted to be thinking about right now.

Sophie's voice in the backseat drew me out of my annoyed spiral. "Why didn't we wait for Daddy to come home, so he could come to the circus too?"

Carissa freed Sophie from her straps and cooed, "Because Daddy doesn't like the circus." She bent forward, pressing her face close to Sophie's and whispered in a conspiratorial tone, "I think Daddy's afraid of clowns." The pair laughed as Sophie hopped from the car and into the parking lot, next to me.

We headed together toward the arena. It was a five storey building, tall and black, with columns of windows that reached all the way to the roof creating amazing horizontal stripes of light in the dark design. Gold letters spanned the front spelling out Aldritch Center in a chunky font. The parking lot was nearly full and people poured out of their cars and into the lot with reckless abandon. Horns honked, people shouted as they all were desperate to get inside for their night's enjoyment.

My phone buzzed again, but I ignored it. Sophie slipped her little hand in mine and we walked, all three of the McConnell girls together, hand in hand for a night of delights, as the advertisement promised.

A second and third text message came in. I finally checked my phone once more as we got our place in line just outside the front doors. Jessica had said, "Want me to beat him up? haha Seriously though, I can't believe he did that to you." She ended her text stream with "Are you mad at me?"

I've burned through a few best friends in the past few years. I can't really say why. I just get bored of the same conversations. The same jokes told in the same way. I get to a point where the glitter of the new friendship fades away and I realize that the person isn't actually as great as I once thought. Then they get mad because I don't want to spend my Friday night watching the same tv show or going to the same mall and they get frustrated that I no longer want to do their favorite things. Jessica and I were at this point. Past the sparkle. Past the wanting-to-do-

everything-together stage. We were dealing with smoking embers here and we both knew it. It's why my momentary silence brought up so much fear in her. I'm not usually quiet. But I just didn't find any solace in talking to her anymore.

I replied back, "No. Just out with my family."

"Let me know if you meet any cute clowns," she answered back.

I didn't have the energy to laugh, so I clicked my phone off once more and put it away. A throng had collected outside the arena's glass doors. Our breath puffed like clouds of smoke as we each exhaled. The weatherman hadn't predicted such a cold night tonight. Carissa wrapped her leather jacket around Sophie as she shivered in line. We were close to the front though and the doors would be opening soon. Every time an employee crept through the doors, a blast of hot air issued from the inside and warmed us momentarily. Those moments were pure bliss, but sadly, short lived and soon we would shiver again.

"What did clowns ever do to Daddy to make him scared? That doesn't make any sense." Sophie decided.

"Oh, honey, I was only joking," Carissa said, stooping down in her heels to get on Sophie's eye-level. "I don't know why Daddy doesn't like the circus, but he seemed pretty upset when I mentioned wanting to go, so let's just keep tonight between the three of us."

I knew. I knew why.

My mother left my dad and me at the circus fourteen years ago. Just disappeared in the crowd and never came back. No signs of foul play. Nothing. She was just gone. I was two. I remember the day. It's my first memory of life: my dad frantically searching, paging my mother over the loudspeaker over and over. The police officers that came to take his story and investigate. They gave me a little teddy bear to hug while my dad stood around, answering questions. I still have that bear, but he doesn't know that. I keep it in the back of my closet, with all the other stuff I don't want to talk about.

I'll never tell his secret though. All of the hurt he has surrounding something so innocent. A childhood pleasure. I kept my mouth shut and the line mercifully began moving. Carissa handed me my ticket and the usher scanned it, letting the three of us pass through the doors and into the blessed warmth of the inside.

People crowded the entryway where programs and light up toys were being sold. "Mommy! Can I get a tiara?" Sophie practically choked on the prospect of owning a light up tiara. The three of us headed over to a middle-aged man in a bright yellow shirt the color of the arena's logo, hocking the toys. Sophie grabbed a tiara that lit up with purple lights and feathers and placed it on her head as if it were some precious jewel. Carissa turned to me and asked, out of habit more than not, "Do you want anything?"

I quirked an eyebrow at the prospect of being bought a cheap light up toy from the circus and Carissa laughed at herself. In her efforts to treat me as much like a biological child as her own daughter, she constantly forgets the age difference. She has a good heart. She does.

Newly illuminated, we headed to the hallway that led to our seats. A crowd of people had congregated, all shuffling their way to get to their own seats. Locked butt to gut in a crowd, I saw, out of the corner of my eye, a sight so familiar it stung: Robbie. I could recognize his curls anywhere. He wasn't with Ellee, fortunately, but I wondered why he hadn't mentioned that he would be coming today. He knew I was coming. I had hoped he would invite himself along, but he didn't. And now—

I tried to make eye contact, to get his attention, but I was too short to stand out in the crowd. On my tiptoes, I could just barely see over the shoulders of the men that surrounded me. But I could see that Robbie had changed directions and was no longer headed into the arena, but back toward the snack area.

Without knowing why, I turned to Carissa and told her I would meet her at the seats. "I saw a friend back there and I want to say hello." Carissa nodded and I pushed my way through the crowd, whispering my apologies for every bump and knock along the way. I followed the back of Robbie's head down the hall. I didn't want to call out to him. The rejection, if he heard me and continued on, would be too much to bear. I just wanted to catch up to him. I had no plan further than that. Just a desire to see his face. Part of me wanted to slap him. Another wanted to profess my love for him.

I followed him down the hall. Past the food vendors and souvenir shops. Around a group of tourists listening to a tour guide and through a pair of double doors marked "Staff Only". It dawned on me, right then, that he might be going to meet someone. That I might not like it if I saw who he was walking so briskly to go see. I slowed and let him fall out of my eyeline. He turned a corner and I stopped dead.

I could cry here, I thought. I wanted to so badly. To just let loose. Why was I still chasing after him when I knew he didn't want me?

As I made the decision to actively forget Robbie existed, the dressing room door next to me flew open and a woman wearing a bad, blonde, banana curl wig and too much caked on makeup popped her head out of the door. "You," she shouted, "What are you doing here? Get out! Get out!" Her features were intense, angry. And her clownish makeup made the sight all the more surreal.

I stumbled backward, catching myself on the wall and ran back through the double doors, past all the shops and tourists and vendors and back to the hallway where I left Carissa. The crowd had thinned out a bit in my absence and I was able to navigate down the narrow staircase three floors to our seats at the ground level.

I scooted into the aisle seat, next to Sophie who stood, hanging onto the railing right in front of her, giddy with how close she would be to all the action. Carissa leaned over. "Did you see your friend?" she asked.

"It wasn't him. I followed the wrong guy," I answered. I tried to laugh, but couldn't help the sad expression that washed over my face. Mercifully, the lights dimmed and Carissa became too engrossed in the experience of Sophie's first circus to ask any follow-up questions.

CHAPTER 3

The circus was bad. Really bad. The clowns were ancient and tired. Their painted on smiles the only sign of happiness in the show. The ringmaster was tubby and barely fit into his waistcoat. He spoke with a lisp and spit so much when he spoke that he became a bigger joke than anything the clowns could do.

Sophie was excited for the trick riders she had seen in the commercial, but when they came out there were only two small ponies hobbling around the ring at a slow gait and a frumpy woman on top who looked like this was her first time on horseback. The commercial that featured this woman so confidently standing on the back of two full grown horses must have caught her in the fifteen seconds before she fell if this performance was anything by which to judge. When the lion tamer came out, Sophie sat down, the excitement of the circus finally waning from her little body. She looked unhappy, the corners of her lips turned down in disappointment. The twinkle in her eye from just moments ago had dimmed to a fatigued expression. I grabbed her hand and when she looked over at me, I gave her a small smile. She returned the same smile and then said, "That lion doesn't even have teeth." She pointed to the lion tamer who had his head in the lion's mouth.

"Yeah," I replied, "I've never seen a bored lion before so that's something."

Sophie giggled. In that happy moment, I caught Carissa's eye. She nodded her thanks as she grabbed Sophie's hand and asked, "Do you want to get some snacks, honey?"

Sophie jumped up, "Yeah!" But just then the stage lights faded to nothing and the ringmaster, invisible to the audience at this point, announced, "Ladies and gentlemen. It is our great honor to present to you today the three-time World Illusion Champion, straight from his show on the Las Vegas strip and with us today for a single night, the incomparable, the illustrious," his voice lowered to a sultry tone, "the handsome, Alfonso the Incredible!"

Sophie and I looked to each other immediately. "Ooo, Alfonso," we said with a shimmy in unison. Carissa laughed.

"You can't miss Alfonso," I pretend pled with the pair.

"No, mommy. We can't miss Alfonso," Sophie said to her mother.

Carissa laughed once more. "Okay, let's sit back down and go after his act."

A single light beamed up from the center of the ring, vibrant blue, and ominous music blared. Sophie jumped into her seat, pressing down the skirt of her white dress and leaning forward in utter fascination. Her eyes widened. I loved seeing her so rapt. At once the beam multiplied exponentially: two, then four, then eight until the entire stage became a blue cube of light. It was so bright we all had to shield our eyes for a moment before the lights dropped to a single warm yellow spotlight beaming down from the ceiling and, in it, a man in a black tuxedo. I clapped without thinking. Because everyone else was clapping.

"Thank you. Thank you," Alfonso bowed with no hint of accent in his deep voice. "Ladies and gentlemen, it is my absolute honor to be here with you tonight.

He began a fairly normal magician's act: doves appearing from nowhere, scarves and balls floating, making bottles appear out of thin air, multiplying every time he raised a shiny cylinder from the table before him. My head was heavy in my hand, as I pressed my elbow into the arm rest to keep my gaze up. I had seen this act before and wished in that moment that I was in line for a soda and popcorn or one of those giant bags of cotton candy that venders were carrying around on their heads when, at once, a spotlight shined directly on me.

I shot back in my seat and covered my eyes from the blinding light. "What is your name?" Alfonso asked, suddenly at my side. The audience erupted in cheers. How had he traveled so far so fast? My heart was beating in my chest so quickly I couldn't think. I looked at him, horrified, incredulity gripping my hands to the armrests. Carissa shoved me a bit to wake me up. "Amelia," I said timidly, into the microphone he had pointed at my mouth.

"Beautiful name," he responded. "Everyone say hello to Amelia!"

The entire arena erupted in a round of "Hi Amelia!"

This was all far too intense for me. I didn't know what to do or how to act. He held out his hand to me and asked, "Will you help me with this next act?"

Thankful for the prompt, I placed my hand in his. I turned to Sophie, expecting to see a scowl of jealousy—she had dressed to perform after all—but she was so beguiled she couldn't sport any expression but honest amazement.

"A hand for my lovely assistant," Alfonso called and the audience clapped once more. I turned bright red. I could barely move my feet, I was shaking so badly. A few steps ahead of us was a half wall separating the ring from the audience. He helped me climb up to stand on top of the half wall, realizing at that moment, that everyone, including Robbie, would now be staring at my garish outfit. I wished I was one of those girls who cared what she looked like. Then I wouldn't have found myself in an arena full of people with a spotlight shining on my stained, mono-toned outfit. My knees were shaking as he he deftly climbed up next to me, throwing both our arms into the air with a true performer's flourish. The audience kept clapping, Carissa and Sophie loudest of all. I glanced back at them and Carissa gave me a double thumbs up. Sophie was practically falling out of her chair with excitement.

"Now, for my next act," Alfonso announced, "I want to make sure you all get a good look at my helper, Amelia, here." He snapped his fingers and a puff of smoke enveloped us. Before I knew it, we were in the center of the stage with the audience surrounding us on all sides.

My jaw dropped. "How did you do that?" I asked him, my voice picking up on the microphone though it was nowhere near me. The audience laughed and Alfonso winked—a gesture alluring in a way high school boys just couldn't muster. Up close he was more handsome than I had initially appreciated: olive skin, dark hair and eyes, strong jaw, full lips. His skin was clear and smooth, just the beginning of a stubble starting to sprout on his cheeks. He was young, perhaps in his mid-twenties, tall and lean. He towered over me. And his hand never lost its grip on mine. It felt right. Natural.

His attention turned from me to the audience. Our shared moment was broken by the reality of standing in front of thousands of people, all of them watching me ogle him. Robbie fluttered to my mind momentarily, but Alfonso's voice brought me back to the moment.

"Amelia, I would like to make your greatest wish come true right now." I blushed as his eyes fell on me once more. "I have a feeling you would like to be anywhere else in the world right now than up here in front of all these people. Am I right?"

"Yeah," I laughed. And so did the audience.

He put a hand to his temple and closed his eyes, taking a visible breath before continuing, "I see a lovely green field, lush with flowers. A bright, blue sky that reaches out to eternity. Trees. Lots of trees surrounding the glade. A scent of lavender carrying on the breeze. Sunlight warming you from every direction. Is that the place you were thinking of going?"

"Yeah," I breathed. It wasn't. I was thinking of hiding away in my bedroom with the lights off forever, but the sound of his voice was so intoxicating I couldn't think of any word but yes.

He smiled at my lie. "Now Amelia, can you confirm for the audience that you and I have never met."

"Right."

"You've never performed this act before?"

"Right," I answered, more confident than before.

"We've never talked about running away to a castle by the sea and eating bon bons by the fire?"

"What?" I asked. He kissed my hand as the audience roared with laughter.

"Worry not. That's for later," he said, patting the back of my hand. A woman clad in a sparkling red and white leotard with a black sequined skirt walked on stage from the wings. I recognized her immediately from her banana curl wig. It was the woman who shooed me away earlier as I followed Robbie. She was pushing a black box that was taller than her even in her stiletto heels, a scowl fixed on her face.

Her presence unnerved me. The magic of Alfonso's gaze was overpowered by her angry presence. "Ah, Tanya, thank you." Alfonso said, pushing me into position and taking control of the box. "The lovely Tanya, everyone!" He announced, gesturing to the woman. She raised a black evening-gloved hand and waved to the audience, a forced smile contorting her face into an ugly expression. As Tanya got closer to me, she caught my eye and her smoldering anger burned through my body.

Alfonso began manipulating the box. "Now, ladies and gentlemen, if you'll allow, I would like to have Amelia examine this box to assure you that there are in fact no false walls, no trap doors, nothing to allow access in or out of this box save this door here." As he spun the box to show the whole audience, he opened its door. Once he stopped spinning it, I glanced inside and nodded my head in agreement. "Why don't you knock on each wall just to be sure," he suggested. I awkwardly knocked my fist into each wall of the box and nodded my head again, having no idea what a false wall or trap door might sound like.

"All right. No way out. No way out. But is there? Amelia, if you would be so kind." He took my by the hand and guided me into the box. Tanya held the other side of it, keeping it steady as I stepped in. The box shifted a bit on its wheels as it bore my weight, but Alfonso steadied me and I turned around to face the audience once more. He spun the box and me around with the door open and then closed the door and gave me one more spin.

The darkness was disorienting. I held onto the walls to steady myself. Worry set in. I had never helped a magician before. What if I messed up his trick? I didn't know what to do. The world stopped spinning as the box came to a halt. It was hard to hear Alfonso through its thick walls. I could just barely catch his words as he shouted, "Now, Amelia, I want you to picture that perfect place. That lovely warm field in the middle of the woods. I want you to see it in your mind. Okay? Hold that image in your head and wish for it as hard as you can. Now, ladies and gentlemen, if you will help me, I believe we can make this young girl's greatest wish come true."

His voice was muffled but the sound of the crowd was unmistakable.. My muscles tensed. I tried to imagine a meadow and the flowers in my mind, but couldn't get past the claustrophobic vulnerability of the box.

The audience's collective voice ricocheted off every wall of my sarcophagus. "Five, four, three, two," the voice of the crowd came over me. At the sound of the roaring, "One," the door flew open.

But there was no more audience.

I stood at the edge of the stage area, inside a bright-lit tent, blinded by the spotlights that bore their luminensence into my corneas. There were no laughing children, no tourists. The tent was empty save the performers as they practiced their acts. A pair of acrobats tumbled over my head clad in the most vibrant red leotards I had ever seen. A lion roared at my side, his ferocious maw wide with pearly teeth that even Sophie couldn't mock. A band struck up a deafening chorus of calliope music. Pasty-faced clowns in every color of costume traipsed their way through the tent. The ground beneath me crunched with gravel.

I was so small. Each act seemed to fill the great space of the tent. They were grand, magnificent. I gawked at each performer that passed by.

It was all too much to take in. I had to avert my eyes. Looking down I saw that I was not dressed in messy too-blue outfit anymore. Rather, I was sporting a white gown with lace around the collar and sleeves. A simple smock of a dress that looked like it was out of some history textbook. My shoes were black booties that laced up to my mid-calf with a small heel that made me stand up even straighter than my sneakers ever did.

Everything in the tent sparkled with practiced perfection. This wasn't the circus I left. These weren't the performers I mocked. Alfonso, however he managed it, took me away from all my problems just as I had wanted.

CHAPTER 4

"EVANGELINE!" A VOICE CALLED OUT. "EVANGELINE! IT'S SO GOOD TO see you." Suddenly my arm was being pulled away from the spectacle of the silk dancers that descended from the upper scaffolding. As I pulled my focus from the women in bodysuits meandering their way up and down the silk ropes in mid-air, my eyes focused on the figure before me. A woman, robust in size. Clad in a floral print dress with a crisp white apron, her hair styled in cropped curls that clung to her scalp. At once, her face came into focus and upon it was the fullest beard I had ever seen in real life. Mostly brown, the same color as her hair, but with flecks of copper hidden throughout its twiny hairs.

I needed a moment to process.

"Who are you?" I demanded, digging my heels into the dirt ground just before we made it to the tent flap. The hint of a bright day peeked through: blue sky, green grass. The very idea of sunlight warmed me a bit.

The bearded woman looked at me quizzically. "How many bewhiskered ladies do you know?"

I searched my mind for an answer. "None?"

"Oh honey," the woman continued. "Did you hit your head again? You know you're supposed to use a net when you practice." She wrapped her arm around me and I recoiled involuntarily.

"Who are you?" I asked, less angry this time. More scared.

"Honey, it's me. Dolores. Why don't I get you a little spot to lay down? How's that?"

She pushed the tent flap open and a surge of sunlight blinded me.

I blinked against its brilliance as she dragged me into the outdoors. I pulled against Dolores' grip, but she was much stronger than me.

Trees encircled the site and, if I took a deep breath, I did smell the lavender Alfonso had mentioned. The place was idyllic, but chaotic with bodies of people everywhere all busy with some important task or other. Some sat on boxes playing cards. Some hammered stakes into the ground to keep the tents supported. Conversations about last night's conquests carried on the wind by a lascivious man who looked Dolores and me up and down. I gave in to Dolores' grasp, finding more comfort in her company than in the ribald man's gaze. The path we took was well-worn, muddied with recent rain and the pummeling of hundreds of feet upon the grass.

As we passed a second tent, I was able to keep my eyes open long enough to peer inside its red and white striped canvas. An elephant took up nearly the entire area as a man in a dingy white undershirt and ripped black trousers held up by matching black suspenders cracked a whip. The animal was frightened. It trumpeted and reared up as the man shouted something—a word I had never heard. His whip cracked and the elephant backed away, seating itself like a dog: its front legs straight, hind legs pushed back so that the bottom of its hooves faced forward. I had, perhaps, never felt closer to an animal as I did in this moment.

We arrived at a teal caravan wagon with pale yellow trim and stairs. Red roses were painted along the doorway and windows, a thick green vine connecting all of the blossoms. Its domed roof sloped down so sharply it seemed impossible that an adult could fit inside.

Once up the steps, Dolores knocked on the yellow door. Footsteps resounded within and the door was thrown open. A thin, old woman answered. Her gray hair was pulled back in a long braid. Her face showed little signs of aging. Only the bulge of her eye from the wearing of time suggested she was any more than fifty. Her lips were thin and pulled into a line, her eyes sharp and half-lidded. She seemed unamused by our appearance on her doorstep. She folded her arms over a pashmina shawl that wrapped around her shoulders. White lace peeked out at her collar and sleeves. A brown skirt and belt spanned the rest of her small frame.

My head was pounding at this point—whether from fear or simply trying to understand what was going on, I couldn't tell. Only that behind her I could see signs of a newly made bed that simply begged to be lain on.

"Madame Chantilly," Dolores began, "Would you mind if our dear Evangeline has a lay down here? She's had a rather nasty tumble and seems a bit off."

Madame Chantilly eyed me for an uncomfortable moment. She did not move. Only her lips parted as she spit out, "Fine."

Dolores pushed me past the old woman and sat me on the bed. It's linen was crisp, firm, and scratchy. A perfect symbol of its elderly owner. The caravan was more spacious than its exterior suggested. Dolores and I, though neither being particularly tall, were able to walk completely upright throughout its length and Madame Chantilly, with her slightly shorter stature fit perfectly.

"Now you just lay down and have a little nap. I'll be back in a bit to check up on you," Dolores said, forcing me to lay down and covering me with the patchwork quilt at the foot of the bed. The pillow was thin and filled with feathers that poked me through the casing like a thousand needles. I closed my eyes only to feel even more feathers pricking the back of my neck and head. Minutes past and the bed didn't get any more comfortable. I wondered how in the world this old woman could sleep like this when her footsteps reminded me that she was still there.

She stood over me, her gaze burning holes into me. I opened my eyes. "Thank you for letting me rest here," I offered, but her scowl persisted. Her arms seemed permanently glued to their crossed position. "If it's too much of a bother, though," I continued, "I could leave."

"You're not Evangeline." Her voice was wobbled and gravelly with age.

I moved to get up, but my head spun and I fell back down.

"Lay still, girl. You're weak. It takes much energy to enter into our realm."

"Where am I?" I asked, relieved to talk to someone with any information.

"You're not Evangeline," she repeated.

"No. I'm not."

"But you have her in you."

Her words baffled me. "I'm Amelia," I offered, hoping for more information from her. But Madame Chantilly looked off into the distance as if listening to some far off conversation.

"Sylas knows you're here. You must get out." Her face morphed from undue sternness to an urgency that startled me. My heart beat fast in my chest. I stood again, too fast, and lost my balance, but Madame Chantilly caught me. She slowly led me to the door as I found my footing, whispering something under her breath that I could not make out.

"How do I get out?" I asked.

But a knock at the door silenced us both. "Evie," Dolores' voice called. "I know you just laid down, but Sylas is asking for you." I looked to Madame Chantilly for advice. "It's too late," was all she said as the door opened and Dolores' smiling face came into view.

On seeing Madame Chantilly holding my arm, Dolores rushed to my side to help me walk. She was right. I was very weak. And the prospect of meeting this Sylas that Madame Chantilly so feared stopped my feet from working entirely. Dolores was strong, though, and practically carried me out the door and through the web of tents, big and small, past cages of animals as confused and miserable as me and two more caravans equally as decorous as Madame Chantilly's, until we got to a great red caravan with golden letters on the side that I couldn't quite read from my perspective. Dolores knocked on the door and rubbed her hand against my back. The sunlight didn't seem to warm me as much anymore. My eyes could barely stay open and I couldn't support my own weight.

The door burst open with an emphatic flourish as a man appeared, dressed in clean clothes where everyone, save the women I'd met, seemed rather dirty. His light gray vest showed the chain of a gold watch that he kept in his pocket. His black pants and white shirt were all pressed neatly. He looked as if he rarely did a moment's manual labor. His jaw was strong and clean shaven, his skin tan from days out enticing visitors to his tents in the daylight. His hair was dark and thick, his eyes intense and black. I understood at once the phrase devilishly handsome. And then recognition set in. It was the magician, Alfonso. His clothes were different, but it was the same man. The same face. I was frightened, but could not stop staring.

"Evangeline," he hummed, hugging me on the doorstep, "Come in, come in! We've much to discuss."

His hand, warm and firm, pressed against the small of my back. I looked over my shoulder as Dolores waved her goodbye and walked back to the bustling din around the mainstage tent. He closed the door behind me and we were plunged into a temporary darkness. I felt him guide me through the cramped interior to a seat: a mattress not unlike the one I had just come from. My muscles seized. I had never before been in the dark with a man, let alone on a bed in the dark with a man I was warned to run away from. As if reading my tension, he cracked open a shutter such that a single beam illuminated the ornate interior. On every inch of wall, colors mixed together, forming a domed garden overhead. I wanted to reach out and touch the beautiful work, but my nerves would not let me unclamp my fingers from their intertwined state atop my lap. He followed my gaze and regarded the handiwork himself.

"I never had the heart to paint over your work. These flowers always brought me such joy." He gazed at me for a long while with complete adoration, the way I had always wanted to be looked at. I lowered my eyes, his beaming love too intense for me at the moment when his black leather boots came into my focus. His hand reached under my chin and he tilted my face to meet his. He laid his lips on mine so gently I barely knew they were there. I felt immediately a rush of shock and confusion and even the slightest bit of embarrassment. It was my first kiss and I didn't know if I would be any good at it. He pulled his face from mine, pressing his forehead to my own and whispered, "I have missed you so."

Tears sprang to my eyes. I wanted to run away. I didn't know what was happening or who to trust and I just wanted to go home. He wiped away the first tear he saw and sat next to me. "Evie," he said, taking my hands, "I knew you would return. Welcome back to the *Cirque des Spirits*.

I recognized his French. The words caught in my throat. "Am I dead?"

A look of bewilderment flashed across his face. "You seem more alive than you have ever been. Dolores did tell me you hit your head. Would you like to lay down?" His hands moved to my shoulders as if he would lay me down himself.

"No," I said, batting his hands away. "I'm not Evangeline. I don't know who that is."

"Don't be silly," he replied. "I would know your soul anywhere. In fact, I brought you here to let you know that we are having a dance in your honor tonight to celebrate your homecoming."

I couldn't summon a single word to utter in reply. I was completely perplexed by everyone and everything. "I want to go home," I mustered, crying.

He wrapped his arms around me, "You are. You're here with me."

At once, a chorus of screams filled the air and a loud thud as the center post of the main tent collapsed. "Dammit!" Sylas shouted. "Idiots." He jumped up and grabbed his hat and coat from the table top next to the bed. He grabbed the doorknob before turning back to me. "I have a gift for you, there, on the table," he gestured where his coat had been covering a brown box wrapped in a red silk ribbon. "It's for tonight." He tipped his hat to me before popping it on and storming to the hubbub mere yards away.

I watched him through the slit in the shutter. People seemed so afraid of him. And Madame Chantilly's words had me frightened. A party. Homecoming. The kiss. Why did everyone think I was someone else?

My gaze turned to the box on the table. I pulled the ribbon, the knot unwinding into nothingness, and lifted the lid off. On top of the tissue paper was a note:

To my greatest love.
—S.

My stomach lurched. I pushed away the golden tissue paper and found within the box a gown of pure scarlet. The bodice was bedecked with crystals that shined even in the dark caravan. The skirt was a loose tulle with sparkling underlay that moved with ease as I picked the garment up.

A knock at the door startled me. Dolores, again, I predicted and was correct. "Come in," I shouted after she had already begun opening the door.

"We have to start getting ready for the party. It's supposed to start soon—if the men can figure out how to get the tent back up." She laughed at her own joke before interrupting her enjoyment. "Oh that is so very lovely," she said, touching the gown with something akin to reverence. "You are going to look absolutely stunning. Let's go," she shouted, placing the gown back in the box and carrying it while she dragged me by the hand.

My body was exhausted. I just wanted to lay down and sleep, but Dolores would hear of no such thing. She dragged me into a small tent off to the side of the main three. This tent was of a simple white canvas. Judging by the rolled up mattresses and clothes scattered everywhere, the groups of people dabbing makeup on themselves and each other in every corner, this was where all the performers slept and got ready each day. The room silenced as I walked in. Their quiet stares drew the breath from my body until I thought I might suffocate at any moment. But then, as if queued by some invisible conductor, they each turned back to one another and their private banters began again.

Dolores pulled me past a small circle of women in various stages of undress as they examined each others' handiwork: three sewing their costumes, another batting on an extra layer of face powder to stem the sweat as the day grew hotter. She sat me on a small wooden stool and handed me a gilded mirror. She began brushing my hair as I gazed at my own reflection. My simple features were all the same: dark hair, dark eyes. The little freckles that summer brings each year still spotting my cheeks and nose. Still nothing special, and yet, an object of admiration. I didn't see what all the fuss was about. Dolores wound my hair into curls that she pinned and greased the stray hairs into place with some sort of aromatic oil. The process was tedious and I tired of looking at myself. I laid the mirror on my lap and closed my eyes, praying for a few minutes rest in the interim, but the sudden appearance of a new clown turned my plans upside down.

"Good morrow ladies," he called out.

"Rodin, you know you're not supposed to be in here when the women are dressing." The circle of women gave disapproving looks, but said nothing to protest his presence.

"As if any of you could pique my interest in the slightest." Rodin bit into an apple, his white face paint beginning to cake on his sweating brow. He was completely bald and wore his cream white tunic three sizes too big. The large orange and green pom poms hung sloppily from his chest.

He flopped into a chair right in front of me and placed his elbows on his knees, his chin in his palms. "Who are you?" he asked in an almost blasé tone.

I tried to look around, but Dolores had a tight grip on my hair.

"Nice way to speak to the guest of honor at the social event of the season!" Dolores answered.

"Ah, the famed Evangeline. I thought you'd be prettier—what with the way everyone talks about you."

"Me too," I answered. A glimmer of amusement made Rodin's cheek quiver into an almost smile.

"She's a tightrope walker and the best trapeze artist I've ever seen." Dolores pitched in. I smiled, but said nothing. I tried to stop myself from massaging my hands: a nervous tic Carissa liked to point out every time I tried to get a white lie past her. Everyone believed I was Evangeline. I silently prayed they wouldn't ask me to perform Evangeline's skills.

"Ah, another equilibristic act," Rodin interrupted my anxious spiral. "How gauche. You should try juggling. Now *there's* a skill."

"Just because something is difficult for you, doesn't make it the hardest skill in the world. I've seen donkeys juggle," Dolores spat back.

"But did he make it look effortless?" Rodin asked, standing from his stool. "Aye, there's the rub. It's not enough to masterfully manage an infinite number of objects as they soar through the air. One must do so with a an unbroken smile and relaxed shoulders, while standing on one foot and singing *La Marseillaise*." He pulled the pom poms from his tunic and began juggling them, turning his back on Dolores and myself as he strutted out of the tent singing in a robust tenor, *"Allons enfants de la patrie, le jour de gloire est arrivé."*

"Pretentious clown," Dolores muttered under her breath as she brushed and picked and pulled my hair, beating it into submission.

"Are they all like that?" I ventured, hoping a rapport with Dolores might work in my favor.

Without looking up, she answered, "No. Just him. The others are nice enough not to speak." There was a severity in her tone that set me on edge. I doubted very much that their silence was voluntary around here.

I could feel the other women in the tent casting glances at me over their shoulders. Was it pity or jealousy they were shooting at me like darts? I couldn't tell. Only the tug of Dolores' hands on the roots of my hair cemented my impression of this dream world I was in. Pain, isolation, entrapment. Fear. Always fear. Not the blood-pumping, heart racing, cold sweat kind. No. It was the kind of fear that set the hairs on the back of your neck on edge. That prickling, queasy feeling when you know something is off.

Despair cast over me like a shroud and I doubted very much in that moment whether I would ever see my family again.

CHAPTER 5

My hair was done, curled and clipped into an ornate updo that complimented the shape of my face in a way I had never experienced before. Dolores applied a light layer of makeup that accentuated the deep tones of my hair and eyes without looking overdone like some of the other performers in their full stage makeup. I was beautiful. Looking in the gilded mirror, I barely recognized myself, but then I saw myself through the mask. It was me. And I was so lovely.

Dolores helped me into the gown, hanging it over my head in a cloud of crimson. The satin lining felt so nice against my skin and the boning of the bodice barely pinched. It felt natural, right. The skirts made a swooshing sound as I walked through the now empty tent. Everyone was in place already for the celebration to begin. The celebration of me: invisible me.

My breath caught as I managed a glance of myself in the full length mirror just outside where the entire circus cast checked their reflections before performing. I looked right. As if I had always imagined looking this way. As if my entire life I had been trying to be this version of me, but never knew where to begin. I never would have guessed the answer was a red dress outside a magic circus tent. Carissa popped into my mind. I wished she could see me like this. I thought she'd get a kick out of me looking beautiful versus my usual sloppy get-up. I looked like her, in a way. Well, more like her than I ever had. I felt finally like a part of my family. And that realization hurt worst of all. They wouldn't see me. Not in this dress. Not like this. They were somewhere else. I was somewhere else. Thought I didn't know where.

The din of the tent broke my painful reverie: shattered glass and a shout of complaint. Dolores' hand on my back urged me toward the slit in the red and white striped tent and my feet followed though my mind protested. Bodies blocked the path. Where had they all come from? I hadn't seen this many people working the whole day. The scant number of performers and laborers seemed to multiply by an obscene number.

Night had come, casting its shadows over the trees and grass, but inside was bright with yellow stage lights illuminating the ceiling of the tent. Lanterns strung outside gave off an ominous glow.

"Excuse me," Dolores pleaded, pushing me forward still. "Make way. Make way. Coming through."

People obeyed without looking, engrossed in their own conversations. Dolores was still wearing the same floral print dress. The people we past were all dressed in their casual clothing. Only, I was the only one dressed up in the slightest, let alone wearing a gown bedecked with rhinestones and beads, a spectacle in scarlet. As we made our way through the crowd toward the center of the tent, I could hear the faint playing of an orchestra of sorts: a violin, a guitar, an accordion, an organ. Just the faintest workings of music off in the distance.

The people parted before me, forming a circle—in the center of which stood Sylas. He wore a sharp tuxedo. Clean, pressed, neat, impeccable. His shoes, so highly polished, reflected the light as he approached me. At once I could feel every eye on me and a hush came over the tent.

Then music.

The orchestra played a haunting waltz as Sylas smiled at me. He bowed and I, out of instinct or some memory from a past life, curtsied. He held out his hand for mine and I took it. He drew me in as the band played. His hand on my waist controlled me. I went where he wanted. Together we danced in circles around the floor for what seemed like a pleasant eternity. All the fear had left my body. I could feel myself smiling, laughing. The band came to a ritardando, the music slowed and Sylas dipped me, looking deep into my eyes and I could feel every cell in my body shouting, "Yes," at once. Then the tempo picked up and we were off again, making our way through around the circle once more. We beamed at each other, perhaps brighter than all the lights in the tent.

When had our fingers interlaced? When did I lean my body against his? The music came to an end and a blush spread across my face as the audience encircling us applauded loudly. Cheers, whistles. It was louder than the music had ever been. Sylas bent down to whisper in my ear over the shouts of the audience's approval. "We have a special show prepared for you," he said.

He waved his arm in the air and Dolores was back at my side, leading me to a group of attendees who had not made the cut for this evening's performance given the inflated number of performers around. Two women and three men: the women in plain dresses, the men in slacks and white undershirts. A waiter came by in a white shirt and black bow tie with a tray of champagne in crystal flutes. He held it out to me and I looked around, confused.

"Oh, I don't drink," I said nervously.

"Since when?" Dolores asked and the group erupted in laughter. Blushing, I took the drink from the tray and sipped it, the sparkling contents immediately giving me a headache.

The lights dimmed and the circle widened to give more room to the performers. A spotlight shone on a man holding a unicycle in his hands. The woman next to me visibly rolled her eyes and giggled at the man to her left. The performer continued. He placed the unicycle on the ground and steadied his weight atop it. Riding around the circle's perimeter, pulling out three small balls and juggling them passively, nodding his head to whomever he locked eyes with as he made his rounds. He was met with a bored applause and so he upped the ante. Heading into the middle of the circle, still atop the unicycle, he dropped his three balls to the ground and pulled out four knives, demonstrating for the audience how sharp they are by slicing his finger. After a brief moment, a drop of blood emerged and my insides tightened.

He balanced himself in the jerky way unicyclists must and started juggling the four daggers, tossing them in the air as if they were nothing more than the balls he used earlier. He made his rounds again, around the perimeter of the stage area and we all clapped vigorously. He paused a moment to absorb the applause before tossing each dagger into the ground and alighting from the unicycle. He held the one-wheeled contraption over his head and we all cheered as loud as we could, thankful, myself, that the stress of witnessing his act was over.

Next up was a pair of acrobats: a married couple wearing red and blue body suits. He walked onto the stage with his wife seated on his shoulder as the cyclist walked off, his time gone. The wife stood up on her husband's shoulders and motioned for the audience to cheer. When she was satisfied, she tucked her head and flipped down to the ground where she landed in a straddle split. Her husband picked up her legs by her feet and flipped her back up into the air where she stood on his hands, waving to the audience that cheered wildly. She balanced herself on one of his hands and lifted her other leg into the sky, holding it there as her husband marched in a circle, carrying her in the precarious pose until he returned to the center of the stage and she cartwheeled out of his hand and stood next to him.

It wasn't until she held her arms in the air in her final pose that I realized my hands were clasped against my face. Countless times I thought her joints would break or she would fall as her husband seemed to toss her around the stage like a rag doll, but each movement was performed with a bright smile on her face and absolute control. It was astounding. I wished I were that flexible or strong.

The couple backflipped their way off the stage, seven in a row, sticking the last one and waving as they disappeared back into the crowd and the next performer took the stage: a strong man. But I wouldn't watch him.

"Sylas is evil," came a voice behind me.

"What?" I asked, peering around to see if anyone could overhear. "Who are you?"

"Penny. Your grandma was right about him." A woman with unnaturally red hair appeared to my left. I hadn't noticed that the group around me had changed. Penny wore a black corset with thick shoulder straps laced all the way up and a skirt with black and white vertical stripes that reached only down to her midcalf. Black boots covered all that should not be seen by society's standards. Her hair wound itself into voluptuous pigtails that framed her highly made-up face.

"My grandma?"

"She told me about him a long time ago. Told me to get away, but I didn't listen."

"I don't understand."

She rolled her eyes. "All of us know that you're not Evangeline. He just wishes you were."

"Am I dead?" I asked, uncomfortable that I had to ask this same question twice in one day.

"No. But you're not really alive either. It's hard to explain, but when your soul comes too close to a black hole like Sylas, he can just," she made a slurping sound, "suck you into his realm."

I spotted Sylas at the side of the tent, preparing the next performer. "Alfonso…"

"That's his stage name. He doesn't want people up there knowing who he really is."

My mind reeled. Up there. What did that mean? Were we in Hell? Purgatory? Hades? "Is he a—" my mind searched for the word. "A demon?"

"No," Penny whispered, "He's an evil man with a lot of power. Everyone here is trapped in the construct of a madman's imagination."

"We're," I began, but my thought sounded too ridiculous to continue on. I pushed through though, "We're in his head?"

"It's all an illusion. All of it. Can't you hear the music? He delights in mocking us."

I strained my ears to listen and picked up the softest woman's voice singing along to the circus waltz that played loudly over her.

"He keeps us where he wants us
and he wants us close at hand.
Whatever you have dreamed of,
that's what the man has planned.

He gives you pure illusion,
your life in ecstasy
Until you dance the dance he loves,
The Soul Collector's Rhapsody

My cheeks burned at the words: Soul Collector. I looked to Penny who stood stock still with a grim expression on her face. She had heard the song before.

Had I given up my life already? With one dance? My first. I couldn't think. Only a picture of Sophie flashed in front of my eyes and would not go away. Her little face. Those squishy cheeks she's had since she was a baby that I always loved to mush. Her wispy almost-white hair. Those deep blue eyes. Would I ever see her again? Or Carissa? Or my father?

The song picked up its tempo. I hadn't been listening as I thought of my family, but it caught my attention once more.

Time is up, my dear, let's go.
You haven't got a chance.
He's been searching so long for you—
this century's old romance.

Over, under, through the hoop:
we jump at his command.
Sylas makes his call
and you must join his band.

"You have to get out," Penny breathed to me.

"But how?" I asked through tears.

I could feel at once behind me a malevolent presence. Rage has that certain feeling that radiates throughout the air.

"Do I not give you food to eat?" Sylas asked of the redhead. "A bed to sleep in? When I found you, were you not begging for scraps of food, freezing in the cold?"

Her countenance shifted. Fear etched itself through her every feature. She turned and walked briskly away before Sylas turned to me. "And you. You don't drink," he said, taking the glass of champagne from my hand.

"I didn't want it," I stuttered, fearing his ire.

"Good. Then it won't be missed."

He threw the glass over his shoulder and grabbed me by the elbow. His grip was fierce and harsh. It stung the bone. I could feel my brow furrowed into a fearful expression. No one seemed to mind the scene: bumping into other guests, the fury in his eyes as he dragged me to the far end of the tent and threw me through a new flap that led only to darkness.

CHAPTER 6

Sylas was gone. I was alone for the first time in what felt like eternity. There was the vaguest sense that I was in some kind of hallway. A slight chill in the air and the echo of my shoes reverberating into the ether suggested the passageway of some drafty, old house though I couldn't find the walls. I hugged my bare arms against the cold, my breath twisting in wisps as I exhaled smoke. A vague glow appeared at the end of the hallway. Just the faintest tendril of golden light like the crack of a door. I hesitated, unsure what awaited me ahead, but only darkness lay behind, so I pressed forward. Warmth radiated from the doorway, blanketing the surrounding area with its comforting aura. I pressed my face against the door jamb and peered, blinking, into the light.

Inside was a study: ornately carved wood paneling decorated the walls without bookshelves. Leatherbound tomes of green and red and blue filled the shelves. Next to the fireplace, which illuminated the room more than the brass sconces on the walls, a gray-haired man stood, leaning his forehead against the mantle as he leaned in frustration against the fiery hearth.

"Evangeline," he pleaded and the name caught my ear. I turned my head in the crack of the door to find the subject and, seated in a red leather armchair was a black-haired woman with my own dark eyes. I saw the resemblance immediately and wanted to call out. She seemed older than me, but not by much. Perhaps in her early-twenties at most. Her hair was curled in ringlets that framed her simple, pale face. Her white dress glowed ivory in the yellow light of the fire. Her face was turned down, focusing on the oriental rug beneath her feet. Her hands clasped together in her lap, mouth closed tightly. "Why must you test me?" the man continued. "I raised you to be better than this. Years of tutors and training, etiquette school and for what? So you could run away with the circus?"

"Papa," Evangeline pled, "I love it. I love performing so much. And I'm good at it. I never dreamed I could feel so much joy."

"It's that boy you love, that magician," he spat. "He's no good for you. I won't hear anymore of this. My decision is final. Now, go to your room."

Evangeline stood. She was taller than me and thinner. It seemed as if she was wasting away, but she held herself with the deportment of a warrior. "Papa," she said, her voice stern, but choking back tears, "This is what I love to do. This is what I want. This is how I want to spend my life. I'm going. I love Sylas and I'm going with him. Any other life would be meaningless." She headed toward me, toward the door before she paused and turned back to her father. "I didn't want to leave like this. I wish you could have been happy for me."

"Happy?" he shouted. "Happy that you are throwing your life away? Happy that you are bringing disgrace to this family? Happy that you consider this life, our life meaningless? I'd rather see you dead than gussied up like some common whore, begging for money while your fleabag husband leaves you once the slightest tinge of youth fades from your cheek." He picked up the fire poker from beside the fireplace and banged it against the metal cage in front of the fire. "I'd rather see you dead!" I could see her muscles tense at the sound and she spun around to run away. He threw the poker to the side and ran toward her. "Get back here," he shouted. "You will not leave." He tackled her to the ground, pulling her hair and beating her face. She fought against him, slapping him and kicking her legs, but she was too weak to fight him off. He pummeled her, throwing punch after punch that would have left even the strongest man weak. When his energy ran out, he sat atop her limp body, gazing down at her bloodied features. He caught his breath a moment and cooed, "Evangeline?" But there was no answer. He pushed a lock of matted hair from her sweating face as life slowly escaped her body.

I was immediately sick and scared. I clung to the doorframe trying hard not to breathe to avoid making any noises. Where could I go? What could I do? Should I have jumped in and saved Evangeline? Is that what I was brought here to do? Why me? Why her?

Questions flooded my brain, but before I could even fathom what to say or do a cry cut through my thoughts.

"No!" Sylas' voice called out from down the hall. Another small crack of light appeared ahead of me and I stumbled away from the murder scene to follow the voices. I needed to gather myself a bit before I could muster the strength to look inside. I took a breath and opened my eyes then peered around the doorframe. He was in the center of a dark, empty room. The only light shining down from directly above him. He clutched a small photograph of Evangeline in his hands. He wept openly, holding the photo to his heart and rocking back and forth.

"You were my love," he cried, "You were my only love. We were supposed to be together. We were supposed to travel the world. To get married and have babies and live on our own terms. Couldn't they see the joy? Couldn't they see our love? We were supposed to be together forever. Forever." He broke down in tears and seemed unable to speak, save the words, "My heart. My heart," repeated twice. After a moment, he calmed himself and looked down at her photograph, tracing the lines of her face as he spoke, "He took that. He took that from you. From me. I swear to you, Evangeline. I swear to you that I will find you, wherever your beautiful soul rests. I will find the music of your spirit. I will find the brilliance of your heart. I will comb through Heaven and Hell 'til I find you once more. And I promise with every fiber of my being that you will be happy for the rest of eternity."

My heart broke to hear him cry, to see him so bare. The energy of the building or construct, whatever it was I was in, radiated his emotions. Everything was somehow even colder and darker. He wanted me. Wanted my soul. And isn't that what everyone is always looking for? Someone who loves their very essence? I could give him what he wanted. I could give myself to him. And then, perhaps, he wouldn't need to hurt anymore people. He would have what he wanted. He would have what he had been searching all this time for. And I could live here. I could live in the sparkle of the circus. I could feed the animals and have tea with Dolores and take care of Madame Chantilly. I could live that life if it meant—

A hand reached out and grasped my shoulder, turning my body around at once. A woman stood before me: glowing and brilliant. Blonde-haired and green-eyed. Her clothes were modern enough to stand out from the dress of the circus folk: a tea length skirt and a plain blouse, but I couldn't make out their color beyond the bright light of her aura. I didn't know the curve of her jaw as it formed a heart shaped point from ear to chin or the way her lips turned down at each corner as if she was born to be sad. I didn't know her at all except that something in me reached out to her as her gaze fell on me. Her hand was cold where it lay on my shoulder and I couldn't help but to gawk at her.

"You have to leave," she said.

"Who are you?" I asked, my mind too fatigued to process her demand.

She faded before my eyes and reappeared yards ahead of me. "Leave now," she said. And her body disappeared and reappeared farther and farther away.

I gave chase. She was either leading me to the exit or into danger, but either way something in this building did not sit well with me. Sylas wanted me to stay, yes. But something bigger wanted me to leave.

I ran toward her, away from Sylas' spotlighted monologue. My footsteps echoed loudly, my breath turned ragged.

"Amelia." A woman's voice resounded like ripples on a lake. But it was not the same spirit I was following. A second figure caught my eye as I ran, just the impression of a woman off to the right. As I neared, she came into focus: long, braided hair that covered a t-shirt tucked into her jeans with a thick belt around her waist. "Amelia," she called out again and I paused. Ahead of me the first spirit blinked farther and farther away until her light dimmed to a mere memory. To my right, the new spirit beamed brighter. "Come to me. Let's go," she said.

I closed my eyes. No choice felt right.

"Amelia," Sylas called from behind me. And my legs took off toward the new spirit before my mind could even place his voice. She glowed next to me, lighting the way down the hall. By her light I could see the hardwood floor beneath us with a narrow strip of rug running just beneath my feet. The walls were a forest green and punctuated with paintings every two feet of women from different time periods looking morosely from the canvas.

"There's a way out, but you can't slow down. Keep running, my love," the spirit shouted. It was then that I recognized the rolled up sleeves of her t-shirt. The cuffed jeans and the combat boots. The face I only knew from a single photograph I stowed away when my father cleared out the house in a raging stupor. The woman I had so many questions about, but could never ask for fear of upsetting him.

My mother.

I nearly tripped as recognition dawned on me. My mouth went dry, my legs weak. I could barely keep myself up, but I knew I had to keep running. "Amelia," Sylas taunted behind me.

Tears sprung to my eyes. I couldn't pick which question to ask. Where were we? Why was she here? Why was I here? Where were we headed? How would I get out? Was she coming with me? Back into our world?

"I can't answer everything," my mother answered, reading the concern on my face. "He brought you here to show you Evangeline's fate. To gain your sympathy, but you must not give it to him. *He* killed Evangeline when she refused him. And since that day he has traveled the world, drawing in every woman that reminds him of her. That's what happened to me."

The floor started to shake beneath my feet and staying upright proved more difficult than ever before. It felt like being at sea during a major storm, tossed on the waves like some ragdoll. "He's breaking down the construct."

"What?"

"You're in his consciousness. We all are. We're trapped here, but I will save you. You won't become like us." Her light had grown so bright I couldn't help, but look around. Running beside us was an army of women with clothing from times as early as the Victorian era to what had to be no more than five years ago. All of them charged with the same determination plastered on their face. Skirts swooshed, ponytails bobbed. Each woman was so young. None more than even twenty-five years old. Were all these women lost to the world like my mother? There one moment and gone the next? How many mothers were missing? How many daughters?

"Amelia," Sylas taunted once more.

I felt a cold shove from behind as a brilliant flash of light blinded me. My mother's voice called out, "The only way out is through his heart." I could feel the explosion of energy dissipate at once. The women, my protectors, were gone.

Once the light faded and I was able to open my eyes once more, I found myself in the same study where Evangeline had died not minutes earlier with Sylas staring back at me.

CHAPTER 7

SYLAS STOOD BEFORE ME, SMILING. "MY DEAREST AMELIA, DO YOU know who you are?" He took a step toward me and an audible crack of electricity tensed his body up. They were still with me.

"Yes," I answered, "Do you?"

He grinned. "I knew you before you even existed. You possess within you the bloodline of a very strong woman. My Evangeline. Your light shines like a beacon. I could find you anywhere." His words felt like a threat. He knew I was trying to leave. "It's so very nice to meet the newest incarnation of my beloved." He moved toward me again and another zap of energy annoyed him.

"I'm not your beloved. I'm Amelia McConnell. I'm a sophomore at Great Falls High. I'm in the art club and I work at the movie theatre on Fridays and Saturdays." I said, standing. With their protection, I felt emboldened. I was speaking up to him for them. For the ones who couldn't.

"Your soul is so old. Did you know it dates back to Cleopatra?" His voice was low and suspiciously calm. He seated himself on the edge of a desk set in the back corner of the room, eyeing me ravenously. The windows were covered with thick red curtains that blocked any light that might have entered the room, if there were any. I could not tell what time of day it was nor if time even existed in this world.

"I have Cleopatra's soul?" I asked, unamused. In the real world I would have been delighted to be told such a thing. But here, under these circumstances and by Sylas, I was not interested. Everything felt like a lie.

"Part of it, at least. Souls fracture with loss and rejoin with love. That's why it was so important for me to find you. So that I could rejoin with the soul of my sweet Evangeline and go on for eternity with her." He peeled his gaze from me and landed on a portrait above the fireplace of Evangeline, sitting uncomfortably in a green armchair.

"All those women," I said, searching the room for a weapon and finding the fire poker Evangeline's father had thrown earlier, placed back in its proper place on the stand by the fire. I would have to get close to Sylas to get to the weapon. And that I would have to do slowly. Seductively. I wanted to puke at the thought, but there was too much at stake. "Evangeline looks so like me. It's clear we share the same soul," I lied, "So why did you go after all those other women?"

"It was all in pursuit of you," he said, pushing himself off the desk and receiving a shock, though it seemed less intense than the last two as he smiled through it. Either he was becoming accustomed to them or the spirits were losing power.

I walked toward him, steeling my nerves as best I could. "I do so love to see those eyes once more," he breathed. He touched my face and instantly I could feel the hatred coursing through him. I could see Evangeline crying before me. Hear her tearful voice cry out, "I won't go with you, Sylas. I do not love you." I could feel his rage build, feel the fire burn. I watched as his hands wrapped around her neck. As he bashed her head against the pavement of the alleyway they had stolen into to have a private chat. I saw the life leave her body by his hands, her eyes staring vacant, face bloodied and broken. And then her face changed to the face of the first spirit I encountered here. It changed to the ponytailed cheerleader. To Penny. To Madame Chantilly. Dolores. He killed them all and I saw their final moments. The last face to cross my view was my mother's, alive. She was headed to the ladies room during a break in the circus performance when I watched him lure her out of the arena, sending a decoy spirit disguised as a toddler to run through the exit of the arena. She chased after what she thought was her own child, broken away from my father's careful watch, and found, instead Sylas, yearning to be loved. He tried to charm her, but she wasn't interested, being more concerned with locating her daughter than a man on the street. And when she rejected him, he consumed her.

I could feel the next zap as it shot him backward, convulsing on his back atop the desk. Papers shifted under his weight. He knocked a gilded photo frame onto the decorative rug beneath. This was my chance. I rushed to the fire poker and grabbed the metal handle. It was heavier than I had anticipated and I struggled to keep the cumbersome weapon aloft. He groaned, unable to sit himself back up at first, but sensing my preparedness to puncture his pericardium he rose up nonetheless.

"Amelia," he said in a manner too calm to be sincere, "You are everything I have searched for in this world. Years. Years I have longed to see those eyes. Those soulful eyes that know me without knowing me. My love. My only love. Though time separates us and memories do not keep, I know that you are there. I know. If you would only close your eyes and see what I see."

He pushed himself from the desk once more and this time no zap prompted him to keep back.

"I have seen what you see. I know what you have done and no one would do those things out of love," I shouted.

He took a step toward me and then another. It was as if he had not suffered a blow at all. He was confident, smiling once more and I hated him all over again. My heart raced. My hands became instantly clammy and I struggled to find the strength to grip the poker let alone keep it up much longer. My arms trembled in time with my knees. I bit down to steady my teeth so that he wouldn't hear them chatter.

"All the pieces need to be together. Our family. Our friends. These spirits are the souls of our loved ones. Each a piece of the beautiful picture we dreamed up together."

"I didn't dream anything with you." I dug my heels into the ground as he took another step. And another.

"I know. It's been so long, my dear. And I am happy to woo you all over again if you will only put the poker down and remember the wonderful world I built for us."

"A circus? That's your wonderful gift to your beloved? A circus of tortured performers, half working against you? This is what you've taken countless lives for? For my soul? I don't remember you and *if* I promised you my soul it would be a soul that doesn't remember you. Evangeline never came back for you. Don't you see that? She didn't want you. You've been chasing this girl for centuries, destroying every life you come into just so you could try to recapture the heart of someone who didn't love you back in the first place? Why would I say yes to you? How do I know you wouldn't just keep on collecting spirits for your *Cirque des Spirits*? Do you even remember what you loved about Evangeline or only *that* you loved her.

Fury swept across his face. My mother's words rang through my head. The only way out was through his heart. But this man had no heart. I doubted he was even a man. My mind flitted back to the room where he wept. Where he rocked back forth, clutching the photo to his breast.

"Everyone who came with me here, came by choice. They wanted to be with me and I, them. Even your mother."

My blood boiled instantly. It would feel so good to shove this makeshift spear right between his eyes. "Don't talk about my mother."

He lunged toward me and time slowed to an almost standstill. I gripped the poker as tight as I could. Before he could reach me, with mere millimeters separating us, I smashed the pointed end of the weapon through the portrait of Evangeline. The portrait tore away like paper and the walls crumbled as I bolted through the opening and away from the grasp of Sylas.

His protests echoed through the darkness, but I didn't dare look back.

CHAPTER 8

Before I knew what was happening, I found myself on the stage of the Aldritch Center. Tanya stood beside me beaming, her arms raised up in a triumphant fan above her head as she and I both stood atop a long black box. Alfonso was below us, on the ground at my other side, his arms in the same celebratory Y, though far less enthusiastic than his assistant. It looked as if he had just performed the "Sawing His Assistant In Half" trick. How apt for him. It was clear from his expression that he had not expected me to reappear.

The audience roared. How long had I been gone? It felt like days. As I hopped down from the box after Tanya descended, Sylas—or Alfonso in this world—looked as if he wanted to eat me alive. But with an arena full of witnesses, what could he do to me? I scampered offstage, past the chain smoking clowns sat on boxes of props and overworked security staff trying not to freak out about the lion roaring feet away from them, however toothless the king of the jungle may be.

Through the double doors and into the fluorescent-lit hallway with the beat-up tile floor, and beyond the double doors marked "Staff Only" that I had gone through earlier that night, I spotted, out of the corner of my eye, the head of the boy I'll never forget. He ducked through the exit doors and I fought the urge to run after him. The memory of my mother's path forever burned into my psyche.

Carissa and Sophie were there. They were waiting for me. They wanted me to be with them. And, what's more important: I wanted to be with them. I pulled my gaze from Robbie's curly locks disappearing through the door and made my way through the central hallway of the arena, into our section and down the steps where my little sister could barely remain seated.

"How did you do that!?" she shouted at me. Half-delight, half-bewilderment.

"A girl can do amazing things with the right pair of shoes and a good attitude." I spoke with a nasal, transatlantic accent and raised my eyebrows several times in rapid succession.

Sophie giggled hysterically. Carissa winked as she reached behind Sophie and draped her arm around me as well. The three of us tilted our heads into a family hug as Alfonso left the stage and the bumbling ringleader stepped back into the spotlight.

"Do you think we can go?" I asked Carissa, the desire to get as far away from Sylas or Alfonso or whoever he was as quickly as possible finally setting in.

Carissa and Sophie nodded emphatically. "I can't imagine the rest of this show being any good."

"Not without Amelia starring in it," Sophie added as she hopped out of her seat and led the way into the central corridor and out the doors to the packed parking lot.

"Where did I park?" Carissa asked, fishing her keys out of her purse as I grabbed Sophie's hand. The evening had warmed up considerably and Sophie no longer needed Carissa's coat to stay warm. The streetlights cast their downward light on the rows of cars. No movement in sight. Everything was calm and peaceful.

As we stepped off the curb, a small breeze caressed my cheek. It felt warm and familiar. "Amelia," I heard a woman's whisper carry on the wind and I knew. I knew my mother was there with me. That she was watching me now, in my world, and no longer trapped in the construct of Sylas' mind. That the spirits of Sylas' circus were at rest at last and the cycle was broken.

I freed them. They saved me and I saved them.

A thought nudged at me as the three of us walked to the minivan. Alfonso was still around. He still walked the same streets as me. What was to stop him from returning? Or trying to collect another soul?

I didn't know. Only that I would prepare myself as best I could in case that day should come. The library would be my best friend and, where that failed, the occult bookstore two towns over. I would learn. And I would teach others to protect themselves.

And I would never go to the circus again.

ABOUT C.M. LANDER

C. M. Lander is an emerging voice in the fantasy and science fiction genre. She holds a bachelor's degree in Creative Writing from Hofstra University where she focused on her first love—poetry. She has been featured as Tumblr's Poet of the Day, placed 2nd in the Bartleby Snopes' Dialog-Only Contest, and has been published by Newsday and ProtestPoems.org, among other publications.

Ms. Lander is currently a student of law and is devoted to marrying her love of writing with philanthropic causes.

CONNECT ON SOCIAL MEDIA

facebook.com/authorcmlander
instagram.com/authorcmlander

ALSO BY C.M. LANDER

Friendless: A Novella

THE RINGMASTER

JESSICA JULIEN

CHAPTER 1

MY BOOTS SQUISHED INTO THE MUD AS I FOLLOWED MY FATHER'S bouncing top hat and twirling cane. It didn't seem as though the guck was even bothering him as he stepped quickly and lightly through the puddles that had accumulated from last nights downpour.

"This really couldn't have waited until the ground dried up? we had to come out here *today*?" I asked him with a heavy sigh and shook off the thick mud that stuck to my sneakers.

"No, of course not. We have to begin working now if we want to draw any sort of crowd for the fall," my father said not looking back at me. His eyes were glued to the mass before him—a pile of red and white striped fabric rustled in the soft summer breeze.

"I don't understand, what is it?" Before today, my father had been very cryptic and mysterious about the special surprise. I overheard him speaking with my mother one night about it, saying it was going to be our new "family thing", but my mother opposed the secret right away, telling him he was "chasing the impossible".

"You'll see," he said rubbing his hands together with excitement. A group of men approached from behind the mound with poles and stakes in their hands.

"Sir," a man with broad shoulders and a thin mustache said, bowing his head slightly in a gentle tilt.

"Yes, let's begin." He motioned to the others with his cane before leaning on it heavily. I watched as it slowly sank into the mud and rolled my eyes. We stood watching the men lift and heave the thick material up onto the poles, listened as they argued over how to assemble it correctly, and finally after a final grunt effortlessly lifted the massive form up off the ground.

It was enormous and unlike anything I've ever seen in person. The red and white stripes that lined the circumference were faded and dull but held firm against the breeze that wafted through them. The arched top reached high as if attempting to touch the sun itself, casting a thick, dark shadow behind it.

"Seriously?" I turned to look at my father whose smile reached from ear to ear. He was beaming, excited, and looked ten years younger. It was as if this monstrosity released a new kind of light within him, softening the wrinkles and wear and tear from his life working in the mill. A twinkle shone in his faded blue eyes as he shifted to see me.

"Isn't it great?" He chuckled.

"Dad," I sighed shaking my head. It was just another one of his business schemes—another one that wouldn't work—and I knew he had just wasted our entire savings on it. My mother was right to tell him it was a bad idea. "This is...I just...why?"

"We could make a fortune off of this, don't you think?" He was watching the men stake down the edges of the tent with a new sense of determination.

"How? We don't know how to perform or anything," I ran my fingers through my thick hair and wiped the sweat from my brow. "This is just another one of your insane ideas." I turned to leave but felt his long fingers wrap around my arm and pull me back.

"Don't talk to your father that way, you will respect me whether you want to or not," his happiness was replaced by anger—an emotion I often saw. My father's voice was filled with deep hatred for me and I felt it pulsated toward me. We stood there glaring at each other as we both attempted to calm down, knowing we were in public, not behind the closed doors of our home where people didn't know what transpired with our hatred.

"Mr. Monroe?" one of the men called from the tent. My father turned toward them with a smile, and I pulled my arm free of him and ran across the muddied field back to the parking lot, where my bike was parked next to my father's rusty, dented car. I was still six months away from getting my license—not that I'd get a car when I turned sixteen—so I was left to hop on my bike and peddle home.

My mother was cooking dinner when I rushed through the front door.

"Can you believe him?" I walked to the fridge and yanked the door open. Grabbing a can of brown soda, I flopped down into our small breakfast table. The edges were cracked, and the thin table runner covered the wear and tear from years of breakfasts I shared with my mother before running off to school.

"Huh, dear?" My mother asked looking over her shoulder at me. The steam from the pot of noodles wrapped around her already frizzy bun. My mother was lovely, and at one point she was probably beautiful, but the ravages of time from our father were held heavy in her face. She herself had to cover it up just as we did the table.

"Dad," I shook my head. "He's insane!"

"So you've seen it?" I heard her sigh heavily.

"Yes, what is he thinking? We can't possibly run something like that!"

"You know how your father is," she forced a smile. "He gets so excited about these new adventures. We need to just support him." She placed her small, frail hand on my shoulder, and I nodded my head.

"Okay," I said standing to give her a quick kiss on the cheek.

"Go wash up. Dinner will be ready soon."

As I came down the stairs, I heard the front door slam shut. I froze waiting to hear where the footsteps would lead. My father stormed into the kitchen with a trail of fury behind him. It was as if I could see his anger drifting around him in a hazy grey hue. I shook the image out of my head and tiptoed down the steps.

"Where is he?" He growled, grabbing my mother's arm hard. I saw her wince and pulled myself out from my hiding place.

"I'm here," I said quietly.

"How dare you embarrass me today like that. Do you know how hard I work to ensure this family has a roof over their heads and food on the table? Do you think your school clothes and books are free?"

I looked to my mother who stood with sad eyes and wrapped one arm around herself.

"Answer me!" he shouted, and I saw my mother's aura shift from a worried blue to a pulsing orange of fear.

"N-No, I know they're not free," I stuttered.

"Then why would you go out of your way to make me look like a fool in front of my new crew by running off like that?"

"I'm sorry, I just don't understand," I said, as my father slammed his fist on the table making the silverware jump and a glass of water to tip over. Quickly, my mother reached for a towel and began blotting it up with shaking hands.

"You would understand if you stuck around to listen to our plan, but you decided it was better to just leave. Now my crew thinks I have no control over my idiotic son."

"I'm sorry, dad. It won't happen again." I hung my head to show my submission, a trick I learned very young to avoid a painful recoil if I continued to look him in the eye.

"I know it won't," he took a beer from the fridge, slammed the lid against the counter making the top clatter to the floor, and sat down at the table. "Tomorrow you and your mother will join me to finalize our game plan. We need to get the show up and running as quickly as possible."

"Yes, dad."

"Good, now sit. I'm starving. Tonight we eat, tomorrow we begin."

I took a seat across from him and let my mother fill my plate with cheesy pasta and a small salad. Without looking up from my dinner, I ate and listened to the sounds of my father and mother discussing how they would conduct and run our very own family circus.

CHAPTER 2

MY DAD HAD A GIFT—A TALENT I SUPPOSE—TO BE ABLE TO MANIPULATE people's thoughts. It was some psychic thing he claimed, and as I sat there watching him interview act after act for the circus, I could see him using this ability to ensure he would get the best ones. He spoke with acrobats, lion tamers, clowns, magicians, and more and with each one he gripped their hands between his and looked them in the eyes asking them to join his new troop.

"We would *love* to have you join us. Please say yes," he said to each one, and as if falling into a trance his favorite acts slowly nodded with glassy eyes. As he released his hold on them, I watched as they shook off the pull of persuasion and regained their former consciousness, as they signed the contract that would hold them to a promise they didn't know they made.

"Why don't you try this time?" My father asked me. He had always hoped that I would have the same power as him and be able to get anything I wanted out of life. I never understood why he didn't use this gift to get a high paying job or use it to gain a role in the ownership of a bank or agency, but he refused and only used it to control his own creations—like the circus. He said he wanted it to be his very own, to be his and no one else's, and he wouldn't take someone else's idea from them. It didn't make sense to me, but I was not my father.

"No, I can't." I shook my head, knowing that no matter how hard I tried to get people to do what I wanted — give me a candy bar from the gas station, A+ on a science paper—no one fell into my deadly trap.

"Maybe if you just *tried*," he glared at me, reaching for my arm. "Here, Ms. Tink would like to go next. She has a tiger act." I rolled my eyes and stood next to my father who waved over the next act. Ms. Tink took the stage under the big top, and my heart dropped from my chest.

She was radiant, gorgeous, and the most beautiful person I had ever seen. Her aura glowed a brilliant pink around her, as she twisted and turned around a small tiger cub that danced on its hind legs and spun in circles. Her ebony hair was twisted up into a tight bun on top of her head with a few trailing curls that fell around her face. I could see the mossy green of her eyes glowing from where I stood as she laughed and cooed at the tiger cub.

When her act was finished, my father clapped and reached for her as she walked toward him.

"Well done, very well done indeed Ms. Tink. That was absolutely amazing." He held her hand tight as she tried to pull away.

"Thank you," she smiled and nodded her head, glancing a look at me.

"Tell me, how do you get the tiger to listen to your commands?"

"I'm just good with animals I guess," she began, but quickly I saw the pull of my father's gift take control as her eyes glazed over and went into a deep stare into nothingness.

"Tell me the truth, how do you manage to control them?" he asked with a stern voice.

"They can hear me," she said. "I can hear them. We communicate in a unique way."

"Ah," my father looked at me. "She has a gift too. Here, take her hand and get her to sign a contract." He shoved her hands into mine and watched me strain to push the ability he thought I had out and around her. My father had told me before it was like a blanket that you wrapped around the person. With deep concentration, you could force the thought or idea into their head. As soon as you could get it locked into place, they accepted it and took it as their own. It was something I had tried a hundred times before and failed at. All it did was make me look like a creep.

"We would love if you joined us," I began watching her eyes lose their glaze. She blinked and looked at me as if forgetting I had been here the whole time. "Please join us."

"Y-yes, of course. I would be thrilled to join," she squeezed my hands and pulled away as my father clapped her on the shoulder and handed her a pen to sign the contract. My stomach was filled with butterflies and knots as the feeling of excitement and horror filled me. Ms. Tink could be the greatest thing that I've seen, but she had no idea what she was getting herself into.

"I look forward to working with you. We meet next week to being rehearsing and will have our show schedule by then as well." Ms. Tink nodded at my father, shot me an eager smile, and raced off to her friend that had driven her and her two tiger cubs to the tryout.

"I'm glad that your ability is beginning to come through," my father said to me as he shuffled the contracts and slipped them into his briefcase. Putting his satin top hat back upon his head, he left. It was the first time I had ever felt as though my father were proud of me, and I couldn't make myself tell him the truth—I didn't persuade her, she decided on her own. For fear of what could follow at home if I were to reveal my empty ability, I kept it to myself.

It was the worst mistake I could have made.

CHAPTER 3

WHEN MY FATHER DISCOVERED I DID NOT, IN FACT, HAVE THE ABILITY to manipulate or persuade people, he took it out on me with a new kind of force that landed me in the hospital with a dislocated shoulder, a black eye, and two bruised ribs.

"Jacob, can you tell me how this happened again?" The third doctor asked. This one wore a different colored set of scrubs and had a thick file in his hands. His white hair was slicked back and the wire-rimmed glasses in his pocket were bent and scratched. Looking over the chart at the end of the bed, he began jotting down notes.

"It was a bike accident, just I-lost control of it I guess," I shrugged.

"Well, some of these injuries don't line up with that kind of crash. Are you sure nothing else happened? No fights with a friend or anything like that?" He continued to question. This doctor didn't buy my story, and I couldn't blame him. How does someone get a black eye from crashing their bike? Answer: they don't—not normally anyways.

"No, nothing like that. I only have a few friends and we don't fight like that." I clicked the TV on and flipped through the few channels they provided until I saw a *Star Wars* movie and stopped. I wasn't paying enough attention to know which one, and I didn't care. I just wanted to distract myself so I didn't tell him the truth and get myself killed. I heard him sigh and felt the bed shift as he sat at the end.

"Is everything okay at home?" he said, carefully watching my face for any sign of deception. What he didn't know was that this wasn't the first time I had been admitted, not the first time I spun lies to make them believe something else, and it wouldn't be the last. I was good at this. This was a game I had been playing since I was very young.

"Yes, everything is great actually. My dad is starting up his own circus," I forced a smile and hoped it reached my eyes. My mother came back into the room holding a cup of coffee and a small bag of snacks.

"Oh, hello," she nodded at the doctor. "I'm Jacob's mother, can I help you with anything?" The old doctor stood and shook his head.

"No, I'm all set here, thank you." He turned to me one last time. "Jacob, if you ever need anything, anyone to talk to, my office is on the third floor. Come find me." I gave him a nod and thanked him as he left.

"What was that about?" my mother asked, sitting in the chair and sipping her coffee.

"Nothing, just more routine questions," I told her, as she nodded slowly.

I was released the next day with a prescription for painkillers that I would never fill. I never did, as the pain would remind me to tell the truth from now on until I healed completely. It worked as a personal punishment to myself to ensure it never happened again.

My father was muttering over a messy stack of papers on the kitchen table, a bottle of bourbon next to him. He looked up as I grabbed a glass to fill with water.

"Everything good?" He glared.

"Yeah, just some bumps and bruises," I gulped.

"Good, sit down." He drank down the last of his glass and refilled it with what I'd learned quickly were three shots of dark amber liquid. The time I only measured two, I ended up with a bloody nose and a broken finger. Since then I was careful to be exact, and I knew precisely where the liquid would hit in the glass.

I looked over his pile and saw maps with arrows and scribbles, and a pad of paper with cities listed with a few scratched out. Sipping my water, I watched him tap the pen against the table and quickly write down another location. He circled it on the map, connecting it to a nearby one.

"Are these for the show?" I asked carefully. He nodded and turned the map toward me.

"We can start here," he pointed to our city. "Since people know us, we can spread the word quickly. Then we will move east," he continued moving the pen to the next circle. "And continue north before looping back west and dropping down south."

"So, we do a big loop around the country," I asked.

"Precisely." He pulled the map back to him and examined it again.

"What about those states in the middle?" I wondered, noticing the big gap in the center of the map.

"If we can make time, we will hit them. Especially here," he pointed to Utah and a few surrounding locations. "Once our name is out there, we can certainly add extra stops along the way but for now these are the biggest cities where we will draw the most attention."

"Oh, I see." We sat at the table, the only sound was the pen scratching across the paper and my father swirling the ice in his glass. My mother came into the kitchen with a bright face and began pulling out pots and pans.

"How goes the plan?" she asked, peeking over his shoulder.

"Great! Once we sell the house, we can begin moving east."

"Wait, sell the house? We have to sell the house? But what about our stuff?" I said in shock. We had lived in this house since I was a baby and the thought of selling it made me mad.

"It's just stuff. You'll pack the important things, and we will leave the rest. We don't need it anymore." My father looked at me with a glare in his eyes.

"But where will we live? In the car? There's no way!" I yelled.

"I sold the car."

"What!" I stood.

"I'll be using your bike until I find us a better vehicle to travel in. It's summer so you don't need it to get to school." I looked to my mother for help, but she shrugged and stirred a pot of onions and peppers that were sizzling, causing steam to rise around her nervous orange aura. Looking at my father, I tuned into his aura and saw a hazy grey turning into an ugly brown as he grew more frustrated with me by the second.

"You can't—" I began, but my father slammed his glass against the table.

"You can, and you will. This is *my* house and *my* car, and I will do as I please. You are my son, and you will listen to me. Trust me, if I could persuade you to be more obedient, I would. It would sure make my life a hell of a lot more bearable."

"Then why don't you just *do it*!" I shouted at him, feeling the blood race through my veins. I pushed my chair out of the way. It clattered to the ground, startling my mother.

"Jacob," she gasped. I saw her aura shift from orange to a deep purple and felt her shock and disappointment hit me.

"If I could, I would, but you know as well as I do that we share blood. Which means, we can't manipulate each other." He watched me with eagle eyes.

"Is that what you do to mom every time you want her to forget about the beatings," I said, before I could stop myself. My father moved like a snake, slithering and jumping at me all at once.

"How dare you," I felt his hand slap against my face, causing my head to fling to the side. The sting radiated to my ears, causing them to buzz. His hands grabbed my arms, and I knew his tight grip would leave finger sized bruises behind. "Your mother has never been under my control, but she knows her place and how to keep her mouth shut. *Unlike you.*" He shoved me back. My head flew against the wall, the plaster cracking slightly under the impact. Tears pricked my eyes as I turned to face my father. We stared at each other, breathing heavily, and I watched the aura around him turn an inky black as it crawled over his entire body, absorbing him in darkness.

"Jacob." My mother's soft voice pulled me back.

I looked at her with a now soft, sad, blue aura.

"Why don't you go begin packing your luggage for the trip."

When we didn't move she spoke to my father.

"Honey, let him go organize. The quicker he packs, the quicker we begin our trip."

The vice on my arms released, and I quickly brushed past him and ran up the stairs slamming my door behind me. I tossed myself onto my bed and allowed the tears to fall freely. Crying in front of my father would show weakness—another lesson he had taught me when he saw me crying after a bike accident. I was very young and new to the two-wheel concept and lost control colliding with a tree. He dragged me inside and spanked me with a wooden spoon until I stopped crying.

"Men don't cry," he repeated. "You will remember that."

And from that day on, I never let him see me cry.

CHAPTER 4

WE SOLD THE HOUSE AND PACKED OUR BAGS, AND BEFORE I COULD blink, we were driving down the road in a dusty, dirty, smelly old motorhome that my father found for a "steal". Passing through county after county, our new home creaked and groaned into our first destination—a sleepy, full town in the center of Arizona.

I had never been to Arizona before, and from the moment I stepped out of the vehicle, I knew I hated it. The heat wrapped itself around me, and I began to sweat instantly. My shirt stuck to me, and the air I breathed in was hot and dry. I felt like I was suffocating.

"Whoo," my mom cried, fanning herself instantly. "That is some heat!" Her face was beaming with excitement as she shielded her eyes from the scorching sun.

"Who's idea was it to begin in Arizona...in the summer?" I asked her, but she only bumped my shoulder and laughed gently. A dust cloud of vehicles rolled in behind us, as the new circus troupe arrived. Quickly, they parked their rigs and began setting up camp, attempting to stay inside their air-conditioned trailers or cars rather than stand outside and melt.

My father observed them, dressed in his regular velvet jacket and satin top hat, looking as though the summer rays never touched him. He remained cool and commanding as if he could persuade his own body to never sweat.

"Let's get the tent up; it will be the most difficult. Then we can begin handing out fliers and practicing the acts." He said loudly as the troupe gathered around him. "I want to see and observe each act personally with my son to ensure you are pushing yourself to be the best. I have posted a schedule in the dining hall; please be prompt and prepared."

"Or else," I muttered under my breath, kicking the bottom of a small cactus by my feet, and I felt my father's glare on me instantly. Not risking a glance at him, I turned and headed to the dining hall to put the cases of water and snacks into the fridge and to find some relief from the heat. I watched as the men lifted the tent, just as they did before, and begin hauling in folded metal stands and different pieces to create the seating arrangement around the cement stage.

"It sure is hot here," I heard a female voice behind me, and I jumped at how close she was. She laughed and put her hands up in defense. "Whoa, sorry. Didn't mean to scare you." Unscrewing the lid of the half-frozen water bottle, Ms. Tink took a swig and sighed heavily. Her thick braid was draped over her shoulder, and I could already see loose pieces of hair sticking to her neck and forehead. Sweat lines dotted her white tank top, highlighting her bra, and I quickly averted my eyes before she noticed me staring.

"It's okay, I just didn't hear the door open." I looked up as the group of acrobats strolled in and headed to the fridge for water.

"Can you believe this is really happening? Oh, I'm so nervous to perform." She squeezed the water bottle between her black polished nails and held a wide grin.

"You shouldn't be nervous you're act is really good."

"Really?" She looked at me with emerald puppy-dog eyes.

"Yeah, who else can find tigers and learn to train them. That's impressive." I crossed my arms and leaned against the support beam next to me.

"Thank you," she said. "I should get back to them actually. They may be jungle animals, but we haven't exactly left California before. I just ran in to check the schedule and grab extra water. I'll see you in rehearsal. I look forward to seeing your act!" She winked and ran off with the bubbly pink aura bouncing around her.

I watched her run back to her trailer where the tiger cubs were sleeping inside, and thought about how this show could ruin her light aura forever.

After watching the acrobats fly through the air, the clowns juggle and play tricks on each other, the magician create illusions and perform card tricks, and everything in between, it was finally Ms. Tink's turn to rehearse again. I watched her dance gracefully with the tiny beasts and saw how they fell into a soft trance at the look in her eyes. They followed her every command without hesitation or fear, as she spun her arms in the air around herself.

"That was just magnificent," my father clapped when she and the tigers bowed. Quickly she leased them and shuffled them off to the thick cage on wheels.

"Thank you," she said, bouncing with excitement. I saw the sweat on her face as she wiped it away, shaking the drops out onto the ground.

"Are you worried about how they will behave in front of a crowd of people?" he asked, watching her intently. I could tell he was slowly making his way into her mind to ensure she would tell the truth. The last thing my father needed was a lawsuit or a mangled body on his hands from a scared tiger.

"Nope," she beamed. "Not one bit. They are very well behaved, and I can control their feelings to make sure they aren't scared. I can comfort them if they begin to worry."

"Fantastic!" He clapped. "Thank you, we will see you tonight for dinner." She walked off, pulling the small tiger trailer behind her. My father turned to me and grabbed my arm hard. "Is there a reason you decided to act all *shy* and not say a single damn word this entire time?"

"I...I just didn't have anything to say," I responded unsure of why he cared.

"You are my son, and you *will* play a role in this business. One day this could all be yours, and I expect you to *care*." He pulled me close to his face, and I smelled the alcohol on his breath. "Next time you will be in charge of rehearsal, and I expect you to a better leader than this. Do you understand me?" I watched as he pulled his eyebrows in tight and breathe in a quick short breath. When I didn't answer right away, his grip tightened and he shook my arm.

"Yes, yes I understand. Sorry." I said, reverting my eyes to my dust covered tennis shoes.

"Good, now go help your mother in the kitchen." He pushed me toward the door, where Ms. Tink still stood watching us. Noticing our movement, she quickly moved on. Heat rushed to my cheeks, realizing she was the first person to ever witness my father's anger.

CHAPTER 5

I HATE TO ADMIT THAT MY FATHER HAD ACTUALLY DONE SOMETHING worth uprooting our entire lives for, but he actually did it—the show was a success.

After only performing in five different locations, our name began to spread through newspapers, news stations, and the radio. Every time the reporters would begin to mention the *Ringmaster Circus*, my father would cheer and honk his horn to let the troupe trailing him know they had done it again, which lead to a wave of honking as they flew down the roads.

We had set up in our next location, and I was sent out with a group to staple fliers to telephone poles and hang up posters in local shops. There were six of us, and we had separated to ensure proper coverage of the town, but soon I felt a tap on my shoulder.

"Need help?" she asked, holding up her stapler. I looked at her, taking in her long wavy hair and freckles that had recently sprouted over her nose from the summer sun, and froze. "I uh," she cleared her throat. "I was watching you struggle. Here," she handed me the stack of fliers. "You hold these and I'll staple. Deal?"

I felt my cheeks warm slightly, as I nodded. My arm was hurting from a recent beating from my father and I was trying hard not to let the pain show, but Ms. Tink knew my secret—she just didn't want to pry.

"Sure, thanks." I smiled at her as we continued down the street stapling circus posters to each one. When we had finished, she let out a heavy sigh. I looked over the see if she was okay, as it sounded

286

heavy with worry or irritation, and saw her aura glowing a brilliant yellow around her. She had her head tilted back, and her eyes closed, as a breeze rushed by her, causing her hair to fly back. Fall was coming and that meant the rain, mushy leaves, and cold winds would continue to follow us.

"Don't you just love the wind," she said, taking a spin while the wind died down.

"No. It's annoying and always blowing dirt in my eyes. Who would enjoy that?" I asked her.

"If you close your eyes or run with the wind or spin in circles with it you won't get dirt in your eyes. If you're mean and angry or a grumpy cat, of course, the wind would torture you like that," she rolled her eyes, laughing.

"Did you just call me a grumpy cat, Ms. Tink?" I gave her my best sarcastic tone.

"Why, yes, yes I did. And you can call me Lottie." She bumped my shoulder gently, but it still caused me to wince. Lottie gave me an "I'm sorry" look.

"Lottie?"

"Yes, it's short for Charlotte, my name you know. You're always calling me by my show name but since we are becoming friends and all," she held her fist out waiting for me to bump it.

"Friends, huh?" I hesitated and watched her smile pull higher as she nodded. Shaking my head, I gave her a fist bump. "Come on, let's get some lunch, I'm starving." I nodded to a small cafe across the street where the aroma of coffee and baked goods had been teasing my nose the entire time.

"You know," Lottie said through a massive bite of a turkey and cheese sandwich. "You can talk to me about stuff if you need to."

"Oh, thanks." I felt the blood rush to my cheeks as embarrassment fell over me. I pulled my shirt sleeves down a little more and shifted uncomfortably in my seat. The beatings had become more frequent and brutal, although my father was careful not to send me back to a hospital in fear of delaying his own show. He was trying to force an ability out of me, beat it to the surface or manipulate it out of my mind himself. Nothing worked. The only special gift I had was reading people's auras and that was a pointless gift if you asked my father.

"It's just," she leaned forward. "I saw how your father speaks to you sometimes, and I know how hard it can be."

"No, it's fine. He's just really excited about the show and is sometimes tired when I try to talk with him, so he gets fussy or whatever." I sipped my coke not making eye contact with her.

"You don't have to make excuses for him, not with me. My father beat my mother for years before she got the courage to leave."

I looked up at her misty eyes and tried to imagine an older version of Lottie fleeing from a man like my father.

"I understand," she reached forward and placed her hand on mine. "Just...let me be a friend for you. Someone you can talk to about it or, or I don't know just spend time with. You wouldn't even have to talk, I mean we could just sit in complete awkward silence for however long and then just be like 'cool' 'cool' and move on." We both laughed.

"It's really no big deal, but thank you I'd like having a friend around the troupe. The road is a lonely place," I sighed dreamily and watched her shy, pale green aura shift to a buoyant blue, as she shook her head and smiled. "Friends," I said.

"Friends," she replied.

That weekend, our show put on a performance like nothing else. We had bought more lights, more fog machines, and more decorations and props to ensure the night would be filled with complete magic and entertainment. Our magician thrilled everyone with disappearing rabbits, card tricks, and falling stars that touched a guest and disappeared as their hypnotism worked. Our clowns twisted and folded animals of complete imagination, and the dancers and knife throwers exhilarated the audience with gasps and claps. My mother joined in the troupe amazed by the beauty of the performers. She began small roles walking the tightrope with different weighted items. She smiled with her focused eyes holding their spot at the other end, stepping lightly and carefully across the almost nonexistent rope. It wasn't perfect, but she enjoyed her small moment in the spotlight.

My father spent every penny we had to make it brighter, make it sparkle more, and to make the audience scream with delight—And scream they did.

They screamed as they watched someone fall for the first time in our show.

They screamed as they heard the body hit the concrete floor with a heavy thud and crack against the hard surface.

They screamed as the blood began to seep from her skull pooling quickly and soaking her once lovely hair.

My father inhaled quickly, attempting to stifle a scream, as he watched his performer bleed out before him. He was frozen in place —so was I. The remaining acrobats dropped down gracefully from their perches and rushed to the body sprawled across the floor. My legs were paralyzed.

"Call an ambulance, she's still breathing!" someone screamed, and a wave of silence washed over the audience. They sat staring at the broken limbs set at wrong angles, and they covered their children's eyes. Others left quickly unable to bear the scene before them, the rest sat whispering under their breath. A few men rushed to help if they could but were pushed back to their seats by the strong men who were about to go on stage.

I felt my pulse pounding against my eardrums and saw the auras of everyone before me shift from the excited rainbow of blue, pink, and bright greens to a dull cloud of deep blues and greens filled with agony and sadness. The room began to spin. It felt like a dream.

"Oh my god," my father said between heavy breaths. He stepped as if to move forward but turned to me quickly. "Stay here," he said, as he darted off into the hoard of his troupe. Pushing his way past them all, he fell to his knees next to his wife of twenty years. I didn't realize I had been walking forward, but as I blinked, I saw the group shift and allow me to pass. With tears falling down my cheek, I looked at my mother, broken and shattered—dead—below my feet.

Her eyes were staring straight up, their once brilliant shimmering blue now matte and unmoving. The pretty brown hair she used to braid in the summertime was pulled up into a tight bun and seeping with fresh red blood as it spilled from the back of her skull. Her chest was forced down, air pushed into her lungs, as someone attempted CPR until the paramedics arrived, but I knew it was already too late. I could no longer see her once pulsing aura. Just seconds ago, a happy yellow shone. Now a vast emptiness was left.

"What have you done!" I cried, grabbing my hair in tight fists. This was my father's fault. He had let her perform, and she was thrilled to be part of the show, but she never wanted this—she didn't want to die for the show.

Looking around frantically to try to make sense of what had happened, my eyes landed on the mass of brown strings on the floor, and I realized the net had failed. I saw the ropes that were supposed to secure it laying loose on the ground.

"This is *your* fault," I said, and my father turned his head toward me. He held his satin hat in his hands; his ebony hair was inky and slicked back against his head. His eyes bore into mine with a vengeance I had never felt before. A shiver traveled up my spine, but I held my ground, giving him a look of utter shock and hatred. Hatred for him and everything that he had done.

"What did you say?" He asked, pushing up, so he was standing directly in front of me. I could feel his breath on my nose and heard sirens approaching from the distance like a ringing in my ears. My pulse raced as blood pumped through my veins, faster than I'd ever felt it before. I felt my chest rise and fall in quick, angry breaths, and hot tears pricked my eyes.

"I said, this is *your* fault," I growled, and instantly heard the crack as his fist collided with my nose. Warm blood dripped onto my lip, but I didn't bother wiping it away. Instead, I reeled back and swung hard from the right making contact with his left cheekbone. Shock rippled through him as he grabbed his face. I took a single step back unsure of what monster I had released. I had never hit him, never fought back, but this broke me. My mother was gone, and it was completely his doing.

"How dare you," he spat, shoving me onto the ground. The troupe stepped back unsure of what was happening. One of their own lay dead before them, and now their leader and his successor were throwing fists. I felt his cowboy boot dig into my ribcage. Already bruised and beaten before, they bent to his will quickly sending shocks of pain through my chest and back as they cracked. I heard someone wince as the sound reached them. I felt people trying to pull him off of me, but he held me tight, moving his hands to my throat and applying pressure. I buckled under his weight, unable to move anything but my arms. Wrapping my fingers around his wrists, I pushed against him, hoping he would release the vice so I could breathe. My head was beginning to feel light, and my energy was draining. People were screaming and rushing around me, their auras colliding and melding with each other creating a thin black veil surrounding us. With my last bit of effort, I moved my fingers to his and began attempting to bend them back hoping to allow myself a single breath of air to continue my fight, but something rammed into my father's skull, and he released his hold as he fell next to me. I looked over, coughing, and saw one of the big men holding a paddle that the clowns used—he had struck him and saved me.

Quickly, I rolled on top of my father and began throwing my

fists into his face. I felt them collide with his nose, his eyes, his cheekbones and with each force, I felt all the hatred from my life release into him. This was the payback I had been waiting to give him for a lifetime. The blood from his broken face splattered against my fist, and I felt the warm liquid hit my face in tiny pricks. This was for all the broken bones, fractured ribs, bruises, and threats. It was for all the fear and anxiety he created in me. It was for my mother.

Thick arms were pulling me off him. I was much lighter than my father and easier to remove and I didn't fight them. I wasn't my father —nor did I ever want to be. I knew what I was doing was wrong but life without my mother wasn't life at all, and I reacted to the fear of what my father could and would do to me now that she was gone.

The troupe held us apart. We stood there bleeding as paramedics rushed and attempted to resuscitate my mother. One paused and looked at us, but the strong man waved them off, telling him it was nothing to worry about. We stood there with tears in our eyes as we realized what we had lost, what we had done, what we—together— had shown the troupe. My father wasn't just the monster anymore, I was too. With the men holding him, they released their grip on my arms.

Lottie stood crying as she watched the entire fight. Her arms were wrapped around herself for comfort, and she quickly wiped her nose when she saw me. I gave her a pleading look and approached my father. I opened my mouth to say how much I hated him, how I blamed him for everything, and that I wished he were the one dead, but then I felt a strange pull in my mind and closed it.

It was as if a blanket had been lifted. My mind felt free as it reached out and searched for something to latch onto. As if seeing my own aura, which I never had before, the black tentacles stretched toward my father who watched me with curious eyes. The strands licked his face and rounded to his ears where they moved in and wrapped around his mind. My father inhaled quickly looking at me, he knew I was in his head and he was scared.

"No," he said in a whisper. "W-what are you doing?" Everyone turned toward me and I felt a sly smile creep onto my face.

"Nothing, I don't know what you mean." I felt his memories and his power, his ability was sitting right there and I could wrap myself around it. He winced as I pulled, tugged, and ripped it from his mind. The scream that escaped him caused his back to buckle and he fell to his knees. Drawing in the tendrils back to my own mind I felt his power, the hunger it eased inside me, and it sent an ecstatic shiver down my spine.

"You...you," my father stuttered.

"Yes, me." I inhaled deeply feeling the new rush of energy flow through my veins. It was as if his abilities were powering me up—as if my batteries were finally full. Looking at my father standing between two muscular men I saw—for the first time—a sense of pride glance across his face.

CHAPTER 6

MY MOTHER'S FUNERAL WAS HELD A FEW DAYS LATER. I COULD ONLY get my father to delay the circus tour by a week and even that was pushing his temper. We learned quickly that he could no longer manipulate others—he lost his ability and it made him angrier than ever. I attended the funeral with a black eye and busted lip over the bumps and bruises of the fight we had. No one commented or looked at me.

I held back my tears through the service, but once I was in the comfort of my trailer I allowed myself to finally feel the loss—to mourn. My father would be out drinking at the local bar so I knew I could toss myself in the small attic bed, pull the curtain closed, and weep.

A soft knock sounded at the door but I refused to acknowledge it. The door creaked open and I heard a familiar voice.

"Jacob?" Lottie called into the dark trailer. I held my breath and lay perfectly still. The last thing I wanted was for her to see me this way. "Jacob, I know you're in here." I heard her climb the ladder up to my bed. She gently pulled the thick plaid curtains back and looked at me with wide wet eyes.

"I just want to be alone," I said rolling over to face the wall.

"Let me be here for you," she offered, setting her arm on my shoulder. I could feel the warmth radiate through the thin t-shirt I wore and I rolled onto my back letting my head fall to look at her. She winced as she saw my face. "If anything, let me get you some ice at least. You look like you're about to turn into a zombie and wander off at any second."

I let her get an ice pack out of the freezer and place it over my eye. Crawling up onto the bed, she lay next to me pulling the curtain closed behind her. We lay there together in silence, as she let me cry for my mother, and slowly, I felt myself drifting off to sleep with Lottie's head resting on my shoulder. I could feel her soft breath against my collarbone and saw her aura fade into an almost nonexistent comforting midnight blue of sleep.

Every passing day became easier with life and the circus. My father kept his distance from me, as if he were afraid of my new ability. I still wasn't sure how to control it, but I was not about to let my father find out and use for himself. The new power made me feel like a new person—like I could conquer the world—but I needed to know how to use it.

Since the fight, I no longer was afraid of my father. I did what I wanted, said what I needed, and began enjoying the circus around me. I learned card tricks from the magician who now always brought around his little toddling boy. Baby Daniel would be the next biggest star when his father's time was up, I could see it in the way he watched his father—moving his hands and making things appear. Using magic as if it were real. The tigers grew, and we obtained two full-grown lions that the zoo had been going to ship back to some farm in Africa. My father outbid the farmer using all our money and was able to take the big cats for himself. Ms. Tink—Lottie—cared for them with as much love as she did her tigers and she allowed me to help her feed them. Soon, they grew to know me and trust me as they did her. The trapeze artists continued their air acrobatics and flew high above me. Every day, I ensured the net was secured and unable to move in fear of another falling to their death as my mother did. Each time they let go and soared, my heart rate quickened until they were firmly attached or connected to their next landing.

I could still see everyone's aura, but now I could feel their energy around me like living breathing things. The warmness of happiness and love, the electric buzz of nerves and excitement, the shaking of fear and worry, and the heat of anger and passion—it surrounded me, reached out to me as if I were a beacon to its power.

Along with feeling and reading auras, I had stolen my father's power as well. The night we fought I reached in and took it for my own and he was taking it out on me with retribution, wanting it back. This time, when he tried to fight me, I fought back and soon he realized he would never be able to beat me—I was too powerful now, my confidence had been empowered.

Eventually, he gave up and slowly we began working as a team making decisions and setting up new shows together. We met new acts along the way and hired more people than ever. I also began collecting fireworks, mechanical items that shot tiny pieces of paper into the air, new contraptions that threw flames, exotic animals and dancers, and more. Our circus was making a name for itself, and I indented to keep it growing.

For the next year, our circus developed into the show of a lifetime and people paid extraordinary amounts to be tricked and hypnotically entertained. It didn't matter that it wasn't real to me, because the profits and the successes gave me a sense of pride and determination that my family had never given me, and I wanted more.

* * *

"I want to run the show tonight," I told my father who was walking quickly to the tent. The afternoon light had begun to darken as nightfall was approaching.

"No," he said without looking at me. I followed him, his greying hair flying around the satin hat in need of a cut and some gel. Ever since my mother died he had allowed himself to fall apart and slowly he forgot to take care of himself.

"Why not," I said pulling his arm and forcing him to look at me. His eyes were wild and the faded blue made him look almost completely *bl*ind.

"It is not your time," he growled as he reached back as if to slap me, but shaking his head he turned and walked toward the entrance where flames danced around the open curtain. I followed him, wanting to tell him that I was ready, that this was my time, that he needed to let me take control, but I was absorbed into the river of people entering the tent behind me laughing, and pointing at the amazing sights.

The center stage was surrounded by tiers of stadium seating, metal and hard, but easy to put up, take down, and transport. Every opening was quickly being filled with another warm body and clowns were blowing up balloons and twisting them into animals for the children who squealed with laughter. Young handsome men walked up and down the rows offering goodies—caramel corn, sweet candies, and water. Music boomed through the speakers set high up in the ceiling of the tent, the bass rumbling and shaking their stands as lights twirled and spun around the entire area, casting a rainbow of colors to dance around the crowd.

I moved behind the stands of people and into the back room where the troupe was preparing for their performances. The acrobats twisted their hair up into tight buns to ensure nothing would get in their way, their small sparkling outfits fit snug against their skin. I found Lottie adjusting her hat and stopped to look at her.

Her ebony hair was curled and gently tucked up into a low bun allowing a few pieces to fall around her face. She pinned a tiny top hat—red sequin—at an angle and shifted her head left and right in the mirror to admire her work. Taking the makeup brush, she dabbed powder onto her cheeks, making the pale skin glow a fresh pink, and covered her lips with a sticky red paste. Lottie's jacket was simple — black and silver with bedazzled edges—but was open at the top showing a lot of flawless skin I couldn't move my eyes from. The tiny shorts she wore drew the eyes down and down to her long legs wrapped in fishnet stockings and held up with simple black heels. Looking up in the mirror, she saw me and smiled batting her long black lashes. I waved and saw her wave back with a cheerful, quick hand motion before returning to her work.

Pulling myself away, I found my father in the back dusting off his jacket and taking a shot of bourbon.

"Real nice," I scoffed. "Don't you ever do anything sober anymore?" I sat down in the folding chair and watched him as he buttoned the faded jacket.

"It's none of your business how I get through the show."

"Don't you care about these people?"

I saw him sigh, reach for his glass and begin to lift it to his lips. Before the amber liquid could touch his skin, I slapped it out of his hands sending it to shatter against the hard ground into a thousand pieces. "That's enough!" I yelled and just as quickly my father turned and slapped me hard across the face.

"You should have been the one," he screamed, breathing heavily. "It should have been you." He poked his yellowing nail into my chest.

"It should have been me, what? It should have been me that died?" I finally realized what he was saying. He wished I were the one dead, not my mother—sometimes I wished it too. "Well, sorry to continuously disappoint you, Dad, but I'm still here and I plan to be here for a long time."

"Give it back," he said and I gave him a curious look. "Give. It. Back." He said louder.

"W-what?" I asked, but he grabbed the collar of my shirt and pulled me close. The smell of alcohol burned my nose and sent a shiver down my spine. His breath was hot against my face and I felt his hands tremble on my shirt.

"Come on, enough of this already." I heard a man call from outside the small room. I looked over my shoulder slightly and saw the magician—Theo—standing there with his arms crossed. "Do we really need to go through this again?" He looked at my father.

"You'll give it back to me." He glared, releasing my shirt and grabbing the bottle of bourbon. "If it's the last thing I do." He took a deep swig and set it back down. Heading toward the door, he paused. "You don't deserve such a gift. It's wasted on you." I understood now what he was demanding me to return—his ability. Even if I could find a way to return it, I wouldn't. At this rate, I feared he would manipulate someone to kill me to make up for the death of my mother.

I watched the show from the back, peeking out through the curtain as much as possible. I saw my father stumble over his words, trip one too many times, and place his hands in inappropriate spots on performers as he introduced them or dismissed them. The acrobats flew through the air, flipping and spinning toward each other and a few dangled down, dropping quickly from thin fabric that caught them at the last possible second. Our fire dancers sent the audience in awe as they caught the stage and even the tiers on fire and called it back to them as if it were their pet.

When it was Lottie's turn, I fell into a trance as she called the animals around her. Tigers, lions, elephants, and more surrounded her and she stood smiling with no fear in her eyes. The crowd fell into a hush and watched with intensity as the animals danced, twirled, and spun around on the stage. They cheered carefully as the tiger cubs—who weren't so little anymore—stood up on their back legs and waved their big paws at them. They clapped as the lions balanced on small stands and jumped through different sized hoops, and they whistled with excitement as the group stood together and took a bow before padding off the stage. Sparkling confetti fell around them as the magician appeared almost out of thin air. Little did they know he had been there the whole time, sneaking onto the stage as the tigers and lions drew their attention away from him.

Our magician was very talented and could make you see things that couldn't be possible. He hypnotized a small group of people, making them believe they were a football team and huddled together. When he said the magic word "llama" the quarterback began to quack while the others acted as ducklings and followed him around the stage. The audience laughed and cheered for them. Danny, now a scrawny five-year-old, stood next to me watching his dad with wide eyes and a grin that reached ear to ear.

"Someday, I want to do that," he gleaned pointing at his father. I ruffled his shaggy brown hair and laughed.

"You will, kid."

Together we watched him pull items out of his hat—impossible items such as an umbrella that opened up and was raining on the inside, a rabbit, two rabbits, ten rabbits, which he let run around the stage. With a wave of his wan*d they disappe*ared all over again in a pop, pop, pop. I knew he had to be holding some kind of special ability, one that was strong enough to move a crowd, but it wasn't something I wanted to take from him—we needed him for our show. Looking at little Danny, I wondered if he held the same power as his father.

CHAPTER 7

MY AFFECTION FOR LOTTIE GREW EVERY DAY BUT I HAD YET TO MAKE any sort of move, afraid that she did not feel the same way I did about her. I watched her one evening as she sat inside the tiger cage petting the large head that lay on her lap. We had recently acquired a large male tiger who had been in another circus but was getting too old for the shows. Lottie insisted we take him in, wanting to provide him a safe, comfortable place to live the rest of his life. She was whispering under her breath to the purring beast while her tiger cubs curled around her outstretched legs sleeping peacefully.

I dragged my feet in the gravel to ensure they heard me approaching. The last thing I wanted was to spook a tiger and have them attack Lottie. The tiger in her lap raised his ears slightly as I came near, Lottie looked up and smiled at me.

"Hey," she said quietly.

"Come here often," I winked leaning against the bars of the cage. She laughed and it pulsed her aura out with a warm honey tone that glowed like gold. It was mesmerizing and I wanted to wrap myself in it and never let go.

"How do you think the show went today?" she asked but what she really wanted to know was how things were going with my father.

"Not bad, I think the animals could use some exercise. Casper here is looking a little round around the thighs." I pointed to the smaller tiger who lifted his head when hearing his name.

"Oh, well look who's talking. How many donuts did you eat this morning?"

"It's not my fault someone bought powdered ones, those are my favorite. They are like a drug," I sighed dramatically. "Their powdery goodness is addictive and I could inject myself with that raspberry filling." I feigned an elated shiver. Lottie laughed again and I felt the edges of her aura touch the spidery edges of mine.

"So," I asked turning toward her and petting the tiger carefully. "What were you two talking about? I hope nothing scandalous." I raised my eyebrows at the tiger who glared at me. I raised my hands in defense before crossing them over my chest.

"Oh, no. Nothing as exciting as a scandal. Although," Lottie thought, looking up into the sky. "I did hear a rumor that Brutus and Claire were going at it all night in their trailer. Apparently," she leaned over the tiger and covered his ears lowering her voice to whisper to me. "They like to roleplay and the clowns were parked a little too close. They thought a pack of coyotes was prowling around their camp."

"Wow, I did not need to hear that." I shook my head and chuckled. We sat in silence as I waited for the real answer. Lottie sighed heavily before answering.

"I was just telling him how sorry I was."

"Sorry? For what?"

"Just.." She shook her head and stopped petting the tiger. "I don't know, he has no family. He was going to be taken and just thrown away."

"But they weren't. They're here, with you," I offered, feeling the tendrils of my power begin to ooze out to her welcoming aura.

"I know, but the idea of someone just giving them up, sending them back to their home where they are destined to die because they weren't raised in the wild, is just...sick. They have no family and are all alone now." She leaned over the tiger's large head and wrapped her arms around him in a gentle hug. The tiger *purred* with love.

"But he does have a family," I said kneeling down next to her and reaching out toward the tiger. I rested my hand on his head and pet his face. "You are his family now." I smiled at Lottie who looked at me with sad eyes. "He's lucky to have such a compassionate person taking care of him now." I watched her face for a moment, feeling the warmth of trust and comfort radiating from her pink aura and saw the ghost-like trails of mine reaching for it. Standing, I waved at her and headed back to my trailer not wanting to risk even pulling the tiniest piece of her power away from her. She was too good—too kind—to deserve that.

Closing the squealing door behind me, I threw the lock and kicked off my shoes. I had passed my driving exam and recently found a small trailer that I acquired to keep away from my father attached to a beat up old ford explorer I may have persuaded someone to sell me for very cheap. We needed our space and if we continued to share a living space we would undoubtedly end up killing each other.

It wasn't anything special—four somewhat straight walls, a small bed, a tiny table, an even tinier kitchenette, a bathroom that doubled as a shower, and a few petite windows that let in just enough light to let you know it was daytime—but it was all the room I needed.

Throwing myself onto the bed I rolled my head to the side where a picture of my mother and I sat. The photo was faded and wrinkled from being packed in the few boxes we had brought but I smoothed it out and found a cheap frame at the local thrift store and hung it up to always remember her. It was my favorite photo of her as her face was filled with a genuine smile. I had just finished playing at the local pond and was covered in green algae. My mother had told me I looked like an alien so I chased her around the yard pretending to shoot her with a ray gun until she grabbed the hose and knocked me down. When my father came home and saw us laughing, he grabbed the camera and snapped the photo. It was one of the only times my father seemed to enjoy his family, our life, and what he had and even though that night ended with a bloody lip and me crying myself to sleep, the memory of my mother will always be there.

A light tapping brought me back from my memories. I sat up in bed and waited to make sure I heard it and not imagined it. It came again and I scooted off the bed to open the door where I was face to face with Lottie.

"Hey, what are you—" I began but she stepped up into the trailer and kissed me. Her lips were cold from the night air and the smell of wet leaves and fall wafted in around her. Before I could think, the door had clasped shut and she stepped forward forcing me to take a step back. I felt the edge of the table against my spine. A shock of pain traveled up and down my back but I pushed it away as I pulled her against me. Her warm hands were on my chest, trailing up and down, sending quivers of delight through my body. I ached for her, I needed her, and I couldn't stop myself from allowing her hands to roam under my shirt and lift it over my head.

I groaned as her soft lips trailed down my chest, her delicate skin against mine. As she stood to kiss me again, I lifted her up and her legs wrapped around my waist. I took her back to my bed laying her down gently. Her long hair was undone and flowing out around her, mirroring the inky tendrils that flowed from my aura and they mingled together as our hues crashed into each other and held on. I felt her breathing heavily as I gently lifted her shirt and kissed her stomach and as my lips pressed against her porcelain skin she moaned with delight.

Without realizing what was happening and not being able to control my power, it wrapped around hers and began chipping away, pulling pieces of it out and placing them in a safe place in my mind. As we made love, I absorbed her ability, and yet she seemed completely at ease; as if the pain mixed with our tender kisses was giving her a new sense of pleasure.

It wasn't until the screams woke us that I had understood what I had done.

Lottie snored softly in her sleep. I smiled at her delicate features that seemed to glow more in the night time and kissed her bare shoulder. After we made love we lay in bed wrapped around each other talking about our lives and how different—yet similar—they had been. She fell asleep in my arms and I couldn't bring myself to wake her so I had allowed myself to sleep against her silky hair that smelled like fresh rain and peonies.

As I drifted off into the dreamworld letting the Sandman control my slumber, I dreamt of finally being free of my father and living my own life— one I wanted to have with Lottie. When my dream shifted into a nightmare was when the screaming began and awoke me instantly. Lottie jumped in my arms, startled by the sudden noise and looked around forgetting where she was.

"What?" she said in a sleepy tone.

"I'm not sure," I said as another scream sounded nearby. Exchanging looks of fear we raced to put on our clothes and leave the trailer.

"Oh, my god." Lottie covered her gaping mouth with her hands and looked at me with wide concerned eyes. Everyone hurried from their trailers and gathered around the one where the screams were coming from—my father's.

All the lights were off inside but the moonlight was casting shadows against the windows and as the trailer rocked from side to side a horrifying roar echoed through the camp.

No one moved, we were all unsure of what we should do. Surrounding the trailer we stood like a still from a movie waiting to see what would happen next. Lottie shifted her weight as if to run forward.

"No," I said grabbing her arm. She gave me a stern look before pulling away and running toward the trailer. I ran after her, my busted sneakers hitting the ground as I rushed to intercept her. There was no way to know if the animal would attack her—or me— but I wasn't about to risk her life in hopes of saving my father.

As Lottie reached for the door a sudden silence washed over us and left us in an eerie haunted haze. I heard the blood pounding in my ears with my rapidly beating heart, my breath came out heavy and I slowly put my hands on Lottie's shoulders to draw her back to me. Pulling her slightly behind my stance, I reached for the door and as carefully as I could I opened it.

Before I looked inside I already knew exactly what I would see. I knew the inside of the door would be splattered with fresh, crimson blood. I knew that the floor would be spotted with pools of warm red liquid and that as I stepped into the trailer the tiger would be crouched over a body on the bed. I knew that if I looked closely I could see a severed hand under the table and part of a shredded scalp smeared across the bathroom door. I knew because this had been the nightmare I had just before the scream woke me.

I gasped and the tiger turned his attention toward me. His large lumbering body was covered with streaks of blood and he had a large gash in his left side. Holding up my hands to show him I had no weapons I took a firm stance and looked him in the eye willing him to hear me.

"*Please, please,*" I thought pushing the words to him. I saw the snake-like whisps begin to reach out toward the beast and gently caress its face. The tiger began to purr as I continue to urge him to remain calm. "*I don't want to hurt you. I am here to help.*" I thought, giving him the best calm face I could. He responded by turning his full body toward me and leaping off the bed. I shuddered as he padded toward me and sat at my feet his wide black eyes never leaving mine.

"*You called,*" I heard his thoughts in my mind as they played out in a type of hazy image. The animal was communicating with me through pictures. I created an image in my head—a memory, of me petting him just earlier that day to show him I meant him no harm. As if he understood, he nodded slightly.

"*Bad,*" He thought showing me a picture of my father slapping me across the face. "*Bad man.*"

"Yes," I said out loud with a shaking voice. "He was bad."

"*No more,*" he shifted the image from my father hitting me to one of his current state. "*Safe.*"

"Yes," I repeated nodding my head and lifting my hand to his head feeling the warm fur between my fingers. The tiger changed the image again manipulating it into a calming picture of Lottie hugging his neck and the feeling of comfort and safety wrapped itself around me. He purred beneath my hand and pushed a bloodied ear against my palm. "Safe," I told him.

"*Let's leave and return to your cage.*" I drew a picture of his cage with me leading him into the door and again he nodded once. I shifted my attention to Lottie who was watching me carefully. She knew. She had to know. I had taken her gift and used it to my own will, to take out my biggest threat, my greatest fear. But I did so unknowingly and it would be something I needed to explain to her.

Backing out of the trailer slowly, everyone stepped back to give us room to exit and make our way safely to the cage. The blood-dripping tiger looked around at the circle of people and whined softly.

"Shh," I tried to keep the animal calm pushing thoughts of safety and comfort into his mind, replaying the image of Lottie holding him and my hand against him to let him know he was still okay.

"Tongo, it's okay no one is going to hurt you," Lottie said reaching out to touch the animal gently. He noticed her and watched her carefully as if remembering who she was.

"He-he doesn't hear me," she said to me not letting her eyes wander from the beast. "I don't understand, I don't feel his mind." She shook her head and finally looked at me when Tongo turned his attention back. He purred at me and padded forward to my outstretched hand, resting his nose against my palm. Someone shifted their position in the circle and Tongo immediately swung in their direction to see what it was.

"No," I yelled holding up my hands to the troupe around me, but it was too late. I heard the cock of the gun before I could find who held it and a loud shot rang throughout the camp. It echoed off the trailers and slowly vanished into the midnight air leaving everyone standing in utter shock.

"What have you *done!*" Lottie cried running to the beast. Tongo lay on his side breathing heavily, a large wound was spilling blood against the hard ground. He looked up at Lottie with wet eyes and blinked. I felt the confusion, the pain, the suffering coming from his mind. He didn't understand what was happening to him and he was scared.

"Shh, it's okay," I reassured Tongo petting his head gently and pushing the feeling of love and affection toward him. I wanted to erase his pain, to take it away like I was taking powers but it wasn't something I could wrap my tendrils around and hold. Tears stung at my eyes as I watched his breathing slow. Lottie had lifted his head gently and placed it on her lap, she bent over and kissed his face petting him over and over and telling him what a great friend he had been, what a good tiger he was and that she loved him. Everyone stood in silence as we watched Tongo take his final breath, sending me a single memory of seeing Lottie for the first time and pushing the emotion of happiness and joy through his mind to mine. It wrapped around my aura like a warm blanket and tears fell from my eyes.

"No. No, no, no," Lottie cried pulling the tiger up to her face and rocking him back and forth. "No, stay with me. Please." I pulled her against me and tried to push the memory Tongo shared with me into her mind. As it created itself again for her, I saw a small smile play on her face, glistening against the tears that stained her cheeks. "Oh, Tongo. I'm so sorry."

I felt the life fade away from Tongo and taking a heavy breath stood up slowly. Surveying the group around me my gaze landed on the person holding the gun. Seeing my glare, the clown known as "Giggles" stepped back in fear.

"I-I didn't...He was about—" He stuttered as his round pale face begin to drip with sweat. I walked toward him in steady, even paces.

"About to what? Eat me? Jump on me? Tear me apart like he did my father?" I spat. "No, he wasn't going to do any of that."

"Y-you don't know that," he began but I was in front of him standing eye to eye and I saw his pupils widen in panic.

"Yes, I do. I had him under *control.*" I reached for the gun and pulled it out of his hands. Lifting it quickly I aimed it at his head, the rifle warm against my hands. His aura jumped from a saddened blue to a pulsing red and orange of fear and worry. "What are you about to do? Should I kill you too because maybe," I pushed the barrel forward into his cheek as he turned away, "You will attack? Maybe you want to kill me and tear me apart." Standing still against him I felt my aura reach for his and tickle the ends of his fear. He gasped as if feeling a darkness sweep over him. I didn't know if he had any abilities but my power would seek it out. Urging my aura to close in around his mind I felt it, a small bubble filled with the ability to shift emotions to laughter. Feeling a chuckle in the back of my throat I began to laugh.

"Jacob?" Lottie stood behind me now, her soft yoga pants covered with fresh tiger blood. It angered me, but all I could do was laugh as I turned and ripped out his ability, taking it for my own, adding it to my collection inside my mind.

"What have you done!" He shouted.

"I took a piece of you," I growled letting the weapon down so I could lean close to him. "You took a piece of our troupe, it was only fair." Shoving the weapon back into his hands, leaving a red circle from the hot barrel on his cheek, I stepped back. "You're done here. Pack your things."

"You can't do that," he replied. "You're not in charge."

"My father is dead," I said loudly to make sure everyone heard me. Lottie put her shaking hand on my shoulder to let me know she was here for me. "He is dead and I am next in line to take over. This circus is mine now and you *will* do as I say."

"No, he's alive!" Theo yelled from the trailer door. "Someone call 911." Frantically everyone began checking their pockets for a phone or any way to call for help. A blonde trapeze artist held up her Nokia and began dialing. I heard her asking for help at the fairgrounds but rushed back to the trailer to see for myself.

Peering over the mutilated body still spilling blood from the fresh wounds, I noticed a slight rise and fall of the chest.

"Oh my god," I gasped. Theo pushed by me and felt his neck for a pulse careful not to press on any open gashes.

"He has a pulse, its faint but it's there. He may be able to survive this yet." He looked up at me.

"He's pretty badly mauled, there's no way to know for sure." Deep down, I wished he may not make it through, knowing that he would return as an even-worse version than himself—if that were even possible—knowing his torn face would never be able to run the show again. Hearing the sirens waining closer and tires hit the rocky surface, I pulled myself away and back to the table where pieces of my father were left.

Paramedics carefully lifted his mangled body, strapped it to a gurney, and took him to the nearest hospital. I declined their offer to ride along and wait for him, knowing there was nothing I could do—honestly there was nothing I *wanted* to do to help him.

"Psshh," Giggles scoffed and I trained my glare on him again.

"What?" I sneered. "You think you're still allowed to be here just because he *may* survive?"

"Well, yeah." He threw his arms up. "You have no say here."

"Get out," I snapped. He didn't move and I stepped quickly to him. He flinched as I neared but puffed out his chest trying to show the others he wasn't afraid of me. I inhaled with my nose pointing at him then leaned in close.

"I can smell your fear, *Giggles.*" I kept my voice low so the others wouldn't hear. Everything around me faded into oblivion and it was just him and I standing nose to nose. His aura bounced quickly around him in an orange and brown hue of fear and confusion. I felt my aura reaching toward his and begin to consume it slowly. Giggles winced as if feeling his aura being drained and I watched as his skin paled.

"Something wrong, Giggles?" I asked feeling a sly smile creep onto my face. Pushing the black tentacles out and around the clown, I saw his face shift from worry to glee. His lips pulled at the side and his mouth opened wide releasing a loud, boisterous chuckle.

"Stop," he laughed. "Please, stop." He winced but continued to smile through the invisible pain I was causing him.

With every inhale I drained his aura more and with every bit I took I felt my own power build within me. I knew I was causing him pain, even though I was using his own ability against him, the tears that fell were not tears of joy—I couldn't stop though. The jolt of adrenaline was a feeling I never wanted to let go of and I may not have if Lottie hadn't placed her hand on my shoulder.

"Jacob," she said quietly. "Don't make a scene." I exhaled a breath I didn't realize I was holding and stepped back from Giggles. His face fell and he was breathing heavily, sweat dripped down from his brow.

"Get out," I growled.

Giggles huffed and stormed away toward his trailer. Within a moment, the truck hauling it rattled to life and chugged its way out of the campsite. Taking Lottie's hand, I lead her away and back to my trailer but before I opened the door I turned back to the group that was beginning to close in on itself and spoke.

"Take the trailer and light it on fire. We will move in two days and I expect you all to be ready."

"And the tiger?" someone asked. I paused and looked at the beast laying motionless on the ground now looking like a sleeping pet.

"There is a vet coming to take the tiger," Lottie said through her tears and I nodded that I heard her.

"Cover the tiger with a clean sheet and someone wait for the vet. Come get me when they arrive." I squeezed Lottie's hand and opened the door to my trailer letting her in before me, I closed the door and sat at the table letting myself fall apart at her hands.

"What have I done?" I asked her letting my head fall into my hands. She sat in the booth next to me and wrapped her arms around my shoulders.

"It's okay. We will be okay. We just...just...need...hell, I don't know but right now there's nothing we can do but wait and see if your father recovers and go from there."

"I'm so sorry, Lottie." I looked at her and grabbed her hands. "I know how much you loved that tiger." She bit her lip trying to force herself not to cry again but she sputtered and fell to pieces letting herself fall into my chest. I held her close and ran my fingers through her hair.

"He was so kind, so gentle. I don't understand why he would do this." She sobbed. I felt her tears begin to soak through my shirt but it only made me hold her tighter.

"It's my fault," I confessed. "I did this."

"No, it was just an accident. I mean, I don't know why he did it but—"

"Shh," I stopped her, pulling her close to me again.

"I will explain it all in the morning," I pulled her face up to mine and looked her deep in the eye. "I promise I will explain everything." I kissed her wet lips and her cheek and pulled her against me again.

The vet arrived quickly and gently took the tiger with him letting Lottie know where she could come to claim the ashes if she wanted them.

"Thank you," she said taking his card and watching as he drove away with her friend.

"You okay?" I asked wrapping my arm around her shoulder, her sad blue aura fading in and out around her.

"I will be," she looked up and gave me a soft smile. "Let's go see your dad."

"Lottie…" I began.

"No, you need to see him, if for anything, to say your goodbyes. If he doesn't make it and you're not there you will never forgive yourself."

"Would I, though?" I asked hoping she would answer what I had been asking myself the whole time.

"The guilt would eat you alive."

"Okay," I gave in. "Let's go."

The doctor explained to me that they put my father into a medically induced coma because his wounds were so extensive his body couldn't handle the amount of pain. They told me he may never wake up, that even if he did he would never be the same person he was before—whether that was a good or bad thing I hadn't decided.

"So, what do we do now, just wait?" I asked the doctor as I stood at the end of my father's bed. He was hooked up to multiple machines beeping, pulsing, pumping, and dripping fluids into him. A tube ran down his throat helping him breathe and his chest rose and fell as it breathed in and out.

"Yes, we never know how long it will take someone to heal and with the wounds his body has it could be days, weeks, months."

"*Months!*" I felt faint. I knew I couldn't wait around for him for months, not if we were going to keep the circus running plus we didn't have insurance and there was no way for me to pay for all these expenses.

"I know it seems like a lot, it can be very overwhelming, but we will just take it one day at a time."

"I can't just sit around and wait for him, I have a job—people that count on me."

"No one said you had to be here by his bedside the entire time, we have nurses and staff that will monitor him. You are free to come and go as needed and we will call you if there are any urgent changes in his condition." I nodded as he spoke but my eyes would not move from my father before me.

It was one of the first times I had seen him so vulnerable, exposed and hurt. He looked at peace. Lottie's warm hand slipped inside mine and I squeezed it for comfort.

"How is his brain activity?" she asked the doctor.

"It's weak, but there is still some. You can see here." He reached over and pointed to a machine that was printing paper with spikes and lines. "These show that the brain is still functioning."

"And what happens if his brain stops?" I asked.

"Jacob, you can't think like that." Lottie looked at me with moist eyes.

"I'm just trying to be prepared, Lottie. I need time to process it all if the worst happens." She nodded, understanding everything had happened so quickly.

"Well, if the brain activity stops then the machines will continue to work and keep him breathing."

"But he'll be dead," I remember watching medical TV shows and recalling that brain-dead patients are only kept alive at that point for organ donation.

"Yes, his body will only be working because the machines are doing it for him but I assure you we are doing everything we can to prevent that."

"Okay, thank you." After giving the doctor a number to reach me, he and Lottie left me alone with my father. Moving around the bed I leaned close to his ear.

"I'm sorry," I whispered, feeling tears sting the corner of my eyes. "But you did deserve this." I pulled away as if to leave but guilt hit my stomach like a brick knowing I had already lost my mother and now...if he were to pass I would have no family left in this world.

"I love you." I left the hospital that day not knowing if I'd ever be back to see him. Little did I know I would never get the chance.

CHAPTER 8

My affection for Lottie grew every day but I had yet to make any sort of move, afraid that she did not feel the same way. I watched her one evening as she sat inside the tiger cage petting the large head that lay on her lap. We had recently acquired a large male tiger who had been in another circus but was getting too old for the shows. Lottie insisted we take him, in wanting to provide him a safe, comfortable place to live the rest of his life. She was whispering under her breath to the purring beast while her tiger cubs curled around her outstretched legs sleeping peacefully.

I dragged my feet in the gravel to ensure they heard me approaching. The last thing I wanted was to spook a tiger and have them attack Lottie. The tiger in her lap raised his ears slightly as I came near. Lottie looked up and smiled at me.

"Hey," she said quietly.

"Come here often?" I winked leaning against the bars of the cage. She laughed and it pulsed her aura out with a warm honey tone that glowed like gold. It was mesmerizing and I wanted to wrap myself in it and never let go.

"How do you think the show went today?" she asked but what she really wanted to know was how things were going with my father.

"Not bad, I think the animals could use some exercise. Casper here is looking a little round around the thighs." I pointed to the smaller tiger who lifted his head when hearing his name.

"Oh, well look who's talking. How many donuts did you eat this morning?"

"It's not my fault someone bought powdered ones, those are my favorite. They are like a drug," I sighed dramatically. "Their powdery goodness is addictive and I could inject myself with that raspberry filling." I feigned an elated shiver. Lottie laughed again and I felt the edges of her aura touch the spidery edges of mine.

"So," I asked, turning toward her and petting the tiger carefully. "What were you two talking about? I hope nothing scandalous." I raised my eyebrows at the tiger who glared at me. I raised my hands in defense before crossing them over my chest.

"Oh, no. Nothing as exciting as a scandal. Although," Lottie thought, looking up into the sky. "I did hear a rumor that Brutus and Claire were going at it all night in their trailer. Apparently," she leaned over the tiger and covered his ears lowering her voice to whisper to me. "They like to roleplay and the clowns were parked a little too close. They thought a pack of coyotes was prowling around their camp."

"Wow, I did not need to hear that," I shook my head and chuckled. We sat in silence as I waited for the real answer. Lottie sighed heavily before answering.

"I was just telling him how sorry I was."

"Sorry? For what?"

"Just," she shook her head and stopped petting the tiger. "I don't know, he has no family. He was going to be taken and just thrown away."

"But they weren't. They're here, with you." I offered, feeling the tendrils of my power begin to ooze out to her welcoming aura.

"I know, but the idea of someone just giving them up, sending them back to their home where they are destined to die because they weren't raised in the wild, is just...sick. They have no family and are all alone now." She leaned over the tiger's large head and wrapped her arms around him in a gentle hug. The tiger *purred* with love.

"But he does have a family," I said kneeling down next to her and reaching out toward the tiger. I rested my hand on his head and pet his face. "You are his family now." I smiled at Lottie who looked at me with sad eyes. "He's lucky to have such a compassionate person taking care of him now." I watched her face for a moment, feeling the warmth of trust and comfort radiating from her pink aura and saw the ghost-like trails of mine reaching for it. Standing, I waved at her and headed back to my trailer not wanting to risk even pulling the tiniest piece of her power away from her. She was too good—too kind— to deserve that.

* * *

Closing the squealing door behind me, I threw the lock and kicked off my shoes. I had passed my driving exam and recently found a small trailer attached to a beat-up old ford explorer. I may have persuaded someone to sell it to me for very cheap. My father and I needed our space, and if we continued to share a living space we would undoubtedly end up killing each other.

It wasn't anything special—four somewhat straight walls, a small bed, a tiny table, an even tinier kitchenette, a bathroom that doubled as a shower, and a few petite windows that let in just enough light to let you know it was daytime—but it was all the room I needed.

Throwing myself onto the bed, I rolled my head to the side where a picture of my mother and I sat. The photo was faded and wrinkled from being packed in the few boxes we had brought, but I'd smoothed it out, found a cheap frame at the local thrift store, and hung it up to always remember her. It was my favorite photo of her as her face was filled with a genuine smile. I had just finished playing at the local pond and was covered in green algae. My mother had told me I looked like an alien, so I chased her around the yard pretending to shoot her with a ray gun, until she grabbed the hose and knocked me down. When my father came home and saw us laughing, he grabbed the camera and snapped the photo. It was one of the only times my father seemed to enjoy his family—our life. Even though that night ended with a bloody lip and me crying myself to sleep, the memory of my mother will always be there.

A light tapping brought me back from my memories. I sat up in bed and waited to make sure I heard it and not imagined it. It came again and I scooted off the bed to open the door. I found myself face to face with Lottie.

"Hey, what are you—" I began but she stepped up into the trailer and kissed me. Her lips were cold from the night air and the smell of wet leaves and fall wafted in around her. Before I could think, the door had clasped shut and she stepped forward, forcing me to take a step back. I felt the edge of the table against my spine. A shock of pain traveled up and down my back but I pushed it away as I pulled her against me. Her warm hands were on my chest, trailing up and down sending quivers of delight through my body. I ached for her, I needed her, and I couldn't stop myself from allowing her hands to roam under my shirt and lift it over my head.

I groaned as her soft lips trailed down my chest, her delicate skin against mine. As she stood to kiss me again, I lifted her up and her legs wrapped around my waist. I took her back to my bed laying her down gently. Her long hair was undone and flowing out around her mirroring the inky tendrils that flowed from my aura and they mingled together as our hues crashed into each other and held on. I felt her breathing heavily as I gently lifted her shirt and kissed her stomach, and as my lips pressed against her porcelain skin she moaned with delight.

Without realizing what was happening and not being able to control my power, it wrapped around hers and began chipping away, pulling pieces of it out and placing them in a safe place in my mind. As we made love, I absorbed her ability and yet she seemed completely at ease, as if the pain mixed with our tender kisses were giving her a new sense of pleasure.

It wasn't until the screams woke us that I had understood what I had done.

* * *

Lottie snored softly in her sleep. I smiled at her delicate features that seemed to glow more in the night time and kissed her bare shoulder. After we made love, we lay in bed wrapped around each other talking about our lives and how different — yet similar — they had been. She fell asleep in my arms, and I couldn't bring myself to wake her, so I had allowed myself to sleep against her silky hair that smelled like fresh rain and peonies.

As I drifted off into the dreamworld, letting the Sandman control my slumber, I dreamed of finally being free of my father and living my own life— one I wanted to have with Lottie. As my dream shifted into a nightmare, the screaming began and awoke me instantly. Lottie jumped in my arms, startled by the sudden noise and looked around forgetting where she was.

"What?" she said in a sleepy tone.

"I'm not sure," I said as another scream sounded nearby. Exchanging looks of fear, we raced to put on our clothes and leave the trailer.

"Oh, my god." Lottie covered her gaping mouth with her hands and looked at me with wide concerned eyes. Everyone hurried out and gathered around the trailer where the screams were coming from —my father's.

All the lights were off inside, but the moonlight was casting shadows against the windows, and as the trailer rocked from side to side, a horrifying roar echoed through the camp.

No one moved, we were all unsure of what we should do.

Surrounding the trailer, we stood like a still from a movie, waiting to see what would happen next. Lottie shifted her weight as if to run forward.

"No," I said grabbing her arm. She gave me a stern look before pulling away and running toward the trailer. I ran after her, my busted sneakers hitting the ground as I rushed to intercept her. There was no way to know if the animal would attack her—or me— but I wasn't about to risk her life in hopes of saving my father.

As Lottie reached for the door, a sudden silence washed over us and left us in an eerie haunted haze. I heard the blood pounding in my ears with my rapidly beating heart. My breath came out heavy and I slowly put my hands on Lottie's shoulders to draw her back to me. Pulling her slightly behind my stance, I reached for the door and as carefully as I could I opened it.

Before I looked inside I already knew exactly what I would see. I knew the inside of the door would be splattered with fresh, crimson blood. I knew that the floor would be spotted with pools of warm red liquid and that as I stepped into the trailer the tiger would be crouched over a body on the bed. I knew that if I looked closely I could see a severed hand under the table and part of a shredded scalp smeared across the bathroom door. I knew because this had been the nightmare I had just before the scream woke me.

I gasped and the tiger turned his attention toward me. His large lumbering body was covered with streaks of blood and he had a large gash in his left side. Holding up my hands to show him I had no weapons, I took a firm stance and looked him in the eye, willing him to hear me.

"Please, please," I thought pushing the words to him. I saw the snake-like whisps begin to reach out toward the beast and gently caress its face. The tiger began to purr as I continue to urge him to remain calm. *"I don't want to hurt you. I am here to help,"* I thought, giving him the best calm face I could. He responded by turning his full body toward me and leaping off the bed. I shuddered as he padded toward me and sat at my feet his wide black eyes never leaving mine.

"You called," I heard his thoughts in my mind as they played out in a type of hazy image. The animal was communicating with me through pictures. I created an image in my head, a memory, of me petting him just earlier that day to show him I meant him no harm. As if he understood, he nodded slightly.

"Bad," he thought showing me a picture of my father slapping me across the face. *"Badman."*

"Yes," I said out loud with a shaking voice. "He was bad."

"No more," he shifted the image from my father hitting me to one of his current state. *"Safe."*

"Yes," I repeated nodding my head and lifting my hand to his head feeling the warm fur between my fingers. The tiger changed the image again manipulating it into a calming picture of Lottie hugging his neck and the feeling of comfort and safety wrapped itself around me. He purred beneath my hand and pushed a bloodied ear against my palm. "Safe," I told him.

"Let's leave and return to your cage." I drew a picture of his cage with me leading him into the door and again he nodded once. I shifted my attention to Lottie who was watching me carefully. She knew. She had to know. I had taken her gift and used it to my own will, to take out my biggest threat, my greatest fear. But I did so unknowingly and it would be something I needed to explain to her.

Backing out of the trailer slowly, everyone stepped back to give us room to exit and make our way safely to the cage. The blood dripping tiger looked around at the circle of people and whined softly.

"Shh." I tried to keep the animal calm, pushing thoughts of safety and comfort into his mind, replaying the image of Lottie holding him and my hand against him to let him know he was still okay.

"Tongo, it's okay no one is going to hurt you," Lottie said reaching out to touch the animal gently. He noticed her and watched her carefully as if remembering who she was.

"He-he doesn't hear me," she said to me, not letting her eyes wander from the beast. "I don't understand, I don't feel his mind." She shook her head and finally looked at me when Tongo turned his attention back. He purred at me and padded forward to my outstretched hand, resting his nose against my palm. Someone shifted their position in the circle and Tongo immediately swung in their direction to see what it was.

"No," I yelled holding up my hands to the troupe around me, but it was too late. I heard the cock of the gun before I could find who held it and a loud shot rang throughout the camp. It echoed off the trailers and slowly vanished into the midnight air leaving everyone standing in utter shock.

"What have you *done!*" Lottie cried, running to the beast. Tongo lay on his side breathing heavily, a large wound was spilling blood against the hard ground. He looked up at Lottie with wet eyes and blinked. I felt the confusion, the pain, the suffering coming from his mind. He didn't understand what was happening to him and he was scared.

"Shh, it's okay," I reassured Tongo, petting his head gently and pushing the feeling of love and affection toward him. I wanted to erase his pain, to take it away like I was taking powers, but it wasn't something I could wrap my tendrils around and hold. Tears stung at my eyes as I watched his breathing slow. Lottie had lifted his head gently and placed it on her lap. She bent over and kissed his face, petting him over and over and telling him what a great friend he had been, what a good tiger he was and that she loved him. Everyone stood in silence as we watched Tongo take his final breath, sending me a single memory of seeing Lottie for the first time and pushing the emotion of happiness and joy through his mind to mine. It wrapped around my aura like a warm blanket and tears fell from my eyes.

"No. No, no, no," Lottie cried pulling the tiger up to her face and rocking him back and forth. "No, stay with me. Please." I pulled her against me and tried to push the memory Tongo shared with me into her mind. As it created itself again for her, I saw a small smile play on her face, glistening against the tears that stained her cheeks. "Oh, Tongo. I'm so sorry."

I felt the life fade away from Tongo, and taking a heavy breath, I stood up slowly. Surveying the group around me, my gaze landed on the person holding the gun. Seeing my glare, the clown known as "Giggles" stepped back in fear.

"I-I didn't...He was about—" He stuttered, and his round pale face begin to drip with sweat. I began to walk toward him in steady, even paces.

"About to what? Eat me? Jump on me? Tear me apart like he did my father?" I spat. "No, he wasn't going to do any of that."

"Y-you don't know that," he began but I was in front of him standing eye to eye, and I saw his pupils widen in panic.

"Yes, I do. I had him under *control*." I reached for the gun and pulled it out of his hands. Lifting it quickly, I aimed it at his head, the rifle warm against my hands. His aura jumped from a saddened blue to a pulsing red and orange of fear and worry. "What are you about to do? Should I kill you too because maybe," I pushed the barrel forward into his cheek as he turned away, "You will attack? Maybe you want to kill me and tear me apart." Standing still against him I felt my aura reach for his and tickle the ends of his fear. He gasped as if feeling a darkness sweep over him. I didn't know if he had any abilities but my power would seek it out. Urging my aura to close in around his mind I felt it, a small bubble filled with the ability to shift emotions to laughter. Feeling a chuckle in the back of my throat, I began to laugh.

"Jacob?" Lottie stood behind me, her soft yoga pants covered with fresh tiger blood. It angered me but all I could do was laugh as I turned and ripped out his ability and took it for my own adding it to the collection inside my mind.

"What have you done!" he shouted.

"I took a piece of you," I growled letting the weapon down so I could lean close to him. "You took a piece of our troupe, it was only fair." Shoving the weapon back into his hands, leaving a red circle from the hot barrel on his cheek, I stepped back. "You're done here. Pack your things."

"You can't do that," he rebuttelled. "You're not in charge."

"My father is dead," I said loudly to make sure everyone heard me. Lottie put her shaking hand on my shoulder to let me know she was here for me. "He is dead and I am next in line to take over. This circus is mine now and you *will* do as I say."

"No, he's alive!" Theo yelled from the trailer door. "Someone call 911." Frantically everyone began checking their pockets for a phone or any way to call for help. A blonde trapeze artist held up her Nokia and began dialing. I heard her asking for help at the fairgrounds but rushed back to the trailer to see for myself.

Peering over the mutilated body, still spilling blood from the fresh wounds, I noticed a slight rise and fall of the chest.

"Oh my god," I gasped. Theo pushed by me and felt my father's neck for a pulse, careful not to press on any open gashes.

"He has a pulse, its faint but it's there. He may be able to survive this yet." He looked up at me.

"He's pretty badly beaten, there's no way to know for sure." Deep down I wished he may not make it through. He would return as an even worse version than himself—if that were even possible—knowing his torn face would never be able to run the show again. Hearing the sirens wailing closer and tires hitting the rocky surface, I pulled myself away and back to the table where pieces of my father were left.

Paramedics carefully lifted his mangled body, strapped it to a gurney, and took him to the nearest hospital. I declined their offer to ride along and wait for him, knowing there was nothing I could do—honestly there was nothing I *wanted* to do to help him.

"Psshh," Giggles scoffed and I trained my glare on him again.

"What?" I sneered. "You think you're still allowed to be here just because he *may* survive?"

"Well, yeah," he threw his arms up. "You have no say here."

"Get out," I snapped. He didn't move and I stepped quickly to him. He flinched as I neared but puffed out his chest trying to show the others he wasn't afraid of me. I inhaled with my nose pointing at him then leaned in close.

"I can smell your fear, *Giggles.*" I kept my voice low so the others wouldn't hear. Everything around me faded into oblivion and it was just him and I standing nose to nose. His aura bounced quickly around him in an orange and brown hue of fear and confusion. I felt my aura reaching toward his and begin to consume it slowly. Giggles winced as if feeling his aura being drained and I watched as his skin paled.

"Something wrong, Giggles?" I asked, feeling a sly smile creep onto my face. Pushing the black arms out and around the clown, I saw his face shift from worry to glee. His lips pulled at the side and his mouth opened wide releasing a loud, boisterous chuckle.

"Stop," he laughed. "Please, stop." He winced but continued to smile through the invisible pain I was causing him.

With every inhale I drained his aura more, and with every bit I took, I felt my own power build within me. I knew I was causing him pain, even though I was using his own ability against him. The tears that fell were not tears of joy—I couldn't stop though. The jolt of adrenaline was a feeling I never wanted to let go of, and I may not have if Lottie hadn't placed her hand on my shoulder.

"Jacob," she said quietly. "Don't make a scene." I exhaled a breath I didn't realize I was holding and stepped back from Giggles. His face fell and he was breathing heavily, sweat dripped down from his brow.

"Get out," I growled.

Giggles huffed and stormed away toward his trailer. Within a moment, the truck hauling it rattled to life and chugged its way out of the campsite. Taking Lottie's hand, I lead her away and back to my trailer, but before I opened the door, I turned back to the group that was beginning to close in on itself and spoke.

"Take the trailer and light it on fire. We will move in two days and I expect you all to be ready."

"And the tiger?" someone asked. I paused and looked at the beast lying motionless on the ground now looking like a sleeping pet.

"There is a vet coming to take the tiger," Lottie said through her tears and I nodded that I'd heard her.

"Cover the tiger with a clean sheet and someone wait for the vet. Come get me when they arrive." I squeezed Lottie's hand and opened the door to my trailer, letting her in before me. I closed the door and sat at the table, letting myself fall apart at her hands.

"What have I done?" I asked her, letting my head fall into my hands. She sat in the booth next to me and wrapped her arms around my shoulders.

"It's okay. We will be okay. We just...just...need...hell, I don't know but right now there's nothing we can do but wait and see if your father recovers and go from there."

"I'm so sorry, Lottie." I looked at her and grabbed her hands. "I know how much you loved that tiger."

She bit her lip trying to force herself not to cry again but she sputtered and fell to pieces letting herself fall into my chest. I held her close and ran my fingers through her hair.

"He was so kind, so gentle. I don't understand why he would do this." She sobbed. I felt her tears begin to soak through my shirt but it only made me hold her tighter.

"It's my fault," I confessed. "I did this."

"No, it was just an accident. I mean, I don't know why he did it but—"

"Shh," I stopped her pulling her close to me again.

"I will explain it all in the morning," I pulled her face up to mine and looked her deep in the eye. "I promise I will explain everything." I kissed her wet lips and her cheek and pulled her against me again.

* * *

The vet arrived quickly and gently took the tiger with him, letting Lottie know where she could come to claim the ashes if she wanted them.

"Thank you," she said taking his card and watching as he drove away with her friend.

"You okay?" I asked wrapping my arm around her shoulder, her sad blue aura fading in and out around her.

"I will be," she looked up and gave me a soft smile. "Let's go see your dad."

"Lottie..." I began.

"No, you need to see him. If anything, just to say your goodbyes. If he doesn't make it and you're not there you will never forgive yourself."

"Would I, though?" I asked hoping she would answer what I had been asking myself the whole time.

"The guilt would eat you alive."

"Okay," I gave in. "Let's go."

* * *

The doctor explained to me that they put my father into a medically induced coma because his wounds were so extensive his body couldn't handle the amount of pain. They told me he may never wake up, that even if he did he would never be the same person he was before—whether that was a good or bad thing I hadn't decided.

"So, what do we do now, just wait?" I asked the doctor as I stood at the end of my father's bed. He was hooked up to multiple machines beeping, pulsing, pumping, and dripping fluids into him. A tube ran down his throat helping him breathed and his chest rose and fell as it forced air in and out.

"Yes, we never know how long it will take someone to heal and with the wounds his body has it could be days, weeks, months."

"*Months!*" I felt faint. I knew I couldn't wait around for him for months, not if we were going to keep the circus running, plus we didn't have insurance and there was no way for me to pay for all these expenses.

"I know it seems like a lot, it can be very overwhelming, but we will just take it one day at a time."

"I can't just sit around and wait for him, I have a job—people that count on me."

"No one said you had to be here by his bedside the entire time, we have nurses and staff that will monitor him. You are free to come and go as needed and we will call you if there are any urgent changes in his condition." I nodded as he spoke but my eyes would not move from my father before me.

It was one of the first times I had seen him so vulnerable, exposed and hurt. He looked at peace. Lottie's warm hand slipped inside mine and I squeezed it for comfort.

"How is his brain activity?" She asked the doctor.

"It's weak, but there is still some. You can see here," he reached over and pointed to a machine that was printing paper with spikes and lines. "These show that the brain is still functioning."

"And what happens if his brain stops?" I asked.

"Jacob, you can't think like that." Lottie looked at me with moist eyes.

"I'm just trying to be prepared, Lottie. I need time to process it all if the worst happens."

She nodded understanding everything had happened so quickly.

"Well, if the brain activity stops then the machines will continue to work and keep him breathing."

"But he'll be dead." I remember watching medical TV shows and recalling that brain-dead patients are only kept alive at that point for organ donation.

"Yes, his body will only be working because the machines are doing it for him but I assure you we are doing everything we can to prevent that."

"Okay, thank you." After giving the doctor a number to reach me he and Lottie left me alone with my father. Moving around the bed, I leaned close to his ear.

"I'm sorry," I whispered, feeling tears sting the corner of my eyes. "But you did deserve this." I pulled away as if to leave but guilt hit my stomach like a brick knowing I had already lost my mother and now...if he were to pass I would have no family left in this world.

"I love you." I left the hospital that day not knowing if I'd ever be back to see him. Little did I know I would never get the chance.

CHAPTER 9

The next morning, I sat at the table with Lottie and explained everything. I told her about my father, the beatings, the psychic abilities—how I didn't have one and then I suddenly did—how I stole my fathers, how I accidentally stole hers, and how I can sense people's auras. She listened to the whole story without saying a word. Sipping her coffee slowly, she nodded at appropriate times letting me explain in full before making her decision if I was insane or not.

"And that's how I was able to control the tiger last night. It was just an accident. I didn't know what I was doing," I leaned back against the seat wrapping my hands around the barely warm mug and watched her.

Lottie sat curled up, her legs crossed under her, and her hair was twisted up into a loose bun on her head and the circles under her eyes made her look tired and sad. Her finger tapped against the mug as she watched the steam rise from the black coffee inside. When she stopped tapping she looked up at me with wide eyes and nodded once.

"Okay," she said, and I waited for more but she sat there unmoving.

"O-okay?" I said like a question, leaning forward on the table.

"Okay, I believe you."

"You do?" It seemed too easy.

"Yes, why wouldn't I?" Bringing the mug to her lips, she sipped it slowly, the steam wrapping itself around her freckled nose.

"Um...I don't know maybe because it sounds completely insane, unreasonable, and maybe I might be some lunatic who is just running around pretending I'm some special alien species with the ability to steal psychic powers, just trying to persuade you to fall in love with me so I can probe you."

Shaking her head, she giggled.

"I have no reason not to trust you. I can sense you are an honest person and I know you well enough by now to know you wouldn't lie to me." She paused blowing out a gust of air. "It may seem far-fetched, yes, and quite strange I'll give you that, but I had an ability, so why wouldn't I believe you that you had one too? I always knew I wasn't the only one out there." Lottie reached across the table and wrapped her warm fingers around mine pulling them toward her. "We will figure this out. Together."

I nodded at her as my father's old cell phone rang.

"Hello," I answered, holding the thick phone up to my ear. It smelled of cigar smoke and was covered in dirt and grime from being carried in my father's back pocket for so long. After a short conversation to the caller, I hung up and let myself fall into the dining table seat again.

"Who was that?" Lottie asked, watching me cautiously.

"It was uh.." I cleared my throat. "That was the hospital. M-my uh, they said his brain activity stopped this morning."

"Oh, Jacob." Lottie moved to the other side of the table and grabbed my hands. "I'm so sorry."

"I need to go down there and tell them my decision."

"Decision?"

"Whether or not to keep him on life support or pull the plug."

Lottie went with me to the hospital before anyone at the camp was awake. She sat by me as I signed the papers to end life support, held my hand while I agreed to allow the hospital to donate his body or whatever they wanted, and stood by me while we watched them turn off the machines keeping him breathing one by one.

The lights had been dimmed and slowly they removed the tubes and detached the wires and I.V.'s and then left us alone while we waited for him to stop breathing naturally. We stood in silence as his chest slowed and when it finally stopped I pulled Lottie's hand and left without saying a word.

Lottie made coffee without saying a word. She set box-mix muffins in front of me, steaming still from being baked in the tiny oven, then she puttered around the trailer wanting to give me space to do whatever I needed to do. As she began folding towels, a knock sounded on the door.

"It's open," I called, pulling the mug up to my mouth to drink the bitter coffee. The trailer door swung open and the magician stepped inside.

"Morning," he looked at me, then Lottie.

"What do you want?"

"Well...the troupe is waiting to hear what you want them to do."

"About what?" I leaned back against the seat, my hands still wrapped around the hot mug.

"Last night..." he hesitated, shifting his weight uncomfortably as if I could have forgotten the incidents that occurred.

"Yes, yes. I'll be right there." The trailer door clicked shut and I pinched the bridge of my nose where stress sat heavily from the hunger in my mind.

Running my fingers through my hair and shaking out the weight that had fallen on my shoulders, I reached into the tiny drawers that held the few items of clothing I had and pulled out a clean polo shirt. It smelled stale as if it had come with the old trailer, so I pumped one spray of cologne onto it. I heard Lottie inhale the fresh scent.

"Oooh," she cooed. "That smells wonderful!" She stood and placed her hands on my chest. "It reminds me of a cozy night looking at the stars."

"What?" I smiled pulling her away to look at her face. Her eyes were closed and she breathed in again.

"Yes, it's like a mix of fresh rain, a handsome man," her eyebrows went up and down, "and a little bit of romance." Finally opening her eyes, she winked at me, pushed up on her toes, and kissed me once.

"And what exactly does *romance* smell like?"

"It's like the scent of the nighttime air, cool and crisp, that relaxes your nerves and makes you feel so safe and comfortable. Like when you're laying outside on a warm summer night looking at the stars, you know? The grass fresh against your skin and the crickets chirping. I really like it."

"Wow," I forced my eyes open wide and picked up the cologne bottle. "Maybe I should be more careful with this stuff."

She smacked my shoulder gently and reached to put on her shoes. "I'm glad to see you smile."

I felt her lips on my cheek and I stood wrapping her in a tight hug. "Thank you, for being here."

She nodded and took my hand, we walked together to the crew that was now waiting for us outside my trailer.

"Good morning," I said loudly and with a deep, powerful tone. The troupe responded in their own morning greeting and I looked around at each of them. They carried heavy faces and slouched shoulders, their auras were a mix of sad blues, greens, and purples that were soft and hazy, blending in and out of each other as if they were all sharing the loss we had last night. Clearing my throat, I continued.

"I know last night was a bit of a...traumatic night for us all." Some people grumbled or snorted. "Early this morning, my father was found braindead and we have decided to end life support. He is gone but we will continue our show. It's what he would have wanted."

"The show must go on," Lottie said with a sad smile. I squeezed her hand to let her know I understood the pain she and I were both feeling. I could sense it in the deep blue aura that washed around her like a pool of tears.

"So what, we just forget it ever happened and move on? We lost our leader, our boss, your *father*," one of the trapeze women said, wrapping a thin, baggy sweater around her petite frame.

"We could..." someone began, and I searched for who had said it.

"Yes?" I urged them. A young boy, one of the snack attendants stepped forward. I nodded, willing him to finish his thought.

"I think we should hold a moment of silence at the beginning of our next show, you know, in honor of your father," he said.

"And what about the tiger?" Someone else asked.

"We will hold a moment of silence for *both* of them. It's a good idea, thank you." I turned back to the group. "It was just an accident, nothing more—"

"And how exactly does a tiger *accidentally* release itself from a *locked* cage?" One of the male tightrope walkers began his accusation.

"I'm...I'm not sure exactly but—"

"It seems really fishy that after what happened between you two, a tiger suddenly gets set loose and *only* goes after him."

"Yes," Lottie took over. "Jacob's father wasn't the most honorable or kind man but he was still his dad. He would never purposely hurt or kill him, he was his only family."

"And how do *you* know it wasn't him?" He asked.

"Because he was with me all night," she responded and a wave of scoffs washed through the crowd. "Look, accidents happen. It could have been my fault for all we know. I was distracted last night and maybe I didn't push the lock in fully. Maybe a bar was loose on the cage. I don't know, weird shit happens all the time."

"I know it doesn't make sense. Hell, I can't even wrap my head around it fully either but I do know that he would want us to continue, to move forward and keep the show up and running."

The trapeze woman began to cry, turning herself into the man standing next to her. Murmurs spread throughout the camp and their auras began to shift to an orange and yellow pulse of worry.

"Everyone. Everyone!" I called. "Please, trust me that I have your best interest at heart. I want us to be the best, be better, be the most spectacular, magnificent, amazing show anyone has ever seen. But I can't do it by myself. I need you—all of you."

Holding my breath, I looked at each one of them and saw their questioning faces and furrowed brows, I saw their mouths open and close trying to make a decision, I watched them cross, uncross, fold, and drop their hands trying to understand the choice they had to make.

"Okay," the tightrope walker said, nodding. He looked at those next to him and urged them to follow his lead. Slowly everyone began to mutter "yes" and "okay" under their breath while nodding their head in agreement. "We're with you."

"Alright, let's begin then." I took a deep breath and began giving orders. Together we came up with a plan to create the best show we could possibly imagine. Everyone provided their ideas, changes, modifications, and upgrades to their acts and the production itself. We had a game plan—one that would ensure we could be famous and keep our show the greatest circus around.

I felt the rush of energy in the room as their auras flickered with bright greens, blues, and yellows of excitement for what we had in store and they reached out as if wanting me to touch them—and I did.

As if in slow motion, I watched as my inky black aura trailed through the people in front of me and began taking tiny pieces of their powers. Before, I had no idea how many of our members held special abilities, but now, it was apparent that almost all of them carried some sort of psychic awareness. With each bite, gulp, and token taken from those around me, I felt myself grow more powerful, as if I had taken a drug that finally woke me up inside. My nerves were sensitive and I felt their emotions, heard their cheers, and drank in their eagerness to enlighten myself.

I should have been scared of this ability and this type of power, but I wasn't. I had never felt this kind of urgency—this need—to take from someone else and yet as I filled myself with the smallest pieces of their abilities, I found myself smiling, laughing even, and rejoicing in the new man I was becoming.

CHAPTER 10

WE CONTINUED ON OUR SET TOUR, TRAVELING FROM CITY TO CITY WITH me as the new showman. I was in complete control and everyone was accepting me as their Ringmaster. It was as if I had been doing it my whole life, it came so naturally to me.

Eventually, I was able to give Lottie her ability back—mostly. We sat holding each other's hands as I attempted to pull it from the collection in my mind and release it back to her, but when I pulled it away—like ripping off a band-aid—it left a little residue behind. I could still feel the emotions of animals and predict what they were thinking, but I could no longer control their actions like Lottie could. She was thankful for getting her power back and I watched as she embraced the two tigers who had once been so small, but now stood with their heads against her chest.

I sought out those with special abilities like myself and Lottie. I found them easily, as I could sense their psychic power and see it in their auras—fire dancers that could control the flame, trapeze and highwire acrobatics that didn't need a net as they never fell, clowns that could alter the emotions of those around them to ensure happiness and laughter, psychics who could actually see the future and read palms, and more. Gaining these abilities in our circus became like a hobby for me—they were my collection and one I could profit off of.

Our troupe became the biggest name in the states and caused excitement when our posters magically appeared overnight. We were a circus that made children beg their parents to take them to because of the power they felt. We were the best but it wasn't enough. My ability wanted more, it was hungry—always hungry—and I had to find ways to feed it and keep it at bay.

I took little bits of psychic power from everyone around me. The more people I hired to work our show, the less they noticed the drain. Eventually, all their power would be gone and I would harness their full ability leaving them dry and empty and soon after they all ended up going insane—some even killing themselves from the constant poking around on their minds. We went through many acts before I learned to control how much I wanted to take. Like a vampire, I drained just enough to give me a jolt of energy—sometimes it was just a sip; others a little more. The power was intoxicating—a high I never wanted to come down from—and the energy of the circus itself was invigorating and complete ecstasy.

Our shows were pure magic. People paid good money to be tricked and hypnotized into seeing whatever we wanted them to see. Soaring birds, bats, balloons, baboons, whatever we thought of they could see. We had so many different acts it kept them entertained and the new fear factor of no net, moving fire, knives, guns, and live animals was enough to keep them addicted—but it wasn't enough for me.

"Ladies and gentleman," I yelled from center stage and the crowd cheered with excitement. Their auras began dancing, spinning, and twirling around themselves in hues of brilliant pinks, blues, and greens. "Welcome to the *Ringmaster's Circus!*" Everyone was on their feet screaming with joy. I smiled as my aura reached out and latched itself onto a few auras that were thick and eager. I took a little, watching it thin, but ensuring their emotions weren't hindered or changed and allowed their excitement to fill me with the power to run the show.

"Please, if we could," I waited for them to quiet down and settle again before continuing. The new jacket felt stiff and tight against my skin—the fabric shimmered of gentle black and silver and the ruby buttons glistened in the show lights. I took a deep breath and continued, feeling the weight of my fathers satin hat upon my head. "I would like to take a moment of silence for all those we have lost so recently. Not only were the members part of our troupe but they were family. As you know, my father—who was our original showman—has passed away following the death of my mother and one of our beloved tigers, Tongo. So please, take a moment to remember them and honor them before we enjoy our magical night." Everyone sat in silence, some bowed their heads as if in prayer while others sat in a respectable quietness shushing their children who didn't understand what we were doing. The large screen that dropped down the back of the stage filled with photos of my father, my mother, and the tiger we had lost.

"Thank you." I smiled at the audience, holding back a tear that threatened to fall from the pool in my eyes. "Although they are gone from our show, they will forever be in our thoughts and hearts. But now, as my father would insist, we must go on." I beamed and spread my arms and yelled, "Let us begin!"

Music screamed above us as the speakers jolted from the bass and the trapeze artists flew through the air as if flying like a bird. They rolled and tumbled through the air barely being caught by their partner or ring while others fell from the top of the tent and were caught inches from the floor with the almost invisible fabric that allowed them to spiral down. Their sequin outfits sparkled with the twirling lights that shone a rainbow of colors around the tent and audience and their smiling faces glowed against the fear the crowd held for them. Tightrope walkers balanced on wires that bent below their weight. Stepping lightly, they moved one foot after the other while holding or juggling different items and the audience gasped as one lost their step and almost tumbled, realizing they could not see a net below them. Little did they know the performers could never fall as their abilities provided them perfect balance and control.

As they disappeared into a haze of fog, dropping down to the ground and vanishing, the fire dancers appeared tossing flames across the stage, burning the fabric and ropes the acrobats and trapeze artists had just held on to, and let the heat wash over the crowd forcing them back and down into their seats. Their shiny black unitards glistened against the red and orange flames that seemed to never touch their skin or burn them—and that was exactly what their ability allowed them to do. After eating the fire, letting it lash out at certain members in the audience, and tumbling through flaming rings, they finished their act with a bang as fireballs rained down from the sky.

The crowd screamed with fright covering their heads, but before the flames touched their skin, they morphed into cool pieces of confetti that kissed them gently. Theo, the magician, stood center stage hypnotizing the audience into seeing whatever he wanted. Cards appeared and disappeared in certain hands, grew to unimaginable sizes and scurried about like mice on the stage and in between the feet of the crowd. Children squealed as cards took shapes of elephants, cats, dogs, and their favorite creatures such as dragons and flew about the tent.

Theo pulled all kinds of things out of his hat. Everything from rabbits to snakes, from flying squirrels to even a dinosaur. They all ripped through the surface of the top hat and ran around before disappearing in a loud *pop* of smoke.

Our show was pure magic. After Lottie and the remaining acts performed, everyone cheered, standing up in hopes to have just one more show; one more moment of excitement, one more thrill as their adrenaline was pumping through their veins.

As I took the stage for the final farewell, I saw the auras waving alongside everyone and reached out allowing it to freely feed off anyone and everyone, taking in their emotions and fueling myself with them.

"Thank you, everyone, for attending tonight," I called with my loudest showman voice. "We hope you enjoyed the show and we will be back!" I clapped my hands and the stage lit up with dancing lights and loud music as the troupe came out for their final bow and disappeared within the fog that had drifted over and wrapped itself around everyone.

To this day, my power remains hungry—starving for more psychic abilities and I have struggled to find enough energy to ease the pain it causes. Lottie has caught on to the amount I have been taking and worries that someday the ability will take total control of my humanity—that I will lose myself to its needs.

Most days I worry as well.

It wasn't until I accidentally took too much too quickly, allowing my ability to take what it wanted that I realized how right Lottie had been.

As I watched the trapeze artist convulse on the ground unable to save her, I understood that my power was becoming its own entity and I was falling into its deadly trap.

There was no way to control it anymore.

"You must find a powerful ability, one greater than all our own put together, one that could sustain your hunger for a very long time," our psychic, Madam Svetlana, said in her withered old voice. I came to her for help, wanting to know if she could see my future downfall and maybe, just maybe help me save myself and those around me.

"How am I supposed to do that?" I asked her, feeling defeated.

"There is one, a girl. She is young now, but her power is strong; stronger than I ever felt before."

"How do I find her?" I leaned forward on the table watching her as she searched inside her crystal ball for the answer.

"You will sense her when the time is right. Her ability can not hide forever and your power will seek her out. Follow your mind and let it lead you to her. She could fill the hunger for eternity." She looked up over the glowing ball filled with shifting smoke and grinned. "She has the ability to see the past, present, and future, but we will make sure she does not see us coming."

"What?" I asked confused. If the girl has visions, she would surely know when they were coming after her, and their end game.

"Allow me to explain. I see that soon she will want to hide her power, push it away and deny it exists as death and despair fill her life. Once forgotten, it will be time for you to find her and push her ability to release itself again. Once regained, her psychic power will be the greatest you've ever felt and too much for her. She may even give it to you willingly to ease herself of the pain it causes."

"And I'll never need to feed again?" I wondered.

"The satiety will fade slowly, but so slowly you will not notice. By the time the hunger peaks again your time in this world will end." She folded her hands together, the many bracelets jingling together as she moved and looked at me with faded brown eyes.

"And what will happen to her when I take her power?" I didn't want to hurt anyone anymore.

"She will fade away." She flipped her hands as if it were just a bug being squished.

"Thank you," I told her, standing to leave. It was something I needed to think about and plan. If Svetlana was right, I still had time to prepare, time to find her, and time to figure out a way to take her power without hurting her, maybe. Right now it was up in the air, there was no way to know what could really happen. For now, I needed to find a temporary way to ease the hunger growing inside me. I felt my power beginning to awaken after its slumber from the recent feeding. It gently pulsed at the edge of my mind to let me know it was ready for more.

I gulped, not knowing what would happen next, but I knew I needed to do something. If one girl's life would save the however many hundreds my ability would need to take to continue thriving, then maybe it would be worth it.

I will not take another human life for myself. Not yet anyways.

Hungry. So hungry. Need more. Want more.

He lets me go and I feel free as I spin through the air toward the human before me. I sense their power, feel their power, and I want it. I must have it. It will be mine.

My master sets me loose and I will take what I want. I feel her mind and find the deepest part of it where it is nice and cozy and filled with her favorite, more cherished memories.

Those ones taste the best.

I take them.

Eat them.

Devour them like a sweet treat

They are mine.

But I am still hungry, hungry for more.

I see her mind shift as I push through the folds and spaces, my smokiness allowing me to move easily as I see a brilliant feast.

She is special. She has a power too. Her power is weak and can not fight me.

I touch it to let it know I'm there and as if saying hello it pulses at my connection. Reaching slowly, sending sparks of curiosity, it feels the edges of my need.

It is scared.

It pulls back.

But I snatch it like a ripe berry and devour it in one bite.

More.

I need more.

Hungry, so hungry.

The human vessel is stronger now because of me. I feel his senses become enlightened as I let my energy flow through him. I need him to be strong to keep me alive.

I can tell the female mind is crumbling as it begins to collapse within the spaces I made.

And yet I need more.

I fill myself with anything I can find and eventually there is nothing left to take.

There's too much blood.

I can not see.

I pull away and drift back to my keeper who welcomes me with an open mind. I settle back into my space, safe within his mind, and close the barriers around myself so no one can touch me. I protect him. He protects me.

Someday I will not need him.

He will always need me. He can not live without me now. Not after he has felt the power I give him.

I pulse lightly letting him know I am here, reminding him of my presence, and letting him know I am always inside his mind.

My color fades around me as the energy begins to lessen.

Hungry, so hungry.

ABOUT JESSICA JULIEN

Born in the picturesque state of Washington, Jessica Julien is an online ESL teacher to students in China, a stay at home mom, wife, and wanderluster. When not in the virtual classroom, she spends her time writing young adult novels focused on the paranormal and supernatural inspired by her love of all things dark and twisty. With her vivacious imagination, witty personality, and ability to bring sarcasm to a new level, Jessica creates unique worlds and characters that readers can't help but hate to love and love to hate.

CONNECT ON SOCIAL MEDIA

jjulienauthor.wix.com/author

facebook.com/jjulienauthor

instagram.com/jjulienauthor

twitter.com/jjulienauthor

We All Fall

Helen Vivienne Fletcher

CHAPTER 1

THE AIR WAS STILL THE DAY SHE ARRIVED. WE'D SPENT WEEKS BATTLING a strange, hot summer wind, the big top closed several nights as flapping tent sides turned to thundering, drowning out the music and scaring the punters. There were no creatures to spook, of course. Those days long gone as animal-cruelty had been replaced with long hours of training human bodies to complete impossible feats.

Not that *I* did impossible feats these days, unless you counted reviving well-worn, ripped costumes and sewing sparkles in the minimal light of early morning. The world often had a pink shine to it when I opened my eyes—the result of rouge sequins stuck to my eyelashes. I'd let my hair grow long since I'd stopped performing, as I no longer had to tame it into a bun each day. The wild and wiry curls claimed the sparkles too. No matter how often I washed my hair, there was always a shimmer to it, and a few sequins falling from my shoulders to leave a trail behind me wherever I went. I swore they were sentient, breeding and moving when I wasn't looking.

We all watched as the new caravan rolled in. The fortune teller's tent was already set up, waiting for them. It had been months since we'd had a psychic travel with us. The last one had taken her role a little too seriously and gone mad with the visions she saw.

I was supposed to be in the costume room, fixing one of the clown's suspenders. Apparently, it wasn't so funny if her pants fell down when it wasn't planned.

I'd snuck out when I'd heard the rumour of their arrival whispered around the tents. The caravan door opened, and an older woman wafted out. She was draped in a black lace shawl with an impractical fringe. If I hadn't already heard the talk, I would have mistaken her for the teller. Instead I waited, holding my breath, for the girl to appear.

"Myra, what are you doing?!"

I spun around at the sound of my mother's voice. I lost my balance as I did, sprawling in the dirt.

My mother stepped back, wincing at the sight of me. It looked strange on her. She was always so poised; her glittering stage makeup and perfect bun replacing her real skin and hair almost constantly. Negative facial expressions broke the effect and were therefore rarely allowed.

I pulled myself up on to my hands and knees, wincing too at the never-ending tenderness in my right leg. "I wanted to see her arrive," I said.

My mother didn't reply, her attention seemingly taken by something just over my shoulder. I knew there was nothing there; she just couldn't bear to look at me. I hadn't seen her eyes meet mine since the day of my accident.

She nodded absently, accepting the explanation, or perhaps simply acknowledging that I had stopped talking. She held out a leotard. "I need this fixed for tonight."

I sighed, glancing back towards the teller's caravan. The door was closed, the girl already inside the tent.

My mother followed my gaze and smiled slightly. "I'm sure you'll get a chance to meet Giselle later. Maybe you can even get a reading."

I scowled. "I don't believe in psychics."

My mother chuckled. "Well, perhaps she doesn't believe in trapeze artists."

"It's a good thing I'm not one of those, then." My tone was harsh, and I watched her face fall. Her eyes flicked towards my leg, then she closed them, a shudder working its way up her body.

"Don't let anyone hear you say you don't believe in the teller," she said, her voice flat. "We must always—"

"Keep up the show," I finished for her.

She nodded, her expression tired suddenly. She turned to head back to her rehearsal, then paused. "Do you need any help getting up?" she asked.

I thought of the pain I would feel, once my weight was back on my feet, and the wobbling uncertainty of those first few steps. A hand—

an arm to link through—would ease some of that, making me feel safer.

"No, I'm fine on my own," I said.

She nodded curtly, then walked away. I waited until she was out of sight before biting my lip and pulling myself to my feet.

I don't know if it was a sign of a lack of parental bond that led my mother and father to send me flying through the air. Maybe it was a misguided belief that the bond was so strong it could conquer gravity. Either way, gravity had won. My leg had shattered in three places, and my feet had been firmly on the ground ever since.

I didn't mind. Well, of course I minded the lingering pain and the limp that made me question every step. But I liked my new role working on the costumes. Not so much the mending, but when I had the chance to make something from scratch. I liked being able to create something that's beauty would last longer than the fleeting moment of thrill my tricks in the air had been. It was a chance to put my own ideas and design into the world, rather than just repeating the same choreography my parents had come up with over and over.

I finished mending the suspender and my mother's costume as quickly as I could, hoping I would have a chance to catch a glimpse of Giselle before the gates opened to the public that night, but by the time I'd attached the last sequin, there were already hoards milling around outside her tent, curious about the new attraction. I knew she wouldn't get a chance to step outside until the night was done.

I walked down to the smoko area as my parents' act began. My mother wanted me to watch their routine each night. To "keep it fresh" in my mind. She was still deluding herself that my injury would heal, and I would be returning to join them someday. I couldn't stay in the big top, though, not even to make her happy. If I watched them flip and twirl one more time, my leg wouldn't be the only thing that snapped.

I took my home-school work with me, settling down with my books in front of the trash can fire. I was hoping to finish another assignment and send it away in the morning. The workers sitting on their breaks were rowdy, but they mostly left me out of it. They were hardly the most polite when it came to women, but they either felt harassing a fifteen year old was going too far, or they were scared stiff of my father's right hook, powered by years of the most intense upper body workout the circus had to offer. Of course, the performers avoided me too, the superstitious fear of someone who'd fallen keeping them away.

"Hey, Myra."

I glanced up as Luca sat down next to me. I hesitated, then closed my book, welcoming his company. At seventeen, he was the closest to my age in our traveling family. He was a performer, but he was a sceptic through and through, and made a hobby of tempting fate just to watch the superstitious ones squirm.

"You met the new girl, yet?" he asked.

I shook my head. He obviously held the same hope I did, that another person our age would bring some sense of youth back to our lives.

He grinned. "You think she knows she's entering the land of the damned?"

I laughed. "Got to be damned already to come here." Making exhibits out of body abnormalities was no longer politically correct, but the circus was still full of freaks either way.

"If I were her, I'd be running in the other direction."

I reached out, touching Luca's arm to quiet him. He had been saying things like that a lot recently. If he wasn't careful, leaving wouldn't be his choice anymore. The ringmaster did not take kindly to complaints.

He took a breath, letting go of his frustration. His face softened as he took my hand from his arm and squeezed it. I'd left a sparkle on his shoulder. He would flick it off when he saw it. I could see another glinting in amongst his dark curls. I ran my hand through his hair, plucking it out.

His eyelids fluttered as I did, and he opened his mouth to speak, but I handed him the sequin before he could.

"A present for you," I said.

He laughed and took the sparkle from me, pressing it to the back of his hand. "I'm always covered in these after I hang out with you." He often complained about me leaving my marks on him.

"I saw her mother," I told him, bringing the conversation back to the subject which had been occupying my thoughts all evening. "Bathed in faux-mystique. If the teller's anything like her, they'll be raking it in."

Luca shook his head. "Another mother-daughter pair, eh?"

Luca nudged my side, and I forced a laugh to avoid the moment becoming awkward. Though he was jaded now, and perhaps regretting the decision, he had joined the circus of his own volition. He couldn't understand what it was like to be born into it. I wondered if Giselle felt the same way I did about growing up like this. It would be hard to say, given I was never sure from one day to the next how I felt about it myself.

"You hear she's blind?" Luca asked.

I shrugged. "You think it's for real?" I'd heard the rumours, but no one seemed sure whether it was true or just part of the act. There was an added layer of mystery to a young girl telling fortunes by feel alone. Even the most sceptical had to find that interesting. Curiosity had always been the main draw of the circus. The crowds gathered to catch a glimpse of a world—of people—that didn't quite match up to the rules of their own.

Luca sighed. "I think it's an act," he said. "Gotta know by now, none of this is real."

"So cynical, Luca. Where's your sense of wonder at the show?" I tried to keep a straight face as I quoted our ringmaster's familiar pep talk.

Luca shook his head. "There's no wonder here, Myra. Sleight-of-hand magic, threats of danger all carefully controlled to be perfectly safe..." He trailed off, and I could tell he'd suddenly remembered my snapped safety line.

His pity filled the space between us, coating both of us thicker than grease paint. I felt my face heat up and I turned to the fire, as if I could pass it off as warmth from the flames.

He cleared his throat. "I'm sorry. I didn't mean—"

"Hey, it's okay," I said quickly. "Nothing's ever perfect, not even safety, right?"

"Right."

We didn't mention the growing number of accidents that had happened recently. None of the others had been as catastrophic as mine—most were simple slips, failures of props or sets, leaving performers with sprained ankles or bruises to ice. We'd blamed the weather—the heartless wind that had been raking its way through all of us and shaking us in more ways than one, but there was no denying the wind wasn't the only thing to blame. There were some in the group who thought I'd brought a curse down on all of us the moment I dropped from that platform into nothing.

"I don't think she's lying," I said.

"Huh?" Luca's thoughts had wandered, and it took him a moment to return to me and our discussion of Giselle.

"The new girl. I think she's really blind."

Luca gave another shrug. "Could be. Guess we'll find out."

I gazed into the fire, letting my eyes soften. I didn't bother to try explaining it to Luca, but I wanted it to be true that she was blind. I couldn't even entirely explain it to myself, but I felt like something would change for me if she were.

CHAPTER 2

I DECIDED TO TAKE MY MOTHER'S SUGGESTION TO GO GET A FORTUNE from Giselle. She wouldn't know that I was a freak—one of the circus folk—so I would get to see what she was like when performing and fooling the normal—unless she really was psychic, of course, but I didn't believe it. In that department, I was just as cynical as Luca.

I didn't get the chance for the first few days. The excitement of a new attraction had brought in a new boon of punters, and the ring-master had added more matinees. I was kept busy mending and making new costumes for the daytime alternate performers. Even if I hadn't been, there was no way I would have been able to get the chance for a reading. Word had spread of the new fortune teller's strangely accurate work, and lines of people circled her tent as if they planned to strangle it.

For three days, all I saw were glimpses of her. A small peek through the gauzy curtains as one customer left, and another entered the tent. Those stolen glances only gave me a fleeting impression. She had long blonde hair, which draped her face, obscuring it from my viewpoint, and she wore appropriately mystical sweeping clothing. The effect was of someone shrouded from the world, swaddled in enough layers to keep her safe…or to keep the world safe from her. Perhaps the layers were supposed to hold the magic in.

Each time I peeked, I saw her mother hovering in the tent too. I didn't know her role in the act. The child psychic was the draw card; the lace-draped mother just seemed to be a power-hungry add-on. Of course, I was bringing my own damage into that thought. My mother may as well have hovered over every flying leap I'd made before my fall.

I took to spending my evenings, once the late performances had started and the other tents had closed down, walking on a loop that took me past her tent. Or limping in a loop, rather. I would get slower and less steady as the evening wore on, the pain growing with each step. Somehow, I couldn't make myself stop though. Passing her tent wasn't the intention, of course. I had no desire to stalk the girl, but I found myself drawn back there each night.

Finally, on the afternoon of the fourth day, a lull in the crowd outside her tent coincided with my finishing my mending. I hovered, unsure whether or not to go in. Her lace-cloaked mother caught sight of me and beckoned me forward.

"Don't be shy, dear, the spirits welcome all." Her voice quavered, a poor attempt at creating mystique.

I suppressed a smile and made my way between the swathes of brightly-coloured and bejewelled fabric curtaining the entrance. A strong smell of incense greeted me, though I couldn't see any burning.

"Sit down." She gestured grandly to a stool perched in front of a small table covered by a lace table cloth much resembling the shawl she wore. "Giselle will be with you shortly."

The interior of the tent was partitioned off by more of the gauzy, colourful fabric and lit only with candle light. She slipped between one of those partitions, leaving me seemingly alone.

Though I'd never worked the fortune teller's tent, I knew enough of the tricks of the trade to guess that they were watching me now, observing my body language and making educated guesses about me. I sat down on the stool wondering what it was I was telling them.

A tap against the floor made me turn. Her mother held the swathes of fabric back as Giselle came forward. I saw now why I'd never been able to see her face, earlier. She wore a white veil covering her eyes, hanging to just above her lips. She felt her way forward, tapping a white stick back and forth to guide her. I frowned as she bumped a table, the candle on top of it shuddering, threatening to fall. The drapes and candles seemed a dangerous mix given the circumstances.

Her stumbling, unsteady progress reminded me of my own unsure steps. Just like me, each careful footstep was an act of faith, bravado and fear. But she crossed the room safely, coming to sit opposite me. She took a deep breath, and I found myself do the same. It was strangely calming to match my inhales and exhales to hers.

She held out her hands. "Please."

I hesitated, then placed my hands in hers.

She ran her thumb along the lines of my right palm. It tickled, and I had to resist the urge to pull away. Her palms were cool, and she sat calmly, at one with the supposed spirits surrounding her.

"You wish to see the future," she said. Her voice was low and steady, none of the forced drama her mother had feigned.

I shrugged, then realised that was not an answer I could give when she couldn't see the movement. "I saw the tent," I said, still not admitting to working here. "It seemed interesting."

She nodded. "The future always draws us." She turned to business then, dropping the mystique a little. "It's five dollars for a fortune, ten for a *good* fortune and twelve for a fortune and a wish."

I frowned. I'd heard others mention the teller's strange method of charging double to only hear the positive parts of what she saw. I'd assumed it was a joke, but here she was offering me the chance to tint the future in a rosy glow.

She smiled recognising my confusion without having to see it. "It's very rare you can change the course of the future. Why hear the bad stuff if you can't do anything about it?"

"I don't believe in psychics." I surprised myself with the bluntness of my words. I hadn't meant to tell her that, but something about the setting made my natural guards drop away and honesty slip out.

"I'm not a psychic," she said. "I just tell fortunes."

I puzzled over the difference. She didn't seem offended by my words, and she didn't ask why I had come if I didn't believe, perhaps having seen this all too often. I reached into my pocket, sorting the coins stashed there. I had eleven dollars, enough to ask her to edit out the things I didn't want to hear. Curiosity made me want her to tell me everything though, and I knew choosing the good fortune would mean spending the night sleepless, wondering about the parts she'd withheld. Even though I didn't believe it was real, I still wanted to hear her whole prediction.

I placed five dollars in her hand. "Just a fortune," I said.

She tilted her head slightly. "You're a brave one."

She said it like a statement of fact, and I couldn't tell whether she was praising or making fun of me. She left her hand lingering on mine, and I felt my breath quicken, a strange warmth starting in my stomach. It spread to my cheeks, making me light-headed. I drew my hand away.

She was still for a moment then folded her hand over the money. "I'll give you the wish for free," she said. "Circus-worker discount."

I gaped at her, and her lips curled up, smirking at my surprise.

"I bet I'll have seen every one of you enter my tent by the time we're done here." It was an off-hand comment, but something about her tone made it sound ominous.

She took out a pack of tarot cards, spreading them across the small table. I watched, fascinated by the beautiful artwork. Each was painted in dark purples and blues, with flecks of silver catching the light and bringing the designs to life. Swirling patterns surrounded the figures on each card.

She laid them out—Le Chariot, La Roue De Fortune, Le Diable, L'Amoureux, La Lune…

I blinked as the last card seemed to move, the image coming alive and twisting under my gaze. The silver flecks flashed, and Giselle jerked her hand away, dropping the card as if it was burning. Her breath caught, then she hesitated, her fingers hovering just above the cards.

"Did that just…" I trailed off, realising I couldn't ask her if she'd seen what I'd seen. I shook my head, trying to clear it.

The images on the cards were motionless now. Their patterns colourful but two-dimensional. A trick of the light and my own exhaustion, I told myself. But still, I found my gaze flicking back to the card, checking for movement. Sweat crept down my temples, as I waited for her to speak.

Giselle's mother cleared her throat. I started and glanced at the lace-cloaked figure in the corner of the room. I'd forgotten she was there, hovering and watching. Now that I'd become aware of her, her presence was hard to dismiss.

Giselle shook herself slightly and returned to spreading the cards. "The spirits have a lot to say tonight, it seems."

I shivered as she began to tell me my fortune, but her words were fairly generic. Be wary of strangers entering your life… the wind will bring with it big changes and trials.… There was nothing specific and nothing to make me rethink my position on psychics.

I brushed the perspiration from my forehead and tried to concentrate, but my interest was gone, and it was a struggle to keep my focus from wandering around the room.

Finally, she gathered the cards together, patting them into line between her hands. "If you have any final questions for the spirits, ask them now."

"No," I said. "Thank you," I added, not wanting to sound rude.

She cocked her head slightly, surprised by the speed of my refusal. I watched for any more movement from the cards, but there was nothing. They were just a prop, I had decided, and not a terribly well-thought-out one either. Whether the blindness was part of her act or not, it meant she couldn't read the cards. Instead she just shifted them back and forth making pretty patterns with no meaning.

"Not a single question. Perhaps not so brave after all."

This time I was certain she was making fun of me.

"Make your wish tonight," she said. "It must be the last thing you think about before you fall asleep."

I'd forgotten about the wish and her circus-worker discount. I wondered again what had given me away—what had outed me as part of the circus. I could have asked her, but then I would have had to admit I'd been trying to fool her by coming here without announcing myself properly. I suppose it didn't matter either way, but I'd wanted to be able to pass for normal, even if it was just for one night.

She tilted her head again, as if she were thinking. "Lavender," she said finally.

"Huh?"

She smiled. "That's your flower. You must sleep with some under your pillow. Mother, do we have any?" Giselle turned, her head vaguely aimed towards the corner where her mother stood.

Her mother nodded, grandly, and stepped towards the gap in the drapes. "A beautiful offering, my dear. I'm sure that will please the spirits greatly." She slipped through the opening, disappearing into the depths of the tent.

I made to stand, really wanting to leave rather than wait for a sprig of some flower I wasn't sure I even liked, but Giselle grabbed my arm before I could.

"Be careful, Myra," she whispered. "The spirits have taken a liking to you."

"How do you know my name?" I tried to pull away, but she gripped me tighter.

She shook her head, fiercely. "They saw you fall," she hissed. "They wanted to claim you, but you cheated death. They don't like to be cheated."

"Wh-what?" I couldn't help the stutter forcing its way through my lips.

She pulled me closer, pressing her cheek to mine and whispered. "We must fight them, you and I. They want to cause us to fail. We must fight them, or we will all fall."

She released my arm, sinking suddenly into the chair. I sat frozen, too scared to move. Her mother wafted back into the room, the scent of the lavender trailing after her.

Giselle didn't speak again, her head drooping under the veil as if exhaustion had overcome her.

Her mother pressed the lavender into my hand. "Under your pillow, dear." She quavered. "It will make the wish that much stronger."

Giselle didn't speak again, and I felt her mother's hands on my shoulder, urging me to stand and guiding me towards the door.

I stumbled out. Afternoon had turned to evening while I was in the tent, but the temperature hadn't dropped any. For once, I wished for the feeling of the wind whipping against my face; something to cool my burning cheeks. I wondered whether we were, in fact, cursed. We had gone from the damaging wind to a thick, damp heat, both of which left us begging for air, or rain, or just anything to break the tension.

There were still hordes of people milling about the grounds. It seemed strange. There was a quiet to the teller's tent, the noise dampened somehow. Coming out into the intensity of people and light felt wrong.

I searched for Luca, wanting someone to share the experience with, someone to hug me and bring me back to the real, solid, earthbound world. But one glance inside the big top showed me he was working. He was covering one of the concessions stands, one of his most hated jobs. But still he played the part with joking banter, and the occasional moment of flirting when it was right for the customer. I could see the strain behind his smile, and the lack of energy in his laugh.

He caught my eye, spotting me as I hovered half-in, half-out of the doorway. His smile turned genuine, but it lasted only briefly. He made a face and mimed something to me. I wasn't sure what the individual gestures meant, but I got the gist as "so busy, will see you tomorrow".

I shrugged and nodded my assent back. Without Luca, there was no one else I wanted to talk to. Behind him I could see my father's strong upside-down hands swinging back and forth, back and forth, waiting for my mother to leap into them. I could go in and watch, but the thought made a sickening shudder work its way up from my stomach to my throat. The ground seemed to tilt beneath me every time I even thought about heights, let alone watching my parents swing in them. I walked away and wandered around the grounds instead, avoiding the teller's tent this time.

The smell of lavender trailed after me. Every few minutes I would catch the scent of it as I inhaled, and Giselle's words would float back into my mind. I thought of tossing the flower, but somehow, I couldn't bring myself to do it.

The incense smoke had permeated my clothes too, making my throat tickle with a cough that wouldn't form. I took to breathing shallowly, just to avoid the sensory assault, until I got dizzy and my head started to pound.

I returned to my caravan, craving the silence and softness of my bed. Despite my reservations, I did place the lavender under my pillow, following the instructions I'd been given. I lay my head down, once more breathing in the natural perfume.

I couldn't clear my head enough to wish, though. No matter what I did, all I could think about was her.

CHAPTER 3

I STILL FELT UNSETTLED THE NEXT MORNING. I IGNORED THE PILES OF costumes I had waiting for mending and skipped breakfast in favour of going for a walk. The pain in my leg began to scream, protesting against the amount of pacing I had done lately, and I found myself limping back towards the smoko spot as a place to rest.

Luca was there, waiting for me after not being able to talk last night. He grinned as he saw me, and I smiled, happy to have the distraction.

He took my hand, helping me to a seat, then sat down next to me. His arm was pressed against mine and I frowned at the closeness. The warmth of his skin was too much now the days of wind had finally stilled.

"Did you hear there was another fall last night?"

I shook my head. I had been asleep when my parents came back, but it's not like they would have told me anyway. They both tended to avoid mentioning anything that came too close to the subject of my accident.

"How bad?"

"Worst since yours. She'll be okay though."

I didn't ask who it was. In all honesty, I didn't care. By this point, it seemed like it didn't matter. We had all either fallen or would probably be the next to drop. Each name whispered around the grounds, joining the list of the unfortunate.

"So, you went to see the teller last night?"

I let out a short, humourless laugh. We were all so starved for entertainment; any simple act could become gossip. I had been desperate to tell him about it, last night, but today in the daylight, I felt too silly. Luca would scoff the moment I mentioned spirits, and he wouldn't believe me about the shifting patterns on the cards.

"She plays her role well," I said instead.

Luca nodded. "Don't we all." There was a bitterness to his words. He'd grown bored with his routines long ago, but there was no other part for him to move into, other than filling in on odd jobs like the concession stand last night. The rest of the time, he was stuck in an impish act, welcoming and teasing guests with a few simple stunts as they made their way into the show. It was better than the concessions but not by much.

"Is she really blind?" he asked.

I frowned, replaying the events of the night before in my head and trying to work out whether I knew the answer. If she wasn't, the act had been convincing, but there was nothing to make me sure either way.

"I don't know," I said finally. "We probably won't be able to tell until we hang out with her outside of hours."

Luca shook his head. "Fat chance of that happening. She never leaves her caravan except to sit in that tent. Her mother even takes her food back there for her."

I thought of her mother's looming presence in the tent. There was something so oppressive about her, even in just the few minutes I'd spent there.

"That's a shame."

"Is it? She obviously doesn't want to be around us. Must be a stuck-up snob," Luca spat the words out. I knew his anger wasn't really about Giselle, but still it made me uncomfortable. I'd barely met the girl, but I found myself wanting to defend her.

"It's her mother," I said.

Luca made a noise in his throat. "Another stage-mum?"

I frowned. "I don't think it's that …" I trailed off, realising again I wouldn't be able to explain it to him. There was something not right about the dynamic between them and with their tent in general. The way she was shrouded, and the whole cloying atmosphere of the candles and incense. I didn't think it was Giselle's choice to keep herself separate.

Luca shook his head. "It's this place. It makes us crazy."

I nodded. That was one thing we could agree on.

Luca stared at me, his bottom lip folded between his teeth as he chewed on it. He took a breath, but then let it go without saying anything.

I sighed. "Spit it out."

"What?"

"Whatever it is you want to ask me. I can practically see the words forming behind your tongue."

Luca chuckled and pushed my arm, gently. "You know me too well, Myra." His hand lingered on my arm. I let it for a moment, before shifting away, trying to make the movement seem natural.

"I've been saving," he said. "I reckon in a couple of months I'll have enough to get out of here."

"For a trip?"

He gave a sharp shake of his head. "No, like *out of here* out of here. Go do something else, see the world."

I frowned. "But you love performing," I said. For all his complaints, I knew deep down he had a passion for the circus. He wouldn't have run away from home to join us if he didn't.

"I do. But this isn't it."

I fell silent, unable to disagree with him. I knew the roles he'd been given didn't challenge him. There was supposed to be a level of growth and training to working here, but since the accidents, everything had stagnated.

"We could get work somewhere else. Maybe study? We could do something real."

I blinked, surprised at being included in his plans. "Something real," I repeated. I thought of the costumes I'd been making. I was good—good enough that I didn't even feel conceited saying that. With some training, maybe I could do something with that. Make costumes for movies, or work towards becoming a fashion designer.

"I don't know, Luca," I said. "What if there's nothing better out there?" Of course better things existed, I knew that. But what if those things weren't for us? Neither of us had even finished school, and who would want to employ failed circus performers?

"There has to be, Myra. There just has to be."

The desperation in his voice made a similar panic start in my stomach. I couldn't tell whether mine came from the thought of going with him or the idea of being stuck here alone after he left.

"I don't know," I said again. I had no money to travel, and I couldn't ask Luca to spend his on me. Guilt twisted in my stomach as I realised, he would. If I said yes, he would take me anywhere I wanted to go no matter how much it cost him.

Luca sighed. "Just think about it, Myra? I can't stand it here much longer."

I thought of pointing out that he could go alone, but I didn't want him to. I didn't want to lose my friend.

I nodded. "I will, but I have to get to work." I had ignored the mending pile for long enough.

I pulled myself to my feet, and he stood, too, automatically reaching out to steady me, as I wobbled.

"Don't take too long to decide, okay?" He pulled me into a hug.

I hugged him back, surprised and nervous at the gesture. The hug lasted too long, and I felt something unpleasant in the pit of stomach.

"You're a good friend, Luca," I said. I wondered if he could hear the worry in my voice as I said that.

He sighed and let go. "Yeah."

I looked away. The unpleasant something in my stomach grew, as I realised him leaving without me wasn't the only way I was at risk of losing him as a friend.

CHAPTER 4

THAT NIGHT, I FOUND MYSELF ONCE MORE OUTSIDE HER TENT. THERE was a small gap between the curtains, and I craned my neck, trying to see through it. The candles had been blown out, and I couldn't see anyone inside. Their caravan was quiet and still too. In fact, the whole grounds were strangely silent, as if a curfew had been imposed and everyone had hunkered down for the night already.

I sighed and ran my hands down my face. What was I doing here? I needed to let go of this obsession or the spirits wouldn't be the only things causing me to fail.

"I've seen you watching."

I gasped at the voice and spun around, losing my balance. Her hand shot out, clasping my arm before I fell. Something fluttered from my stomach up into my chest. We were face-to-face, so close it was almost intimate.

She smiled, amused by my shock at having been caught peeping. The veil was gone, and her face was as soft and pretty as the blonde hair which floated around her. I had an urge to reach out and brush the strands back from her cheek.

"So, you're not blind," I said.

She laughed, a light tinkling sound, and I blushed, horrified that those were the first words out of my mouth.

"I'm sorry," I croaked, embarrassment making my throat clench. "I didn't mean—"

"It's okay, Myra. I've heard the whispers."

I swallowed. "There are always whispers here."

Her eyes narrowed a little at that, and she studied my face. I dropped my gaze, my cheeks flushing again.

I snuck looks at her. She seemed paler in the moonlight. Yesterday the candles had washed her with a warm glow, despite the dark theatrics of her tent. Tonight, she was cold and pale, her hair bleached bone-white by the darkness. It made her seem more ethereal. It was almost like I could see the spirits she spoke of swirling around her.

"I am blind," she said.

I looked up, frowning, and she laughed again at my confusion.

"Legally blind," she added. "I can see a little, but I find it hard in bright light. It's easier in the dark. That's why I don't come out much during the day and why I wear the veil."

I nodded. It was similar to my leg, I guessed. I wasn't completely paralysed—I could walk a little—but it still changed things, made them more difficult. It was easier at night when there were less people to navigate through.

"Totally blind works better for the act. It makes things more mysterious."

I nodded again, not sure how else to respond. It was as I had suspected—the fortune telling was just an act—but I couldn't help but feel disappointed to hear her admit it. She had almost drawn me into believing she was really able to commune with something beyond us. I guess I had needed to believe that. It was like Luca with his plans of leaving. We all just needed to know there was something else—something *more*—out there.

She smiled. "You're easy to see, though. You're magic."

I frowned. "I am?"

She reached up, pulling a sequin from my cheek.

I blushed again. "I work in the costume room. They're everywhere."

She smiled. "It's pretty."

My words disappeared again at that. It wasn't like she was calling me pretty, but I still didn't know how to take a compliment. She watched me, clearly amused by my inability to respond, then she moved her hand, looping her arm through mine.

"Come for a walk with me, Myra?"

We walked through the circus grounds. I thought of pointing things out to her, but she didn't seem to want a tour. I asked about her life instead, the other places she and her mother had worked. She had moved around a lot, but it all seemed much the same. Each new place meant long hours and many faces filing past, none of them making an impression. I liked listening to her talk, though. She had an interesting way of looking at the world, and she made me laugh with her stories.

She asked about our circus, and I told her about the accidents; the rumours of the curse. I didn't tell her people thought I'd caused it, nor did I go into details about my fall. The evidence was obvious in my limp, even without her being able to see clearly.

She didn't repeat her words about the spirits, though I was sure they must be crossing her mind as they did mine. I wondered if perhaps she had already heard the rumours, and that's where her urgent warnings had come from. Another trick to add validity to the act. Afterall, someone must have told her my name; it wasn't a stretch to think they could have told her more.

She asked a few questions, mostly about the people who worked here. I answered as best I could, but I mostly kept to myself, so I only knew the superficial basics about the people around me. Eventually I told her as much.

"Your mother's like mine," she said.

I frowned. "I didn't—"

"You didn't have to. You're a fifteen-year-old working in a circus."

I shook my head, confused. "What does that have to do with anything?" I heard the defensive note in my voice and was surprised by its presence. I had criticised my parents many times for their choice to raise me in a circus, but it was different to hear it coming from someone else.

Giselle didn't answer. We had circled back to where we had started, and she stared at her caravan, her expression hard to read. "She won't let me out," she said quietly.

"Your mother?"

She didn't answer, but I took that as a yes.

"Because of your sight?"

Giselle made a noise in her throat. "That and other things."

I touched her arm, wanting to say something comforting but feeling unsure of what that would be. "It must be hard to be stuck inside all day," I said.

"It would be all night too, if she had her way. I have to sneak out when she falls asleep."

I shook my head, frustrated on her behalf. I thought of my mother's strained hovering each time I left our caravan. She never tried to stop me, but she made it clear she didn't think I should be going anywhere except the sewing room.

"My mum's scared of me falling if I go out alone," I said, "but she can't bear to watch me struggling to walk so she won't go with me either."

Giselle's and my disabilities were very different, but they caused a lot of the same problems. Perhaps this had been why I was sure things would change when Giselle arrived. Maybe all I really wanted was to talk to someone who understood the life I lived now.

Giselle was quiet for a moment, then she turned to face me, stepping in close to me again and taking both my hands. "Then we make the perfect pair, don't we? I'll help you balance, and you'll be my guide." She leant forward, kissing me lightly on the cheek.

I breathed in, catching the scent of incense on her hair. It didn't make me want to cough this time, it just smelt nice. My stomach fizzed with something I wasn't sure I'd ever felt before, and my face heated up again.

She let out another little tinkling laugh. "You're blushing," she said.

I noticed her cheeks were pink too and her eyes sparkled. For once I wasn't ashamed of the way my skin heated red everytime I experienced the slightest emotion. I wanted my feelings to be on display. I wanted her to see them.

I leant forward, kissing her lips. They were soft, and they tasted of strawberry. The heat in my cheeks turned to burning.

I gasped and stepped back. "I'm sorry. I'm so sorry." The words rushed out, my embarrassment making them overlap.

I heard her inhale, but I didn't wait for her to speak. I broke into a limping, stumbling run, making my way as fast as I could back to my caravan.

I slammed the door behind me, leaning against it and sliding to the floor, my knee giving way. The pain in my leg screamed, and a groan escaped my lips. I had kissed her. I had kissed her and ruined any chance I had of keeping her as a friend. In the morning, I would be the gossip whispering around the grounds.

At first, I was almost glad of the physical pain. It came in waves, mirroring the embarrassment I felt and distracting me from it. But as the pain increased, it made my stomach churn and became a reminder of everything that was wrong with my life here.

I crawled up onto my bed, mortified tears leaking out and coating my face. From under my pillow, I could smell the lavender, and it made me cry harder.

Luca sat with me at breakfast. If he'd heard, he didn't say anything. I still couldn't look at him though. My cheeks burned so hot and so long I was sure everyone must think I was sunburnt, though that was pretty unbelievable today. The day was overcast—neither windy nor burning hot for once.

The breakfast tables were set up outside, the weather finally allowing us to eat in comfort rather than crammed between caravans, crouching low for shelter. Even so, I felt like everyone would judge the blush of my skin, labelling me from the moment they caught sight of me. I didn't raise my face for them to see. I kept eyes on my uneaten eggs and just hoped Luca would be kind when the whispers inevitably reached him.

"No accidents yesterday," Luca commented.

I nodded, but I was well beyond caring.

"Perhaps we should start a pool, earn some money guessing who'll be next."

I nodded again. I could tell he was trying to bait a reaction from me; expecting me to either chide him for his callousness or laugh along with him, topping him with an even darker joke. But my mind was not on the falls, other than my own from grace.

"Are you okay, Myra?" He reached out, touching my hand.

I jerked my hand away, nodding. "The pain's bad today." I thought it was an explanation he wouldn't question, especially as there was truth to it. The ache from last night hadn't subsided and that along with everything else had kept me awake all night.

Luca frowned. "It's not just that, though, is it? I know you, Myra. What's wrong?"

I sighed. He was right, he did know me, and sometimes that was both a blessing and a curse. I studied his face, wondering how he would react.

"I did something stupid," I said finally. He was my friend, and it would be better if he heard it from me, I supposed, but it didn't make it any easier to say aloud.

"You can tell me. What was it?" Luca's brow knotted together, and he reached for my hand again.

I opened my mouth to speak, but a gust of wind rushed through the grounds, disrupting the plates around us. Luca's and my attention were drawn away, as startled chatter started up around us, and people rushed to hold down objects the wind was trying to steal.

A familiar tapping across the ground made me turn. Giselle was making her way across the grounds, her mother at her side, their arms tightly linked. The wind whipped the shawl around both of them, the tassels like tentacles, slithering their way around the two. Giselle's face was covered by the veil again, presumably to block out some of the light. It swished gently against her hair as she moved, but it still kept her hidden.

"Huh. So, they've finally come out to play." Luca had turned back as the gusts settled again. He watched them approach, his expression unreadable.

I stood, suddenly, unsure whether to run in the other direction or towards Giselle, ready to beg forgiveness.

CHAPTER 5

LUCA WAS STARING AT ME, SURPRISED BY MY BEHAVIOUR. HE GLANCED from my shaking hands to the pair approaching us.

"Myra, did they do something—?"

"Giselle!" I surprised myself by shouting. She and her mother both stopped as did several other people around me. I found my tongue had now gone slack, no other words forming to explain my outburst.

Giselle tilted her head towards her mother, speaking softly, then they resumed their slow approach.

I sat down with a thump, horrified that I had just made everything even worse.

Luca put his hand on my shoulder, leaning in to speak quietly. "Seriously, Myra, what is it? What's wrong?"

I just shook my head, shame sealing my lips.

Giselle's mother led her over to our table. Giselle reached out, finding the back of the chair beside me. She slid into the seat, her incense-smell washing over me as she did.

Her mother sat down opposite. "So lovely to eat outside, isn't it? It will please the spirits greatly that we are spending time in nature."

I felt Luca's eyes on me, his smirk at her mentioning "spirits" barely contained. I nodded, still too embarrassed to speak.

"Who is at the table?" Giselle asked.

I frowned. Surely the overcast sky wasn't so bright that she couldn't see us at all? But perhaps she was not ready to admit to everyone that the blindness was in part an act. Luca was clearly waiting for me to introduce him, as I was the one who had met her already. I wasn't sure I could force words out, given how paralysed with embarrassment my tongue felt, but I opened my mouth anyway.

"Myra," I croaked. "And my friend Luca."

"Nice to meet you." Luca's face was surly, and his voice came out just as croaky as mine. He wasn't good with people when he wasn't performing; there was a reason I was his only friend here.

"Myra." Giselle's face lit with a smile. "I thought that was your voice."

The knot in my stomach eased a little. She wasn't running from me at least. That had to be a good sign.

Her mother stood. "Giselle, will you be alright alone for a few moments?" She hovered, and the overprotectiveness Giselle had mentioned felt palpable in the air.

Giselle nodded. "Myra will look after me."

Her mother headed off towards the food tables. I nudged Luca. He frowned at me, so I nudged him again.

He finally got the message and stood, following after Giselle's mother. "Let me help you," he mumbled. He glanced back over his shoulder, giving me a look which I interpreted as both "you owe me" and "you better explain later."

I mouthed "thank you" in response.

The knot had tightened again at the thought of being alone with Giselle, but I needed a chance to explain or apologise, or perhaps both. I was glad of her veil. She was sitting so close to me, and I felt like I would have dissolved had I been able to see her beautiful face right next to mine.

I kept my eyes on the table. Though I had made Luca leave in order to have this time with her, I was searching desperately for something to say but coming up with nothing. Just as I was ready to drop to my knees and crawl away in shame, I felt her hand creep under the table, reaching for mine. She found it and squeezed my fingers tight.

"I'm glad you're here," she whispered, leaning over towards me. "I spent all morning persuading Mother to let me come out, just in hopes of finding you."

I stared at her, my mouth gaping. I'd been sure she was going to ask why I'd run away last night, or worse, what on earth I'd thought I was doing kissing her.

It took me a moment to find my voice. "I ... I thought you might be mad."

"No? Why would I be mad?" Her face broke into a smile. "I'm happy."

My chest squeezed with a different kind of pain to the one I'd been carrying with me since last night. I felt like I would burst with excitement and joy, turning into nothing but sunlight and the scent of lavender.

"Ohh," was all I managed to say. My face broke into a grin though, and I was sure she would be able to feel it, even if she couldn't see it for herself.

"I forgot to ask," she said. "What did you wish for?"

"Huh?" I looked up.

Giselle squeezed my fingers, bringing me back to her. It took me a moment to remember the wish—the whole reason she had given me the lavender in the first place.

"I'm not supposed to tell you that, am I?" I said.

She laughed behind the veil. "That's just a superstition."

I had to laugh too, at the fortune teller dismissing superstitions. She definitely looked different in the daylight. She wasn't quite as magical without the ghostly paleness, but the warm sunlit glow on her hair was beautiful.

"I'd thought you might have wished for your leg to be better," she said. "But it was something else, wasn't it?"

I frowned. It was strange the way she said that—so certain—and I wondered how she knew I hadn't. Honestly, it hadn't even occurred to me to wish for that. The disability was difficult—painful—but it was a part of me now. Wishing it away would have almost seemed like a betrayal. I didn't say that aloud though. I knew she may have spent many wishes hoping for her sight to return.

"I couldn't concentrate to wish," I admitted. "After the fortune... I just kept thinking about you." The dread that had followed me since last night came back a little at that. I couldn't see her expression behind the veil and the fear that she found my behaviour creepy started to build up again. If she hadn't been holding my hand, keeping me grounded, I think I would have run again, despite the pain it would have caused me.

But then she smiled, slowly. "Then it sounds like you got your wish." She laughed, and I joined her, delighting in the cheesiness of what she'd just said.

I'd never realised until that moment what people meant when they said their heart skipped a beat. I felt a little flip inside my chest, and the meaning was more than clear.

I tried to force myself to stop grinning as Luca and Giselle's mother re-joined us. Giselle dropped my hand as soon as her mother returned. My stomach dropped too, then I remembered her words about her mother's over-protectiveness and tried not to take it personally. It was hard when all I could think about was whether I would get to kiss her soft, strawberry lips again.

I could see Luca glancing between me and Giselle. He knew me well enough that he would have instantly noticed my change in mood. Even so, I didn't look at him or try to explain anything. He could wait. For now, I would just enjoy the light, bubbly feeling coursing through me at knowing Giselle was happy.

CHAPTER 6

We didn't have any plans to meet, but I sought out Giselle that night, hoping she would have snuck out of her caravan too. I hovered outside her tent, as I had done the night before, waiting.

"I hoped you'd come."

I turned at the sound of her voice behind me, and her hand was on my arm, steadying me, before I even began to stumble.

"You've got to stop creeping up on me." I kept my tone light, and I couldn't stop the smile spreading across my face, so the admonishment didn't hold much weight. I didn't want it to.

She grinned back, slipping her arm through mine. "How can I creep up on you when you're coming to find me?"

I smiled at her logic.

"Your hair's full of magic again." She reached up, pulling another sequin from my hair. She dropped it behind us, like she was intentionally marking our path. "You leave trails of it wherever you go."

Luca said the same. He said he always knew when I'd been somewhere, because I left the sparkles like breadcrumbs.

"I like it," Giselle added. "It means I can always find you, shining in the dark."

I grinned, her words warming my cheeks.

We did the same as we had the night before—walking around the grounds, talking, our arms linked; me her guide, her keeping me from falling. It was different though. A different energy coursing between us; the touches of our skin felt more charged, even though it was just the insides of our elbows meeting.

I didn't rush to kiss her again, and she seemed in no hurry to kiss me either. It didn't matter. I just wanted to be around her, to hear her stories and that tinkling laugh in response to mine.

She leaned her head against my shoulder as we walked. "Can I ask you something?"

I nodded. "Anything." I really meant that too. It felt easy to be honest with her.

"How do you feel about your leg?"

I raised my eyebrows at the question.

"Only if you want to tell me," she added.

I frowned, thinking it over. "I feel okay about it. It bothers me when it hurts, but I guess I've just got used to it now." There were things I couldn't do anymore, and sometimes that was frustrating, but mostly I didn't think about it. This had become my new normal. I'd reached a point where I was just thankful for the movement I did have, rather than aching for the bits I didn't

She chewed on her lip. "So, if someone said they could fix you, you wouldn't do it?"

I stopped and looked at her. "I don't need to be fixed, I'm not broken."

She stared at me for a moment, then we started walking again. I could almost hear her thoughts buzzing, puzzling over that. I hadn't really answered her question. If someone gave me the opportunity to have the pain go away, I think I would take them up on it, but I had made peace with the rest of it. If it were a case of reversing time, having the accident never happen, I don't know if I would do it. I liked most of my life now, and I couldn't be sure I would have ended up on the same path if it wasn't for my fall.

"How do you feel about your eyes?" I asked.

"I hate it," came the immediate answer.

I nodded, not questioning it. There had been times I'd felt like that too.

My limp became more pronounced as the pain increased. I tried to hide it, to keep moving, but after a while, Giselle stopped.

"You're hurting," she said.

I shrugged, in an attempt to downplay it. "It's okay."

She didn't answer, just waited.

I sighed. "I've been walking too much." I didn't want to admit the pain running away from her had caused, and it was true I had already been sore from my many laps around the grounds. "I can do a little, but I get tired. It starts to hurt more."

She frowned, and I dropped my gaze, not wanting to see the pity I'd seen from everyone else twisting her features, especially after the conversation we'd just had. She brushed her hand down the side of my face, making me look up. She kissed me, gently, on the lips. My stomach and chest exploded with sparks, and I felt like I was disappearing into the scent of her incense hair.

She pulled back to look at me and cupped my face in her hands. "Then we will not walk anymore." She kissed me once more and then took my hand.

She led me over to the big top. The late show was still going, music greeting us before we reached the entrance. I wasn't keen to watch, having seen it all a thousand times, but I realised it was still new for her. I resigned myself to making that a thousand and one times, but then suddenly Giselle changed course. She led me around the side, heading to the back entrance.

We slipped inside, finding some chairs and hiding in the shadows, backstage. Giselle peered out through a gap in the scenery, watching the acrobats' routine. I wondered why she had chosen to come around the back if she really wanted to watch the show.

"Is it too bright out the front?" I asked.

Giselle was staring at something on the stage and didn't answer at first. Then she nodded. "There is definitely too much light out there… And my mother."

"What?"

I looked through the gap. It didn't take me long to spot her mother. She sat in the audience, looking out of place still wrapped in her black shawl when everyone around her was dressed in celebratory bright colours.

"She shouldn't be here," Giselle said. Her face and her tone were both dark.

I felt the niceness of the evening we'd spent together slipping away, ruined by the pain in my leg and the pain in Giselle's side that was her mother.

I touched her arm. "It's okay, she can't see us back here."

Giselle nodded, absently. She was still watching something out the front—whether the performers or her mother, I wasn't sure. Her hand slipped into mine, though, and she squeezed my fingers.

"They're so high up," she said.

I looked through the scenery to the stage, as she pointed. The performers were balanced one on top of the other, making a dramatic human pyramid. It was nothing compared to the heights I used to fly through on a daily basis, but my stomach still clenched. The girl at the top wobbled slightly, making micro-adjustments to counter the movements of the others below her. I knew the deal—knew it was all perfectly normal and under control—but the tension in my body still built at the seemingly precariousness of her position. I felt myself start to sweat. Her image blurred, double-vision-induced ghosts dancing around her. I realised I was dizzy and looked away.

I tried to meet Giselle's eye, to give her a cue that I wanted to leave, but she stared at the performer, transfixed. I suspected I could wave my hand in front of her face, and she would just keep staring. It was a look I'd seen many times. If you didn't know the way things worked behind the scenes, much of the circus was mesmerizing.

I watched Giselle's mother instead. She held herself tightly, her gaze also fixed on the performer at the top of the pyramid. Her jaw was clenched, all the tension I felt displayed on her face too. She said something to herself, whether a prayer or an incantation I wasn't sure.

"Your mother—" I started to say, but a gust of wind interrupted me. It rushed against the side of the tent, blowing it into us. I caught hold of Giselle, and we braced each other.

I heard a scream, a sickening thud. "No!"

Giselle's gaze was still fixed on the point where the performers had been, but her mouth had dropped in horror.

I turned, not wanting to see the crumpled body I knew would be there, but something forced me to look anyway.

Suddenly, she snapped out of it. "We shouldn't be here!" She grabbed my face, not letting me look. "Come on." She pulled me from the tent.

There were more screams now. The other performers surrounding the fallen girl, and audience members rising from their seats, unsure what to do. In the middle of it, I could see Giselle's mother just standing there, still whispering to herself. I stared at her, over my shoulder, as Giselle pulled me away.

It was too far away to be sure, but she seemed to stare straight back at me.

I was still shaking when we got back to Giselle's caravan. We'd run the whole way, both of us stumbling as Giselle struggled to see the path and I tried to ignore the pain blaring in my bones.

We stopped, both heaving as we gasped in air, trying to catch our breath.

"It's okay, Myra, it's okay," Giselle was saying.

"She fell!" I realised I was saying it over and over.

I'd heard people gossip about the falls, Luca had told me about each one. But this was the first one other than my own that I had seen. I found I was laughing, a strange, humourless, hysterical sound.

Giselle held my face, kissing my cheeks and my lips, in a panicked attempt to calm me. I laughed more at the irony of that.

"It's okay," she said again. She started to laugh too, until we were both holding each other, nervous giggles working their way through us.

I leaned my head against her shoulder. "Do you think she'll be okay?" I asked.

The question sobered both of us up a little.

Giselle gave a firm, single nod of her head. "She will. She wasn't hurt badly, I promise."

I nodded too, trying to reassure myself. I had fallen from far higher, and I was okay, I told myself; in pain, but still okay.

Giselle had gone quiet, and her grip on me had changed. It felt less desperate now. More like she was holding me because she wanted to, not because she had to.

I moved my head, so I could look at her. She held my eye, and my fear dissipated. I felt safe in her gaze.

"I'm glad you came out tonight, Myra," she said. "I… I like being with you."

She sounded shy, for once being the less-confident of the two of us. It made the fluttering feeling start up in my chest again.

"I like being with you too."

In the distance, we could still hear the commotion caused by the fall. I felt some guilt at my happiness now, but I knew that on the night I had fallen there would have been couples sharing moments as I was rushed to the hospital. In every day, there were so many different mini-worlds overlapping each other. We couldn't always feel each other's pain, just as we couldn't always share each other's happiness.

Giselle sighed. "I better go inside. My mother will be back soon."

I frowned, thinking of how Giselle's mother had behaved during the girl's fall. There was something not right about it, but I shook the feeling off. Giselle didn't need to know about my imagined fears.

"My mother…" Giselle paused, biting her lip, and for a moment I thought she had read my thoughts. "We mustn't say anything in front of her—about us."

My stomach dropped, and I knew my hurt must show on my face, but Giselle rushed to continue.

"Not because of you, I mean. Just because I'm not supposed to be outside. She would be mad if she knew I was sneaking out."

I nodded and sighed. Mine would be too, I realised. We were not children, but sometimes our disabilities made our parents think we were. I wondered how my parents would react to my growing feelings for Giselle. Somehow, I thought they would be happy for me— the fact that Giselle was a girl wouldn't make a difference, I didn't think. But they would only be happy once they accepted I was old enough to date at all. My mother wasn't ready to do that, and it was clear Giselle's wasn't either.

"This will just be for us, then," I said.

A smile broke across her face, and she kissed me. "Just for us," she said.

CHAPTER 7

IT CARRIED ON THAT WAY FOR THE NEXT COUPLE OF WEEKS. DURING the day, I felt shut out of Giselle's life. She either avoided me completely by staying locked inside her caravan, or when she did venture out, she kept up the blind act, which made it harder to feel close to her. I couldn't relax around her when she was pretending to be someone else; at least not the way I could at night.

I tried not to take it personally. My stomach dropped each time she looked straight through me, but her mother's presence during the day gave a clear explanation for why her behaviour was so different. I still wasn't sure what I'd seen just before the performer fell, or if I'd seen anything at all. Something didn't feel right, though. I wasn't sure how much Giselle knew—or didn't—so I kept quiet regardless.

My evenings with Giselle made up for the daytime weirdness. When we'd both finished for the night, and everyone else was occupied with the late performances, we would slip out and I would come find her, waiting in the shadows by the fortune telling tent. Then just like she had said that first night, I was her guide and she kept me balanced. In more ways than one, I realised. The nights with her made the long days sewing and the pain from my accident easier to bear. My father even commented that I seemed happier, that I was smiling more. My mother's shoulders relaxed a little at that, as if some of the guilt had slipped away.

There had been more accidents, though. I didn't know many of the details, I'd just heard the rumours. Some said they saw ghosts around people just before things went wrong. That frightened me. It's what I'd seen before the girl fell from the pyramid—ghostly double images dancing around her as my eyes blurred. I told myself it was a coincidence and pushed that idea to the back of my mind, but it lingered there, not letting me ignore it completely.

The girl from the pyramid wasn't hurt too badly—two sprained wrists and a concussion. She hadn't returned to work, though. A few other performers had left as well, claiming the curse was more dangerous than it was worth. My parents hadn't mentioned it, but I noticed they spent little time in our caravan now, presumably filling in for the missing acts. Luca probably would have been able to tell me exactly who was gone, but I'd been avoiding him. I felt bad for it—I knew how much my friendship meant to him—but I had never been able to keep secrets from him, and I wasn't ready to share this one yet. His friendship meant a lot to me too, but I needed time to explore what was happening between me and Giselle, and I hoped he would understand that.

Giselle and I never spoke about the falls. I'm not sure if she'd heard about them—she didn't really spend time with anyone other than me and her mother. I could have told her, but I didn't want to spoil the nice safe space we had built between us.

Over the nights, she explained some of her fortune telling methods to me. "I used to watch their body language," she told me. "Most of the time you can tell pretty quickly what it is they're wanting to hear. That works best for the good fortunes, then when they ask for a full, you just have to throw in a couple of warnings. Usually about strangers and taking risks."

I laughed, realising that's almost exactly what she'd said for me. "How do you do it now? When you can't see their body language."

She smiled. "Get them talking, mainly. Listen for tiny changes in their pitch, the smell of sweat when they get nervous." She squeezed my hand. "And I measure their pulse rate, when I take their hands."

I glanced down and saw her finger had slid to the vein on my wrist without me noticing. "That's very clever."

"It's sneaky, I don't know that it's clever." She sighed. "Of course, the spirits help me too. Whispering things I need to know when the time is right."

I looked up at her. Her face was serious, no hint that she was being facetious, but she had to be, didn't she? She had told me it was all an act.

"Why did you say that, about the spirits wanting to claim me?" I felt cold, remembering the fear her words had laid on me at the time.

"Huh?" She stared at something in the distance in front of us, either ignoring or oblivious to my puzzled stare.

"When you told my fortune. You said they had taken a liking to me...Then something about us needing to fight them or we would all fall."

The words seemed darker, given the accidents. Even knowing that her fortune telling was all an act, I couldn't help but see it as having been an ominous premonition.

Giselle frowned as I spoke. There didn't seem to be any recognition in her face, and I wondered if she remembered saying it. If I was more given to superstition, I would have thought perhaps the spirits had taken her over to speak those words. She was staring intently into the middle distance, the way she had just before the girl fell the other night. Her hair seemed even paler. Wisps of it floating around her face like cobwebs, drawing attention to her colourless cheeks and the dark circles under her eyes.

"Are you okay, Giselle?" I asked.

She turned to me, blinking, as if she'd forgotten I was there. I looked towards where she had been staring. A figure was watching us, shrouded in a shawl. If it was her mother, Giselle had to know that, even with her weakened sight.

"La Lune," she said.

"What?"

"That was your final card, wasn't it? La Lune—the moon." She glanced up at the full moon above us.

"I think so. I don't remember." I shivered, despite the warmth of the night.

"The card of deception and trickery."

I looked from her to the figure in the distance. She said it like it was supposed to mean something to me, but it seemed stupid when the whole reading had been an act of deception and trickery.

I wondered what her mother wanted by following us. Giselle had said her mother would be bothered by her sneaking out, but she was making no move to come after us, simply standing and staring. I started to wish she would come over—drag us both back home—just to get it over with. Her presence in the distance was giving me chills.

"Is that a playground?" Giselle asked suddenly.

I followed Giselle's eye to the playground just outside of the circus ground. "Yeah, there's one on the other side of the fence."

Giselle smiled. "We should go."

"To the playground?" I squinted. I could barely see the play equipment myself, I wasn't sure how Giselle had managed to spot it. I glanced back at her mother, but Giselle avoided looking that way again.

She took my hand. "Let's pretend we're children again."

Part of me wanted to press her. To ask what was really going on between her and her mother. There was more to it than just the desire to keep her inside at night, that much was obvious. But Giselle bit her lip as she waited for me to answer, and I found myself nodding.

"Okay, let's go."

I let her lead me to the fence, then I took over, showing her where there was a gap we could squeeze through.

She ran over to the swings. "Come on, I'll push you!" She laughed, sounding happy and childlike.

I followed her, reluctantly.

She was light on her feet, dancing, too excited to stay still. "Come on, Myra!"

I sat down in the swing, though my stomach twisted at the thought of it. "How did you see the swings, Giselle?" I asked.

She pushed me into the air instead of answering. I leaned back, bending my legs on the backwards swing to build the momentum.

She seemed so confident in her steps tonight, no hesitating or checking the ground ahead was stable, and she had run right to the swings. I wanted her to give me an explanation—to tell me that she had seen the light glint against the mental chains of the swings or that she had been here before and mapped out the playground in her mind.

"Go higher, Myra!" she shrieked, laughing. She pushed me harder, sending the swing wobbling towards the sky.

An unpleasant thought crept its way into my mind. Perhaps the legal blindness was an act too, a lie on top of a lie. I stretched my legs out, trying to slow the swing, but she pushed me again, sending me shooting back up.

Why, though? Why would she pretend to have limited sight, when she had already admitted to me that she wasn't totally blind? My stomach jolted as I hit the top of the swing's arc and started to fall. I stretched out my legs again, hoping to catch the ground on the way back, but it suddenly seemed very far away.

The circus was full of con people—in a way, it was our job. You might think there would be a code of honour against duping each other, but you'd be wrong. We were all so used to gaining the trust of strangers and breaking it just as easily. It was a hard habit to quit. Her blindness was what made me trust her.

I hit the top of the arc again and felt the sickening drop in my stomach as I fell back to earth. "Giselle, I want to stop!" Panic made my voice rise. I twisted around, trying to look at her, but that just made the swing wobble and shoot higher. "Giselle!"

Her tinkling laugh floated back to me. "No, go higher, Myra. Go all the way to the sky! Fly up and we'll be stars together." She pushed me again, sending me shooting back up.

"Please, I want to stop!" In the distance, I saw the cloaked figure. "Giselle!" I shrieked. "Let me off!"

I grabbed the swing's chains, making it jerk dangerously back and forth. I lurched forward, getting my feet on the ground, but my leg gave way. I scrambled forward, looking for her mother's figure in the distance.

Giselle had stopped, frozen with her hand on one of the swing's chains. She stared into the distance. No, not into the distance. She was staring at her mother, transfixed like she had been the night the girl fell from the pyramid.

She suddenly snapped out of it, coming back to herself. "Myra?" She stumbled forward, the hesitant steps returning as she tried to find me. "I'm sorry, I thought you were joking."

I looked back to where her mother had been. The figure was gone, having left now I was on the ground. Perhaps that's what she'd wanted all along—for me to fall again.

"Myra?" Giselle reached for me, her soft, beautiful face scared, taking on my panic. "I'm so sorry, I should have known the swing would scare you after your accident."

I took her hand, helping her find her way down to the ground beside me. She cupped my face, peering into my eyes, trying to calm me.

I felt my breathing start to slow. Of course—my fall. The swings mimicked the sensation of dropping through the air. That was why I felt panicked, and why I had started to have doubts.

Up close, I could see her eyes were unfocused, darting back and forth much quicker than eyes normally did, as she tried to see me properly. It wasn't an act. Her new confidence had come from me— from us—and I had just trashed that.

"I'm so sorry," I whispered.

She folded me into her arms and held me.

Something changed after that night. Giselle and I still met up each evening, and I still loved spending time with her, but the ease of the first few weeks we'd spent together was gone.

Her mother's figure haunted us. Giselle became jittery every time she was near, though she still acted like she didn't realise we were being followed. I didn't press the issue, wanting to avoid the confrontation, but my fears and suspicions about what her mother wanted grew. The accidents continued, and though I couldn't prove anything, I felt like she had something to do with them.

Another figure had started to follow me too—Luca. I saw him everyday at meals, or when I ventured down to the smoko area. But after a few minutes, I would make up an excuse to get away from him.

We were friends, and I tried not to make it obvious I was dodging him, but I knew he must be suspicious. I wasn't quite sure why I hadn't told him what was going on. It was obvious Giselle's mother knew now, so there was no real reason to keep up the secrecy. I just couldn't get past the feeling that things would change between me and him, once the news was out.

Of course, things were changing between me and him anyway. He stopped approaching me, knowing I would disappear on some flimsy pretext if he did. Instead, he was just always there, everywhere I went, on the edge of my peripheral vision, trying to catch my attention.

It was unkind of me to keep avoiding him, I knew that, so when I saw him hovering nearby one evening as I waited for Giselle to finish her last fortunes of the day, I waved him over.

"Luca," I called. "Come sit with me."

He hesitated, perhaps thinking I would change my mind and walk away before he reached me. "Hey, Myra. I feel like I haven't seen you in days."

"That's because you haven't." I grinned. "Been busy. So many new costumes." It wasn't a lie, there had been a lot of work in the costume room, altering outfits to fit replacement performers as more and more people left. I still felt my cheeks flush at my lie by omission.

"Oh…" Luca's posture softened. "That's good. I thought you were avoiding me."

I looked down at the ground, scuffing my feet in the dirt.

"Because I asked you to come with me, I mean," he added.

I'd forgotten about Luca's plan to leave, and his offer to take me with him. With everything else going on, it had completely slipped my mind.

I'd been undecided before, but now with things between me and Giselle, there was no way I could go. I opened my mouth to tell Luca as much, but then I stopped. I wasn't quite ready to tell him about Giselle, and I didn't know how else I could explain my rejection of his offer.

His face fell, before I managed to say anything. "You're not going to come," he said.

I dropped my gaze. "I'm sorry, I can't."

"Your parents would understand, Myra." He took my hand, squeezing it. "I promise."

He was wrong, they wouldn't, but that wasn't the point.

I shook my head again. "Luca, I—"

He touched my shoulder, interrupting me and making me look up. He had a sparkle in his hair, a rouge one that had migrated from my unruly locks to his. I reached up to brush it away, but he misinterpreted the gesture. His hand slipped from my shoulder to my cheek and he kissed me. I froze, surprise and confusion overwhelming me for a moment.

Then I pushed him away. "Don't!"

His face fell. "I thought…"

I couldn't look at him. "I love you, Luca. You're my best friend, but—"

He looked away, not letting me finish. This is what I'd been afraid of, I realized. I'd tried to ignore it, but I'd known how he felt. I'd known that if I told him about Giselle, I might lose him.

"It's not you, Luca, it's—"

"Don't, Myra." He shook his head, still not looking at me. "You don't need to pull out the platitudes." He stood, not quite walking away from me, but putting distance between us. His cheeks were burning in a way I'd felt on my own skin many times, embarrassment taking over him.

"No, you don't understand." I stood, clumsily, reaching for his arm to balance against. "It's really not—"

He shook his head again and started to back away, moving out of my reach. "Please, just don't."

"Luca…" I leaned against the caravan instead, frustrated by my inability to follow after him. In a second, I would find my balance, the pain in my leg easing, and I would be able to walk after him. But in a second would be too late.

"I'll talk to you later, Myra."

He walked away, and I had to let him. I wanted desperately to explain about Giselle, to make sure he knew it really *wasn't* about him, but I could see he needed time. I hoped I wouldn't lose him as a friend, but I wasn't sure I would be able to control that. In all honesty, I'd known for a while how he felt, and I'd known I didn't feel the same. But it had taken Giselle arriving to show me why.

"What was that about?"

Giselle stood behind me, watching Luca walk away. I didn't understand how she managed to creep up on me every night. I was beginning to think she was doing it on purpose, just to watch me jump.

I shook my head, not ready to talk about it. "Nothing, it's not important." My cheeks flushed at that lie. It was very important, but only to me and Luca.

Giselle frowned, and her lips pinched together. I wondered how long she had been listening. Something about her expression told me she had heard the whole thing. I waited to see if she would ask, but instead she held out her arm for me to link through.

We walked around the grounds as usual. My leg was still sore from getting up too quickly, so we took it slowly. Giselle was strangely quiet though, and she was holding herself tightly. I found myself growing tense too, drawing discomfort from her. I knew I should tell her exactly what happened, to clear the air, but I couldn't bring myself to do it. I felt bad for Luca and it seemed like a breach of trust to discuss his embarrassment further.

Giselle paused across from the big top, staring. Luca dangled from a bar set above the entranceway. As people entered, he'd steal hats from their heads and other simple pranks before they noticed him. To anyone else, the performance would have looked as it should, but I knew him too well for that. He was distracted, his mind wandering, and his movements were slower than usual, everything a beat late. I cringed internally, knowing I was where his mind was wandering to.

Giselle frowned as she watched.

"Giselle…"

She didn't look at me. The wind picked up around us. The dirt swept up and seemed to dance in the air. Summer was coming to a close, but it seemed the strange, hot winds would be following us into the fall.

I sighed. "You saw what happened, didn't you?"

"You kissed him." She still didn't look at me.

I shook my head. "It wasn't like that. He kissed me, and I pushed him away."

"But you said you love him."

The wind dropped away again, but the bits of dirt still seemed to move, swirling in patterns around us. Giselle's hair swirled around her too, the strands wafting across her face.

"I love him as a friend, Giselle. He doesn't know about you. You wanted us to keep it secret."

Giselle made a noise in the back of her throat.

"I don't mean it like that. I'm not blaming you. I just mean..." What did I mean? It wasn't Luca's fault, but I could still understand why Giselle was hurt. From her point of view, he had crossed a line. One he didn't know existed, but it was there nonetheless, and his kiss had breached it.

I went to brush the strands of hair back from her face. They swirled away, my hand seeming to go straight through them. I frowned. The dirt was still shifting, patterns appearing and disappearing around us, and her hair seemed to do the same. She had an aura of colours around her, ghostly double images, just like the others had before they fell. I stepped back as I felt dizzy.

"Giselle?" I said again.

She looked at me, her eyes shifting away from Luca for the first time. She held my eye for a moment, then she gasped. "My mother," she said.

I turned. Her mother was standing outside the big top, watching us. I reached automatically for Giselle's hand, wanting to comfort her. She squeezed mine tightly, her nails biting into my skin.

Her mother didn't approach, just stared at us. The wind picked up again, and it seemed to focus on her, whirling in circles around her. It changed as it did, becoming opaque. I stared, open mouthed as white wisps of wind wrapped themselves around her, until she was bound tightly by them. She clenched her fists as her sides—trying to fight or control them, I wasn't sure.

She looked from us to Luca, dangling in the entranceway. And then he screamed.

"Luca!" I started forward.

I didn't see him hit the ground, the crowds hiding that from view, but I heard the collective gasp as it happened.

I turned back to Giselle, knowing I couldn't leave her to find her own way home. She studied my face for a moment. I was sure she would see my fear and guilt written across it—fear for my friend and guilt that my rejecting him had been the distraction that made him fall. I hoped she could also see how much I cared for her, and that none of my feelings about Luca changed that.

"Go," she said. "My mother will help me get home."

I nodded. "Thank you."

She touched my face, gently running her hand down the side of my cheek. I kissed her lightly, then limped over, pushing my way through the crowds surrounding Luca.

CHAPTER 8

I DIDN'T GO OUT TO MEET GISELLE THE NEXT NIGHT. I JUST KEPT seeing Luca's face in my mind, his hurt written across it. Was it my fault he fell? I should have told him about Giselle earlier. He was my best friend, and I should have told him.

He'd landed on his head and had a concussion. That's all I knew. The medic team had pushed me away, not letting me stay by his bedside. If it had been a day earlier, Luca probably would have insisted I stay with him. I would have happily been the one to look after him, to wake him every hour until he was out of danger. As it was, he didn't acknowledge I was there nor protest when I was asked to leave.

The sound of his scream kept playing over and over in my head and there was something else niggling at the back of my mind, but I couldn't quite face it. The way the wind had changed around Giselle's mother, I had to wonder how much she was controlling. She had looked at Luca just before he fell.

The colours and patterns that had floated around Giselle weren't normal either. I had dismissed her talk of spirits as part of the act, but it was getting harder and harder to do that. I thought of the rumours that people had seen ghosts dancing around the performers before they fell—I'd seen it myself, just before the girl from the pyramid dropped to the ground. I wondered if the ghosts I'd seen around Giselle meant the next accident would be hers. I cut that thought short before it could fully form.

My spiralling thoughts were interrupted by a knock at my

caravan door. I hesitated, wondering if I could pretend to be asleep. It would likely be someone coming to give me news of Luca's state and I wasn't sure I could deal with hearing it.

"Myra? Are you in there?" Giselle called.

I got up, opening the door. "Giselle, how did you get here?"

She gave that tinkling laugh. "I walked, of course."

I wrapped her in a hug, so glad to feel her warmth against me. "I meant how did you see to get here? You shouldn't be wandering alone, it's too dangerous."

She laughed again. "You sound like my mother."

I pulled back to look at her. She didn't seem to have any hesitation at mentioning her mother, no guilt or fear around it. Perhaps she hadn't seen what I had. The wisps of wind were so light and flighty, easily missed even with perfect sight. I shook my head, questioning again whether they were only in my head.

"I had to come," she said. "You didn't come to me."

I felt a pang of guilt at that. She was right. I had waited outside her caravan every night since we met. She must have been confused to find me missing, but I just hadn't been able face going out when things had gone so wrong last night.

She touched my face. "You've been crying."

I nodded, bowing my head as I felt like it was going to start again. "Why?"

I looked up at Giselle, frowning. How could she need to ask that? We had watched Luca fall. She had seen him make his feelings clear and me reject him. She must surely know how much it had hurt us both.

"Because of Luca, of course."

She stared at me, her expression hard to read. Was she still upset by the fact that he had kissed me? It seemed so trivial now, so unimportant when he was injured.

She smiled. "You need a distraction." She took my hand, trying to pull me out.

I kept my feet planted, letting my arm stretch between us. "No, I can't...my mother said I can't." I flushed at the lie, my cheeks giving me away as usual.

Giselle went still, dropping my hand. I wrapped my arms around myself, familiar shivers working their way up my body.

"So, both our mothers are trying to pull us apart now."

Her tone was cold, and I didn't like the hardness to her voice. Again, the image of the wisps surrounding her mother came into my head. There was something really wrong here, and Giselle getting caught in it scared me.

I stepped out into the night, taking her hand again. Whatever else was going on, the feeling of having her close to me still felt right. "Okay, let's go out," I said. "But just for a little while."

Giselle insisted she had a surprise for me. I let her lead me through the night. My misgivings hadn't settled. It felt wrong to be wandering around so freely when Luca was hurt. But Giselle pulled on my hand and chattered as we walked, keeping me distracted.

She led me into the big top, a skip in her step.

I hesitated. Everything was closed down for the night—the late performance cancelled due to the number of performers absent. I wasn't sure we were allowed to be in here after hours, especially after all the falls.

"Giselle, I don't think—"

She took both my hands. "No questions. This is my surprise."

She led me inside, then skipped away from me. Her steps were surprisingly confident. I realised her arm hadn't been linked through mine all night, and she'd made her own way over to my caravan. I felt the same doubt I'd felt in the playground. I tried to push it away again. Her confidence was growing perhaps, her feet having learned the way through the grounds. The doubts refused to be quashed. I was happy to see the ease with which she moved, but it still left me nervous and confused.

"Close your eyes," she called.

I frowned. "Why?"

Her tinkling laugh echoed around me. "Because it's a surprise."

I sighed, then closed my eyes, covering them with my hands to make it clear I was following her wishes.

"Good girl. Now, don't peek until I say."

I waited, a feeling a of dread growing with every second. There was a rustling sound and then nothing. "Giselle?" I called.

She didn't answer. Outside, I could hear the wind picking up, a low rumbling starting as it caught the sides of the tents.

"Giselle?" My voice was squeaky with anxiety. I dropped my hands, not waiting for an answer.

I couldn't see her. I spun on the spot, looking for her.

Her tinkling laugh rung out from above me. "Naughty girl, Myra. I told you not to peek."

I gasped. She was halfway up the ladder, climbing up to the trapeze platform. "Stop! What are you doing?!"

She turned to look at me, her foot stepping into nothing as she missed a rung.

"Giselle!"

How could she have found the ladder, let alone managed to climb the steep rungs? She laughed, finding her footing and leaning back dangerously. She didn't seem like herself, a wild energy taking over her.

"What are you doing? Get down from there!"

"No, my love, you come up here." She was still laughing, like it was nothing. Was this a punishment? Was she mad about Luca and risking her life in order to make me feel bad about it? She was far too high already but still climbing.

I found I'd moved to the base of the ladder and was staring up at her. "Giselle..." I hadn't been up there since the day of my accident, the thought of doing so making me ill. Even the swings had terrified me. If I was honest, the reason I couldn't watch my parents' routine wasn't just that I was bored with it. Every time they flew through the air, it made my stomach clench.

"Please come down, Giselle."

"No, you have to come up and get me." She leaned back again, watching me.

"Why are you doing this?" I whispered the words, but she heard them anyway.

"You need to face your fears, Myra." Her voice lilted, turning sing-song. "Come up here and face them." She let her foot dangle as she peered down at me.

This was insane. She sounded drunk, or crazy, or... something. Whatever it was, this wasn't my Giselle.

"Myyy-raaa," she called. She leaned her head back to give me an upside-down grin. Her other foot slipped from the rungs, and she swung forward, slamming into the ladder. She shrieked as she was left dangling by her hands.

"Giselle!" I found I was climbing, having started up without thinking about it. "It's okay, I'm coming!"

"Myra, hurry!" The laugh was gone from her voice, terror taking over.

I reached her quickly, climbing up behind her. I wrapped my

arms around her, bracing her so she could get her feet back on the rungs. She was crying, shaking and sobbing, in no state to climb back down.

"Keep going," I said. We were nearly at the top. If we reached the platform, we would have time to rest and for me to calm her down.

"I can't!" she wailed, her tears turning to hysteria. She flopped back against me, nearly causing us both to fall.

"You can!" *You have to*, I added inside my head. "I'm right here, Giselle, just keep climbing."

She took a shuddering breath, then stepped up on to the next rung.

"That's it! You can do this."

She was shaking badly and so was I, but I moved with her, my hands and feet just one rung below hers, matching each step. She reached up, her hand touching the platform. She let out another shriek when she couldn't find a rung.

"It's okay! You're there. Just climb up."

"I can't!" She cowered, clinging tighter to the rungs.

"Shh, it's okay. I've got you." I climbed up over Giselle, reaching the platform myself and clambering up onto it.

She grabbed my wrist. "Myra! Don't leave me." Her face was even paler than normal, terror written across every part of her body.

"I'm not. I won't." I gripped her arms, guiding her up onto the flat surface. "You're okay, Giselle."

She crawled toward me and I held her, letting her cry against me. Thoughts were swirling in my mind, trying to put together what was happening. The pieces were all there, but I couldn't make them fit properly.

"What the hell were you thinking?" I whispered.

"I wanted to help you." Giselle shook her head back and forth, as if she were trying to erase what had happened. "I thought if you came up here again, you wouldn't be so afraid."

I stroked her hair. "It doesn't work like that."

"I know, I'm sorry. I'm so sorry."

"Shh, it's okay." I wanted to believe her, but so much of tonight didn't make sense. The doubts I'd had about her blindness were no longer just doubts. I cupped her face, pulling her away from my shoulder so I could look at her properly. "You're not blind, are you?" I asked.

She didn't answer, just stared into my eyes. As she did something seemed to change. My eyes blurred, and she split into two, the double-vision induced ghost very real suddenly. I dropped my hands, scooting to the other side of the platform

"Please don't be afraid, Myra," she whispered. Marks appeared on her face, little silver lines like cracks. "I thought love would be enough, but they wanted fear."

I couldn't form words. I looked down at the platform. It was littered with sparkles already, shaken from my lose hair. Within seconds, I had left my trail.

"You never have sequins on you," I said.

"What?"

I looked up at her. "I leave them everywhere, but I've never seen one stick to you."

I heard a noise below us, someone entering the tent. I turned, expecting the see her mother, stalking us as she had all the nights before. Instead the figure I saw below was haloed in soft blonde hair, her veil-covered face angled up towards us.

"Giselle?" I turned back, looking from the girl in front of me to the one below.

I screamed. The Giselle on the platform with me covered her ears. I blinked and the one below disappeared, but I screamed again. The world tilted, and I clung to the platform, certain I was falling.

Giselle grabbed hold of me, her arms wrapping around me trying to comfort or kill me, I wasn't sure which. "Shh, they get stronger with fear. I'm so sorry, Myra. I'm so sorry. I'm sorry."

She kept saying it over and over, and I kept screaming, unable to do anything else. I pressed my face into the platform, doing anything I could to avoid seeing the way her form was splitting.

I felt the vibrations of someone else climbing the ladder to the platform, but I couldn't look. It would be the second version of her; the veiled one. I couldn't bear to see the two of them closing in on me with no escape but to jump.

"Myra? Myra, it's me."

I heard the voice and felt the hands shaking me, but I couldn't look.

"What's wrong with her? Why are you up here?"

It was Luca's voice. I opened my eyes, but I couldn't make myself turn and look. They were playing tricks on me. She and her mother were in it together.

"I brought her here." Giselle's voice was shaking. "I thought it would help."

Luca made a noise in the back of his throat, his anger at hearing that obvious. "Myra, come on, please. It's me; it's Luca." He lifted my shoulders gently, turning my face towards him.

His face was bruised, a cut crusted in dried blood at his hairline, but it was him. I risked a glance at Giselle. The cracks on her face were gone, and there was only one of her, but I still shuddered as I remembered the way she had split in two.

She stared at me, her lip still shaking. A tear made its way down her cheek. She shook her head, in what seemed like a desperate attempt to communicate silently with me.

"I'm so sorry," she said again.

She reached for my hand, but I cringed away, not wanting even the slightest contact with her.

Luca sniffed then cleared his throat, his discomfort clear. It wasn't fair that he was having to rescue me, when I'd hurt him, but right now I needed him.

"How did you know we were up here?" Giselle asked, her voice low.

He shook his head. "I couldn't sleep, I was walking. Heard you both screaming."

I covered my mouth, feeling another scream building up at the memory. Luca's face pinched up with worry as I did.

He shifted, moving towards the edge of the platform. "Let's get you down from here, ay?"

Giselle visibly flinched at the idea of climbing down, and I felt myself do the same.

"Okay, okay." Luca responded to our unspoken protests. "We'll go slowly, one at a time."

He took Giselle down first. I stayed huddled on the platform as they made their slow descent. He climbed behind her as I had done on the way up. I didn't watch, just waited for the vibrations of the ladder to stop, signalling that they were on the ground safely.

I heard their muffled voices at the bottom, but none of the words were clear. I was glad. There was nothing either of them could say that could make sense of this. I felt Luca start his ascent, then his head appeared over the edge of the platform.

He squinted slightly, assessing my position, still curled up in a ball, my arms locked tightly around my legs.

"You ready?" he asked.

I nodded but didn't move.

"I won't let you fall, Myra."

His words would have meant more, if he hadn't just fallen himself, but somehow, I still trusted him. I scooted over to the edge and let him guide me back down to the ground.

Giselle wasn't waiting at the bottom.

"She said she had to get back to her mother," Luca said, when he saw me looking around.

I nodded. I wasn't sure whether I was relieved or just confused by her absence. I knew I would have to unravel what had happened, but none of it made any sense. I started to cry again, thinking of how she'd been fooling me. Did she ever really care for me, or had that been an act too?

Luca touched my shoulder, then wrapped his arms around me when I didn't stop. "What the hell happened tonight, Myra?"

I shook my head, unable to speak.

"Are you and Giselle...?" He let the question hang without finishing it.

I nodded, though I wasn't really sure what we were now. I wasn't sure what she was.

He let out a breath. "Wow." He started to laugh then stopped when he realised I was still crying.

"I'm sorry, it's just...wow."

He walked me back to my caravan. My leg was so sore, I had to shuffle, leaning heavily on the arm he wrapped around me. I could see he had questions, but he had the sense to not ask them tonight. His mood was lighter though, the tension from after he kissed me gone. I was glad he understood now—knew for sure that it wasn't about him. I just wished it hadn't come as a result of whatever it was that had happened tonight. We stopped outside my door.

"Myra..."

He glanced back towards the big top and I couldn't help a shudder working its way up my body.

"Is everything okay?" he asked. "Between the two of you?"

I shook my head. "No. It's really not."

The next day, I stood outside the fortune teller tent for far too long. I didn't go in—only partly because of the crowds. Instead, I watched as she told fortunes, still swaddled in those layers of fabric.

Her words echoed in my mind: *I thought love would be enough, but they wanted fear.* There was fear everywhere now as we all waited for the next accident. We were cursed, even the most sceptical of us couldn't deny it. Or if it wasn't a curse, there was something else unnatural here, and I had a feeling it was too late to fight it.

"Did she tell you how she lost her sight?"

I started at the sound of Giselle's mother's voice. Her hand shot out, just as Giselle's had, steadying me. She withdrew it as soon as I was stable. I could still see the wisps around her, though they were fainter in the daylight. They circled her slowly, keeping her trapped in a tiny, translucent prison.

"Did she tell you?" she repeated.

I shook my head, my throat too tight for words.

"It was an accident." Giselle's mother's voice held the same sadness my mother's did on the rare occasions she spoke about what had happened to me. "At one of the other circuses we worked at. There was an explosion. She was the closest to it. She hasn't seen a single thing since."

I thought of telling her mother that I knew Giselle could see, but she was so determined to keep up the act, it seemed pointless to try dissuading her from it. Besides, after last night, I had to question whether I really knew anything about Giselle at all.

"That must have been very hard for both of you," I said instead. There was an edge to my voice—not quite sarcasm, but a hardness I'd never heard from myself before.

"Oh, it was, it was. Giselle was very angry for a long time. Kept talking about negligence and revenge. She took it very hard and it made her bitter."

I frowned, unable to find anything sensible to say to that. I shifted my weight, stretching out my leg. My muscles were tight, and I was still moving slowly after last night. I ached for an arm to link through, a shoulder to lean against.

Giselle's mother watched my movements. "I'm glad she's met you, Myra. The way you handle your... affliction." She gestured towards my leg. "It's good for her to see."

I wasn't sure about that. I had made the best out of my situation, taking as much joy in my new role in the sewing room as I could. But it was still hard.

"I'm glad I've met her too," I said. "I... care very much for her." Even after everything, that was true. I wouldn't be there, waiting outside her tent, and trying to figure out what on earth was going on if I didn't.

"Yes, it's clear you are very special to each other." Her mother smiled, and I wondered if she knew exactly how much we meant to each other. The thought made me nervous though, as I realised I wasn't sure that was what I wanted anymore. A similar tension has crept into her mother's face.

Her mother sighed. "The spirits have helped her. She turned to them eventually, of course." Giselle's mother's face turned pinched. "But perhaps they have helped her too much," she said quietly.

Her fingers curled, in and out, making fists as she had the other night when I'd seen the webs wrapping around her.

"What do the spirits look like?" I surprised myself with the question. I'd barely made the connection myself before the words were out of my mouth.

Her mother looked up, puzzling over the question. "It depends," she said finally. "Most people don't see them at all."

I dropped my gaze, feeling my cheeks start to heat.

"But… something tells me you do." She whispered the last part, fear crossing her face.

I nodded, slowly.

"Wisps mostly. Changes in colour and light—moving patterns."

I thought of the strands of hair that always floated around Giselle's face, the ones I hadn't been able to brush away. And the cards, the way the designs had changed and swirled.

"Where have you seen them, Myra?" Her voice had gone low, the quavering note she normally affected completely gone as she became serious.

"Around you." I swallowed. "And Giselle. I thought you were causing them at first." I didn't tell her about how I'd seen her watching us. After seeing the veil-covered girl below us last night, I was pretty sure it had been Giselle all along.

"They're wrapped around me, aren't they? Binding me." She nodded to herself, not waiting for an answer. "Sometimes they are stronger. Sometimes they take the shape of a person. But the copy is not the same. It's—"

"Paler," I said, my stomach dropping. "More ethereal."

Giselle's mother nodded, tension written across her face as she read into what I was saying.

"Tell me honestly…" I swallowed, having trouble getting the words out. "Is Giselle really blind?"

Her mother hesitated, a slow breath rattling against her teeth. "Completely," she whispered. "She can't see a thing."

I thought you might have wished for your leg to be better. I remembered her words, and suddenly I understood them. She had made a wish too—she had wished for her eyes to be better. I had wished for her instead, whether I meant to or not, and we had both been granted what we'd asked for.

I looked back at the tent. Giselle sat at the table, the veil over her eyes. Her skin and hair were warm, bathed in the yellow of the candle light. Her hair fell softly around her face, no wisps or stray white strands.

She was the figure I had seen watching us. She had been following us, as the pale spirit form and I had fallen in love.

I thought love would be enough, but they wanted fear. There was still more fear to be had at the circus. There was still more potential for falls.

I turned and limped away as fast as I could. The pain in my leg screamed, but I forced myself to keep moving.

"I'm sorry, Myra. I'm so…"

I heard her mother calling after me, but I didn't stop.

Now that I knew what to look for, I could see them everywhere. Wisps, like cobwebs or stray pale strands of hair, danced over every-thing—over everyone. It was no wonder so many had fallen. They wrapped themselves around all the performers, stretching between their limbs like tripwires.

I found Luca at the smoko spot. "Luca," I called.

He smiled, stepping towards me, but his face fell as he saw the fear on mine.

"Please, Luca, I need your help."

"What is it, Myra?" The bruises on his face had deepened overnight, and I could see him wince as he spoke, the words causing him pain.

"It's her. Giselle. I think she's causing the falls."

He shook his head. "What?"

"There's two of her… I think. But one of them is a spirit. The spirits are everywhere. They wrap around people, and—"

"Myra!" My name came out draped in a laugh. "What are you talking about? You're not making sense." The amusement on his face started to drop, being replaced with concern, as he realised I was serious.

He was right, it didn't make sense. I knew that. But I also knew it was true. She had been growing stronger. It had been happening right in front of my eyes, but I hadn't wanted to see it.

"Please, Luca." I gripped his hands. If Luca didn't believe me, then no one would. "You have to trust me."

He frowned, clearly torn. I had broken some of his trust, and this had to be confusing for him. But he knew me— knew me better than anyone else, and he had to know I wouldn't make this up.

His expression set into one of grim determination. "What do you need?"

"I... I don't know." I cut myself off. I had no plan. Worse than that, I had no idea what Giselle or the spirits that had taken her form were planning either. All I knew was that they were trying to cause fear.

I could see Luca's frustration was growing, my lack of explanation confusing him further.

"The big top," I said finally. "I think that's where she'll be."

The main tent hadn't yet opened for the morning show. My parents were inside, rehearsing a new routine. My mother swung back and forth, building up the momentum to leap into my father's arms. I knew better than to call out to them, not wanting to disrupt their concentration, but I had to get them down. I could see the spirits snaking their way around their limbs, just waiting for the right moment to make them drop.

"They're everywhere," I whispered.

The white wisps were sneaking their way around Luca too. He couldn't see them, but I think he could sense them. He scratched at his throat as they wrapped around it, and his manner grew more urgent.

He stared up at my parents. "We should get them down."

I nodded, glad he was cooperating. "I don't want to distract them, though."

He made a noise of agreement. "I'll climb up, tell them you're sick or something."

I touched his arm. "Thank you." I could see he still didn't entirely understand why we were doing this, but I was glad he trusted me enough to realise it was important.

He gave me a half smile, then he was off. I watched as he climbed the ladder to my dad's platform. I hoped my parents would listen. They were meticulous about their rehearsals, letting very little interrupt them. But Luca could be convincing when he wanted to be, and I hoped this was one of those times.

I cringed as my mother finally leapt. But my father caught her wrists, their hands locking on to each other. He grinned at her, his strong arms holding her, as he had held me many times. I let out a breath. They were safe for now.

Something caught my eye up on my mother's platform. The wisps seemed to be congregating there, swirling around a figure dressed in white.

"Giselle," I whispered.

I didn't give myself time to think. I limped over to the ladder and began to climb.

I hadn't noticed the pain when I climbed up to save Giselle. My focus had been on her, and the adrenaline covered everything else. This time it was difficult, my knee didn't want to bend enough to reach the rungs, and a sharp pain stabbed each time I forced it. My leg started to shake, threatening to give way, but I bit my lip and kept going.

Giselle didn't turn around as I reached the platform. Spirit-Giselle, that was. The other was still back telling fortunes. She knew I was there, though. The wisps fanned out from her, circling me and drawing me to her.

"It wasn't meant to be like this," she said.

I swallowed, feeling like I couldn't breathe with the wisps surrounding me. "How was it meant to be?"

"I just wanted to be able to see again."

I shook my head. "You're not her. Stop pretending, I'm not stupid."

She spun around, grabbing my arms and latching on to them. "I am, Myra. It's me! Don't you understand?"

I stepped backwards, the momentum of her sudden movement nearly sending us both flying off the edge of the platform. She pulled me to her, steadying me and protecting me from falling. I leaned my head against her shoulder. The familiarity of her embrace was too much for me. I wanted to just melt into it, forget everything that had happened. But I couldn't.

I pulled back from her. "You're not real. You're one of those spirits." My voice cracked as I said that. I wanted desperately for her to tell me I was wrong, but instead she started to cry.

Across from me, I could see Luca had reached the other platform and was talking to my parents. They were safer now they were off the ropes, but I would rather they were on the ground. I could see Luca was having trouble persuading them to come down.

"I just wanted to be able to see. They gave a me a way to do that through them. But it's still me in here. They've given me the form, but it's still me!"

Giselle reached for my hand and I took it automatically. I wanted to believe her. Maybe she wasn't like the spirits that coated everything. She seemed different— more in control than the random way the wisps floated around things.

"I didn't mean for any of this to happen. I thought I could stop the falls."

I stepped closer to her, brushing the white strands away from her face. Of course she had tried to stop them. I knew her, she was good. She wouldn't hurt people.

"The spirits needed emotions to fuel this. To give me another form." She leaned her head against my shoulder. "When I met you, I thought our feelings would be enough."

I nodded and pulled her closer to me. My feelings for her were the most powerful emotions I'd ever felt. Without her having to say it, I knew it was the same for her.

"But they still wanted fear," she whispered.

Something sank in my stomach, and I pulled back. "You can't let this continue, Giselle. You can't let anyone else fall." I glanced over to my parents and Luca. They were still on the platform.

She gripped me tighter, her nails digging into my skin. "But don't you see, Myra? I'm getting stronger. It's nearly over."

I frowned. "What do you mean?"

"That day on the swings, I realised what I needed for this to be permanent." Her face lit up, her eyes becoming wide and manic, like they had been when she was on the ladder climbing up the last time. "I needed *your* fear. The spirits have craved it since you fell."

"What are you talking about?" I stepped back, but I was on the edge, nowhere for me to go. I looked for Luca. He and my parents had caught sight of us and were frozen, watching.

Giselle's face turned serious. "Oh no, my love. You don't need to worry. I won't hurt you. I couldn't." She run her hand down my face, but I flinched away. "But I saw how afraid you were when Luca fell. When *I* nearly fell."

I shook my head. "Giselle..."

Tears leaked from her eyes again. "Please don't think I'm callous, Myra. I don't do this lightly."

A gust of wind rushed through the tent, and my mother screamed. She overbalanced, but my father and Luca grabbed for her. My father fell instead. He seemed to hang in mid-air. I screamed, rushing forward as if I could fly through the air and save him. But then he hit the ground. Giselle grabbed me, holding me back.

She pressed her face into the back of my shoulder. "I'm sorry, Myra, I'm so sorry."

I stared down at my father's broken body then spun around, anger seething through me. I wanted to hit her, to claw at her face and make her feel the pain she had just caused me. But something in her face stopped me. The silver cracks were appearing across her skin again.

She sank down to the platform, covering her face with her hands. "No, no, no!" She shook her head back and forth. "I'm so sorry, Myra. I can't control it anymore. The spirits are taking over."

I turned back, staring down at my father's body. I was shaking, and a wailing sound was filling the air. I wasn't sure whether it was coming from my mother or from me.

"I wouldn't have done that. I wouldn't have hurt anyone, you know I wouldn't!"

I didn't know what to believe. The wild look I'd seen on her face, it wasn't her, it wasn't the Giselle I knew, but right now I couldn't be sure I'd ever really known her. It was all so mixed up—what was her, what was spirit?

"I want to stop, but I can't," she whispered.

Another gust of wind rushed through, and Luca was knocked from the platform. He caught the side of it and dangled by his hands from the edge.

"No!" I turned to climb down, but she was blocking my way.

"I'm sorry, Myra, I'm so sorry!"

The wisps floated around her, creating a haze. They were feeding from her, growing stronger. I did believe her, I realised. She was split by this. The spirits gave her strength, but they also took it from her.

She reached for me. "Believe me, I didn't want this."

Luca and my mother both screamed as the platform tilted. It shouldn't be able to do that, but the wisps were wrapped so tightly around it, manipulating everything.

"Please stop this, Giselle."

She stared up at me. "I would if I could," she whispered.

I heard a gasp from below. I turned. Giselle's mother stood in the middle of the tent, the white-veil-covered Giselle beside her, their arms tightly linked. The girl looked weak, growing fainter as the spirit-Giselle's strength grew.

"I tried to fight them, but I failed," the veiled-Giselle said. "Now we will all fall."

The wisps crowded around them. Giselle's mother clutched at her chest. She looked like she was having a heart attack, but the white tendrils creeping around her hand showed the truth. They were killing her, their malice given full flight now.

"Giselle, you have to stop this!" I wasn't sure which one of them I was talking to. Both perhaps. The veiled one stood helpless, while the spirit girl in front of me switched between crying and a wide-eyed manic stare that told me the wisps were taking over.

"There have to be more falls, it's the only way." She stood, joining me at the edge of the platform.

We watched as my mother and Luca scrambled, clinging to the platform as it bent unnaturally. I looked from her mother's gasping form to my father's broken one down on the ground. Finally, I looked to the veiled-Giselle, as she sunk to her knees beside her mother. The wisps were circling her too, smothering and weakening her. She raised her head, pleading with me, from behind the veil.

The spirits wouldn't be done. They may give Giselle back her sight, leave her in this new form after killing the old one. But that wouldn't be the end of it. They would attach to someone else. Split and twist them until they became something they weren't. Cause them to do unspeakable things, preying on their sadness.

"Yes, there needs to be another fall," I said. I turned and pushed Giselle from the platform.

Her mother didn't make it, and neither did my father. Giselle was fine though. The "real" one, I mean, though it felt wrong to call her that when the other had meant so much to me. The spirit-Giselle had broken apart in the air, dissipating into wisps before she hit the ground. My mother had pulled Luca to safety, and we had all climbed back to the ground, too shaken to speak about it.

I still couldn't process that my father was gone. I felt numb instead of grieving, though perhaps that was part of the process. My mother hadn't spoken about it, or about anything. She had sat silently in our caravan since it happened.

The real Giselle was leaving. I don't even know who I heard that from, it seemed to just be collective knowledge. I debated whether or not to go see her. In the end I realised I had to, or it would haunt me forever.

She was sitting outside her tent, and it seemed like she'd been waiting for me. She had her veil on, but she raised her head when I approached.

I hovered beside her, unsure whether to sit or stay standing. A few days ago, I would have wanted to be as close as possible, but now the comfort and familiarity of being in her presence were gone.

"Le Chariot, La Roue De Fortune, Le Diable, L'Amoureux, La Lune..." she said.

It took me a moment to recognise the words. "The cards. But—"

"I couldn't read them, no. But the spirits told me."

I remembered her warnings. I was so caught up in being with her, there was no way her words could have reached me. Would things have been different if I had taken the warnings seriously? I didn't think so. There was no way I could have predicted that the spirits would take her form.

"Do you know what they mean?" she asked.

I shook my head. "No."

She patted the ground beside her, gesturing for me to sit. I hesitated, then lowered myself to the ground beside her. Her arm brushed against mine, and even with everything I knew now, I still felt butterflies in my stomach.

"The Chariot—trouble, upset, change." She spoke as if reading from a textbook, listing each of the cards and their meanings. "The Wheel of Fortune—destiny involving great gain or great loss. The Devil—reversed—physical or spiritual release, overcoming handicaps, enlightenment. The Lovers ..." Her voice cracked, and she took a long breath. Despite myself, I found I was reaching for her hand. She squeezed mine, and I started to cry.

"The moon—a warning against false friends, deception and trickery." She paused, letting me process all of that. "It was all there in the cards," she said. "I just couldn't see it. The reading was meant for me, not you."

"You tried to warn me." My voice rose, turning that into a question. I wanted her to reassure me that she had. I wanted her to say she had at least tried to stop it.

"I did." She nodded, reassuring herself as much as me, it seemed. "But the spirits needed your fear to gain power. They needed the falls."

I stretched out my leg, easing the pain in it. "But the accidents... they started well before you arrived."

She moved her hand, playing with my fingers, then she shrugged. "Your fall... it really was just an accident. Nothing more, nothing less.

But the spirits attached to you after it, like I said. They were already here when I arrived, causing mischief. I gave them something else to focus on." Her voice didn't hold any shame for what she'd done. All the people who had gotten hurt, it was like none of us even mattered.

I dropped her hand. "You made a wish, didn't you?"

She nodded. "I didn't realise until it was too late what it would cost me to take that form."

"So, none of it was real?" I couldn't bring myself to say it properly —the feelings, the kisses we'd shared—none of it had really been her. The spirits had wanted me to feel, so they'd tricked me into thinking they were her.

Giselle hesitated, then slowly she removed her veil. Underneath, her face was scarred, a web of silvery lines scattered over her eyelids. Her eyes themselves were bloodshot and unfocused.

I looked away, blinking as tears beaded in my eyelashes. I wanted to hate her, but she was still just as beautiful as she had always been. She was still the girl who had made me fall in more ways than one.

She touched my arm, but I couldn't look at her. "She was a way for me to have freedom again." The spirits were still wrapped around her, the wisps binding her tightly the way they had her mother. She thought they had given her freedom, but really they had imprisoned her.

I sniffed, hard, trying to stop myself from crying. "You were just using me." I didn't make that a question and I didn't need a confirmation from her.

The energy and the spirits attached to me from my fall had fuelled her freedom. I understood the desire for independence. Every time my leg gave way, or pain kept me indoors, I wished desperately to escape the confining barriers of my life. The accidents we'd had and the consequences of them were hard, but it didn't excuse what she'd done. She didn't have the right to mess with people's lives—with my feelings—in the way she had.

She reached out hesitantly, finding my face with her finger tips. "Everything she felt, I felt it too. She was me. It was real, Myra."

I wanted to believe that she'd felt the same way I did, but even if it were true, it didn't matter. She may have cared for me, possibly even *loved* me, but she had still used and hurt me.

"That's not enough," I said.

She swallowed, the sound audible in the quiet between us. She dropped her hands and shifted away.

I waited with her until one of the workers came and told her he was ready to go. He was giving her a lift to her aunt's place across the city. He treated her with kindness, believing her to be the poor, unfortunate, disabled girl, grieving her mother. There would be no consequences for her, other than losing the spirits that had enabled her to roam at night through them. Half of the circus workers had no idea what had happened, still telling themselves the accidents were just a horrible coincidence. The other half—the superstitious ones, and the ones who had seen too much of what happened last night to dismiss it—knew what she had done, but there was nothing any of us could do about it.

She paused before getting in the car. "Goodbye, Myra. I wish...I wish I had met you earlier—before I made the wish to see again. I...I think things might have been different if I had."

She leant forward, offering a final kiss.

I didn't lean in myself.

"Maybe they would have."

She hesitated, still waiting, then when I didn't return the kiss, she got in the car and closed the door. I watched them drive away, feeling grief for the girl I'd thought I'd known mixed in with grief for the others we had lost.

Luca was waiting by my caravan, a packed bag at his feet. I slowed my pace as I saw him. He'd told me not to take too long to decide whether or not I wanted to go with him. I'd delayed, and now the decision was made for me.

"So, you're leaving too." I couldn't keep the reproach from my voice.

"I asked you to come with me." His tone sounded harsh, but the sulky look on his face told me he didn't mean it. He was sad, not angry.

"I couldn't say yes, Luca."

He surely had to understand that now. I could see how he felt about me, and it wasn't fair to let him think things would have changed if we'd run off together.

"No, you couldn't have." He stared at me for a moment then stepped towards me, taking my hands. "But you can now."

I felt my eyes widen, a flicker of the hope I'd lost returning, but it was fleeting. I shook my head. "Just because of what happened with Giselle, it doesn't change... how I feel. I still like girls, Luca."

He gave a wry smile. "She's not the only girl in the world, Myra." He paused, studying my face. "And neither are you."

I dropped my gaze, embarrassed again for not being honest with him from the start. "I'm sorry," I whispered.

He shook his head. "You don't have to apologise. I love you, but you can't love me back. That's just the way it goes sometimes."

I took his hand. "I *do* love you. Just… as a friend."

Luca frowned, his face pained for a moment, then he squeezed my hand and put his arm around me. "Me too. And as your friend, I want you to come with me."

I met his eye and held it. He was offering with absolute honesty. There was no hidden agenda, nothing he wanted from me other than my company and friendship. He couldn't love me in the same way Giselle did, nor I him, but he would love me honestly as a friend.

"Yes," I said. "I want to come with you."

I thought of sneaking out without telling my mother. Perhaps leaving her a goodbye note or calling her from the road. Instead, I faced up to it and told her I was going.

She went still at my words. "With Giselle?" she asked.

I shook my head. "No, not after what she did. Luca and I are leaving."

She nodded slowly. "He's a good boy. Always been a good friend to you."

I was surprised by her lack of protest. I'd been sure she would try to lock me away, still deluding herself into believing I would one day return to join her flying through the air.

"The circus will probably close," she said, nodding to herself. "Your father and I were one of the only things keeping it together." She started to cry at that, finally beginning the grieving she needed so badly to do.

I wrapped my arms around her, crying too. But after only a few minutes, she brushed the tears from her cheeks, moving away from me.

"I have something for you," she said. She opened her bedside drawer, taking a bracelet from it. She clasped it around my wrist. "Your father gave me that. I think he would want…" She trailed off, emotion choking her voice. It was engraved with a single word—*Fly*.

She took my face between her hands, meeting my eye for the first time since I fell. "I love you, Myra. You call and check in with me every day, okay?"

I nodded, my turn to be silenced by emotion.

We left that night, hitching a ride with another one of the workers who was heading across the city to see his family. My mother was right—the way people were leaving, the circus wouldn't be around for much longer. We couldn't take responsibility for that though.

We didn't have a plan. Luca had some friends he thought might let us stay with them. Beyond that, we had only vague dreams of what we would do.

Luca closed his eyes and took a deep breath as we drove away from the circus. "Can you feel it?" he asked me.

"Feel what?" I was sitting tensely, my bag clutched on my lap.

Luca took it from me, placing it by his feet so I could sit more comfortably. "The spirits are releasing us."

I nearly laughed and reminded Luca of all the sceptical comments he had once made. I could feel it though. Like little whispers across my skin, they were letting us go, peeling back and allowing us to breathe deeply for the first time in a long while.

I thought of Giselle, and how tightly they had been wound around her. I wondered if she would ever escape, or if they would forever be tempting her, offering her promises they could only ever fulfill with fear. I hoped at least this time she would choose better. I hoped she would choose to live the life she had now instead of forever wishing for the one she had lost.

"What are you thinking about?" Luca asked.

I glanced at him, wondering how to explain. "I'm thinking I'm glad I chose to come with you," I said.

And I was. Whatever the future held for us, I was glad I was living this life, with my friend by my side.

I opened the window and let the air rush against my face. It was different from the wind that had plagued us—fresher. I shook my hair out into it, watching as sequins and sparkles flew from it, leaving me to fly back to the circus where they belonged.

ABOUT HELEN VIVIENNE FLETCHER

Helen Vivienne Fletcher is a children's and young adult author, spoken word poet and award-winning playwright. She discovered her passion for writing for young people while working as a youth support worker, and now helps children find their own passion for storytelling through her work as a creative writing tutor. Overall, Helen just loves telling stories and is always excited when people want to read or hear them.

CONNECT ON SOCIAL MEDIA

helenvfletcher.com

facebook.com/Helen-Vivienne-Fletcher-Writer

www.instagram.com/hvfauthor

twitter.com/helenvivienne

ALSO BY HELEN VIVIENNE FLETCHER

Broken Silence

Underwater

The Trespassers Club

THE DOLLHOUSE

CHRISTIS CHRISTIE

CHAPTER 1

IT APPEARED OVERNIGHT WITHOUT WARNING—LIKE A MYTHICAL fortress of high peaks and sloping turrets rising up from the morning fog rolling in off the harbour. Those who lived nearest the boardwalk where the train tracks ended and the shipping yard began, spoke of the eerie whistles drifting through the midnight air and waking them from dreams to darkness, and the call of the steam engine roaring by.

Cirque de Séduire.

Situated in the last lot between train tracks and dockyard, the circus was a multitude of black and scarlet striped tents—consisting of an assortment of sizes ranging from one-person, intimate revelations, to large-scale, hundred-person shows. It was truly a breathtaking sight, silhouetted by the harbour skyline and capped by the large bridge spanning overhead. Intermingled with the tents ran the fairway: booths of games, feats of strength, and tests of wit all lined the route towards the bright and shining apple of the ringmaster's eye —a beautiful carousel of glistening painted horses. Beyond, the slowly drifting Ferris wheel stretched into the murky sky above, with its gently rocking buckets offering a soothing ride into the heavens.

At noonday, the metallic, steam-driven sounds of the calliope filtered out over the surrounding city streets, drifting in on the ocean breeze. With quick snicks of glass sliding into wooden traps, the clouded ticket booth windows opened to reveal beaming clowns inside. From within the circus grounds, a horned man on stilts beckoned people inside, calling for them to come and see all the wonders *Séduire* had to offer.

It was all anyone could speak of, as word travelled quickly through the city of the circus that had sprouted up in the night. Marisol first heard gradual whispers of it in her morning class, as two of her classmates discussed the appearance of the circus down by the docks. Finding their hushed conversation far more intriguing than her English teacher droning on about Dickens' portrayal of the spurned lover in Miss Havisham.

"Papa worked the night shift down at the docks last night, and told me over breakfast this morning that when they finished offloading their last container, the circus was just there, almost like *magic*," Sarah Braeden excitedly informed Kathleen McArthur, her voice rising a little above what was deemed appropriate classroom talk, and thus incurring a reproachful glare from Mr. Thompson.

Their chatter ceased for but a moment, giving just enough time for it to seem like they had stopped, and for Mr. Thompson to become fully engrossed in Pip's travels once more, before they took right back up where they had left off. Marisol found herself leaning in a little more on her desk so that she could better hear what was being said, her long red braid falling to curl up on its surface.

"Magic isn't real Sarah," Kathleen responded in a whisper.

"No, but the point is, it simply came out of nowhere, and no one seems to even know how. They managed to get all of the tents up before anyone could take notice. I'm thinking of seeing if Billy and the others want to skip our last class to go and check it out."

Sarah was brimming with excitement, as was evident in the brightness of her reddened cheeks and the sheen in her eyes. Marisol found herself wishing that she had enough courage to go up to someone like Billy Coulter and invite him and all of his rambunctious, smart-mouthed, oh-so-tempting friends to skip school for an afternoon of fun.

"What if your mother finds out?" Kathleen whispered back, glancing quickly to the front of the classroom to ensure they weren't being overheard, and Marisol wondered what *would* happen if one's mother found they had given in to a day of truancy.

"What if? Don't you think a bit of a scolding will be worth it, if someone like Billy or David wins us a prize at the circus? Think of the rides on the Ferris wheel, Kathy!" Sarah's hand reached out to grip onto her friend's wrist, squeezing tightly in all of her glee. "Or we can have them walk us through the funhouse so that we can cling onto their arms. Please, you have to come with me!"

Marisol slumped back in her seat, slouching down a little with a despondent sigh as her black and white saddle shoes slid out before her on the floor. She would not be leaving school to sneak off to the circus early, instead she would have to wait until tonight, and pray that she could convince her mother and father to allow her to go. If she were able to get her brother James on her side, there was a chance they would be given a few spare dollars to go and enjoy all of the excitement while it was still in town.

By the end of the day, students had ceased even trying to pretend that they were paying heed to anything taking place in their classes, and over half of them had already disappeared from school grounds. Likewise, teachers had long since given up attempting to keep their students' attention on the lessons, and were themselves wandering across hallways to chat with the next teacher about the circus in town. Marisol's best friend, with whom she had the final class of the day, was quite literally ecstatic at the thought of clowns, games and freak shows. Without even being asked, she had accepted an invitation to join Marisol and James that evening.

"I'll just come home with you, and ring mum when I get there to let her know where we're going," Nancy declared as her fingers recoiled a curl at the side of her face, before straightening the red scarf tied neatly around her head.

"Don't you think you should ask permission first?"

"Mar…what have I been telling you? It's better to seek forgiveness afterwards than to ask permission before." Her friend wiggled her eyebrows, eyes sparking with mischief.

If ever they got into trouble, it was always due to Nancy's penchant towards misbehaving, and because Marisol was easily dragged into whatever it was.

"Plus Mar, you know that your father is far more likely to agree if I'm already there."

It was true, despite the fact that he was Marisol's father, he seemed to have a much more difficult time saying no to Nancy, than he did her. Perhaps it was because he wasn't her father, and happened to be polite to a fault when it came to other people. Whatever the reason, it did tend to help them do far more than he might desire.

"Okay, fine, you're right. You come home with me, and we'll tell your mother later."

As if sounding off its agreement with their plan, the bell shrilled the end to the day, which was instantly met by the scraping of chair legs over tiled floor. Packing up her books into her leather satchel, Marisol grinned a little at her friend. While she didn't exactly like doing things without parental consent, the idea of heading off directly to the circus with her best friend was exciting. There was also the added benefit of Nancy pushing her do to things outside of her comfort zone.

"Perfect. Let's get out of here!" Jumping to her feet so that her short curled hair gave a little bounce, Nancy grabbed up her own books and hefted her bag onto her shoulder. Without another word, she moved towards the door, only glancing back to ensure that Marisol was following.

Convincing her parents was not as much of a hassle as she had thought it would be. As it turned out, her father and mother had already chatted between themselves about James and Marisol spending the evening at the circus after a customer spoke to them about it in the general store. While the Chandler family lived in the upstairs apartments of their home, down below was a small shop where groceries, everyday needs, and small amounts of clothing and wares were sold. Both of her parents ran it during the day and closed up the doors just shortly before the dinner hour.

Though they had not been anticipating Nancy strolling through the shop door with her, Marisol couldn't say that either of her parents looked particularly surprised to see the dark haired girl alongside their daughter.

Though from an influential family, Nancy tended to spend a great deal of time with the Chandlers, treating their home much like her own. The few times Marisol had gone to spend time with the Pinders instead, she'd found the house pristine and cold. It had been very easy to see why someone would wish to avoid that atmosphere in preference of the chaotic, yet welcoming, feeling of Marisol's home.

"Really?" she'd cried excitedly when her father had agreed before she'd barely had enough time to finish asking.

He had chuckled and nodded, his eyes crinkling warmly at the sides.

"Yes, really. Your mother and I were talking earlier today, and we decided that you and James have been working hard all semester and deserve an evening out. Mind you, we haven't got much extra to give you beyond money for tickets and a few games or treats, so you'll have to pick your entertainment wisely."

"Don't worry Mister Chandler, I've got some with me, and can cover whatever else they might need!" Nancy added in, a wide grin on her cheeks as she announced this.

Once permission had been granted, and the Pinder's housekeeper had been informed where Nancy was, the girls went off in search of Marisol's older brother, James. Whereas the two girls were in their first semester of their very first year of high school, James was a senior and was already looking forward to heading off to an apprenticeship in the spring. He'd wished to forgo his final year so that he could take up the position at a local mechanics shop right away, but their father had pushed for him to finish school—wished in truth, that he was looking on to better things like using his cleverness to get a business degree, but had settled for a high school one instead.

James had always been clever and more than capable of tinkering with whatever had broken around the house until it was up and running once more. While their father longed for more education for him, Marisol recognized that her brother was happier when he was working with his hands. One day, someone would need to take over the running of the store from her parents, and while she wasn't sure that it would be her, she was positive that it would not be James.

It was no surprise to find him freshly home from school and already crouched behind the refrigerator that had been acting up, working away at something. Nancy, seeing a perfectly opportune moment to go over and practice her flirtations, hopped up on the counter next to the obnoxiously loud, humming ice box and peeked behind it.

"Hey handsome, getting your hands dirty?"

Marisol rolled her eyes as she came to stand before the fridge, her arms crossing over her green, button-up sweater and her relatively flat chest—puberty had not been as kind to her as it had been to Nancy, who had been well-endowed indeed. A fact about herself that Nancy was quickly learning how to best use to her own advantage. James tended to be one of her favourite on which to practice, whether he noticed or not.

There was a slightly incoherent response that came from the direction of the floor, somewhere in the remote area of James' head, which, by Marisol's best guess, was situated at the bottom of the refrigerator. Nancy laughed, having been able to hear him clearly over the loud hum due to her close proximity, while Marisol could only stand there and watch.

"James!" she said sharply, trying to be heard over the refrigerator. "Mum and Dad said we could go to the circus. Come out from behind there."

Stepping up to the blue fridge, she nudged at his foot with the toe of her shoe, trying to get his attention. His foot simply pushed back at her own, as he remained lying where he was. Huffing in frustration and a sense of anxious impatience, Marisol sidestepped to the other side of the fridge and cocked a brow at Nancy.

With a little nod of her head, Nancy winked back at her before leaning back behind the fridge so that she could speak directly to the teen hiding behind it.

"Let's go, sugar, we've got some clowns to see and you've got some games to win."

James sat up just a moment later, though it wasn't due to Nancy's words, but to the fact that the loud humming of the refrigerator had settled down to a soft, almost nonexistent purr. Nancy gave a quick, excited clap as he came out from behind the fridge, climbing to his feet as he wiped his hands on a rag.

"Really? You had to finish the fridge first?" Marisol asked, eyeing him.

James gave a slight shrug of his shoulders, before responding. "I was already down there, and it was almost done."

"Well, now that it's fixed, how about the three of us mosey on down to the waterfront to celebrate?"

The siblings both looked at Nancy for a moment before their eyes locked with each other.

"I suppose she's coming with us then?" James asked.

Laughing, Marisol could only nod to her brother's question as Nancy slipped off the counter and adjusted her bell shaped, felt skirt with its abstract black pattern stitched all around the bottom of it.

"Well?" Nancy asked.

"Yes, Nan, we're going. James...cleanup, we'll meet you downstairs."

CHAPTER 2

THE SUN WAS ALREADY LOW IN THE SKY AS THEY APPROACHED THE circus grounds, and the chill off the ocean was enough to make Marisol shiver and sink further into the jacket she'd slipped on. However, the excitement coursing through her, which only increased as they drew nearer, was enough to help warm her. At the front of the circus, a bright red ticket booth sat, proudly bearing its sign of ticket prices like a stamp of honour.

"Well, hello, kids," chimed the white-faced clown inside the booth, with bright painted lips, and round circles of black upon his cheeks, who leaned out towards them as he drew out each word in a high-pitched voice. "That will be $2.75 each." His flash of teeth was broad and a little terrifying when paired with the curly, black and red wig upon his head.

It was enough to make both Marisol and Nancy teeter with nervous laughter, hands coming to shield their faces as they leaned towards each other until their shoulders were pressed together. James gave a roll of his eyes and pulled out his own two dollar bill and coins, handing over his fare. Still giggling nervously, Nancy dug into her small handbag to pass over admission for both of them.

"You can get the Abba Zaba bars and popcorn." She grinned at Marisol, as she tentatively pulled the tickets from the clown's outstretched hand, being sure to avoid the fingertips peeking out from the ends of cut-off, wool gloves.

Laughing nervously once more as the ticket booth clown leered out at them maniacally, they hurried off to catch up with James who was already passing into the circus grounds.

"How rude, James, don't you think you ought to protect us from terrifying men?" Nancy asked, sidling up to him, and wrapping her arm through his.

With a little shake of her head, and a light tug on the knit cap that sat upon it, Marisol fell into step beside her best friend. While her brother offered Nancy a mildly irritated glance and stated that it was only a man with a painted face, Marisol was busy looking about them.

Overhead were strung bright Edison bulbs that swung gently in the wind and offered happy specks of light, encouraging them further into the grounds. Kids and adults alike passed around them, with excited chatter and happy laughter spilling from the crowd to blend with the thud of a hammer upon a lever, or the rattle of wooden bottles toppling.

She gasped delightedly as two tall men on stilts circled them, leaning down to hold out paper maps of the circus. Their faces were shadowed by the night sky, allowing only the broad white grins to peek through the darkness, and hinting at the horns that rested upon their heads.

"Be sure to check out *all* of our tents," the first said with a suggestive grin.

"Sometimes the greatest adventures are found in the smallest places," informed the other, as the two of them continued to circle around them with long, overstated steps—long pant legs falling around tiny, wooden feet.

They wore suits of red, long tails trailing behind, with the hint of a forked tail peeking out between them. Giant, horned devils that leered and grinned above them; long legs making vast, sauntering steps about the trio.

"Looks can be deceiving, and what is real isn't always." The first swooped down from his great height to tug at one of Nancy's curls, making her teeter in nervous laughter once more.

"And sometimes what isn't, once was."

The girls shared a look, their faces split by large grins as a thrill of the unnatural went up their spines. Marisol was aware that all of this was for show, and that it was just ordinary men with remarkable balance walking around on wooden sticks. She also knew that the man in the ticket booth had only been a man in a wig with a painted face speaking in a particularly spooky manner. Yet, none of that mattered at all as they were swept up in the music and the lights of *Cirque de Séduire.*

Already it felt as if she had stepped into another world, one in which anything could happen because the adults in it were no longer the straight-laced, typical parents or teachers that she saw every day. Instead, they were something otherworldly, and it made her both nervous and blissful.

Both of the men offered dramatic bows, before spinning away to converge on the next unsuspecting group of visitors who squealed and giggled just as much.

"This is so much fun!" Nancy whispered to her, leaning away from James' arm that she clung to, despite his apparent lack of interest.

"It is." Marisol had to agree. "What shall we do first?"

"Games!"

"Food."

Nancy and James chimed in at the same time, both eyeing each other before turning their glances to Marisol to act as the deciding factor.

"Come on Mari," James pleaded. "I'm starving."

"But we're at the circus!" Nancy cried, bouncing with excess energy. "I want to have some fun." There was a whining quality taking over her voice that made Marisol's nose and lip curl a little.

While she agreed with her best friend that they had come to the circus to have fun, she also knew that none of them had stopped for supper before they'd headed out, and she could feel her own belly beginning to stir with the rumblings of hunger.

"I vote some food, and then we head straight into some games." It was the easiest way to make all parties happy, and they'd all feel better with some food in their bellies as they wandered around all of the sights.

"Curse your sibling bond." Nancy sighed, but allowed herself to be dragged over to a red and black wooden stand, with bright white scrolling detail along the roof and sides, as it offered up corn dogs on sticks, and an assortment of treats.

There was a bit of a line, but soon enough the three of them were balancing corn dogs, popcorn to share, and a cone of cotton candy that Nancy had insisted on since she had been denied her games.

"Come on, you big baby, let's go win you a prize," Marisol drawled once their food had been eaten, heading back towards the fairway with its row upon row of games to test your strength and accuracy, while emptying all of the change from your pockets.

"Now Mar," Nancy whispered. "We don't win the prizes, that's what boys are for." With a wink in her direction, Nancy then slid up beside James, pointing out a throwing game. "Oh look, that one's free. Let's see if you can't knock all of those down."

While she couldn't exactly blame her best friend for seeking out male attention where she could find it, Marisol did find it rather annoying that tonight was becoming more about her flirting with James, than it was about simply having a fun time.

As James handed over a ten cent coin for his chance to go, Marisol turned to lean back against the counter. She casually paid attention to her brother's first throw before letting her eyes wander to other people, enjoying the sight of circus entertainers appearing out of places they were least expected, to interact with the crowds. With awe, she watched a woman dressed in a tight black leotard, and a red tutu, juggle five balls in the air while simultaneously balancing upon the shoulders of a man clad entirely in white with a red-rimmed, white cone hat perched upon his head.

She couldn't help but cheer as the balls fell down to the man's hands, and he juggled for a moment before throwing them back up to the woman who worked them back into a spinning circle without issue. Marisol's fingers itched to do something showy and amazing like that, but knew walking across the floor without tripping on her own feet could be hard enough, let alone walking while keeping multiple things in the air.

"You aren't here all by yourself, are you?"

Marisol jumped as the voice murmured close to her ear, and whipping her head to the side, she found herself peering into a set of brown eyes that belonged to Billy Coulter. Finding herself speechless for a moment, her lips opening to release only silence, all she could do was point towards her brother and best friend. What was Billy doing speaking to her, and where had Sarah disappeared to?

Billy chuckled. "With them?"

Swallowing a little, she managed to find her voice at last.

"Yes. My brother, James, and my best friend Nancy," Marisol explained, her heart tripping away nervously in her chest.

"Well, they seem to be doing a poor job including you." His eyes shifted over to the two of them who were in the process of both throwing balls at the stacked bottles.

"Oh, it's fine, really. They're trying to win a toy for Nancy."

"What about you, don't you want a toy too?"

Marisol supposed that it was a nice thing to have a cute stuffed bear to take home, but she wasn't aiming to win one for herself.

"Well, not from my brother." She laughed a little, her nose scrunching.

To her surprise, Billy laughed along with her, looking first to James and then back to her.

"I suppose not." He grinned, and she felt her stomach flop and her knees turn a little bit to jelly.

"What about you? Where have all of your friends gotten off too?" And what was he doing standing here speaking to her, of all people? None of it made any sense, not that she was complaining. But Billy hadn't exactly spent a great deal of time noticing her at school.

"They're all on the carousel for what has to be the tenth time, and I'm a little bored of it. So, I skipped out." He rolled his sleeves up a little as he turned around to face the game stand behind them. "How about I win you a stuffed bear instead. *Before* Nancy gets one."

Marisol laughed, flushing a little as she turned to face the game stall along with him.

"Well, I suppose that isn't such a bad idea." Their eyes met, and she flushed more as Billy simply grinned back.

Ducking her head a little, she tucked a few stray hairs behind her ear, smiling to herself. This was entirely unexpected, but fell in with the spirit of tonight—magical and impossible. She could only stand there and continue smiling as Billy paid for a turn, and was handed two balls. Shifting on his feet he then drew one hand back before tossing the first ball. He managed to clip the top bottle and send it tumbling down, but the rest of the bottles remained standing.

"Oh…so close!" Marisol couldn't help chiming in, and received a grin in return.

"Don't worry, I still have a second ball." He tossed it up into the air, winking at her before snatching it back up.

Marisol held her breath as he tossed the second ball at the remaining stack, groaning when he missed completely. It would seem tonight wasn't going to be *all* magic and success. Beside her Billy let out a grumble, digging in his pocket.

"Well, thanks for trying."

"Oh, I'm not done yet." His hand outstretched to offer the carney —sporting a black horned hat—another ten cent piece.

This time, when he was handed his two balls, he sized up the stack of bottles like they were his arch nemesis, and then let loose with a vicious throw. Marisol yelped in happiness as the bottles went toppling, all of them crashing down behind the stand. Clapping excitedly, she looked over at Billy.

"You did it!"

He flashed her a broad, satisfied smile.

"Pick out which teddy bear you want."

Still unable to believe that this was taking place, Marisol glanced up to all of the stuffed animals lining the small hut and pointed to a white bear, with brown arms, legs and ears, and cute little button eyes and nose.

"We'll take that one please," Billy informed the carney who moved to pluck it down off its hook before holding it out to her.

Accepting the stuffed animal, she clutched it to her chest, squeezing it happily as she felt a shiver of pleasure course through her.

"Thank you, so very, very—"

"Oh golly, Mar, where did you get that bear?" Nancy interrupted before Marisol had a chance to finish thanking him.

Her friend stepped up to her quickly, and being so focused on the bear, she hadn't noticed the male beside her. When her eyes lifted and took in the sight of Billy Coulter she let out an uncharacteristic eep of surprise.

"Billy? Billy!" Nancy looked to Marisol, her eyes big and round. "Billy?"

Marisol could only blush more, knowing exactly why her best friend was so shocked—she wasn't exactly the type of girl who usually drew the attention of the boys at school. Not with girls like Sarah and Kathleen there, or Nancy and her newly blossoming flirty nature.

"Yes, Billy," stated the current object of their exclamations, as he leaned against the booth, that confident smirk tugging at his lips.

"He won me this bear," Marisol supplied, grinning at Nancy before casting a quick glance in Billy's direction.

"Are we done here yet? I don't think I'm going to knock all the bottles down..." James was muttering as he stepped up to them, his words drifting off as he took in the newcomer to their little group. "When did you get here?"

"They really were ignoring you, weren't they Mari?" Billy stated, grinning at her like they were sharing a secret. "Come on, let's go check out some of the sideshows."

"Yes, let's!" Nancy chimed in, bumping her shoulder against Marisol's as she looked at her suggestively, mouthing 'oh my gosh' in a dramatic manner.

CHAPTER 3

EVEN THOUGH MARISOL HAD EXPECTED BILLY TO GROW TIRED OF THEM and quickly head off to find his own group of friends, he stayed by their side. Together, the four of them moved into each new tent to investigate what resided within. The first tent that they slipped into was very narrow, yet stretched sixteen feet into the air, black and white striped, with a red flag at its tip that offered them a melancholy flap of greeting.

Inside, at a little wooden table, sat one solitary man. Dressed in a black shirt and slacks with red suspenders, his blank, sightless white eyes stared off into the distance, looking at something beyond what vision could have offered. Poorly applied white makeup appeared in blotches over his face and looked mostly wiped away, or smeared, causing the three blood red tear drops falling down his cheeks from the corner of each eye to stand out all the more vividly.

Cautiously, the girls stepped inside, gazing at the man unsurely. The boys were not as nervous, and slipped past them to look around the barren tent—all except for the man and his wooden table, with two chairs opposite him. Overhead, hung a single oil lamp that cast an eerie glow down over the sad, forsaken showman.

"Welcome young monsieurs et mademoiselles, come and take a seat."

His words were followed by nervous laughter from both Marisol and Nancy, a glance shared between them as they moved further in. The tent was so narrow that it took only a couple of steps for them to make it to the table. Glancing back at James and Billy, Marisol looked for reassurance and found neither of them concerned, so she pulled out one rickety black chair and sat down.

She felt herself flinch back into the chair as her eyes landed upon the man's face, and she could see more clearly what the blotchy makeup had been concealing. From the top of his brows and down to the bottoms of his cheeks ran jagged scars where it appeared someone had dragged the tip of a knife blade, or something equally as sharp.

"Don't be afraid," he commented, the side of his mouth tipping up in a jarring half smile that she felt was meant to be reassuring. "They're not contagious."

His fingers dragged over his eyes, mimicking the fall of the scars, and down to his cheeks. How he knew of her reaction Marisol wasn't sure—unless it was given so frequently that he simply presumed—but the man was attuned to more than just the darkness of his sight.

From what seemed to be nowhere, he produced a deck of cards that were soon shot into the air, forming a wide fan only to be caught easily by his second hand. Amongst the four of them, there sounded collective ooo's of enjoyment. His fingers flowed with an ease and grace that was otherworldly. The snap of cards quickly moving from one hand to the next sounded again as he worked at shuffling.

"I will show you an act of sleight of hand, and should you be able to tell how I did it, then you owe me nothing. However, if you are unable to see the truth in the trick, then you each owe me a ten cent piece." His white eyes travelled over them, and despite their useless state, held each one of them accountable.

"We can agree to that," James spoke for the group.

Nancy nodded, her eyes wide with interest as she gazed at the man opposite them. Beside her, Marisol grunted softly as her friend's hand suddenly shot out to grip onto her thigh, just above her knee.

"Easy Nance," Marisol muttered to her, understanding the anticipation growing inside Nancy, but not her need for physical touch at this time.

Nancy's grip loosed just a fraction, but remained on her thigh, partially concealing the grey felt poodle patched onto the bottom of her white skirt.

Before them, the performer shuffled the cards quickly, and then fanned them out on the table so that their faces lay downwards. His hand lifted, and a bony finger pointed in Marisol's direction.

"Choose one of these cards. You may show the others, and though I am unable to see, don't show it to me."

Marisol gazed at him uncertainly for a moment, but then reached out to pick a card from the deck. Sliding it across the table until it reached the edge, she then plucked it up to reveal the ace of hearts. Gazing at the stark red ink upon the white backdrop, she felt a strange sense of foreboding. The others leaned in around her to see what it was she had gotten, murmuring in their own responsive ways.

"Now, do you know your card?" He questioned her.

"Mhm."

"Will you remember your card?"

"Yes."

"Then please slide it back into the deck wherever you should choose."

Glancing over at Nancy, she reached out to place the card back into the deck several cards down from where it had originally been taken. With a quick swipe of his hand, the showman gathered them up, and began to shuffle once more. Cards arched up into the air like a stream of water from a spout only to be caught with ease. Once his tricks were completed, he tapped the entire stack of them down against the table. Splitting the stack in half, he placed the top onto the bottom, and repeated this action several times until at last he set the stack face-down upon the table.

Marisol gazed at the stack, wondering what it was he was planning. With a tap of his fingers onto the top of the card deck, she felt the anticipation mounting inside the tent. Pulling the top card off the stack, he held it up in the air so that all of them could see.

"Is this your card?"

Marisol stared at the black three of spades and shook her head, beside her Nancy's shoulders slumped in disappointment.

"No, it's not."

From behind her, Billy snickered, which drew the sightless gaze of the performer directly to him, a dark look upon his old features.

"Perhaps the young disbeliever should check his coat pocket."

They all turned to peer at Billy, brows lifted in disbelief, none of them sure about what was going to happen. Nancy's clutch on Marisol's knee only tightened as they waited impatiently for Billy to check first his left pocket, and then his right.

He did not look impressed, lines of doubt etched upon his features. Until, his hand slipped into his right pocket and then his entire body froze, while incredulity slipped over his face as it began losing all colour. Slowly he withdrew his hand, which held between its fingers a paper playing card. His eyes were upon it first, but

Marisol didn't need to see the face of the card to know already what it bore. All she needed to do was look at Billy. A rush of heat washed over her, as well as the desire to deny it, until he had spun the card around to show them the ace of hearts.

Nancy gasped happily, shaking Marisol's knee a little before she began to exclaim how amazing it was. Gingerly, Marisol reached out to take the card from Billy, her cheeks warm from disbelief, and amazement.

"Is that your card?"

Her head whipped around to gaze at the man across the table, a knowing look upon his grizzled face.

"Y-yes."

"You should be wary of who holds your heart in their hand," he murmured, confirming once more that he knew exactly what card it was, though none had said it aloud.

"How..." she whispered, but Nancy was drowning her out with all of her exclamations of wonder and surprise.

Without question, all of them placed their ten cent pieces upon the table, and Marisol felt lightheaded as they left the tent. All of them had been watching him throughout the entire performance, and he had not moved from his spot. She had to agree with Nancy that it had been a wondrous thing to behold, but it also felt like playing around with something dark that should not be tampered with.

If that wasn't true magic, then what was it?

Their chatter was quick and filled with life as they made their way onto the next tents: visiting acrobats, a juggler who danced with knives, and a man who blew, and then ate, fire. Each tent seemed more grand and more amazing than the last, sending them off to the next with flushed cheeks and excited laughter.

At the end of the field of smaller tents was a short, fat one. Red and black striped, it sat out of sync from the others, and bore a halo of mist or fog around the bottom of it—a nest of clouds, as if it were resting in the sky. Atop the tent sat a large black raven, who cawed ominously at them as they passed a sign that read Madame Tousaught, Guide to the Spirit Realm.

"What do you think she'll tell us?" Nancy whispered as they stepped up to the opening into the tent.

The fog appeared to be steadily rolling out of the open flap, and out from under the bottom of the tent itself, unfurling in soft swirls of wispy fingers beckoning passersby to enter into the canvas structure.

"I don't know," she whispered back, still feeling a little spooked from their encounter with the blind showman.

One by one, they slipped through the narrow opening, and inside. All around the perimeter of the tent stood tall candelabras with numerous black candles burning, wax dripping down the length of them to pool in the white metal cups. From the centre pole of the tent hung long ribbons that curled and coiled until falling in a pool of satin and lace on the ground. Madame Tousaught lounged gracefully upon a series of cushions in the corner, her legs stretched out and crossed at the ankles to show that she wore no shoes, only a gold chain anklet with a series of gold coins attached to it.

As they entered, the woman stood to her feet to greet them. Her skirt—a series of silken scarves stitched together—flowed around her legs as she moved towards them. Her bare arms, clad only in golden bangles, motioned them in towards her.

"Welcome children. Come in and let me take a look at you." As she walked closer, Marisol noted her face makeup which was white as the other's had been, but in the middle of her forehead was painted a red eye, which sat unblinking upon her face.

Something about the art made her feel ill-at-ease, and as if sensing this fact, Madame Tousaught quickly left James' side whom she had been circling. As she stepped up to Marisol, she held out her hands just inches from her face, almost cupping her cheeks but not quite, and closed her eyes. Humming softly beneath her breath, the soothsayer stayed where she was for a moment, and then her hazel eyes snapped open to peer intently into Marisol's.

There was a look within their depths that chilled her, not in the way that the card trick had, but in a far more worrisome way. Her heart began to pick up as her natural adrenaline began to take hold, and a small voice inside of her head whispered, "Run!"

"The spirits are strong around you child," she spoke lowly, a voice that was only for Marisol and no longer for show. "They whisper warnings of guarding your heart against cold hands that would steal it away."

The chill in Marisol only increased, as her words eerily echoed those of the sightless magician. Madam Tousaught's eyes closed for another moment.

"Beautiful things can be terribly ugly on the inside, don't trust the pretty trinkets." Her eyes opened once more, and for a moment they stood silently staring back at each other.

Marisol didn't know what any of these messages were meant to mean, and she was clever enough to know not to trust the random leadings of a circus mystic, but something about Madame Tousaught's words echoed within her.

As suddenly as she had come to her, Madame Tousaught turned away from Marisol and the show was back. Akin to a dancer, her arms trailed about her, curling and waving until she had reached Nancy's side, and then she took her hand.

"You child, need your fortune told, come to the pillows and let us see what the crystal ball has to say for you."

With a happy trill of laughter, Nancy followed her over to the corner where the bed of large pillows lay. Plopping down on one, Nancy folded her legs beneath her and peered down into the crystal ball that perched upon a small table sat on the large pillow. Madame Tousaught sat down across from her, leaning over the ball as she began to swirl her hands around it, singing softly.

Marisol barely watched the proceedings as both Billy and James inched forward to better hear what the woman had to tell Nancy. None of it mattered to her however, as her brain tried to process why both the magician and the mystic would give her warnings about her heart.

Eyes drifting to Billy, Marisol had to wonder if there was more to his presence with them tonight. It all seemed too good to be true, maybe she was better off listening to her doubts than she was to her hopes. Who *was* she to have earned Billy's interest anyhow? Swallowing roughly against the strange emotion rising up in her throat, Marisol looked away from her friends and gazed down into the fog swirling around her ankles.

Perhaps she was putting too much thought into all of this. There was a very strong chance that all of circus performers worked together on this very sort of thing, picking one person in each group that came through to say the same line to. Yet, there had been a cord of truth in Madame Tousaught's eyes that had not felt like an act, but rather an honest note of concern.

"Oh gosh, how did you *know* that?!"

It was Nancy's loud exclamation that broke Marisol from her contemplations, to glance over at her friends. Billy and Nancy were laughing, while even James appeared a little impressed at whatever Madame Tousaught had said to them.

"Marisol, did you hear that?" Nancy was calling out to her, grinning broadly in amazement.

"No I didn't, sorry." Although she wished to stay further away from the mystic, Marisol moved up to the others to engage more in their readings while each took turns having their fortune told.

When it came her turn, Marisol shook her head in denial, claiming she had heard enough already. Once coins had been handed over, the four of them moved back outside. Billy fell into step beside her once more, and she felt concern wash through her. Should she go with her suspicions and tell him to leave now? Would she be saving herself embarrassment and heartache later?

She had no desire to allow herself to be lead down a track of shame if this was only some sort of game he was playing, yet in her arms she still carried the teddy bear he had won her. She didn't want to believe that he was spending so much time with them in order to be cruel, but what was a girl to think?

She had now been warned to be cautious of who she gave her heart to by two separate people on the same night she was hoping to be able to begin giving it away.

"You seem very deep in thought," Billy said, causing Marisol to look up into his eyes.

He really was a perfectly handsome boy, one that Marisol wanted to spend more time with rather than chase away.

"I guess I am."

"What are you thinking about?" he asked her softly as the group continued to walk the circus grounds.

"A lot of things… Billy, I don't know if—"

"Mar! Come quick and see this!" Nancy cut in before she could continue telling Billy it might be best if he go off and find his own friends, rather than continue on with them.

Nancy was adamant, however, waving her arm vigorously for the two of them to catch up to where she and James had gotten to, fifteen feet away. Walking past a cotton candy stand, Marisol stepped up to her best friend and looked beyond to the large tent that awaited them.

CHAPTER 4

THE TENT WAS ENORMOUS, RISING ABOVE THE OTHERS AROUND IT LIKE A mountain predominant on the horizon. Though the greater portion of it was made of black and red canvas, the front was a large, grey house facade, including a front door and a step rather than a tent flap. On the upper story of the house hung a white washed sign, slightly askew with paint-dripped red letters reading, The Dollhouse.

"Isn't it amazing?" Nancy asked, peering up at the large structure before them.

Marisol stared at it in question, unsure of what to expect of the large tent and it's strange frontage.

"What is it...? Have you ever seen a dollhouse at the circus before?" she asked, looking from Nancy to James. Both of them shook their heads.

"No, but don't you want to find out?" Nancy wiggled her brows, and Marisol could only laugh.

"I suppose so." It was a very strange thing to see, and her curiosity had her walking towards the large tent with its wooden facade, her friends and brother following along beside her.

There was a strange light coming from somewhere behind the Dollhouse that gave it an ominous glowing aura all around, an uncanny beacon calling them all forward. Unlike the other tents that had staked signs outside giving an idea of what awaited them inside, there was nothing for this one, only the steps leading up to a wooden door, and a brass doorknob.

Bounding up the steps, Billy took hold of the knob and quickly opened the door, only for them to be greeted by nothing but a dark hallway with a flashing light at the end of it. Marisol felt an instant flash of terror as that darkened hallway stretched out before her, each rapid flash of the light a silent warning. She didn't want to go in there, though she had no idea what was at the end of that hallway, she decided she was okay never knowing.

"What if we were to see what is in the main tent first?" Marisol suggested, attempting to sound casual while she stared down the pit of that dark hallway.

"We've got plenty of time for that later, Mar, I want to see what this is about and we're already here," Nancy said, heading up the steps..

"You're not afraid are you?" James asked, gazing down at her and what was likely her paling features, as the dark hallway loomed before them.

"What? No! Of course not," Marisol lied, trying to swallow down the gurgle of fear rising up in the back of her throat. How could none of the others sense the terror she felt coming from inside of that hallway? Like a low, chilling whisper, it coiled its way around the back of her neck, and down her spine.

Nancy and James had already stepped inside, their bodies disappearing into the darkness as they walked towards the flashing light at the end. Billy stood on the step, waiting for her to join them. Swallowing roughly once more, Marisol climbed the rickety wooden steps and passed by him, to move inside.

Instantly her eyes were struck by the darkness. Blinking rapidly, Marisol tried to adjust herself to the low level of light, the sound of her heartbeat overpowered only by the creaking of the wooden floor beneath her. Up ahead, Marisol heard a shout that sounded like a fearful Nancy, and found herself hurrying faster as the tempo of her heart picked up. Had something awful happened down there beyond that flashing light? In the process of trying to get to where her friend was more quickly, she became tangled up in her own feet and tripped.

It was Billy's arm slipping around her waist, and pulling her back upright, that kept her from falling flat onto her face.

"Are you okay?" he asked, his voice warm in her ear as he spoke from behind her, the press of his body against her back.

"Y-yes…I just thought I heard Nancy scream."

They both paused for a moment, barely breathing as they listened. Again the shout came, but this time it ended in a peal of laughter.

"I think that was a laugh, she's having fun," he responded. "Come on, let's see where they are."

Pulling away from his hold, Marisol tugged on the bottom of her sweater, straightening it around her waist in a desire to feel more in control of herself. Her heart was still beating fast enough that she could hear it in her ears and feel it crashing against her chest, but Marisol told herself that walking down the hallway towards the flashing light was what she needed to do right now, and that her brother and best friend were having the time of their life.

The hallway narrowed in on itself the nearer to the end they got, until it forced them through the small doorway into the next space. Ignoring the hesitation within her, Marisol stepped into the next room and jumped in surprise as she was met with another person before her. Releasing a soft eep of shock, Marisol tensed up in fear until she realized that it was herself she was looking at.

All around her were mirrors, and she had to put her hand before her in order to feel out the next opening. The flashing of the light overhead, and the reflective walls surrounding her left her disorientated. From somewhere beyond drifted another shout of surprise from Nancy, and the deep rumble of James' laughter. They were having fun—it was okay. She would be okay.

Gradually, Marisol slipped through the next opening, which took her further into the mirrored hall that was turning out to be a maze, her own pale and shaken reflection bouncing back at her in an infinite amount of shocked expressions. Behind her, she sensed Billy before his reflection mingled with her own, endless images of him standing beside her now surrounding them both. It made her feel a little dizzy and off-kilter, her mind unable to comprehend which way was which, as every direction bounced from one wall to the next.

"Oh look, so many of us!" Billy laughed, gesturing towards one wall, and a thousand Billy's followed suit.

Marisol released an awkward laugh, trying not to show how uneasy all of this was making her feel. There was something discomfiting about not having a clearly defined path laid out before her.

"I don't know which way to go next..." she informed him, gazing back over her shoulder so that she could see the real him, and not the cold reflections mirrored back.

"I think it's through here." Billy stuck out his hand only to hit glass. "Oh...nope, I guess not."

As a unit they turned, looking for an exit. It took running their hands along the walls to find the narrow gap between mirrors that led into the next section of maze. Marisol didn't want to go through first, but Billy was directly behind her and she felt foolish asking him to go in before her when she had no clear reason for being frightened. Gathering her spirits, she squeezed herself, and her skirt, through the separation in the walls to the newest room beyond.

The light overhead wasn't flickering as quickly as it had been in the other location. Instead, this one came from a swinging halogen bulb on the end of cord, with a small beaded chain beside it to turn it on and off. The light flashed on, before going completely out, leaving her in the pitch black, with only the warmth of what she assumed was Billy behind her—who must have slipped into the room as the light went out and didn't realize how near to her he was. As the next flash of the light came back on, Marisol looked into the mirrored eyes before her, only they weren't Billy's.

They were large, rounded eyes with heavy black circles around them, and a fringe of red yarn obscuring them slightly. Marisol screamed in shock as her brain registered the unfamiliar face. While the light flicked out once more, she spun around, backing away from the strange figure behind her.

With her heart pounding, Marisol did her best to see through the darkness of the room until the light flicked on once more. When it did so, it was Billy standing before her, gazing back at her with a concerned expression on his face.

"Mar, are you okay?"

"There was just—Where did she go?" Her sentences came out in fragments as the surprise ran through her. Twisting her head to the side, she jumped back and hit the wall of mirror behind her.

In the corner stood a girl slumped over a little, her arms dangling at her sides with white mittens upon her hands. She wore a red yarn wig that was braided in pigtails much like a handmade rag doll—one who had bright red lips and a smile that extended wider thanks to jagged stitch marks trailing from each corner and across her cheeks. Bright pink painted circles rested just above the ragged grin, helping the white of her eyes to pop as she gazed directly at Marisol in a lifeless manner that left her even more chilled than before.

Just as this was registering in her mind, the light above went out, and Marisol felt as if she could no longer breathe.

"Bil-Billy?" Her hand began to extend out in search of him and then was quickly snatched back to her body. What if that doll was coming closer to her? The thought of touching something foreign in the darkness petrified her.

"I'm right here," he spoke, his voice sounding right next to her, and quickly she reached out to grab a hold of his arm.

The overhead light flashed back on, and the doll was still there in her corner, except that one mittened hand had lifted and was slowly waving back and forth in a loose, uncoordinated manner as if there were no bones in her body. Her gaze peered across the small room at them, wide and unblinking, while her lips pinched together in a large grin that only made her eyes all the more round for it.

"Where did she come from?" Billy asked, noticing the doll clown for the first time.

"She appeared behind me as soon as I came in here," Marisol explained. "Billy, how do we get out?"

All around them were reflections of themselves, but this time they were joined by the red hair and dead stare of the rag doll in the corner.

Once again, the light flickered out, the bulb giving a little crackling noise as it did, and then blinked back on almost as quickly. In the short period of darkness though, the doll clown moved forward, her legs and arms loose and shaking as she continued to advance towards them, back and shoulders hunched forward as her head lolled about on her neck. Rolling her arms quickly around in a circle before her, she then paused with a jerk that shook her entire body to point to one mirrored panel to their right.

Swallowing roughly, Marisol took this to mean that she was leading them in the direction they needed to go, but that also meant that she would have to pass directly by her. Glancing quickly to Billy, Marisol then began moving that way, her hand still clutched around his arm tightly.

As she neared the doll, her head tipped to the side and she smiled more intently at Marisol, all the while the dark irises of her eyes stared blankly outwards. Just as Marisol reached her, the doll's lashes blinked down over them quickly and with a snap, her head popped up, and the clown was staring at Marisol, a dark smile twisting her painted face.

Jumping, Marisol hurried past her and shuddered as she felt the brush of a white mitten run along her arm. Pulling Billy along behind her, she nearly leapt through the now-apparent hole in the mirrored walls. Her heart was beating fast once more, and she could feel a little faint bead of sweat beginning at her hairline.

Behind her, Billy was laughing, just like Nancy and James. It would appear that he found this to be an amusing escapade. To her, however, it was anything but. Marisol also didn't seem able to stop, as she rushed away from the rag doll, her hands slid along the mirrors until she was able to move on to the next location. By this point she was used to seeing the fearful reflection of her own face repeated back to her continuously.

In her hurry, somewhere along the way she had lost her grip on Billy's arm. No longer did it seem to matter if he was there with her, just putting as much distance between herself and that rag doll.

As she passed through the next open doorway, she found that it lead into a room with yet another living doll. This one was dressed entirely in white, even her face and skin bleached with paint. The only colour besides the crimson spots on her cheeks was a short, curly bob of a silver wig upon her head. Her arms were folded at the elbows so that her gloved hands stuck straight up and she was bent a little at the waist. From her back protruded a large wind-up key that slowly rotated.

As Marisol entered this new mirrored section, the windup doll slowly straightened, her arms lifting and falling while remaining bent firmly. With stiff-legged steps, much like a tin soldier, the doll swung her white stockinged legs straight up before her, walking in a disjointed manner in Marisol's direction.

"Please...don't," she gasped out, feeling the chill climbing up the back of her neck. All around her, stiffly-moving, windup dolls shifted. In every direction, hundreds of them were trying to make their way towards her.

Marisol screamed, leaping forward as a hand pressed to her back, sliding up to rest upon her shoulder. Spinning around with her hands flying up to protect herself, she found not the rag doll from before, but Billy.

"Woah...hey, it's just me, you're okay," he reassured in a soft voice.

"Sorry, you startled me."

The windup doll had paused near them, bent slightly at the waist with her arms stuck in the air. She peered at them with a strange look upon her face—a sort of half smile that looked almost vicious. Unlike the rag doll who'd had eyes that appeared lifeless, the windup doll had a gaze of ice-cold flint.

"Let's...find James and Nancy," Marisol murmured, her words barely above a whisper as she gazed at the doll-painted woman before her.

After a series of more hallways and mirrored confusion, the two of them finally slipped into another portion of the Dollhouse that did not consist of reflective surfaces. However, Marisol found herself in yet another dark hallway, one with large wrought-iron chandeliers hanging from the ceiling that flickered with burning candles. From somewhere beyond, a breeze seemed to blow as they swung just enough to cast a glow of light on different portions of the room at once.

Along the walls were narrow alcoves that each glowed with their own candlelight, but instead of something comforting, what she found inside each small square was a series of broken doll pieces. Bodies with heads, but no arms and legs; eyeless doll heads lying upon their sides, and a number of headless bodies all in a pile together. Wax and feathers spilled from inside their empty forms, creating what looked like an altar of worship for dark, terrible magic.

In the next sunken shelf rested a series of animal bones, and a pile of the dolls eyes. Melted red wax trailed over all of it, cementing each piece to the wood, and in the back corner sat a doll's head upside down with a large red candle protruding from inside it. The flame flickered, releasing the wax to spill out onto the shelf and run down the outside of the wall.

If they were hoping to showcase an exhibition of the chilling and dark side of doll collecting, they had achieved that. Every step took them further down the hallway and passed new displays of horrific and disturbing doll scenes. Each one the example of a childhood massacre.

Her nose scrunched a little in disfavour as they passed a squared, medieval candelabra that bore numerous cobwebs along its frame and stand. Obscenely, at each holder a doll head had been shoved, protruding from the tops of their bare, baby scalps was a red wax candle which trailed its scarlet flow over empty sockets, or drooping marble eyes.

"Do you think they took these from real voodoo witches?" Billy asked as they walked past the wall displays, and a bone wind mobile hanging in the corner as they turned the bend.

"Maybe...but wouldn't that be dangerous?"

"It's only dangerous if you believe in the power of it."

On a wooden pedestal carved to look like a skeleton arm and hand —which she could only hope and pray would not turn out to be real —sat a small human-shaped doll made out of straw and sticks. Its face had been painted on in a crude manner, and the clothes stitched around it were barely the semblance of a shirt and trousers. Stuck all through the torso were a number of straight pins, dissecting across each other through the small form in a vindictive show of hatred and revenge.

Who had this doll been intended for, and where were they now?

In another deep alcove, lit by a row of single tapered candles in brass candlesticks, hung a wooden puppet. His carved, wooden face pointed towards the ground and his jointed jaw hung open. Inside, a spider had made its home, filling the dark hole with webbing until the dummy was being choked by it.

The sticks for his hands were jabbed into the interior of the alcove in such a way that the poor, abandoned thing looked to be hanging limply from his wrists, trapped endlessly in a life forgotten. The only life-like thing about him were his eyes, which peered out of the alcove, and seemed to Marisol as if they were trained directly upon her. Though the white had faded to a yellowish ivory and the paint was chipping off the wood, his irises were a vivid blue untouched by time, or wear.

Inside the depths of them there was a cry for help, a desperate plea to end the suffering, and it caused Marisol to step past the alcove all the more quickly. Her fear and anxiety were getting to her, and she couldn't lend too much significance to the painted gaze of a dummy.

At the end of the hallway there was a door crafted from a series of doll arms fused together, while the knob was an actual doll head that one had to grasp and turn. Marisol could not bring herself to reach out and turn it, the eyeless sockets of the head peering up at her in a demonic fashion that sent a fresh chill down her spine.

Billy, on the other hand, showed no qualms with reaching out and opening the door, only letting out a soft chuckle to show that he was amused.

"This hallway was a blast." Billy cracked a smile in her direction, his eyes twinkling with merriment as the door opened outwards into another room.

Marisol didn't even bother answering as she moved past him and walked through the doorway, she simply wanted to get out of The Dollhouse as quickly as possible.

CHAPTER 5

THE UNIVERSE HAD SOMETHING ELSE IN STORE FOR MARISOL, FOR THE doorway didn't lead out of the large tent they had entered, but instead into another room—one that was vast, and filled with more dolls than she could count.

The walls were the picture of delicate and lovely. White, wooden wainscoting was met halfway up three of them by soft, pink paper scattered with dusty rose peonies and green leaves. The shelves that lined the fourth wall entirely were white and trimmed in scalloped edging that hung from the bottom of each, making it seem like the dolls stood upon a pretty, layered cake. From the ceiling overhead hung a large, armed chandelier with burning candles, and shining pearl chains looped from one arm to the next.

It reminded Marisol of a tearoom, and to prove this point, in the very middle of the room sat a large round table covered in lace, with tiers of lovely desserts and sandwiches presented upon its surface. A delicate china teapot sat on one end amongst a sea of teacups on saucers, all waiting to be filled with their chosen liquid.

There was another rag doll which made her stop short, except this one did not seem to be moving, only sat there inanimately—a doll that had popped off the shelf behind and come to sit at the table with guests.

To her surprise, Nancy and James sat at the table, a big grin upon her best friend's face as she nibbled on a minty green macaron.

"Mar!" Nancy cheered. "We've been waiting for you! Where've you been?" She looked between Marisol and Billy, her brows wiggling suggestively at her.

"We just...got caught up in the hall of mirrors," Marisol found herself stating, even though more than that, it had been her own terror that had tripped them up so.

"Well, took you long enough." James was not snacking away on the small buffet presented, instead he leaned back in the small white lattice chair, his legs extended out in front of him—appearing bored.

Before either Marisol or Billy could respond further, a figure appeared out of some hidden hole in the walls, while another dropped suddenly from the ceiling, thin silken ropes tied about her arms and wrists like the strings of a marionette.

It caused Marisol to startle a little in surprise, while the others let out awed noises of pleasure. James sat up, his face lighting up with interest as he took in the living marionette hanging from the ceiling, her face painted with lines at her mouth and running down the sides of her chin. Bright spots of red coloured her cheeks which also bore several black circles to indicate freckles. Her hair was braided on either side of her head and tied at the ends with small ribbon bows.

Slowly, and with a presence of self that was astonishing, the woman swept her legs up straight before her and then over her head, rolling fluidly in the air. As she rolled the ribbons released magically from her ankles so that she could wind her arms up the silks, closer to the ceiling. Then, as quickly as she had taken herself up to the ceiling, the marionette let herself free fall towards the floor, caught up with a jerk by the red silks at her wrists.

Around her sounded a series of gasps, and Marisol found even herself forgetting her fear of earlier in the wonder of what she had just witnessed.

So as not to be outdone, the other figure that had crept into the room moved to a more prominent position on the floor. She was dressed in a tight-fitting garment that consisted of several spare pieces of fabric stitched together. Her dark brown eyes, which were lined with black, peered out from a face of pure white. Dark crack lines marred the white of her cheeks and forehead, with what appeared to be spaces of dark to mimic the look of porcelain that had fallen away, and been lost.

The broken doll collapsed upon the floor, her entire body arching backwards to curl in upon itself in a manner in which no body should be able to bend. Marisol felt herself gasp, and beside her Billy exclaimed softly in shock. With her chest upon the ground, the doll contorted her form up and over herself until her feet rested on either side of her head, and she smiled up at them.

"Wow… isn't that the niftiest thing you've ever seen Mari?" Billy asked, watching the contortionist with wide eyes.

Marisol had to admit that it was indeed something spectacular and almost inhuman. She had never realized that the human form could bend in such ways before.

"I see that you have met my girls, Molly and Sally."

The voice came from behind them, and caused the four teenagers to turn from the sight of the acrobats, and look in the direction of the main door. There, leaning upon the jam, stood a tall, lanky man in a pinstripe suit, with a red bow tie around the collar of his white shirt. His short, sandy brown hair was slicked down to the top of his head and parted at the side, mimicking in many ways the look of the ventriloquist doll she had seen in the hallway alcove.

His cheeks were hollow and sharp, while around his mouth were dark markings that lined his chin, also indicating what was supposed to be a wooden mouth that would drop down for speaking.

"I am the Doll Collector, welcome to my tea room." His hand swept out to encompass the walls that currently surrounded them. "Please, enjoy your time here and do be sure to look over the shelves."

As he pointed to the wall of dolls, Marisol followed the motion of his hands, gazing at all of the dolls that seemed to show a vast array of difference. So many outfits that resembled the world at large: tiny dolls in miniature, large dolls with wooden faces, stuffed dolls made from cotton and sand, and beautiful dolls of porcelain and lace.

She felt drawn to the shelves, a strange and uncanny sense of being watched taking over her. Though no one but the Doll Collector was paying her any heed, Marisol could have sworn that someone was peering very intently upon her. Though the others seemed content to snack away on the treats laid out upon the tables while enjoying the marionette hanging from the ceiling and the broken doll twisting her body in impossible ways, Marisol stepped over to the Collector's collection.

A little stitched rag doll in a blue dress was the first to capture her eye. It's little button eyes telling a tale of happiness and love. Marisol felt that at some point in the world this doll had been loved by someone, and deeply. The next compartment on the shelf housed a little porcelain baby doll all curled up on its belly, its head pillowed on its hands. She was so lovely, and real looking in her pink sleeper that Marisol had to reach out to ensure that it was indeed only a doll and not actually a living child. The hard little stitched body filled with rice beneath the garments felt unnatural to her fingertips.

A series of lovely dolls sporting dresses from Russia, Mexico and China greeted her, along with a British soldier in his black ostrich hat and red jacket. As she walked, her arms pulled the teddy bear tightly against her chest, an absent motion that brought comfort in the foreign place in which she had come to find herself.

Although the dolls were all strange and curious, they were lovely. Unlike the ones that had been in the dark hallway, these dolls had been cherished and cared for. Each one clean and displayed with intention. Though the styles were all very different, with many countries represented in their tiny forms, Marisol liked each one better than the last.

As she neared the end of the shelf, her feet came to an unbidden halt as her eyes locked with that of a set of green glass gazing back from the shelf. The doll that sat upon the painted wood, with its glass legs peeping out from beneath a white nightgown, clutched in its arms a tiny teddy bear that in many ways looked like her own. Bright red hair was caught up in a single braid that trailed over her shoulder, and upon its head sat a little night cap trimmed in lace. In the second that her eyes landed upon it, Marisol felt a pull, and she counted each one of the ten painted freckles on its cheeks.

"Marisol," a soft whisper echoed in her ears, making the hair on the back of her neck stand up, and her heart jolt with a violent sort of tug.

She looked around her, but found no one within whispering distance. With her heart tripping along quickly in her chest, Marisol looked back to the little porcelain doll upon the shelf.

"That wasn't you, was it?" She heard herself say in a hushed tone, knowing how crazy it was, even while she said it.

"Found one that you like, did you?" This time the voice of the Collector was directly behind her, and Marisol jumped in surprise.

"I..." she didn't know what to say, and so her words faded off without being completed.

"Rosie is a special baby doll, I found her in a small shop while we were visiting England. Still in her box and desperately desiring to be taken home with someone, so I gave her a place here among all my children." As he spoke, the Collector's hand lifted to pluck at the end of Marisol's own red braid.

The way that he referred to the dolls as his children chilled

Marisol, and feeling uncomfortable, she pulled back from his hand, not wishing to have him in her space so familiarly.

"Perhaps like calls to like?" he murmured, his dark rimmed eyes looking into her own in such a way to make her swallow uneasily.

"What?" she whispered, her brows knitting. She wasn't asking to be taken home by anyone—unless that home was her own, and meant being away from this tent.

"Don't you see the resemblance between yourself and Rosie?"

Marisol's eyes lifted to the doll on the shelf once more, her insides tightening a little as it felt as if her stomach had dropped down to her feet. Why it was such a horrifying realization, she wasn't sure, but something innately inside her rebelled against being compared with the doll upon that shelf.

"I...suppose so?" Her arms clutched more tightly about the bear just as Rosie was clutched onto her own.

"She likes you."

Her eyes snapped to the Collector who was peering back at her intently, his round eyes almost bugging out of his features. Something washed through her that Marisol could not explain, except to say that fingertips had reached in and brushed over her spirit and curled around her heart in an intrusive fashion that left her trembling vulnerably in her shoes.

Finding it impossible to respond, she spun away instead, turning from both him and the shelf of dolls to look back at her brother and her friends. She had a strong urge to leave this place finally, and she needed them to come with her.

"Are you all ready to go see more of the circus?" Whether it was the shrill quality to her voice, or her words reminded them that all they were doing was sitting around a tea party eating snacks, the three of them gathered themselves up.

"Yes, let's go catch a show in the main tent before it's too late."

Marisol had never been so grateful to hear her brother speak, as she was in this moment. Steadily both Nancy and Billy seemed to agree, her friend wiping her hands free of cookie crumbs and pulling away from the sweets at last.

"It is a shame to lose you, but thank you for paying us a visit." The Collector was moving across the room, and as his hand pressed to a spot on the wall, a doorway cracked open in the wallpaper and the exit was revealed.

She should have waited for them, but instead Marisol headed

straight for that door, able to see the glowing lights of the fairway beyond, which meant her means of escape.

"*Marisol,*" whispered softly inside her mind once more as she reached the doorway. Feeling the eyes boring into her yet again, Marisol bounded through the door and down the steps that led to the ground, her lungs gasping for the fresh air finally all around her.

CHAPTER 6

SHE NOTICED IT FIRST AS THEY ENTERED THE BIG TOP, HER HAND BEGAN to feel stiff when she reached out for the railing that ran along the bleachers. As they took their seats, she pressed the fingers of her other hand against the back of it and then into her palm. Marisol could have sworn that her flesh felt hard and cold to the touch. While the large tent filled with a parade of amazing animals, and the boisterous ringmaster bellowed out their praises, her vision swam before her—though she saw nothing concrete, she could have sworn another room flickered into view.

Though she was able to concentrate somewhat on the show being performed down below them, at the back of her mind she felt the presence of something else haunting her thoughts. A voice continuing to whisper words that she could not properly make out, but were a fairly steady hum inside her mind that ebbed and flowed with frequency and intensity.

All of it was enough to make her shut her eyes against the strange sensations overtaking her, wishing not for the first time this evening, that she was at home, safe in her bed. Distractedly, she clung to the bear in her arms, and while the circus show faded in and out of her awareness, the teddy bear was the only item that remained unfailingly with her.

Laughter all around her brought Marisol back from her silent misery, and blinking heavy lids, she gazed around her. It felt as if she were listening to the crowd of happy laughter and cheers from behind a wall of solid glass—everything muted and distant. In the main ring down below, a beautiful woman in a white leotard and red tutu was riding on the back of an elephant that bore a black star on his side. She stood upon his back, her crimson hair curling up and away from her head in the loose shape of a heart.

Her eyes feeling heavy once more, Marisol let them fall shut, her vision darkening as she did. Nearby she caught the sound of a man's voice, he was murmuring pointedly to someone else, about what she could not be certain, but his tone was intense and purposeful. When she blinked her eyes open once more, she found that the show was over and most of the bleachers were empty. Nancy, James, and Billy were all standing and looking down at her questioningly.

"Marisol?" James was saying, drawing her eyes up to him in her confusion. "Are you coming?"

When had the show ended? Her eyes had not been closed for that long, she was sure of it. The chill was back, and though she was sure the pounding of her heart had increased, when she placed her hand to her chest she could not feel it.

"Right...of course." Feeling not entirely herself, Marisol stood up and silently followed the others.

Abandoned bags of popcorn and candy wrappers littered the stands beneath her feet as she walked along the bleachers, and carefully made her way back down the steps to the ground level. Marisol found that she had to squint hard to make out the ground itself as she took the final step down, for it had begun to look an awful lot like pink wallpaper and dusty rose peonies.

Billy seemed to sense that something was wrong, because he had stayed back a little to wait for her, his arm moving out to slip around her shoulders and successfully steer her out of the large tent through the main exit.

"Where's your mind at? You seemed to disappear back there," he spoke softly to her as the glow of hanging lights overhead welcomed them back onto the fairway.

"I don't know, I suppose my head just hurts a little."

"How about we go take a ride on the Ferris wheel? You can get a little bit of fresh air, and you don't need to keep walking around."

Marisol gazed up at him, her head tipping back a little so that she could look into his eyes. A part of her wanted to disagree, the warning from the soothsayer flitting back into her mind. Yet, the idea of riding on the Ferris wheel for a little while was tempting, the idea of letting herself slowly shift up and over in the air, while her seat swayed gently, and she didn't have to pay attention to anything but sitting…

"What about James and Nancy?" she asked.

"What about them? They'll be fine. I think Nancy wanted to go on the carousel anyway."

So Marisol found herself being led towards the line for the Ferris wheel without really issuing any complaint. It was taking far too much effort to walk anyway. Her knees were beginning to feel like jelly, while her ankles were stiffening up, causing Marisol to walk in a slightly uneven manner.

She was glad to have Billy's arm around her shoulders steadying her, and guiding her—offering a sturdy frame of support. Today she had felt fine, but those words no longer associated with her state, though Marisol was uncertain of what was actually going wrong with her. A very large part of her argued that she should be heading home, that whatever was happening was not going to get better the longer she stayed out.

However, the line moved ahead as the Ferris wheel emptied, and soon enough she was being handed up into one of the small swinging benches with Billy sliding in beside her. As the bar clicked into place before them, Marisol felt a fingertip brush along her jaw, only when her head snapped in that direction it was on the wrong side of her to have been Billy. Billy who was currently leaning over his side of the seat to look below them as their bench swung up into the air, rocking slightly while the next seat was filled with people.

"I think I need to get down," Marisol whispered, her voice raspy and weak as her throat complained at the sudden speech. Even swallowing was becoming increasingly difficult, her head feeling heavy upon her shoulders as if it were a foreign object upon her spine.

"Sorry?" Billy asked, straightening up from where he had been gazing down at the ground to look over at her.

Marisol could only shake her head, though the motion made her vision spin a little. Needing to take a deep breath to clear it, she leaned back against the seat and closed her eyes. Only, as she inhaled —or tried to—her chest seemed to tighten and it became difficult to draw in a breath. Beginning to feel frantic, Marisol brought her hands up to her cheeks in the hopes of grounding herself, except it wasn't warm flesh beneath her palms, but cold, hard porcelain.

Her body jerked violently, which sent their seat rocking

hazardously back and forth as Marisol released a scream of terror from lungs that were finally filling with oxygen. Before her eyes were pink walls and large peonies, and the feel of a wooden shelf below.

It was Billy pulling her into his side, and tugging her hands away from her face, that brought her back, and with a quick blink of her eyes the tea room disappeared from view, and it was his concerned face peering back at her, instead.

"Mari?" He whispered.

"I want down," she sobbed brokenly, tears beginning to pool in green eyes, that for the moment, still felt like her own.

"It's okay," he murmured soothingly, his arm holding her tight into him while the other hand rubbed briskly up and down her arm. He was doing his best to reassure her that everything was going to be all right, but what was happening to her was not all right.

No amount of tight holds and arm rubs was going to prove otherwise.

"I want to go." Marisol turned towards him and buried her face into his shoulder as she plucked her teddy bear back up and clutched it to herself, giving it her best attempt to block out the world.

Only there was no escaping the real dangers plaguing her mind.

Slowly the Ferris wheel circled them down towards the ground and then quickly back up, their seat rocking in a pleasant way that was in fact torturous to Marisol. Had this been any other moment in time, there was a strong chance she would have been holding onto Billy's arm and pretending to be frightened just so that she could be close to him. With her nose buried in his shoulder, she would have been enjoying the masculine scent coming off of him, and doing her best to memorize it.

Instead, each spin of the Ferris wheel was a test in patience and resilience. No more screaming, and no more crying—if she could prevent it.

When at last her feet hit the ground, Marisol nearly collapsed upon it in relief. There was also the factor that the weak feeling had returned to her knees, which she tried her best not to compare to the flattened joint of a rag doll, but with each step forward the only thing she could picture in her mind was her knee folding entirely in two because it was nothing but stitched fabric.

In the end, it was Billy who walked her home. Marisol had wanted the stability of her best friend beside her, but he'd assured both Nancy and her brother that he would get her home, right as rain, and that they could continue having fun. Marisol did manage to say farewell to them both, and even felt a small smile on her lips as Nancy shouted after her that she still owed her an Abba Zaba bar.

CHAPTER 7

THE WALK HOME HAD BEEN MORE OF A SILENT AFFAIR, THOUGH BILLY had tried to make conversation with Marisol, obviously worried about her and hoping to make her feel better—but Marisol hadn't wanted to speak. Her mind felt muddled, and her limbs felt both loose and stiff all at once, leaving her thinking more on how to walk down the street than what words she should speak to Billy as they walked.

Once he got her home, she assured him that she was okay, and thanked him for making sure that she got back safe and sound. Standing on the doorstep looking up at him, Marisol wished that this was something she could count on for the future, but the warnings of both the soothsayer, and the magician repeated in her mind.

Who holds your heart?

After thanking him once more, Marisol had ducked inside, trying not to let the surprised and disappointed look on Billy's face affect her.

"Marisol? Is it just you?" Came her mother's voice as she stuck her head out of the kitchen.

Marisol had just finished walking up the steps and through their apartment door, and was in the process of slipping out of her shoes. Toeing out of them, she looked up to her mother's confused face.

"Yes, it's just me. I'm not feeling so well, and I didn't want to force James and Nancy to come home early, so I told them to stay."

Frowning with concern, her mother stepped towards her and

lifted her hand to press the back of it to first her forehead, and then her cheeks.

"You don't seem to have a fever, is it lady problems?" her mother asked the last part in a hushed tone, as if there was someone around to hear the scandalized topic.

Blushing, Marisol shook her head.

"No, Mama, it's not that. I think I'm just going to go to bed early."

"Okay darling, feel better." Her mother pressed a kiss to her cheek. "Let me know if you need anything."

"I will." Marisol offered her mother a little smile that she hoped was reassuring, and headed down the hall to where her bedroom awaited her. She too hoped that she would feel better in the morning.

With a blink of her eyes, Marisol gazed about herself in confusion. She was back in the pink peony covered room once more, only this time she seemed to be gazing over the tea party from a different angle. Strangers came and went, some sitting down at the table and trying to speak with the rag doll who sat lifelessly in her seat, while others merely stood enthralled as they watched the life-sized marionette in the corner, as her body effortlessly wound up and down the silken threads.

Marisol startled as Sarah Braeden appeared suddenly before her, yet in such a scope that made her appear many times larger than herself. Attempting to lift her hands up in order to ward off Sarah, Marisol found that her hands would not lift. Though she could feel them where they sat in her lap, the soft feel of her teddy bear pressed against her wrists, she was incapable of making them move.

As Sarah drew nearer, Marisol tried to lift herself up from the hard surface she sat upon, but much like her hands, the rest of her body was immobile. Like before, on the Ferris wheel, her heart began to pound loudly within her own ears, and her breathing picked up, but unlike before, her chest did not rise and fall quickly with each desperate breath. Instead, there was nothing, just the feeling of being trapped within a stiff, unresponsive cage.

Unwanted, Sarah's hand came towards her, blocking everything else from her view as fingers wrapped easily around her entire body. Fighting against the restraints placed upon her body, Marisol screamed, unleashing all of her fear and anxiety—only her lips did not open, and her throat made no sound. The scream sounded only inside her own mind, bouncing off the walls of her internal confinement.

At the same time as she felt her body lifted from where it sat, she also felt her legs slide lifeless to hang in the air, while her arms remained around the teddy bear against her torso.

"This one reminds me of someone," Sarah was saying, her voice clear and yet also muffled, like Marisol was hearing it through a wall. "Billy, what do you think?"

Marisol's eyes followed the turn of Sarah's head, as her classmate looked to the side and Billy Coulter stepped up beside her, looking bored and not the least bit interested. Yet, all the same, Marisol felt her stomach plummet. Had Billy dropped her off at home only to return to the circus without her?

"It's a doll, Sarah, it doesn't look like anyone."

"No...I could swear it reminds me of someone in my class, her eyes seem so lifelike..." Sarah's voice drifted off as her eyes returned to Marisol, gazing down at her with her brows a little furrowed.

Marisol stared back, her heart beating frantically as she attempted to shout back at Sarah, to make her realize that it was indeed herself that the other girl was holding—crying out for help that didn't seem to be coming. Suddenly though, Sarah gasped as her thumb pressed more firmly down upon the centre of Marisol's chest.

"There is a heartbeat inside this doll's chest!" she announced in shock, her eyes growing a little wider as she pulled Marisol in closer to her face.

"What are you talking about?" Billy asked, leaning in over her shoulder just a bit.

It was at this point that the Doll Collector appeared at Sarah's side, a concerned look upon his face as he reached out to snatch Marisol from her hand.

"What are you doing?" His tone was appalled, as he looked scornfully at Sarah and Billy. "The dolls are meant to be looked at and admired, not played with." Tsk'ing at them in disapproval, he waved them away from the doll shelf, his eyes looking down upon Marisol. "Don't worry, I won't let any harm come to you."

The look in his eyes struck deep into Marisol's chest, as it was one of acknowledgement and understanding. In response, Marisol tried screaming and struggling once more, fighting against whatever was holding her back.

"Not yet," he cooed as he reached out to place her back on the shelf.

Panting and covered in cold sweat, Marisol sat up in the midst of her bed. From her window, filtered in a little bit of light from the street-lamp outside, enabling her to see that she was indeed within her own room and not inside the Doll Collector's tea party.

A shudder coursed its way through her body, as Marisol brushed damp locks away from her face. Everything about that dream had seemed real, far more real than any nightmare to have plagued her before.

From down the hall, she could hear the sound of her father snoring, a sound that while annoying was also comforting in the moment. She was safe, at home, where she was meant to be—the dream had only been the culmination of all her insecurities and fears from the evening. Climbing from her bed, Marisol made her way quietly out of her room, and out into the hall so that she could make her way to the galley kitchen for a glass of water.

She was okay. After a drink and a little time to catch her breath, she would be settled enough to sleep, and everything would be okay once more.

"Marisol? What are you doing up?"

From where she leaned back against the counter, Marisol glanced up to the doorway of the kitchen to see her brother standing partially in the darkness of the hallway.

"Woke up from a nightmare," she responded quietly, not wanting her voice to carry down the hall and wake up her parents—though the likelihood of being heard over her father's snoring was slim.

"You okay?" he asked as he stepped into the kitchen, moving over to the fridge he had fixed earlier that day, to open it up and pull out the glass milk bottle, carrying it over to the counter where he reached for a glass.

James was too good of a guy to drink from the milk bottle, even though Marisol herself had been tempted by the idea a time or two.

"Yeah, I think so." She watched him as he poured himself a glass and then returned the milk bottle to the fridge before taking a sip. "How was your evening with Nancy?"

She had been anticipating that he would scoff in annoyance, but instead Marisol noted the makings of a blush blooming upon his cheeks, and over his ears. It was shocking, to say the least.

"That good, huh?" she asked, a brow lifted in curiosity.

"No, I mean…it was okay, I suppose," he fumbled over his words, his sincere nature warring with his desire to appear aloof.

"I'm glad," Marisol informed him. Though it would mean less time spent with both her best friend and her sibling, she could honestly say that the thought of the two of them together was not a notion that bothered her. "You should take her out some night."

James looked over at her in surprise.

"Really? You wouldn't mind if I did?" This had clearly not been the reaction he had been anticipating from her.

"No, I wouldn't mind." Finishing off her glass of water, Marisol placed the tumbler into the sink and stepped up to her brother, rubbing his arm gently. "I love you both."

Offering him a smile, Marisol left him to his glass of milk in the kitchen, and made her way back to her bedroom.

As she settled back beneath the covers, Marisol was grateful for her conversation with James out in the kitchen. It had given her something else to think about as she closed her eyes and let herself drift back off to sleep. In the morning she would have to head over to Nancy's to see just what her best friend was thinking about all of this.

CHAPTER 8

WHEN HER EYES OPENED ONCE MORE, MARISOL WAS NO LONGER IN HER bedroom. Instead, the dim lighting of the pink papered, peony room greeted her once more. Unlike last time, the space was not brimming with guests, and all of the living dolls had gone away. From her best judgment, Marisol guessed that the circus was closed, and everyone had gone home, or back to their private quarters.

One thing had not changed, Marisol was still stuck firmly in place where she sat, peering out over the empty room. Dread was a cold shower trickling over her, seeping into every pore, nook and cranny —leaving her shivering, and wishing to jump away.

In a desperate attempt to leave whatever fresh, hellish nightmare she had entered, Marisol closed her eyes. She willed herself awake, telling her sleeping mind that she was well aware that this was a dream, and she had no desire to be a part of it anymore. However, each time that she opened her eyes once more, it was still the Doll Collector's tea room awaiting her.

There was an impossible likelihood facing Marisol that she refused to acknowledge. Instead, she struggled and fought against whatever invisible bonds were holding her down. Trying her best to be free of the mental confinement, she continued until an all-too-real exhaustion pulled her down into darkness.

When her eyes opened once more, the Doll Collector was in the room, speaking quietly to a girl Marisol felt like she recognized, although she couldn't place her.

"How many are we waiting on?" the girl was asking.

Though the girl was in normal clothes and a clean face, the Collector still wore his hair slicked down flat against his head, and his face painted like that of a ventriloquist dummy. It was a creepy thing to see, and questionable, but then, did anything ever make sense in dreams?

"Just the one this time, but my hope is that she will prove more useful than multiples usually do."

When the girl turned so that she was facing Marisol's perch more directly, she was able to see that it was the marionette from the corner, only out of costume and looking like any other young woman Marisol may have seen. Except that there was a hard look to her face that had not been so readily seen the night before.

"When will she be here?" the marionette asked.

"I expect any time. The sun is almost up, and she'll need to avoid being seen."

As if on cue, the side doorway that was used as the exit out into the real world opened. The figure in the doorway was backlit by the faint glow of early morning sunshine, so at first Marisol was not able to make out who had just stepped into the room. However, when the door closed with a resounding thud, she felt her breath stolen away from her as the cold shower of dread returned.

It was herself standing in front of the door—or at least the shell of herself. Dressed in the nightgown that she had worn to bed, it was now stained shockingly in crimson that splattered up over her neck and face. Each of her red smeared hands clutched onto a pillowcase bulging with items.

Marisol felt as if she were suffocating, what she was witnessing was not possible, it was also a sight that filled her with the sort of dread that was both all-consuming, as well as shattering. Though she knew, her mind refused to place a name to the red covering her body.

"Oh look, what have we here?" The Doll Collector spoke with a conniving glee, his hands smoothing down his pinstripe suit, before he made his way over to Marisol's body.

She didn't know what else to call it, because even though it was 'her', it was not like watching herself from outside herself—there was no life reflecting back from her green eyes. Instead, what she saw was a moving, reacting body, that truly seemed to hold no spirit at all. Marisol's form held out the two pillowcases as the Doll Collector came towards her, and he removed the items from her hands, seeming entirely unfazed by her appearance.

It was hard to know where to look, as the dummy-inspired man stepped away from her body. Yet, as she just stood there staring blankly off into the distance, Marisol looked instead to the Collector. He had brought the bags over to the table in the middle of the room where he took turns dumping both onto its surface.

From the bags tumbled money in the form of bills and coin. As the coins spun on the wooden table top, they were joined by pieces of jewellery that she recognized as her mother's favourite necklace, and the ring that had been passed down by her grandmother.

"Did you empty the safe?" The Collector asked the Marisol-that-was-not-Marisol.

Her response was the nod of her head as she remained standing docile and silent by his side. Marisol wanted to fight this, to yell at the form of herself that was just standing there, while the contents of her parents' safe was divvied up on the tabletop, and the Doll Collector looked scornfully at her mother's wedding ring that was also caked in crimson. As he discarded it with disdain, Marisol felt a sharp pang in her heart. Though it wasn't much to look at, Marisol was aware of the story behind it. How her father had saved up for so long so that he could ask her mother to marry him, and because of that her mother had cherished that ring—refusing to replace it even after the shop became more profitable, and a new ring could have been bought.

Staring at the red smeared ring laying discarded on the table, Marisol began to feel the pain of loss taking her over. What she had thought was a dream, was beginning to feel all too real. A few other items came to join the discarded wedding band: her father's watch which was nothing more than a simple face on a leather strap, and the small Swiss Army knife James always carried in his pocket.

It caused Marisol to struggle against the bindings holding her, screaming angrily at whatever held her enclosed. This had to be a brutal nightmare, but if so, she wished to wake up now.

"*Wake up! Wake up! Wakeupwakeupwakeup!*" she screamed silently into the void, thrashing, and fighting from the bottom of her soul.

With a jolt, Marisol blinked awake, her body feeling strange and foreign to her in this moment—as if there was the echo of someone else in her mind. It took but a moment for her to realize that she hadn't woken up in her bed from a nightmare, but that she was standing in the midst of the Doll Collector's tea room, a blood soaked nightgown covering her body, and her eyes staring down at bare feet which also bore the stark stain of blood.

Lifting her marked hands up before her, Marisol felt a horrifying realization cascading over her—this was not a dream, and none of what she bore upon her was her own blood. The floor felt too hard beneath her, the air too chilled upon her bare flesh, and the light overhead shone with the sharpness of reality.

Perhaps it was her movement, or a sound of shock that she had released, but the Doll Collector became aware of her true presence back inside her body. From the table, he turned to look at her, a light of shock within his eyes as he peered at her, his glance falling to her hands which were still lifted up before her.

"You're awake..."

Staring at each other for a moment, Marisol watched him look over towards the shelf where the dolls sat. There, upon one lonely shelf, sat Rosie; her own lookalike doll.

"How...defiant, of you," he murmured, taking a careful step towards her.

Marisol, her mind still hazy from waking back inside her own form, felt a wash of forewarning rush over her, and instinctively took a step back.

"Now, now...don't be like that. I mean you no harm," he cooed at her, his hands lifting to reach out towards her, as he began murmuring something dark beneath his breath.

Marisol felt it, the pull at her mind and heart—cool fingers slipping inside her skull and between each of her rib bones, to pull her free of them. Unwilling to go back into the dark, silent confinement once more, she turned away from him to flee, but found her way trapped by one of the silent, living dolls.

Instead of being able to pass through the exit door out into the outside world, Marisol spun on her bare heel and fled past the table, going around the opposite side to place it between herself and the Doll Collector. Frantic, she grabbed a hold of one of the teacups resting on the table and threw it his way. Despite the pounding of fear nearly deafening her, Marisol heard the crash of china breaking upon the floor, and turned toward the first opening that she happened to find.

Finding herself in the dark hallway of creepy dolls once more, Marisol looked around herself in a cloud of panic, trying to find an alternate route to getting out without having to go back through the hall of mirrors.

"Marisol, you're only making this more difficult on yourself." It was the Doll Collector, moving along behind her without any apparent fear, or concern, of her fleeing from him.

"Please…" she begged desperately. "I just want to go home."

"Home? What home?"

Marisol shook her head, she didn't want to think about what he was implying, or what the blood coating her nightgown and hands truly meant. In her fear, she had turned around to look at the lanky man behind her, and not paying any heed to where she was going, she backed into the wall. Her hand slapping out, she found that it had sunk into a hole.

She was beside the alcove that held the wooden dummy, his eyes staring out at her with a lifelike misery that struck her heart once more.

"Marisol…save yourself the trouble and come back to the tea room," he was trying to be soothing, but the true underlying nature of his words was there in every sinister syllable.

As he approached, he began the soft chanting beneath his breath once more, and she could feel the tug at her mind and soul—a pull that was making a hazy darkness close in on her sight. Reaching behind her, Marisol grabbed hold of the dummy that hung there, and pulled him roughly from his spot so that the strings holding him up snapped.

Brandishing the dummy before her as a shield, what she hadn't anticipated was stopping the Doll Collector in his tracks. His eyes fell to the wooden ventriloquist doll and widened just enough to show Marisol that he was concerned at the notion of it being in her hands —which he clearly hadn't intended to give away, for he quickly cleared his expression.

"What do you plan to do with that?" His words were sneered condescendingly, but she had seen enough not to be fooled by this.

Clutching the wooden dummy in her hands, Marisol faced the Collector defiantly, the doll raised up before her.

"L-let me go, and I'll let you have him back," she insisted, struggling to find strength in her tone.

"You're not going anywhere Marisol, just put down the doll," his dark painted eyes were fierce upon her face, as he spoke.

Feeling that she had the upper hand in this moment—which wasn't bound to last the longer she hesitated—Marisol swung the dummy around to slam his head against the corner of the alcove. It landed with a harsh thud that caused the Collector to release a distressed squawk.

"Don't *do* that," he growled angrily, his hand lifting to brush against his forehead, rubbing gently.

"I said to let me go!" Feeling more sure of herself, there was now a forceful quality to her voice that had not been there the first time around.

The Doll Collector was no longer choosing to stand idly by and assume that she was going to passively pass over the doll. Instead, he began approaching her, a sinister look in his eyes. Fearing what would happen if he reached her, Marisol swung the dummy in her hands to smash its carved face against the corner of the alcove once more. This time, there was a sharp crack that followed her motion, and she could tell without having to look that she'd made some damage to the doll in her hands.

The cracking sound was followed by a howl of pain from the Doll Collector, and as her eyes travelled to his face she saw a large gash had opened up on his forehead, almost as if it were his own flesh that had cracked beneath the pressure of the hit, rather than the dummy's. Marisol looked down at the small wooden figure in her hands, and found that his own forehead now bore a crack, and within the dummy's eyes was a look of relief.

"That was a big mistake," the Collector growled, and launched himself suddenly at Marisol.

She had only the time to brandish the dummy up before her with a hefty swing at the furious man before she found herself slammed against the wall behind her. The impact forced all of the air out of her lungs, and her head to strike the hard wall, making her ears ring, and her sight to blacken slightly.

His hand was moving for her throat while the other attempted to snatch the dummy from her clutches. Struggling to break free, Marisol kept a hold of the dummy as tightly as she could, her fingers biting into the crack along its forehead, and delighting when she heard another cry of pain from the Doll Collector looming over her.

"Enough!" He snarled, his hand tightening on her neck enough that she lost all thought of keeping hold of the dummy, and instead, struggled for her breath.

The Collector yanked the dummy free of her hold, and released her at last. Gasping harshly for each struggled breath, Marisol slid down the wall to land upon her bottom on the floor. With each ragged breath she took, her throat ached and burned, tears wetting the corners of her eyes.

Above her, the Doll Collector continued to loom, blood coating the side of his face where his forehead had cracked open from the blow to the dummy. He was furious, it was written in every painted line and defined slope of his narrow appearance.

"You will pay for that," he sneered. Tucking the ventriloquist dummy beneath his arm, he reached for her wrist, and pulled on her. "I told you that this was a futile attempt, and now you've only succeeded in angering me."

Forced to her feet and still breathing raggedly through a throat that felt like it had been crushed, Marisol stumbled after him, her muscles trembling. Her attempt at escape had failed, and she wasn't sure what she could do now.

Marisol. She could hear the voice echoing within her mind once more, tugging at the sensitive hold she still had upon it—weakened by the brutal attack. As she was hauled back into the tea room, her eyes landed upon the shelf where Rosie the doll sat, a shudder of trepidation went through her.

Marisol...Marisol...Come back.

CHAPTER 9

UNLIKE THE FIRST TIME WHEN SHE HAD BEEN ASLEEP FOR THE PROCESS, being physically ripped from her body while awake was a painful endeavour. Much like she would imagine it felt to have your fingernails pulled off, it felt to resist against the pull, and yet she did it, clinging on to some mental hold on herself until there was no more hold to give, and the blackness welcomed her.

When her eyes opened once more, she was trapped back on that shelf, watching the shell of herself listening obediently to the Doll Collector. Marisol wished to scream, and fight, as she heard him speak to her form about Nancy and her family, fear—raw and agonizing—welling up inside of her.

Then she had to sit silently, and unable to sleep, throughout the rest of the day. She watched the Doll Collector as he left to clean himself up, and as the aerialist marionette came out to prepare herself. Marisol knew that she would be awake for the torture of today, waiting to see when her form would return.

She was aware that the circus had opened once everyone was set up in the tea room: the rag doll perched at the round table, the marionette rolled up in her ribbons near the ceiling, the contortionist doll bent up and over herself, while the Doll Collector stood sentry over them all. As the day wore on, hordes of people passed through, some laughing excitedly because of the mirrored maze they had gone through, others screaming in nervous fear and enjoyment.

While her own fear was a tangible thing, it was easy to fall into a numb haze while people came and went, only breaking from the near trance when someone would come too close to her. Just as Sarah had, during that one moment she had believed to be a nightmare. There were a few that felt drawn to her, and picked up the small, baby doll that she was locked inside. It was a surreal experience, to be so tiny while others were so large, towering over her as elephants to a dog.

The day wore on into the night, and at last it seemed that the day had ended, but, instead of just being shut down, the room began to be packed up by other members of the circus. Marisol began to fear that she was going to be packed up as well, trapped forever in this tiny compartment, where all she could do was watch silently as the lives of others passed her by. When the room had been cleared except for the dolls resting on the shelves with lined crates before them, everyone left the room except for the Collector himself.

The tall, lanky man stepped up to the shelves, and plucked 'Rosie' from her small compartment. Gazing up at him angrily, Marisol longed only to be set free. She needed to check on her family, to check on Nancy, to see what had actually happened to all of them.

"You were a nuisance, but useful in the end," as he spoke, his hand which bore a ring that felt strangely familiar, lifted and swiped over her face.

Darkness enveloped Marisol once more, and she felt as if her body were tumbling and turning through a vast void. When at last her eyes opened she knew that she was back in her own body, but she didn't quite understand where she was.

She sat upon the floor, still dressed in the same nightgown as before, though it was now stiff from something dark and stuck to her in some places. Out in front of her stretched her legs, which appeared to be covered in splotches of dark red, more so than even the last time she had seen herself.

Her body feeling ice cold, Marisol slowly stood up, gazing around. She was home, seated inside her kitchen, which for all the quiet that surrounded her, seemed entirely normal.

"M-mom?" Marisol called out, her timid voice echoing in the stillness.

When no response came, Marisol carefully walked across the linoleum floor, her legs feeling unsteady and strange, as if her mind had forgotten what it meant to correspond with a moving body.

The hallway was dim, the windows showing that dawn was just arriving outside. Typically, her mother and father would already be up, and there would be breakfast on the stove waiting for them while her father began opening the shop down below. This morning there were no sounds to greet her.

Slowly, with mounting anxiety, Marisol made her way down the hall, her fingers tracing along the wall as a way to steady herself in this reality. The sound of the floor squeaking beneath her steps was the only sound to greet her until she had entered her parents' bedroom.

It was a massacre. Blood sprayed all over the wall their bed rested against, their blankets shredded and hanging nearly to the floor that was itself a red sea. Upon the bed lay her parents, her father's arm dangling off the edge, a red line falling down along the full length of it where it had dripped off the tip of his index finger that pointed to the red sea below.

Her mother lay beside him as was expected, but her eyes were open and staring with a white sightless haze up at the ceiling, her lips open, and twisted in pain and surprise. The front of her nightgown bore the same faded, and browning red that Marisol's own did, but there was so very much more of it.

She didn't even realize she was running until she had fled the room, hurrying to the opposite side where James' door was cracked open just a little. Bursting through it, a ragged sob tearing from her throat, Marisol flung herself onto her brothers form that was angled away from her, laying on his side.

"James! *Please* wake up! Mom and Dad are-Mom and D-Dad-" her voice broke off as she shook her brother's shoulder and he rolled onto his back, his blank eyes staring up at her with an emptiness that was gut wrenching.

Another scream of horror built up inside of her, but a harsh sob won out. Her form trembling uncontrollably, Marisol shook James' body, refusing to believe what her eyes were telling her.

"P-please James! No! Please wake up, you have to wake up!"

Dropping back onto her bottom on his bed, her hands lifted to her cheeks, a new dampness from his clothes now joining the tears streaming freely down them. Sobs wracked her slender form, shaking her until it was hard to stand up. The Doll Collector had done this, she was sure of it. While he'd had control of her form, while she'd been locked away in that torturous doll, he had stolen her family away from her.

She wasn't sure what caused her to think of it, but in the throes of her misery, Marisol remembered the flash of the ring upon the Collector's hand—and remembered where she had seen it. It was a ring most commonly seen upon the hand of Nancy's father. A ring that he was never without because it was a signature of their family, and the wealth they had accumulated over the years.

A new found dread began to take her over, one that left her shaking even more than before. Without thinking her actions through, Marisol leapt to her feet, and stumbled down the hall. Not stopping to grab anything or to change, she fled from her home, and out onto the street. People were beginning to stir in the dawn: men travelling to work, the milkman making his rounds in his small white van, an older woman sweeping her front step. Marisol ignored it all.

Even as her presence created gasps of shock and worry, Marisol paid no heed to the cries of people as she rushed down the street. A dark certainty was already filling her with the knowledge of what she would find when she reached Nancy's home, but she had to make sure. She needed to see the truth with her own eyes.

Though the soles of her feet were raw from the scrape of the sidewalk against the bottoms of them, she barely took note. In her panic, the trip to Nancy's home seemed to take no time, and no effort at all. As she hurried up the front steps of the large three story home, Marisol paused, her hands resting against the door she steeled herself for going inside. With a deep breath, slowly she opened the door, and stepped inside.

There was noise coming from the kitchen that was the family's housekeeper, but no noise from the family themselves. Marisol tried to tell herself that they simply weren't awake yet, and almost had herself convinced until she saw the trail of red footprints leading from Nancy's room to her parents.

"Please...no," she whimpered, her slow steps taking her down to her best friend's door. Pushing it open carefully, her heart dropped down into her stomach, as her world finished crashing down around her.

Nancy wasn't in her bed, instead, she was laying sprawled out on the floor, several open wounds in her back where she had been taken by surprise. Her light pink, plush carpet was stained in her blood, all of it having soaked into the fibres.

Rushing into her room she fell down upon her knees, her hands grabbing at Nancy's body to pull her up into her arms, her friend's eyes blank and unseeing as her mother's had been, and James'. Clutching her tightly to her chest, she sobbed, rocking her back and forth.

Nancy had been the sister she'd never had, the other side of herself that pushed her to do more—be more. This was too much.

Crying still, she allowed her face to bury in her friend's hair, ignoring the screams she could now hear coming from down the hall in the direction of Nancy's parents' room. Cries for the police sounded out as quick, heavy footsteps rushed past them. At some point someone came into the room and did their best to pull her away from Nancy, but she simply continued holding onto her, not letting anything separate her from the last person she loved.

The police showed up soon enough however, and it was an officer in a dark uniform that pried Nancy from her clutches. She protested, struggling a little, but eventually her weak, aching muscles gave out, and she allowed herself to be hauled up to her feet. Looking up in confusion, Marisol stuttered when metal handcuffs were clasped around her wrists.

"Wh-what?"

"Marisol Chandler you are under arrest for the murder of your family, and the Pinder family. As well as the theft of both valuable property, and monetary goods contained within each home," the officer droned on, keeping his hand upon her upper arm as he spoke.

"What?" She was still confused, her thoughts still too fractured from shock. "No! It wasn't me, it was the Doll Collector! At the circus!" she cried out, beginning to struggle against his hold. "You have to believe me, please! I was at the circus and he stole me from my body, and trapped me inside a doll."

It sounded crazy even as she spoke it, but she pulled, and tugged, as the police officer began to pull her from the room despite her best efforts to brace her feet against the floor.

"Your nonsense won't work for you, and I wouldn't say much more if I were you," he was grumbling as he pulled her through the doorway.

"It's not nonsense, I swear it! You have to stop him, I think he's done this before! And there was a dummy who when it was injured, injured him. I don't think he's human! Please... oh please...you have to go to the circus and stop him before he does this to someone else!"

"The circus has already left."

Marisol was crying once more as she struggled and pleaded, begging for them listen to her about the Doll Collector and all of his strange ways. But they heeded her not at all, and instead she was thrown into the back of one of their police cars, staring up at the

Pinder home that looked far too beautiful, and lovely, for all the horror that had taken place inside.

They'd stripped her down before spraying her off with a hose. As they scrubbed vigorously at her flesh as if she had come to them filthy and diseased. She was then given a pair of socks and a white hospital gown to tie around herself. Despite her protests, several pills were forced into her, a hand pulling her head back while another massaged the pills down her throat.

Once she had been thoroughly manhandled, the nurses dressed in their prim white uniforms and flared white hats, took her down a long hall lined with door after door. Though she couldn't see anyone through the small windows set inside each, she could hear the moans and cries of distressed minds at play. Towards the end of the hall, they reached an open door, and Marisol was forced to step inside, finding herself in a small room with a single barred window, and a narrow bed in the corner.

"You'll be in your room for the next couple of days. Behave yourself, and take your medication as required, and you'll be allowed out in the common areas for meals. Behave poorly, and you'll find this, or the cell a floor down, will be your constant home."

The nurse was trying to be kind in her way, giving her the rundown, but Marisol felt numb. Treading silently over to the window, her hand lifted to slip around one of the bars as she gazed down at the lane below.

Behind her a door clanged shut, closing her into the room, and the sound of a lock sliding into place followed, letting her know that she had been once again trapped inside a cage. This time, however, there would be no escape.

ABOUT CHRISTIS CHRISTIE

Christis Christie was born and raised in a small town in New Brunswick, Canada where she spent most of her time either reading someone else's book, or dreaming of writing her own. Her favourite thing to dive into is an epic fantasy, or anything else magical and wondrous that really allows her imagination to take her away.

She now lives on the East Coast in Halifax, Nova Scotia where she works as an event designer, putting her interior decorating degree to wonderful use. Whenever she's not busy magically transforming venues for her clients, Christis is working on her own writing. Currently she has two projects in the works; a YA fantasy novel, and an adult supernatural short story serial.

CONNECT ON SOCIAL MEDIA

christischristieblog.wordpress.com

facebook.com/christis.christie.1

instagram.com/Tiss.Writes

THANK YOU

Our dear readers, thank you for coming on these journeys with us. We hope you enjoyed our circus-inspired tales, from magical to frightening.

If you savored these selections, we'd love to hear from you! Reach out to the authors and let them know if you fell in love with their stories!

The circus has always captured us, and we hope it captured you as well!

LEARN MORE

To learn more about this anthology and others from Cresent Sea Publishing, please visit crescentseapublishing.com